NIKKI COPLESTON is the author of thre[e?]
Wiltshire detective Jeff Lincoln: *The Price*
Disturbed, and *The Shame of Innocence.*
awards, including the Wells Literary Festi[val]
and she is an active member of Frome Writers' Collective. Born
Somerset and brought up in the Midlands and Wiltshire, she worked
in London throughout her career in local government before moving
back to Somerset in 2012. She writes occasional articles on Salisbury
for *The Fisherton Informer*, and is a member of Stellar Scribes, a trio of
novelists running creative writing workshops in Somerset.

A keen photographer, Nikki takes her inspiration from the landscape
of the West Country, although her novels reveal the darker side of life
in rural towns and the countryside. She is currently living in Wells with
her husband and Harvey the cat.

NIKKI COPLESTON

THE PROMISE OF SALVATION

SilverWood

Published in 2021 by SilverWood Books
for Silver Crow (www.silvercrowbooks.co.uk)

SilverWood Books Ltd
14 Small Street, Bristol, BS1 1DE, United Kingdom
www.silverwoodbooks.co.uk

ISBN 978-1-80042-154-7 (paperback)
ISBN 978-1-80042-155-4 (ebook)

British Library Cataloguing in Publication Data
A CIP catalogue record for this book is available from the British Library

Page design and typesetting by SilverWood Books

In memory of Brenda Edwards and Pete Hobbs
This one's for you

CHAPTER 1

WEDNESDAY 1ST FEBRUARY

When Corky started barking, Barbara abandoned her Weetabix and hurried into the living room to see what was wrong. The little Cairn terrier was standing on his hind legs, pawing at the French windows.

'There's nobody out there,' she said, gently pushing him down. 'It's only the wind.'

Away to the left of her long garden, the towering firs on the edge of Greywood Forest swayed and sang mournfully in the wind. She loved living so close to these woods, in the end house in the terrace, but the trees made her fearful in bad weather – always had, ever since she was little. Now her empty washing line looped and snapped, clattering like a skipping rope. She'd hoped the gale would blow itself out in the night, but it was nearly seven now and the wind was still going strong.

And then a massive roar filled the air, a huge groan like a plane coming down, as a colossal sheet of metal sailed over the hedge and crashed onto her back lawn. Moments later a second sheet landed on top of it.

'Oh no! That's all I need!' She pulled her old mac on over her jumper and skirt, shoved her feet into her sheepskin boots and hurried down the garden, not knowing what to expect.

Two buckled sheets of corrugated iron lay embedded in the grass. The gale must have ripped them off Ploughboy's Pit.

Even as she stood there wondering what to do next, the wind dropped, as if it had had its fun with her and was off to torment somebody else. She looked up towards the house, where Corky was scrabbling at the window, desperate to get outside. She went back indoors, put Corky on his lead and took him up the rutted chalk track towards the edge of the forest.

Ploughboy's Pit was an old well about fifteen feet across, a water tank sunk deep into the ground, a relic of the army camps set up during the Great War. At any other time of the year it would be surrounded by stinging nettles, but now only a few brambles and some rusty barbed wire coiled round it. A brick parapet, waist-high, ran around its circumference, and for years it had been capped by several rusting sheets of corrugated iron —

7

Until this morning, when the wind had tugged some of the iron sheets away and dumped them on her lawn.

When she leaned over the parapet, she was disgusted to see how much rubbish had been surreptitiously shoved into Ploughboy's Pit over the years, posted through the gaps where roof and parapet no longer met: old buggies and half-used tins of paint, builders' waste and scrawny Christmas trees. All hidden by that old tin roof – until now.

'Come on, Corky, let's get away from here.'

But Corky was keen to investigate this new place with its smells and scents and possibilities. Before Barbara could stop him, he'd tugged the lead from her hand and leapt over the low wall. She watched in horror as he slid down the slopes of rubbish. Oh God, was there still water in the bottom of the well, underneath all this mess?

The Cairn's slipping and sliding stopped abruptly as he landed on something solid – a dozen or so discarded bags of cement that had solidified over time and been transformed into a concrete platform.

Corky stood there trembling, then started to yap frantically, refusing to budge when Barbara called him.

'Oh, for goodness' sake!' She hitched her skirt up, clambered over the parapet and trod gingerly down onto broken tiles and soggy cardboard. The uppermost cement bag felt firm under her feet, so she stepped down until she could grab Corky by the collar and haul him out.

And then she saw what he was yapping at.

A body. Well, a skeleton really, with clothes. Well, the remains of clothes.

Barbara put a hand on her chest, her heart thudding so hard she thought she'd black out. And then, with Corky's lead held tight in her other hand, she began the difficult climb out into the fresher air.

CHAPTER 2

Detective Inspector Jeff Lincoln scooped up the post from the doormat. Bills, circulars, a final demand for his council tax – and a postcard showing a pair of cartoon pensioners eating ice creams on Southend Pier. He chucked the bills onto the hall table and turned the postcard over: *Getting stuck into some old library books. Hope you're behaving yourself! Love Trish xx P.S. Wish you were here xx*

He grinned, stupidly pleased by the card, brief as her message was. He'd much rather she were here in Wiltshire than a hundred and fifty miles away, but he was too much of a coward to tell her so. She'd taken a job in Essex, organising the library of an antiquarian scholar who'd been dead for three hundred years, but that was the sort of work she enjoyed. But when would he see her again? Were they still an item? Were they still in a relationship? They'd agreed to stay friends no matter what, but would they ever move in together again, or was that too much to hope for?

He picked his way across his living room, stepping on the joists in the absence of floorboards. He'd been living in the Old Vicarage for nearly a year, and yet there was still so much that needed to be done to it – like new floors to replace the ones that were full of dry rot. The flooring company he'd employed had suddenly decided, a month ago, that they had 'more pressing contracts to fulfil'– a subtle way of telling him they'd gone bust. He had yet to find another company that sounded more reliable than the bankrupt one.

As soon as he opened the door into the kitchen, Tux the cat flew out and bounded up the stairs.

'No sleeping on the bed!' Lincoln yelled after it, but he knew what he'd find when he got home at the end of his shift: the cat curled up like a big black and white dormouse in the rumpled sheets. He didn't really mind. Tux had sort of come with the house. The first time Lincoln had set eyes on the Old Vicarage, a year and a bit ago, he'd noticed the cat lurking in the overgrown garden. Although skinny, it looked too well fed to be a stray but, whoever it had once belonged to, as soon as Lincoln moved in, it had taken the Old Vicarage over as if it had always lived there.

He glanced at the clock. No time for breakfast, but he couldn't function without coffee. While he waited for the kettle to boil, his phone rang. It was Woody – Detective Sergeant Mike Woods – and there was excitement in his voice.

'A skeleton's turned up in Greywood Forest, boss. I said I'd pick you up on the way over there.'

'Sure it's not a team of archaeologists they need?'

'No, I was told to pick you up asap.'

Lincoln made coffee, spooned sugar in, stirred it briskly. He'd planned a morning at his desk at Barley Lane nick, catching up on paperwork he kept putting off, but the chance to act as Senior Investigating Officer at a crime scene was far more appealing.

He'd knocked back half a mug of coffee before Woody's car drew up outside. The horn beeped. Propping Trish's postcard on the mantelpiece, Lincoln grabbed his jacket, mac and phone and hurried out.

He buckled his seat belt as Woody swung the car round and headed out of Barbury. How did his DS always manage to look so smart, even this early on a winter's morning? It was all Lincoln could do to find an ironed shirt and clean tie most mornings. But then, Woody was married to Suki, who managed her husband and their two small sons with unfailing efficiency. Lincoln, in contrast, was on his own and always left things till the last minute.

'So where are we off to?'

'The Bridgeford end of Greywood Forest,' said Woody. 'Sounds as if the bones are in some sort of hole.'

'What, like a shallow grave?'

'No, some sort of rubbish dump, a place called Ploughboy's Pit.'

They drove west through the straggling outskirts of Barbury, past council workers with chainsaws tackling trees blown down in the night. Twigs and rotten branches lay smashed here and there all along the road.

Woody swerved to avoid a particularly large fallen branch. 'Fair old gale, wasn't it? Lose any tiles in the night?'

Lincoln laughed bitterly. The Old Vicarage didn't have many tiles to lose. Still, at least the bright blue tarpaulin covering its roof hadn't flown away in the gale. 'So...what do we know about this skeleton?'

'Not a lot. Small, probably a child. Reckon it's been there a while.'

'How long a while?'

'Too early to say. I only got the bare bones.' Woody chuckled.

They turned off the main road through the small dormitory town of

Bridgeford and drove up a steep lane towards Greywood Forest. At the top, with trees looming over it and police vehicles parked askew below it, stood a terrace of red-brick houses on an embankment. A couple of uniforms were running tape across the lane to restrict access, and fifty yards farther on, at the very edge of the forest, Lincoln could make out the ghostly shape of a forensics tent.

'Looks as if we've been beaten to it,' he said, put out that someone else had already taken over as Senior Investigating Officer.

He and Woody got out of the car and trudged up the chalk track towards the scenes of activity.

The tent had been pitched a bit precariously over mounds of rubbish that all but filled a brick-lined hole, like a big well, twelve or so feet across. It was impossible to tell how deep the hole was: it could be ten feet or fifty.

Lincoln felt strangely uneasy. 'What is this place?'

'Something left over from when the army were up here in the war, I reckon, though with a name like Ploughboy's Pit, it was probably here long before that, and the army just made use of it.' Woody scratched his head. 'Bit dangerous. Surprised it wasn't filled in years ago. Must've forgotten it was here.'

Lincoln snorted. 'It's been pretty much filled in by fly tippers.'

A man came towards them in a white boiler suit and blue overshoes, thirty-something, medium height, slightly built. His beaky nose was made more beaky by the hood that framed his bony face.

'Stop!' he said, squaring up to them as if he expected a fight. 'If you're not booted and suited, you'll have to stay where you are.'

'DI Jeff Lincoln, and this is DS Mike Woods.' Lincoln showed his ID, not sure of the necessity of a forensics suit if the bones had been lying in the brick pit for decades. There'd be precious little evidence left to destroy or contaminate. 'And you are?' he asked, resentful of some Scenes of Crime jobsworth bossing him around.

'I'm the SIO. Detective Chief Inspector Dale Jacobs. Are you the lot from Barley Lane? You took your time getting here, didn't you?'

Lincoln was about to protest, but Jacobs cut across him.

'Spare suits in the boot of my car,' he snapped, nodding his white-hooded head in the direction of a dark Astra Estate.

Lincoln exchanged a look with Woody and they both tramped back to get suitably attired.

'Is he Bryn's replacement?' DCI Bryn Marshall had recently taken early retirement on health grounds – at least, that was the official line.

'Could be.' Woody fought his way into a paper jumpsuit and slipped his shoe covers on. 'I heard he's come across from Avon and Somerset.'

'That's no excuse for acting like a prick.'

As they stepped over the low brick parapet and approached the tent, a familiar figure emerged from it: pathologist Ken Burges, a dapper man in his late fifties, his thinning hair combed over in a vain attempt to hide his bald pate.

'This is a tricky one,' he said, after greeting Lincoln and Woody. 'The remains are lying on a concrete ledge, but everything else is somewhat precarious and liable to slide down.' He swiped the tent open and led them inside.

'Taking any evidence with it.' Lincoln gazed glumly down onto a tumble of abandoned bikes, broken furniture and rubble that had slipped round the stack of cement sacks like water round a river boulder. 'How deep is this pit?'

'It's only about ten feet now,' Ken said, 'but it would've been a lot deeper originally. Looks as if they pumped some concrete into it, chucked the rest of the cement bags in, slapped some sheet metal over the top and left it at that.' He stepped down carefully into the morass of rubbish. 'And there's your body.'

A muddle of grey bones lay on top of some cement bags about three feet below them. Ken clambered down first, Lincoln and Woody following him, taking care not to dislodge anything.

As Lincoln's eyes got used to the low light, the bones took shape: the skeleton of a child, curled in a foetal position. He crouched down to get a better look. A plastic hair slide was tangled in the brittle folds of dull brown hair that had slipped away from the skull. A little girl, then. A deep sadness invaded his heart, pushing aside his irritation about the new DCI.

Scraps of clothing clung to the bones here and there, but they'd rotted too much to reveal their original colour or pattern – at least, not in this artificial lighting. A stained plastic sandal that must once have been pearly pink still encased the bones of a foot. The other sandal would probably turn up when they sifted through everything.

Lincoln stood up again, his knees protesting. 'Could she have climbed in here and got trapped? Gone to sleep and died of exposure?'

Woody scratched his head. 'The houses aren't that far away. She'd have cried for help, wouldn't she?'

'If we can find out when these cement bags were left here, it'll give us a rough date for when she died.' Lincoln glanced hopefully across at

Ken. 'I suppose it's too soon for you to give us an estimate of how long she's been here?'

'More than ten years, less than fifty. Can't say any more than that until I've got her back to the mortuary. And the sooner I do that…' Ken shooed Lincoln and Woody ahead of him back up the banks of rubbish.

Out in the open again, they were confronted by DCI Jacobs.

'What was this thing used for?' he wanted to know, arms folded, feet apart. 'Wasn't built as a rubbish dump, was it?'

'Water storage during the First World War,' Ken told him. 'There were army camps all over Salisbury Plain and this part of Wiltshire, all through Greywood Forest. No mains water up here in those days, of course.' He waved his hand at the row of houses. 'Those wouldn't have been here then.'

Jacobs frowned. 'Who owns it now? The MOD?'

Ken shrugged. 'Whoever owns the land here, I suppose – the Riverbourne Estate, probably.'

'The Riverbourne Estate?'

'As in Lord Riverbourne,' Woody said. 'He's the big landowner round here, lives at Greywood Hall.' He nodded in the general direction of Bridgeford, a town that probably owed its continued existence and prosperity to the Earls of Riverbourne.

Jacobs grunted. 'Whoever it belongs to, they haven't maintained it very well.'

They all stared down into the messy depths of Ploughboy's Pit.

'Reminds me of the Wall of Death at the fair,' said Ken. 'Remember that? Motorbikes roaring round inside a wooden cylinder? Centrifugal force.'

'Way before my time,' Jacobs said, and stomped off to talk to the SOCO team.

'Makes me feel positively elderly.' Ken reached into his inside pocket for a miniature of Martell.

'You're not that much older than me,' said Lincoln, only a few years off fifty himself, though the arrival of the young, sour-faced DCI Jacobs made him feel overdue for retirement.

Ken unscrewed the bottle cap and knocked back a couple of shots of brandy. 'Helps my stomach.'

Lincoln sighed. 'We'll have to wait a bit, then, before we know how she died.'

'Afraid so.' Ken took another crafty shot of brandy. 'And of course, after all this time, we may never find out.'

CHAPTER 3

While Lincoln and Woody were inspecting Ploughboy's Pit with DCI Dale Jacobs, DC Graham Dilke was talking to Barbara Trent, whose Greywood Terrace house was the closest to the forest and the pit.

'So it was you who found the body, Mrs Trent?' The young detective constable, conscientious but still inexperienced, wasn't sure that was the right word. Bones, that was all it was really. Bones, and a few scraps of material. Still, the new DCI had told him to talk to the woman who'd dialled 999, so here he was.

'*Miss* Trent,' she said with a quick smile. 'And actually it was Corky who found it.' She crouched beside the wicker basket, where a ginger-coated terrier lay with his head on his paws, one ear cocked, one eye open. 'He's a little hero, my Corky, finding that poor child.'

'He certainly is.' Dilke's Aunt Jocelyn had a dog like Corky, a Cairn or something, nippy and not to be trusted. Its erratic behaviour had put his mother off dogs for life. 'Good boy.'

Miss Trent stood up and crossed to the fireplace, where an unlit wood burner stood four-square on the hearth. She leaned down and switched it on. Electric, instant. Not the real thing after all.

'Can't seem to get warm.' She crossed her arms and rubbed her shoulders. 'Must be the shock.'

She was a bit older than his mother, Dilke guessed – mid-sixties, stocky and neat in a tweed skirt and Fair Isle jumper. Her iron-grey hair was thick and wavy, and she kept pushing it back from her forehead as if she was fed up with it.

She told him how she'd gone up the track to Ploughboy's Pit after sections of its roof landed in her garden.

'Will someone need to examine that?' She nodded towards the rusty metal sheets that stuck up out of her lawn like the lids of supersized sardine tins.

'Not sure,' he said. 'So it was for water, was it, this pit?'

'That's right, for water storage. There was a whole string of them, all through the woods.' She pushed a plate of assorted biscuits towards him – Duchy of Cornwall, he noticed, as he helped himself. 'Dad knew all about it,' she went on, a trace of wistfulness in her

14

voice. 'The other pits got filled in, but this one's always been covered over, though that hasn't stopped the world and his wife using it as a rubbish dump on the sly.'

'There's a load of cement bags in there. Who—?'

'Oh, that was the council. They had a half-hearted go at filling it in years ago.'

'You don't remember how long ago that was?'

She smiled triumphantly. 'I do, actually. The family next door, the Joneses – they're not there now – their son got a job with the council straight out of school. First job they gave him was to help fill Ploughboy's Pit in, so that'd be July '96. His mum was pleased because she could have him home at lunchtime. They pumped in a load of cement. The machine was going all day. Not that I was here, of course. I was at work, but it drove Mum up the wall.'

Dilke sighed. How could they hope to solve a crime – if that was what this was – after so long?

Then, as if she were thinking aloud, Miss Trent said, 'Of course, it could be that little girl.'

He sat up. 'What little girl?'

'She went missing at a funfair in town the weekend Diana died.'

'Diana?'

'Princess Di. 1997. You'd be too young to remember that. She was only eight or nine. Got separated from her mother and then vanished. An unusual first name, foreign-sounding. *Yazmin.*' She pounced on the name as it came back to her. 'That was it. She was never seen again. You must have it on file.'

He jotted it down, suddenly more alert. 'Remember anything else about her?'

'Sorry, no.' Miss Trent stared down the garden. 'Oh, it'd be just like that lad next door to leave the job half-done.' She pushed her hair back with an irritated shove of her hand.

The living room had grown warm while the electric flames licked rhythmically over the imitation logs. Dilke felt she'd told him all she could.

'Nice pictures,' he remarked as she showed him out. The living room was lined with paintings – a few modern landscapes but some much, much older. Originals, he could tell, not prints.

'I'm a bit of a collector,' she said bashfully. 'I worked at Greywood Hall for many years. You develop an appreciation for fine art when you're surrounded by it for so long.'

15

He'd had to visit Greywood Hall when he was in middle school, and had hated it: paintings of horses and religious scenes; tiers of portraits of the Buckthorn family, who'd owned the house since the Stone Age. He'd rather have been climbing trees and exploring the parklands that spread for miles around the Hall.

'What did you do there?'

She beamed, pleased to be asked. 'Ran it, virtually. I was Lord Riverbourne's right-hand woman. The *previous* Lord Riverbourne, that is. Howard. His son's running it now.' She sounded less enamoured of the son than of his father. Then she pushed her hair back and said, almost shyly, 'I know this little house isn't Greywood Hall, but it's so uplifting, having beautiful things to look at.'

CHAPTER 4

Lincoln filled the kettle and dumped it down on top of the filing cabinet. Over the years, rust had etched an irregular ring in the metal surface where successive members of Barbury's CID team had been less than diligent in their making of teas and coffees. Barley Lane nick was long overdue for a makeover but was unlikely to get one now. Instead it was expected to close, its personnel transferring to the larger, more modern Park Street police station in neighbouring Presford – not a move to which Lincoln looked forward with any enthusiasm.

He switched the kettle on, keen to get some caffeine inside him as soon as he could. He should eat something too.

Why did he find it so hard to get into a routine in the mornings? Probably because he was always in a rush, half-awake. He went to bed as late as he could, hoping he'd be tired enough to fall asleep easily. Instead he lay awake into the small hours, dozing off for a few minutes then rushing up out of sleep, his heart racing.

Stress, that was what it was. Anxiety. Too much on his plate, too much unfinished business, cases unresolved, his house still unfinished.

When he'd got back from Greywood Forest an hour ago, he'd searched the Internet for anything about the abduction Barbara Trent had mentioned to Dilke. He'd found disappointingly little, apart from the essential facts: Yazmin Fletcher, eight years old, had been abducted from a funfair in Presford in 1997, on the August bank holiday weekend. Her father, Bruno Bartek, had been the prime suspect because he and Yazmin's mother, Sonia, had been in dispute over her custody. However, when Bartek returned from a trip to Poland, as distraught about the child's disappearance as Sonia was, it was evident that he knew nothing about her whereabouts.

The hunt for Yazmin had continued for months before quietly fizzling out, along with any media interest.

He printed off a school photo taken only a few weeks before she disappeared. Dark blue eyes gazed out from her small, heart-shaped face, her light brown hair falling straight and shoulder-length. Her skin was very fair, with the faintest suggestion of mauve shadows under her eyes. Something about her gaze unsettled him, though, as if she wasn't quite present – distracted by something, troubled. Was this the child whose bones had lain in Ploughboy's Pit all these years? Sadness washed over him despite his resolve to stay dispassionate. He wouldn't be human if he didn't feel at least a little sorrowful.

His desk phone rang. Dilke picked it up before Lincoln could reach it, but quickly handed the receiver over.

'Youngman here,' the DCS barked down the line. 'I gather from DCI Jacobs that the remains could be from a case twenty years ago. That right, Jeff?'

Lincoln recounted what he'd learned himself within the last hour. 'And of course, sir, because Yazmin went missing in Presford rather than Barbury, it was the team at Park Street who took charge of it.'

DCS Youngman sighed unhappily. 'May not be her, of course, but either way, I want Barley Lane and Park Street to work together on this one. Collaborating on a case like this could lay the foundations for consolidating the teams.'

Lincoln loathed management bullshit. Consolidating the teams? Closing Barley Lane and moving everyone to Park Street nick was what Youngman meant. Everyone who was left who hadn't opted for early retirement, that is.

'I'm sure we can work together, sir.'

'The *Messenger* will be all over it, naturally, although the publicity might jog a few memories. Sorry I couldn't forewarn you about a new DCI arriving, by the way,' Youngman went on, not sounding at all sorry. 'I'd hoped to bring Dale over to Barley Lane, introduce him properly, but then this case cropped up and there was no time for niceties. I wasn't expecting him to go to the scene himself – which shows you how keen he is.'

We don't need keen, Lincoln thought, staring out of the window at the flat, colourless sky. We need steady. We need someone we can trust.

He switched the kettle on again, and as if by magic DC Dennis Breeze appeared beside him, his leather biker jacket creaking as he leaned across to put a couple of Yorkshire teabags in his mug. A detective in his forties unlikely to get promotion or even seek it, Breeze was Lincoln's bête noire: no matter how many training courses he was sent on, no matter how often he was reminded of correct procedures and protocols, he always did things his way, at his own pace.

'Bloody cold out!' Breeze blew on his hands and rubbed them together. 'And not much warmer in here. This a new economy measure, boss, turning the thermostat down?'

18

'Nothing to do with me, Dennis. You'll soon warm up with a cup of tea inside you.'

Breeze pulled his chair out, the springs protesting as he sat down on it and leaned back. He sucked on some nicotine gum. 'So what's this body up the woods, then?' He jabbed a thumb towards the whiteboard, where Woody had begun to put up scene photos and a sketch map.

'It's just a skeleton,' said Dilke. 'Possibly a little girl who went missing in 1997. The woman who found it—' He broke off as DC Pam Smyth came in, her face flushed with the cold. She dumped her cycle helmet down on her desk and ruffled her short blonde hair back into shape.

'Who's gone missing?' She peeled off her waterproof jacket and draped it over the back of her chair, sounding eager to get cracking on this new case. Conscientious and keen to learn, Pam had been part of Lincoln's team for the shortest time of all of them, but she'd already impressed him with her ability to think laterally, even if it meant they sometimes disagreed.

He scanned the faces of his team: Woody, Dennis Breeze, Graham Dilke and Pam Smyth. Only now they'd be DCI Jacobs's team…

'Yazmin Fletcher,' he said, 'abducted at a funfair on Presford playing fields in 1997. Eight years old. Her parents had split up and couldn't agree on access arrangements. When she disappeared in broad daylight, everyone assumed her dad had snatched her, but they soon found out he'd been in Poland at the time. I don't know if there were any other leads. We'll know more when the files come through.'

'And now she's turned up,' said Dilke. 'Or her bones have. At least, it's *possibly* her.'

Pam stared intently at the scene photos on the whiteboard. 'She was found on a rubbish tip?'

'The locals call it Ploughboy's Pit,' Lincoln explained. 'It was sunk into the ground to use as a water tank during the war, but it's had rubbish and rubble dumped in it over the years, including a load of cement that's formed a kind of platform a few feet down. That's where he left the body. He *or* she.'

'The woman who found the bones remembers council workers filling it in during the summer of 1996,' Dilke added, 'so that's when the cement bags date from.'

Pam frowned. 'How are they going to know if it's Yazmin or not, after all this time? There'll be no DNA worth testing, will there?'

'Her dental records are on file, according to one of the newspaper reports I read when I got back here,' said Lincoln. 'The team at Park Street got hold of them soon after she went missing – never guessing it'd be twenty years before anyone would look at them again.'

She groaned. 'God, her mum's had to go all those years not knowing. How do you manage that?'

'You take one day at a time, I suppose.' Lincoln wondered where Sonia Fletcher was living now, whether she'd married and had other children, whether she was even still alive. She'd be in her early forties now, Bruno Bartek about forty-seven, about the same age as Lincoln himself. 'There's going to be a lot of media interest in this – lots of speculation.'

'I vaguely remember the case,' said Woody. 'The family had moved here from Southampton.'

'Maybe they moved back there after what happened,' Pam suggested.

Lincoln took a sip of his coffee. He'd left it standing too long, and now it was lukewarm. 'I haven't a clue. It happened before I came down here. As for what happens next, it's no longer up to me. I'm not in charge any more.'

The room went quiet around him.

'How do you mean?' A spring in Breeze's chair twanged.

'A new DCI's turned up,' Dilke said, twiddling a pencil between his fingers. 'Dale Jacobs. From Avon and Somerset. He was there this morning, at the scene.'

Breeze snorted. 'DCIs don't usually get their hands dirty like that. Where is he now, then?'

Lincoln surveyed the CID room – *his* CID room. 'I expect he's on his way.'

'She might as well have been wearing a GPS tracker,' DCI Jacobs declared on his arrival a few minutes later. 'Bloody social media!'

Sonia Fletcher had been traced by the Tweeters and Facebookers who'd picked up the *Messenger*'s newsfeed. She hadn't moved back to Southampton, as Pam had suggested; she was still right here in Barbury.

'Still, Twitter's saved us a bit of legwork, eh?' Jacobs stared round at Lincoln and his team. 'Where's Brewery Court?'

Pam started to tell him, but he cut her off. 'You free, Inspector Lincoln? See if you can find her?'

'If you've got the address, sir, I'll go with DS Woods.' He grabbed his coat.

'Spare desk anywhere?' Jacobs looked round him in an exaggerated way, as if he'd somehow overlooked one that was right in front of him.

20

Breeze lumbered to his feet. 'Shauna's desk's free.'

'And where's Shauna?'

'Maternity leave,' said Lincoln. DC Shauna Hartlake was expecting a baby in May. Soon after Christmas, though, she'd had a threatened miscarriage and had gone on maternity leave early. 'She won't be back for a while.'

Breeze lifted a stack of memos and briefing papers from Shauna's desk, deliberated about where to dump it, then dropped it unceremoniously next to the photocopier.

Jacobs glared at him. 'Shouldn't that material be filed?'

'Of course,' said Breeze, retrieving it and dropping it onto his own desk with a thud. 'I'll sort it first. Sir.'

Jacobs scowled as he took his tablet out of his case and his phone from his jacket pocket. He set them down on Shauna's desk. The desk that used to be Shauna's. He lined them up. He straightened her pen pot – a chipped souvenir mug with *We Have Seen the Lions of Longleat* on it – and her empty wire tray. Straightened her desk phone on its mat.

Woody picked up his keys and exchanged a glance with Lincoln, rolling his eyes.

Jacobs glanced up. 'Okay, then, you two? Off to Brewery Court?'

'Off to Brewery Court,' Lincoln agreed, following Woody as he headed for the door.

'He's wearing a suit,' said Woody as they drove away. 'With a patterned lining. Did you notice? Looked expensive.'

Lincoln had noticed. His new boss was evidently a smart dresser, but when you were that slim you could get away with it. Even so, DCI Jacobs's charcoal-grey suit with its bright blue lining was a bit flash for everyday wear. Or maybe that was how they dressed in Avon and Somerset.

'What are we supposed to say to Sonia Fletcher? We don't even know for sure it's Yazmin we've found, do we?'

'No, Woody, but we need to get to her before the reporters do.'

'Wish I could remember more about the case. She's Polish, isn't she?'

'Sonia? No, but her partner was, though he'd lived here all his life. Bartek. Bruno Bartek.'

'And if it *isn't* Yazmin?'

'We'll cross that bridge when we come to it. It's the next turning, isn't it?'

Barbury Brewery hadn't produced beer for decades, although its name lived on in real ales produced elsewhere in Wiltshire. The brewery building itself had been converted into apartments, but across the street some old outbuildings had been demolished to create a small estate of stone-clad houses called Brewery Court.

Sonia's mid-terrace house looked clean and cared for, if rather compact.

Lincoln lifted the brass knocker and rapped smartly on the door. No answer. Woody bent down and peeped through the letterbox. Straightened up, shaking his head. 'Reckon she's out.'

'Reporters, are you?'

They both spun round. An elderly woman had come out onto the step of the house next door, a fleece round her shoulders against the cold.

Lincoln flashed his card at her. 'We're looking for Sonia Fletcher.'

'So it *is* her little girl you found.'

'We can't confirm anything yet. We need to speak to Sonia as soon as possible. You know when she'll be home?'

'She'll be at work, I expect. Not sure where, though. She does all sorts – dog walking, house-sitting, shelf-stacking at the supermarket.'

'Got a mobile number for her?'

The woman sighed. 'Somewhere.' She went back indoors, returning a minute later with a number written carefully on the back of an old envelope.

Lincoln handed her his business card in exchange. 'Thanks. If you see her, ask her to call me straight away. And not to talk to any journalists.'

As soon as he was back at his desk, Lincoln looked through what he'd downloaded from the Internet earlier. He probably wouldn't be able to get hold of the original files for another twenty-four hours, so the more he could find out now the better.

According to Sonia, Yazmin had been wearing a blue cotton summer dress when she went missing, a pattern of yellow and white flowers round the hem. On top of the dress, she'd been wearing a white knitted cardigan. Allowing for the deterioration of the material over nearly twenty years, the scraps Lincoln had seen this morning matched the description of the dress, but he couldn't remember seeing even the remnants of a cardigan near the child's bones.

'What are jelly shoes?' he asked Pam.

'Jelly shoes?'

'Says here that Yazmin was wearing pink jelly shoes.'

'They're those plastic sandals kids wear at the seaside. You can go in the water in them.'

'Right. Didn't know that's what they were called. That's like the sandal we found, then. I'm just reading the description of what she was wearing that day. "Pink jelly shoes. Bangles." Can't remember any bangles, Woody, can you?'

Woody looked up from his keyboard. 'No, but the SOCOs won't have finished yet. Reckon there's still loads of rubbish to go through. The other jelly shoe could turn up, and the bangles. Sounds like it's her, though, doesn't it?'

'So far, yes. And the dental records should confirm it, one way or the other.' Lincoln looked up, suddenly realising something – or someone – was missing. 'Where's the DCI?'

'Got called back to Park Street,' said Woody. 'Something about an assault at Press Vale Country Club.'

Lincoln had last visited the country club over a year ago, when he'd been investigating the murder of Holly Macleod, a local businesswoman. A stately mansion on the edge of Barbury, Press Vale boasted sports facilities and a shooting range, a health spa and a casino. Its orangery was a popular venue for celebrity weddings, featured far too often, in his opinion, in the *Messenger*. After Holly Macleod's death, though, Pete Doubleday, a member of the syndicate that owned Press Vale, had left the country, and two of its staff had been jailed for attempted murder. Prestigious it might be, but some of the people who owned it had dubious connections.

'Did he say what kind of assault?'

Woody shook his head. 'He shot off before I could ask.'

'Couldn't it wait?'

'Reckon an assault takes priority over a cold case like Yazmin Fletcher.'

'Huh! Might be a cold case to Jacobs, but it's not a cold case to her mother.' Lincoln sat back from his screen. 'DCS Youngman's expecting us to work with Park Street on this one.'

'Reckon he's paving the way for us all to be merged?'

'It's been on the cards long enough.' And yet the powers that be seemed to be biding their time.

Pam looked apprehensive. 'You fancy a move to Park Street, boss?'

'No,' said Lincoln, 'but I doubt if I'll have a choice.' Move or quit. He didn't fancy either.

The door opened and DCI Jacobs swept in, a slim bundle of manila folders tucked under his arm. 'The Yazmin Fletcher file,' he said, slapping the folders down on Woody's desk. 'Courtesy of Park Street.'

Lincoln had been expecting the file to be much thicker, but before he could say anything his new boss plonked himself down at Shauna's desk.

'But don't get excited,' Jacobs went on. 'We'll have to hold fire on that for now. We've got an attempted sexual assault at the country club to deal with.'

'So I hear. What's happened?'

'Girl called Amy Cartland says one of the guests tried to rape her on Sunday night. She took drinks to his room and he grabbed her, threw her on the bed, climbed on top of her.'

'And she's only just reported it?'

'She was scared to come forward, but then her dad persuaded her. She's given a statement, but it's pretty sketchy.'

'So she's on the staff at Press Vale? I can see why she was scared to report it.' The sort of men who belonged to the country club were the sort that stuck together, covered for each other, held all the power – or so it would seem to a young girl whose job was to keep the customers happy.

'Any witnesses?'

'Only one – a guy who was playing poker there that evening. Promised her he'd give a statement if she went to the police. Name of Hugh Buckthorn. I've got a number for him.'

'Hugh Buckthorn?' A name Lincoln hadn't heard in a while, or seen in print. What was Hugh doing these days, apart from gambling away the family inheritance?

Jacobs looked up. 'Ring any bells?'

'Buckthorn's the family name of the Earls of Riverbourne,' Woody told him. 'Of Greywood Hall in Bridgeford.'

The DCI snorted. 'Bloody upper classes! Nothing better to do with their time and money than gamble it away, eh? Fix up to speak to him, find out what he knows. If it sounds promising, get him to come in and give a statement. Okay?'

'And Yazmin Fletcher?' Lincoln asked.

'Drop it. For now, at least. The media can speculate all they like. We're not obliged to tell them anything.'

'But her mother's going to—' Pam began, but Jacobs cut her off.

'Sod what her mother's going to do! This assault takes priority.' He pointed a bony finger at her. 'I'm Senior Investigating Officer and you

24

take your orders from me. Got that?'

'Yes, sir.' She bent her head, her cheeks ablaze.

'A little courtesy—' Lincoln started to say, but he too was cut off by his new boss.

'You, Lincoln, ring Buckthorn, go and see him asap. He's probably the *Honourable* Hugh,' Jacobs added with a snarl, 'but I trust I can rely on you to address him correctly, yeah?'

'I'll be sure to check *Debrett's* before I call on him.'

But Lincoln's sarcasm was wasted on him. Jacobs flipped open Shauna's laptop. The laptop that used to be Shauna's. He frowned at the dinosaur stickers decorating the lid, and snatched a Post-it note off her track pad. 'Huh! So much for keeping passwords secret and secure!'

CHAPTER 5

Barbara knew the media would get hold of the story of the skeleton in Ploughboy's Pit, but she hadn't expected quite such a flurry of interest. Although the police had blocked off the lane below Greywood Terrace, a couple of enterprising reporters had worked out another way of getting near the crime scene: through the field that ran along the back of the houses as far as the woods.

One of her neighbours had let them through the gate at the bottom of his garden, so they didn't even have to climb over any fences. They'd probably bribed him, she thought angrily. It wouldn't take a lot.

She glared out of her window. The young detective who'd interviewed her had promised to let her know if she could move the buckled sheets of iron or whether they'd have to be looked at first. He hadn't got back to her, but then what did she expect? He didn't look much more than a teenager. She'd have to get someone in to do it. Did people still come round and take scrap metal away?

Unable to settle, she took Corky for a walk along the footpath beside the railway and round the field. She couldn't stop thinking about the child she'd found – the remains of a child, her dress little more than tatters, her pathetic skull so small Barbara could have held it in her own cupped hands.

What mother would have let her child come to such an end? How could that little girl have lain there so long without a soul coming to look for her?

Oh God, had she climbed in there and not been able to get out? Barbara couldn't imagine what the child might have been through, crying for help and not being heard.

She hadn't been back indoors more than a few minutes when the doorbell rang. Oh no, not those journalists!

She marched down the hall and yanked the door open, ready to send them packing, but instead she found a man standing there. A man she knew.

'Hello, Barbara,' he said in that authoritative way of his. 'It's been a while, hasn't it? I saw you on the news. May I come in? We've got a lot to talk about.'

CHAPTER 6

Lincoln dropped his phone and keys on the kitchen table and went in search of food. The night was cold, threatening to be frosty, so he grabbed a tin of tomato soup from the pantry shelf. One day he'd follow Trish's advice and plan his meals for the week ahead. One day, but not yet. Soup would do for now, though, and he might even have some bread left to go with it.

Before he left Barley Lane, he'd phoned Hugh Buckthorn to ask about the incident at the country club, but Buckthorn hadn't picked up and he'd had to leave a message. While he waited in vain for his call to be returned, he'd started to go through the folders Jacobs had brought back from Park Street.

On the last Saturday of August 1997, Sonia Fletcher had taken Yazmin to the bank holiday funfair in Presford, meeting up with her sister, Julie Miller, who'd brought her two young sons along. Soon after they got there, Sonia left Julie in charge of all three children while she returned to the car for something.

Distracted by one of the boys, Julie had turned away from Yazmin just long enough for the little girl to drift away from her side. When Julie looked round for her, she saw her trotting calmly away with a young man she was sure was Bruno Bartek, Yazmin's father.

Julie had shouted after him, but the crowds closed behind him and Yazmin, and she lost sight of them. With two small boys in tow, she couldn't follow them until Sonia got back a minute or two later, but by then the man she thought was Bruno had vanished. And so had Yazmin.

If only Julie Miller hadn't been so sure it was Bruno! She'd been so certain it was him, the team at Park Street nick seemed to have made no attempt, in those first crucial hours after her disappearance, to look for anyone else.

Only when Bruno had turned up at Park Street, having heard on the news that his daughter was missing, did DCI Soloman apparently consider other possibilities. Bruno had been in Poland all the previous week, returning to his flat to learn that Yazmin had vanished the day before. He'd driven straight to the police station to show it wasn't him

27

they should be looking for. Julie had to admit that she'd been mistaken, but by then it was too late.

The investigating team at Park Street had had their work cut out: many of the workers on the funfair were unskilled labourers or travellers who followed the funfair circuit to pick up employment where they could. The men hiring them hadn't always insisted on full names and addresses, so tracking down every last one of these workers had proved impossible. Once the team had traced and eliminated local sex offenders and the few names they'd received through anonymous tips, they ran out of suspects.

Lincoln turned the pages, imagining the thankless task of tracking down the dozens of men, inadequately documented, who'd worked on the funfair that weekend. He relished the opportunity to reopen the case, but he was afraid DCI Jacobs would decide to shelve it until the attempted rape at Press Vale had been investigated.

Now, at home in his kitchen, he was pouring hot soup into too small a mug when his mobile rang. He dumped the pan back on the stove and hunted for his phone – until he found it under a tea towel.

'Inspector Lincoln? Hugh Buckthorn. I've only just this minute got your message.'

Lincoln sat down at the table, pushing the mug of soup aside. 'Thanks for getting back to me. It's about an incident at the country club on Sunday evening. I understand you—'

'Amy's come forward after all, then?'

'She's come forward, yes. You saw what happened?'

'Not really, but I promised her I'd make a statement if she went to the police. Look, why don't you call round tomorrow sometime?'

'Of course, but—'

'Speldon Magna. Corner Cottage. Opposite the pub. You can't miss it. One o'clock?' Clearly expecting the arrangement to be perfectly acceptable, Buckthorn hung up.

Lincoln sipped his soup and tried to imagine the life Hugh Buckthorn lived these days. He'd take bets on Corner Cottage having tiles on its roof, floorboards in the living room and a larder with more in it than a few tins of soup and some packets of rice.

He recalled the days, long ago, when Buckthorn was rarely out of the newspapers. The younger son of Robert, the ninth Earl of Riverbourne, he'd been a bit of a rake in his twenties, clubbing with models and dukes' daughters, jetting off to the south of France and generally having a whale of a time. As a teenager only a few years younger than him, Lincoln had envied the young man – even though, like so many aristocratic sons and daughters before him, Buckthorn had seemed destined to crash and burn.

And yet clearly he'd survived, outliving his older brother, Howard, who'd died suddenly last August after only a few years as the tenth earl. What was Hugh like now, the one-time playboy aristocrat? Lincoln would soon find out.

He finished his soup, wishing he hadn't had to eat it alone. Trish Whittington had left Barbury for the Essex coast a few months ago, to take over the running of a private library built up towards the end of the seventeenth century by scholar Charles Lundy. Lincoln was doubtful whether any but the most dedicated researchers would traipse all that way to consult the works in his collection, but Trish seemed to be enjoying the challenge.

Not that she'd had much choice. The previous spring she'd unwittingly assisted in a campaign against her own employers. She'd done some research for a young colleague, Linus Bonetti, only later discovering he was on a quest to expose corruption in the council's Social Services department. He'd been suspended, then dismissed. In despair, he'd killed himself.

Months later, Lincoln had found himself investigating the murder of a teenage runaway Bonetti had been trying to help. Allegations of corruption had resurfaced. When a journalist began to explore the story behind Bonetti's death, he had been aided by an anonymous source who passed him information Bonetti had gathered, revealing the extent of corruption among council officers.

That anonymous source had been Trish, who hadn't wanted to see Bonetti's efforts wasted.

Lincoln knew she didn't regret what she'd done. Still, she'd been sufficiently scared of being identified, then disciplined or dismissed, that she'd leapt at the chance of a job a long way away from Barbury.

He'd hardly set eyes on her since she'd started this new job. When she came home for Christmas she'd spent most of her break with her daughter, trying to make up for lost time. Against Trish's expectations Kate had refused to move to Essex with her, and was living with Woody and his wife, Suki – Trish's older sister.

'I'll be back in Barbury at half-term,' Trish had told him over the phone at New Year. 'I miss Kate even more than I thought I would. And you, of course,' she'd added quickly. 'I miss you too.'

'Why don't you stay here with me that week?' he'd suggested. 'That's if you don't mind the flapping of tarpaulins in the night.'

'That'll be the least of my worries.' He could hear the grin in her voice. 'As long as you've got heating and hot water and that nice big bed, I'll be fine.'

But she hadn't got back to him yet, and the half-term holiday was only a couple of weeks away.

He was doing the washing-up when his mobile rang. Hugh Buckthorn calling back?

'Mr Lincoln? It's Sonia Fletcher. I've seen the news. Is it Yazmin?' Her voice was fearful.

'We can't confirm the identity yet,' he said. 'Shall I come round? This isn't easy to talk about over the phone.' Indeed, it wasn't easy to talk about, full stop.

'What, now?' She sounded uncertain.

He checked his watch. Seven thirty. 'I'd rather not leave it till the morning.'

He reached Sonia's house in Brewery Court in fifteen minutes. Light streamed out from the living room window and a lamp was burning in the hall too, shining through the diamond-shaped panes in the front door. He banged the brass knocker a couple of times. Where did she park her car? The space marked out in front of her house was empty.

As he lifted the knocker for a third time, he felt the door give and then drift open. He stepped inside and called out. Went to the foot of the stairs and hollered. Went through to the narrow galley kitchen, where lights beamed down from gaudily painted cabinets onto a clean but cluttered worktop.

A cup stood on the drainer, half-full of tea. He touched it. It was still faintly warm.

Maybe she was in the bathroom. He waited a couple of minutes, but she still didn't appear. He brought her number up on his phone and rang it. After a few seconds he heard the ringing of an old-fashioned American telephone. Traced the sound to a small patchwork bag sitting beside the sofa in the living room, her iPhone sticking up between her wallet and her hairbrush.

He tried not to jump to a sinister conclusion. She could be round at her neighbour's house. That would explain the lights left on, the door unlocked, the phone still here. He went outside, leaving the front door on the latch.

The woman he'd met before came to the door with her hair wrapped in a towel.

'Ah, Mrs—'

'Best. Joan Best.'

'Is Sonia with you? She's expecting me, but she doesn't seem to be in.'

Mrs Best frowned at him as if he was a bit barmy. 'Of course she's in. She was running the tap in the kitchen ten minutes ago.'

Filling the kettle for that abandoned mug of tea? 'She's nowhere downstairs and it seemed a bit cheeky to go looking upstairs if she'd only nipped next door to you. Her bag's there, her phone...'

Patting her makeshift turban, Mrs Best pushed Sonia's front door open, calling her name as she went from room to room downstairs while Lincoln hovered in the hall.

'I'll pop up and check she's not in bed with a migraine or something,' she said, and climbed the stairs that went up from the living room. After a minute or two she reappeared on the landing. 'That's odd. She's not here.'

'You didn't hear her drive away?'

As Mrs Best came slowly down the stairs, Lincoln was reminded of Gloria Swanson in *Sunset Boulevard* – except Mrs Best was no ageing film star, despite her floor-length dressing gown and strange headgear.

'I wouldn't have, would I? I was washing my hair. But where's she gone, the silly girl, without her bag and her phone?' Nervously, she patted her turban again. 'She'll have guessed it was Yazmin you'd found. I know you can't say, but she'd have put two and two together, and she's not strong. Mentally, I mean. Gawd, I hope she hasn't gone and done anything stupid.'

'Have you got a phone number for her family in Southampton?'

Mrs Best shook her head. 'No. But *you* should be able to track them down easily enough. That's what you do, isn't it, your line of work?'

'Call me if you hear anything from her, or if she comes back.'

'Of course. I'll pull her door to. No good leaving the place unlocked.'

As Lincoln drove away he, too, hoped to God that Sonia hadn't done anything stupid when she heard her long-lost daughter might have been found. An end to hope.

Nothing more he could do tonight. He'd leave his phone on in case she tried to contact him. Sometime tomorrow, with any luck, he'd know for certain that the remains were Yazmin's – or not.

CHAPTER 7

THURSDAY 2ND FEBRUARY

'No Dale?' Lincoln looked round as he hung his coat up and headed for the kettle.

'He's probably stopped off at Park Street on his way in,' Graham Dilke said. 'Can't be easy, trying to manage his team there as well as us lot.'

'*I* was managing you lot perfectly well before he came along. We need to get hold of Sonia Fletcher's sister.'

'Her sister?'

'I went round to Sonia's last night but she'd gone off somewhere. No bag, no phone, maybe only the clothes she stood up in. I don't want to take any chances. I'm hoping her sister might know where she's gone.'

Coffee made, Lincoln was about to log onto his computer when his desk phone rang: DCS Youngman, sounding grave.

'Bit of bad news, Jeff. Dale Jacobs rolled his car yesterday evening on his way home.'

'Christ! Is he okay?'

'Not sure yet. Still waiting for an update from Presford General.'

'Anyone else involved?'

'Fortunately not. Maybe he swerved to avoid a deer or something, lost control. Easily done if you're not used to the road, and it might've been a bit icy. Avon and Somerset are trying to contact his next of kin. Which isn't to say he won't pull through,' Youngman put in, hurriedly, 'but you need your family round you when this sort of thing happens.'

'Of course.' Not for the first time, Lincoln wondered who'd come rushing to *his* hospital bedside: parents both dead, sister Ruth estranged from him and living in the States, brother Paul busy losing himself in South America – although he might have moved on from there by now, for all Lincoln knew. They weren't a close family, never had been – even less so now that Cathy wasn't around to remind him about birthdays and keep track of addresses.

'This leaves us without an SIO on the Press Vale assault case, of course,' Youngman went on. 'I want you to take over, Jeff, at least until I can draft somebody else in.'

*

32

Hugh Buckthorn may have been raised at Greywood Hall but his house in the village of Speldon Magna looked rather more modest. Corner Cottage was quaint, very old and very thatched, down the steep hill from the parish church and across the road from the Two Magpies – a pub Lincoln had visited several times in the course of his murder investigation last year. He wondered if the cheery Billie Wheeler was still the landlady there.

The only parking space outside Buckthorn's house was already taken up by a silver Jaguar, presumably his. Since the lane was too narrow to park in safely, Lincoln drove into the pub car park instead. The railway embankment loomed over him, carrying the line that ran from London to Bristol, though trains hadn't stopped at Speldon Halt since before the days of Beeching.

He crossed over to the rustic porch of Corner Cottage and rang the doorbell, conscious of the weight of damp straw above his head. He guessed the ceilings inside would be claustrophobically low.

When Hugh Buckthorn opened the door, it was like coming face to face with an old friend. Thirty-odd years ago he'd rarely been out of the tabloids, his dark good looks and playboy lifestyle making him a favourite target of the paparazzi. He'd be snapped sunbathing on some exclusive Mediterranean beach, or waterskiing with a viscount's daughter in the Caribbean. Meeting him at last felt a little unreal.

'Come in, come in.' Buckthorn stood back and waved him over the threshold before leading him down the flagstoned hall. 'Mind your head.'

Lincoln ducked to avoid the ancient beams criss-crossing the hall ceiling and followed him into the kitchen-diner, which somehow combined the charm of a traditional cottage with the practicalities of modern equipment.

'Now: tea, coffee?'

'Coffee, please,' said Lincoln gratefully. 'Black, two sugars.'

A few minutes later they were sitting on opposite sides of a farmhouse-style table, with a cafetière and tall mugs of coffee in front of them. Hard winter sunshine streamed in through the low windows, and a log fire burned merrily in the grate.

'The alleged assault at the country club on Sunday evening,' Lincoln began, opening his notebook.

'Poor little Amy. I'm glad she's decided to come forward. I was afraid she'd lost her nerve.'

'Can you tell me what you saw?'

Buckthorn leaned back in his chair. He was still a handsome man even now, in his mid-fifties, with thick, dark hair streaked with grey at the temples, a couple of wilful curls falling onto his forehead. He had the naturally tanned complexion of a keen sailor or sun worshipper, and the bright eyes of a man who enjoyed life and savoured every moment of it.

'I'd been playing cards,' he said, twisting his signet ring round on his little finger. 'Took a break to stretch my legs, get some air. As I was going along the corridor, a door opened and this young lady came rushing out, straight into my arms.' He gave a lopsided smile. 'Excellent timing. Then I realised she was hysterical, shouting that someone had tried to rape her. Poor kid was trying to cover herself up. Her top was torn, gaping open, so I took my jacket off, put it round her and led her downstairs to the manager's office.'

'Did she say who'd attacked her?'

'She didn't know his name. I expected someone to come charging out after her, but the door slammed behind her. I was more concerned about getting her downstairs, making sure she was safe.'

'Did you see into the room before the door shut? Was it a bedroom? An office?'

'One of the bedrooms the club has for wedding parties and so on. The Abbey Suite.'

Lincoln made a note, though it would probably be pointless checking the room this long after the attempted assault. Any evidence would have been cleaned or tidied away. 'So you didn't see who was in there?'

Buckthorn shook his head. 'I wasn't really looking. My priority was to get her away from there.'

'Had you seen her at the club before?'

'She's served drinks at the tables a few times. Those girls are paid to be invisible, discreet. You're not supposed to notice them. I didn't even know she was called Amy until I took her down to the manager's office.'

'And the manager called the police?'

'He didn't seem to want to, and neither did she. She probably knew she'd be out of a job if she complained.' Buckthorn leaned his elbows on the table as he drank some more of his coffee. 'It astounds me the way some organisations treat their staff.'

'The manager's name?'

'Powell – Olly Powell. I know damn well he didn't take her allegation seriously – or didn't have the balls to confront the bastard who attacked her.'

'And you're still prepared to give a statement about what you saw?'

Lincoln could feel the investigation trickling away: a victim reluctant to report an assault, a manager who didn't want any trouble, and a delay of several days in which vital evidence would have been lost.

Buckthorn took a sip of his coffee. 'I told Amy I'd back her up and I'm as good as my word. If she's been courageous enough to report this, I can't let her down.'

'Did you get the impression she knew who the man was but didn't want to say?'

'No idea. Poor kid was in such a state, she wasn't making sense.' A quick, regretful smile. 'Sorry. I expect you hoped I could tell you more.'

Lincoln tapped his notebook. 'This should help.'

'I won't tolerate men who treat women badly. I saw enough of that when I was growing up. My father bullied my mother, he bullied his staff and he bullied me and my brother. Howard could put up with it, but I got out as soon as I could.'

'And now Howard's son's taken over?'

'Yes, though rather sooner than anyone expected.' Buckthorn's face clouded. 'My brother's death came as a shock to all of us. He was only sixty-three.'

Lincoln had read that the late earl had suffered a massive coronary while out shooting. His son, Laurence, had acceded to the title of Lord Riverbourne soon after his twenty-fifth birthday.

'Are you involved in running the estate too?'

'Not the day-to-day stuff, no,' Buckthorn said, 'but I've made a start on cataloguing the paintings – a job that'll probably take me from now till doomsday! That's my field of expertise: art history. I may have sown a few wild oats when I was younger, but when I was Laurie's age I went back to college and got my degree. Oddly enough, the tabloids never mention that! I shall forever be the so-called "Playboy Black Sheep of the Riverbournes".' He grinned. 'But yes, I've taken on the task of working through the paintings. I've got Rufus helping me.'

'Rufus?'

'Rufus Rayner. He runs the Cheese Market Gallery in Barbury.'

Lincoln had often passed the gallery on his way to and from the library where Trish used to work. The gallery's artworks were an eye-catching mix of the traditional and the modern, with some striking interpretations of the local chalk downs and river valleys, Stonehenge and Salisbury Plain.

'No one's catalogued the paintings before?'

'My aunt did a rudimentary inventory about forty years ago, but Rufus and I plan to do it properly this time – photograph every painting, see if we can establish its provenance. Far too many of the pictures are shut away in the attics at the Hall. It'd be terrific if we could bring them out into the light.'

'I can't see the point of having pictures if you don't put them on display,' Lincoln said. 'Like having records you love but never play. What's the point?'

Buckthorn laughed. 'Exactly! In fact,' he added, dropping his voice as if he were letting Lincoln into a secret, 'we're planning an exhibition next year – showing some of the paintings that *are* on show, but highlighting some of our hidden gems. You know, somewhere in the depths of the store rooms there's a Caravaggio that hasn't been seen for decades – although I haven't actually located it yet.'

'That must be worth a lot, mustn't it?'

'Oh yes. And even better, there's a wonderful depiction of the conversion of St Paul, attributed to Giacomo Scrabini, a student of Uccello's, but I've got my suspicions it could actually be by Uccello himself. Now, that really would be a showstopper! Sadly, I could never persuade Howard that a big exhibition would be a great way to attract more visitors. All he could do was fret about the insurance.'

'But your nephew's more enthusiastic?'

'Yes, absolutely. I haven't discussed the details with him yet, but Laurie knows he needs to bring some money in. Greywood Hall is rather down on its uppers. Maintaining a house like that is like painting the proverbial Forth Bridge, except you can't simply slap on a new coat of battleship grey!' He laughed. 'Laurie's got his head screwed on. He's more astute than his dad was, knows you've got to move with the times if you want to keep the punters coming in and save the Hall. It'd be tragic if the Riverbournes had to leave there after all these years. And a big exhibition… Well, *that* should draw the crowds. You've been round the Hall, have you?'

'Well, actually, no.'

Buckthorn stood up and went over to a bookcase beside the fireplace. 'Well worth it.' He thrust a folded leaflet at him. 'You'll see some smashing paintings. There's a Rubens, several by Velásquez, quite a few of the Dutch masters. Or maybe you aren't into art?'

'I'm no expert,' Lincoln confessed. 'As the old saying goes, I don't know much about art, but I know what I like. If I'm honest, I prefer more modern artists.'

Buckthorn laughed. 'I always appreciate honesty. But do visit the Hall sometime, if only to wander round the park. You can lose yourself for a few hours, imagine you're in another country. Another century,' he added wistfully, as if he'd enjoyed losing himself there once upon a time.

Lincoln thanked him, slipping the leaflet into his folder as he stood up to leave. 'Not sure if this case will get to court, but you're willing to be a witness if it does?'

'Of course. I'll come into the police station first thing tomorrow and make a statement. For young Amy's sake.'

As Lincoln walked back to his car, a train rattled by on the embankment above him, a two-carriage unit sprinting out of sight, heading west. He wondered if Buckthorn envied his nephew living at Greywood Hall while he had to make do with a cottage, albeit a very desirable one.

He headed back to Barley Lane, happy to be in charge once more.

'Sonia's family haven't heard from her in weeks,' Dilke said as Lincoln was hanging his coat up. 'And you might want to keep your coat on, boss. The boiler packed up not long after you left, so the heating's gone off.'

Lincoln left his coat where it was but kept his scarf on. It was psychological. He'd expected to have his work cut out finding out who abducted Yazmin Fletcher, but he hadn't expected her mother to do a disappearing act. 'Any word on DCI Jacobs?'

Breeze craned over the top of his screen. 'Mate of mine at Park Street heard he's got a broken leg and a few cuts and bruises. He'll be in hospital a few days at least.'

'Any idea where he lives?'

'Got a flat in Presford, apparently. Someone's going over there this afternoon, make sure he hasn't got a cat needs feeding, or a dog.'

Lincoln turned back to Dilke. 'What's the latest on Ploughboy's Pit?'

'SOCOs are still sifting through the rubbish.'

'They haven't found the other sandal, then? Or the bangles Yazmin was wearing?'

Dilke shook his head dolefully. 'There's loads of stuff to go through, and the bangles would only be small, wouldn't they? Must be like doing an archaeological dig, recording all the layers to show how far down things were.'

Breeze chuckled. 'More likely they'll chuck it all into a few rubble sacks and empty it out on a garage floor somewhere.'

Lincoln feared Breeze was probably right.

'We should have the dental records tomorrow,' he said. 'They've been on file since Yazmin first went missing.'

Breeze blew on his hands. 'Should've brought some gloves in. I'm nearly too shrammed to type.'

'Where's Pam?' Lincoln had only just noticed she wasn't there.

'Her grandad's not been well,' said Dilke. 'Maybe he's taken a turn for the worse.'

'I didn't know he'd been ill.' Why hadn't Pam felt able to confide in him? He was about to call her to find out what was up when his mobile rang, a landline number he didn't recognise. 'Hello?'

'It's Joan Best. From Brewery Court. She's back. Sonia. She's home.'

Lincoln drove over to Brewery Court once more, pulled up outside Sonia Fletcher's house and knocked on the door.

'I'm sorry,' she said before he was even over the threshold. 'It all got too much. When you phoned about Yazmin, it was such a shock and it all closed in on me, you know? I got in the car and... I don't know what I thought I was going to do. Crash it into a wall, maybe? Drive it into the river? Anything to end this...this agony.'

Slim but not very tall, she wore her light brown hair in a ponytail that showed off her high cheekbones and heart-shaped face. No make-up, but an armful of bracelets, a chunky rust-coloured sweater that looked homemade, a black pinafore dress on top, baggy at the sides as if it were two sizes too large.

'I wish I could've told you some other way, Sonia, but—'

'I'd always hoped she was still alive.' She spun away and hurried into the kitchen, where she set about making coffee, busily fetching mugs down from the shelf. 'Sounds insane, doesn't it? But I believed what I wanted to believe. That was the only way I could cope. And the longer Yazmin was missing, the more I convinced myself she wasn't dead, that someone else had given her a better life than I could have done.'

'Of course,' he said, 'until we've finished checking, we can't confirm anything.' Nothing he said was going to make it any easier for her.

'Where did you find her? One news bulletin said Greywood Forest and one said Bridgeford. I used to go to Bridgeford, to the chapel there. If I'd known that's where she was...' She shook her head, bewildered.

Lincoln described Ploughboy's Pit, trying to make it sound a more peaceful resting place than it was.

'The gale blew the covers off it,' he explained, 'and a woman walking her dog happened to look inside.'

'It's always someone walking their dog, isn't it?' She laughed bitterly. 'Bloody dangerous, walking dogs. I do it all the time, in between my other jobs, so odds are, one day...' Gallows humour. She laughed through her tears. 'If you've talked to Mrs Best next door, you'll know I haven't been well.'

'She said you were doing several jobs, working hard. Can't be easy on your own, away from your family.'

She pulled a face, suspicious. 'You've spoken to my sister?'

'We were worried about you. You walked out of here without your phone, no money. We had to try and trace you in case you'd—'

'In case I'd had another breakdown?'

'Breakdown?'

She filled the mugs, pushed sugar and biscuits across the worktop towards him. Then she pulled her sleeve up to show him the scars the bracelets hid.

'I was in the Manor House for weeks. I blamed myself for what happened. Still do. Yazmin was my responsibility, and I should've been there for her.'

The Manor House had been a forbidding-looking psychiatric hospital on the outskirts of Presford – not a place to which you'd go by choice. It had closed down a few years ago, redevelopment planned but continually shelved.

She led him back into the living room, where they sat down at the table.

'Sometimes I feel like I haven't grown up at all since I lost Yaz, like I'm still that young mum struggling to cope alone.' She gazed out of the window. 'Like I'm still there, waiting for her to come home and not wanting anything to change in case she won't know me when she gets back. When you said you'd found her—'

'Until we can be sure—'

'In my heart I knew, really. When you told me on the phone, I already knew.'

Lincoln waited a moment or two. 'Tell me what happened the day Yazmin disappeared.'

Still staring out of the window, she began to recount the events of that bank holiday weekend in August 1997. He knew what was on record, but he needed to hear it from Sonia herself.

'My sister Julie was over for the weekend with her two kids, so we all went to the fair together. Finn, her youngest, had this toy dog that went everywhere with him. We were queuing for one of the rides and he started kicking up a fuss because he'd left his bloody dog in the car, so I went back for it.' She brushed tears away.

Lincoln sat back. 'Take your time. It must be hard, going over it again now.'

She sniffed and carried on. 'Julie turned her back on Yaz for a couple of seconds, but that's all it takes, isn't it? She looked round and – no Yazmin. And then she saw her in the crowd with a man who had her by the hand, leading her away. Yaz never looked back, that's the thing, like she was happy to go with him.'

'Is that why your sister thought it was Bruno who'd taken her?'

'Julie was sure it was Bruno, and I didn't want to believe Yaz had gone off with some stranger. I *wanted* it to be him.'

'But then you found out he'd been in Poland at the time.'

'That's right. Julie said he could've put someone else up to it – perfect alibi, him being out of the country, y'know – but when I saw him...' She broke off to compose herself. 'When I saw him at the police station the day after, he was in pieces. I could tell he didn't know any more than I did.'

'Are you still in touch with him?'

She looked down at her lap. 'He changed jobs and moved to Southsea. About six years ago I found out he'd died. Liver cancer. I got a letter from his solicitor to say he'd passed away and he'd left me a few bits and bobs. I didn't even know he was ill.'

'I'm sorry.' If Bruno Bartek had known or suspected who'd taken his little girl, he'd never be able to reveal it now.

She lifted her head up again, fighting back tears. 'I can't pretend any more, can I?'

'Pretend?'

'That she's growing up somewhere with whoever took her. I used to imagine what she'd be doing, where she'd go to school – all that. She'd have been married by now, maybe. And now it's all come crashing down.' She reached her hand out towards his on the tabletop. 'It's not your fault. It was better coming from you than seeing it in the papers or having bloody reporters on my doorstep and not knowing why.' She drew her hand back and picked up her mug, staring into it before putting it down again. 'If it's her, she's been there all along, hasn't she? If she's got that dress on. Those sandals.'

'Pink jelly shoes.'

40

She managed a smile through her tears. 'She kept on and on about those bloody sandals. Kept on until I bought her a pair, and then they rubbed great blisters on her heels. I told her, I said to her, I said, "They may look nice, but you won't want to walk far in them." But she didn't care. Just wanted them because all the other girls in her class had them.' She reached in her pocket for a tissue, blew her nose. 'Will I be able to see her? I mean, I know it's only her bones that's left. I know that. But it's still her. It's still my Yazmin.'

'As soon as you can, I'll let you know.'

He glanced round the living room. The sofa was heaped with brightly coloured cushions, and the chairs were covered in silky fabric patterned as intricately as the material he used to see in sari shops in North London years ago when he was doing his training. Dreamcatchers dangled like feathery cobwebs in the window, and a caravan of small wooden animals processed along the sill.

No photos, he noticed, but then he wasn't a great one for photos himself. He took after his mother, he supposed. She'd always considered a display of family photos rather common.

'I loved Bruno to bits, y'know?' said Sonia, her voice thick with tears. 'I'd always wanted kids, even more than having a career, earning good money. But once I lost her...' She shook her head. 'I don't know how I'm going to get through this now.'

'And there was no one else she might have gone off with so willingly?'

'I've gone over and over it since it happened, and there's nobody. I didn't find it easy to make friends when we moved to Barbury. It was all right for Bruno. He was working with a bunch of guys at the garage all day, made friends with some of them, that's how he was. But it was harder for me.'

'And he never brought any of these workmates home?'

Another shake of the head. 'I didn't want them there.'

'Why not?'

She looked away, as if ashamed. 'I suppose I was jealous. He'd made friends and I hadn't, and I couldn't bear to see how happy he was here, after he'd taken me away from my family and the place where I grew up. Okay, he'd done it for us, getting a better job, better prospects, a chance to buy into the business. But having those guys in our home would have been rubbing my face in it.'

'Do you have any more photos of Yazmin, or of you and Bruno around that time? Might help jog some memories. Have any reporters contacted you yet?'

'I've seen people hanging around, but I don't want to talk to them. I went through all that twenty years ago, for all the good it did.'

She got up and riffled through a drawer of the dresser. Lincoln was surprised she didn't have a precious album of her photos carefully put away, but in half a minute she'd retrieved a snapshot for him to see.

It had been taken in a garden in summertime, a panel fence in the background, three men in shorts and T-shirts standing at a barbecue. The two little girls in front of them were scarcely tall enough to peep over the top of it. He recognised Yazmin straight away, a sparkly slide holding her hair off her forehead. She had a wide smile, even though she was missing a couple of her milk teeth.

The other little girl was darker, plumper.

'This guy, Lee, lived next door to us.' She pointed to the taller of the men with Bruno, 'and that's Pip, his little girl. He'd got a new job and they were moving, so they invited us round for a barbecue to celebrate. August '96. Me and Bruno split up not long after that.'

'And the other man?'

'Oh, that was Edgar – Ned, they called him. Him and Bruno were mates because Ned was Polish too, or his parents were. A shared heritage,' she added with a touch of sarcasm. 'He hadn't worked at the garage long. He did repair work for the council before that, labouring sort of jobs, but he didn't like it much, so he went to work at the garage. He was funny, though, Ned, always clowning around. He had the girls in stitches that day. He knew a lot of the kiddies' programmes off the television and was doing all the voices, making them laugh.'

'Can you remember his surname?'

'Ned's? You don't think—' She looked horrified. 'No, Ned was soft as butter, and he worshipped Bruno.'

'I need to make sure we don't miss anyone we should speak to, that's all.'

'Sorry, I can't remember his surname. It wasn't Polish. He'd changed it, or his dad did when they came over here. I only met him once or twice. Like I said, I didn't like Bruno bringing his mates home.'

'You mind if I keep this photo? I'll get it scanned, get it back to you, okay?'

'Of course. Yaz was such a trusting little thing, even though I dinned it into her, *Never talk to strangers!*'

Which suggests, thought Lincoln, the man she went off with was someone she knew.

'You got kids?' She'd sat down again, her hands round her mug.

42

'No.'

'Married?'

'Not any more.'

'We all need someone. It's a lonely old world otherwise. I've found that out over the last twenty years.'

'So after Bruno...?'

She shook her head, gaze fixed on her hands. 'I still loved him. Couldn't fall for anyone else. And then when Yazmin... When I lost Yaz, I couldn't see the point.' When she looked up again it was as if she saw straight through him, as if she'd actually touched him. He felt unnerved. 'But you're not like that,' she said. 'You're a man who needs someone, aren't you? Even if you can't admit it.'

'How's things in Barbury?' Trish's voice on the phone was bright, a cheery tonic at the end of a long day. The Barley Lane boiler had refused to fire up again, despite the ministrations of Woody, who knew about such things. By the time he got home to the Old Vicarage, Lincoln was cold, tired and hungry.

'Well, we found some bones from a twenty-year-old murder,' he was about to say, 'and there's been an incident at Press Vale—'

But would Trish really want to hear all about some randy bastard trying it on with one of the country club staff? About Dale Jacobs crashing his car, and Sonia Fletcher having a meltdown that had him chasing his tail all day?

'Everything's fine,' he said instead. 'Though my floorboards may take a little longer to put down than I'd expected.'

'Still no floorboards? Didn't I hear you say your house was habitable a couple of weeks ago?'

'Habitable as long as I remember where to put my feet when I cross the living room.'

'You could've moved back into my house,' she reminded him.

'Yes, but you need the money from renting it out.'

'Who's to say I wouldn't have charged *you*?' He could hear her grinning. He could hear her breathing.

'How's Essex?'

'Cold. Windy. Grey. But the job's exactly what I needed, something to challenge me, get me out of my comfort zone. And we both know I couldn't have stayed in Barbury.'

He knew she was right. Temporary as the job was, it got her out of Barbury, and gave them both some breathing space in which to decide if they still wanted to be together when she got back.

Make or break.

'I was talking to the Earl of Riverbourne's uncle this morning,' he said grandly, trying to be more upbeat.

'Hugh Buckthorn? I thought he was drinking himself to death in Morocco.'

'He seemed pretty sober yesterday. And nowhere near Morocco. He's living in Speldon Magna.'

'Not at Greywood Hall? I *long* to be let loose in the library there!'

'Maybe if I ask him nicely...'

She laughed. 'Mind you, there's some pretty rare stuff here, when I can find it. Most of it's been in crates since before I started. Lundy's got several works by Isaac Newton—'

'The man who invented gravity?'

'Be serious! Okay, so it's not your sort of thing, but I just love handling all these old books. And lots by Robert Hooke, who's even more interesting. He and Newton famously fell out—'

'Famously?'

'Oh, all right, Jeff, I'll shut up. I realise you don't share my enthusiasm for the Age of Enlightenment. But the good news is I'm getting an assistant.'

'Hooray! You sounded a bit overwhelmed last time we spoke.'

'The trustees have no idea how much work needs to be done here. And now they've cut the length of the contract—'

'Again? They've already reduced it to half what it was!'

'They've cut it down from fifteen months to a year. Giving me an assistant for four or five months must be cheaper than keeping me on for fifteen, and I'm desperate for some help. I'm interviewing him tomorrow.'

'Him?'

'Stewart. He sounds promising.'

'You trying to make me jealous?'

'Ha! I mean he sounds as if he'll do a good job. Which is just as well, since he's the only applicant.'

'Ah.' Lincoln wasn't surprised: from the way Trish described it, the library – in the house where Lundy had lived and died – was miles from anywhere, on a stretch of bleak Essex coastline with few amenities, except for a pub. The nearest shop was a draughty mile away, the nearest restaurant even farther. She'd swapped her tall, terraced house in Barbury for a flat over the library.

44

'Have you been into Local Studies since I left?' she wanted to know. 'I've been wondering what my replacement looks like.'

'Not yet, but I'll need to go over there soon, to look at the newspaper archives for 1997.'

He might have known that would pique her interest. 'Tell me more!'

Briefly he told her about the finding of the child's bones in Ploughboy's Pit, the likelihood that it was a little girl abducted from the funfair.

'Yazmin something? They thought her dad had taken her abroad, but he hadn't. Is that the one?'

'How come you've remembered so much about it?'

'That was the weekend Princess Diana was killed, so we pored over the newspapers, Suki and me. Yazmin's disappearance was there too, only her story got pushed off the front page because of Diana, which seemed terribly unfair. I've never forgotten it.' She broke off. 'I'd better go. The microwave's just pinged. Speak to you soon.'

And he still didn't know if she was coming home for half-term.

CHAPTER 8

FRIDAY 3RD FEBRUARY

Tilly Rayner parked her car in the last space in Bridgeford market square and hurried down Jackdaw Lane to the Old Shoddy Mill, where her brother had an apartment. The conversion of the former textile mill was an ongoing project, so she had to pick her way through piles of building materials and equipment to reach the main door. Since the lift had yet to be installed, she had to tramp up six flights of steep stone steps to the third floor.

Sunlight streamed through the tall windows as she strode along the landing. No wonder Rufus loved this building! He'd seen its potential when others had suggested it'd be better to knock it down. Refurbishing it as twelve flats was three or four times more expensive than starting from scratch, he was warned, but he wouldn't listen. And he'd been vindicated: there was already a waiting list for the other, as yet unfinished, apartments.

'I could earn more from developments like this than from running the gallery,' he'd told Tilly when he moved in. 'Never mind what Dad says.'

Their father, Cornelius Rayner, had started the Cheese Market Gallery in Barbury forty years ago when he was still working for an auction house in Bristol. He'd made a real success of it, but after a series of health problems he'd persuaded Rufus to take over from him.

Rufus's heart wasn't always in it, Tilly knew, but he was determined to keep the gallery going – for their father's sake, for her and for their mother.

Tilly had done her best to make her brother's life easier, helping him keep this new flat spotless, shopping for him when he was away on one of his numerous expeditions in search of potential redevelopment sites, picking up his mail.

'It's about time you got yourself a PA,' she'd teased him. 'I don't mind doing a bit of your housekeeping for you, Ru, but I've got my own life, you know.'

She put down her hessian shopping bag and scrabbled in her pocket for the key. When she opened the front door, she was surprised to see a couple of lamps on, the blinds drawn down.

Anxiety made her stomach flutter. Had Rufus come back early? Did he have someone staying over? She always dreaded walking in on him with someone.

'Ru, it's only me!' she called out. 'It's Tilly!'

She let the door slam behind her and headed for the kitchen to put the shopping away. Hardly anything left in his fridge! He'd starve if it weren't for her.

When she'd put the milk and cheese away, she stowed the rest of the food in the cupboard: muesli, cans of beans and chickpeas – healthy food to offset the junk food snacks he lived on when he was driving round Wiltshire in search of abandoned warehouses and factories. She shut the cupboard door. Glanced through the archway into the living room –

And dropped the bag of apples she'd been about to put away.

A man was sprawled on his back on the sofa, his dressing gown open, exposing his black suspender belt and stockings. A thin rope tied round his neck ran down his body and was knotted below one knee. His face, shrink-wrapped in polythene, was horribly distorted.

He was dead.

She tried to move but couldn't. Her legs had gone weak.

If her mobile hadn't buzzed in her pocket, she might have gone on standing there for minutes on end.

It was her mother. 'Tilly, darling, are you going anywhere near Boots on your way home? Because we're right out of that mouthwash your father prefers, the minty one. Could you pick some up?'

'Yes,' she said mechanically. 'No problem.' She slid her phone back into her pocket. Drew it out again and dialled the emergency services.

A few minutes later she retreated from her brother's flat and waited on the stairs.

Lincoln had often wondered what loft living was all about, and now here he was, standing in the kitchen of an apartment created out of a disused Victorian textile factory. Double-height ceilings, the iron roof beams exposed. Windows high up in the walls, letting in geometric streams of light.

From the kitchen he could see straight into the living room, with its sparse furnishings and studio-like atmosphere, masculine, functional: a couple of leather-covered armchairs, a coffee table that might have been reclaimed from a defunct machine of some sort, a plain metal desk pushed against the far wall.

47

The living room's central feature was a low sofa, on which a man lay dead in little more than a black, lace-trimmed suspender belt, black stockings and a dark blue dressing gown. A cord was looped round his neck and one of his legs.

At first glance the scene looked comical, bizarre, but a second glance dispelled any urge to laugh.

Ken Burges had been kneeling beside the body, but now he sat back on his heels.

'No suspicious deaths for weeks,' he said wryly, 'and then two come along in the same forty-eight hours. And in the same village. But in all likelihood,' he added, standing up, 'unconnected.'

Lincoln hadn't thought they would be connected, but he was still relieved to hear the pathologist say it. 'What can you tell me about this one?'

'White male, fifty-five to sixty years old. Cause of death? Most likely asphyxia.' He pointed to the plastic freezer bag clinging to the dead man's face. 'I estimate he's been dead less than twelve hours.'

A length of twisted cord – the belt from the dressing gown, probably – lay slack around the man's neck. Then it trailed down his body to below his left knee, where it looped round his calf, ruckling the black nylon stocking that encased his leg. His left hand lay across his chest, the fingers resting on the other end of the twisted cord.

His right leg, also stockinged, had slipped off the edge of the sofa, buckling at the ankle. His right arm dangled down, his hand cupped.

Nausea swept over Lincoln the instant he recognised the signet ring on the man's left hand.

'Hugh Buckthorn.'

Ken gasped. 'As in the Riverbourne Buckthorns?'

'I was talking to him less than twenty-four hours ago.'

'Didn't realise you moved in such exalted circles, Jeff.'

'It wasn't a social chat.'

'He was in trouble?'

'He witnessed an incident at the country club. He was supposed to come in to give a statement this morning.'

'Not sure he's going to be doing that now.'

Lincoln swallowed hard. 'Is it murder or suicide?'

'Neither. Accidental, most likely, a solo sex act gone wrong. Auto-erotic asphyxiation – or "scarfing", as it's known in the trade.'

'Cutting off his air supply to get a better buzz?'

'That's the theory. Haven't tried it myself. Haven't needed to.'

'Me neither. See how stupid you look if you screw up!' Lincoln nodded at the prostrate Hugh Buckthorn, a man he'd taken to. He felt like an intruder, witnessing his humiliation.

'The poor chap didn't even go out on a high,' Ken went on. 'I can't see any traces of semen, although I haven't examined him properly, obviously.'

'How horny do you have to feel to take that kind of risk? Don't answer that.'

Ken snorted. 'I wasn't going to! Strangulation during sex is dangerous enough when couples do it, but it's bloody idiotic when you're home alone.'

'But this *isn't* home for him. He's got a cottage in Speldon Magna. That's where I met him yesterday.' Lincoln turned towards the door. 'Better go down and talk to the woman who found him, see what she can tell us.'

He and Woody went back downstairs to find the young woman sitting hunched at the desk in the Portakabin that served as the site office.

In her late twenties, she was shrinking down into her thick tweed coat as a tortoise might retract into its shell. A knitted bandeau pulled her hair back from her face, exposing a rounded forehead and delicate features devoid of make-up. Someone had made her a big mug of tea, and she was clutching it with both hands as if she were warming herself up on it.

She told them her name was Tilly Rayner. 'Is it Hugh?' she asked in a tiny voice.

Lincoln nodded, wondering why her surname seemed familiar. 'Although until he's been identified officially—' As he stepped towards the office chair next to hers he stumbled over her shopping bag, and she hurriedly pulled it back towards her own feet.

'Sorry,' she said. 'Sorry.'

'That's okay. Should've watched where I was putting my feet.' He sat down. 'Bit of a shock, coming home and finding him like that.'

'It's not *my* flat.'

'Then who—?'

The stocky man who must have made the tea spoke up. His name badge, swinging from a bright red lanyard, showed he was Austin Kendall, site foreman.

'It's Tilly's brother's place,' he said, his hand resting on the back of her chair. 'Rufus Rayner.'

Lincoln remembered where he'd heard the name before. 'He runs a gallery in town?'

'Yeah, and he part-owns this building. Tilly looks after his flat when he's away.'

'I need to phone him.' Her voice was little more than a whisper, her hands glued to the mug once more. 'I need to tell him what's happened.'

Lincoln leaned in closer. 'Where is he?'

'He should have been here by now. He's been working in Trowbridge on another project, an old brewery or something.'

'He was away last night?'

'And the night before. Easier than driving back and forth.'

'It's only an hour away, isn't it, Trowbridge?'

'Yes, but this time of year, finishing late, starting early, with the roads a bit icy... It makes more sense to stay there overnight.'

'You know where he's been staying?'

'The Premier Inn.'

Lincoln made a note: they'd need to check her brother's movements during the last twenty-four hours.

Woody turned to Kendall. 'You said Mr Rayner part-owns this building...?'

'Some local businessmen got together to save the mill from being demolished. Now they're converting it, as you can see.'

'Was Hugh Buckthorn one of those businessmen?'

Kendall shook his head. 'He doesn't have that kind of money.'

'You know him, then?'

He snorted. 'I know he doesn't have that kind of money!'

Tilly looked round at him sharply. 'Oz!'

'Any security cameras here?' Woody wondered.

'Will be, eventually,' Kendall said, 'but not yet. Mr Rayner's the only one who's moved in. The other apartments are still being fitted out. He was going to use his for the promotional stuff. Don't suppose that's going to happen now.'

Lincoln hoped some of the other buildings in Jackdaw Lane had CCTV, but when he stepped outside the cabin he saw that even the closest were some fifty yards away along the millstream. Worth checking in case a security camera had picked up Buckthorn's arrival, but since his death looked accidental there'd probably be no need to pursue that.

Farther up the lane, in the other direction, stood a Victorian chapel. It appeared deserted, but maybe it had cameras to deter trespassers. He marched up the lane towards it, realising as soon as he reached it that it was derelict, boarded up with warning notices: *DANGEROUS STRUCTURE. DO NOT ENTER.* His own house should have had a similar deterrent scrawled across it when he first discovered it. Too late now...

He looked up, scanning the building for cameras, but all he saw was a tattered poster stapled to the door: *Church of Heaven's Promise. They are not dead, only gone on before. Believe in this and Salvation is yours.* Was this the chapel Sonia Fletcher said she used to attend? It didn't look as if it had been in use for a good few years.

Though it must once have been a thoroughfare, Jackdaw Lane had been turned into a dead end by a wall of metal barriers erected a few yards beyond the chapel. The barriers didn't look as if they'd been moved recently, and anyway you'd need a crane to shift them.

He walked back towards the Old Shoddy Mill, a stately brick building – one hundred and fifty years old, he guessed. It would have been criminal to pull it down, even though it was uncomfortably close to the mill race and still in need of a significant amount of refurbishment.

Tilly had abandoned her tea to step outside the Portakabin. 'I can't believe what's happened,' she whispered. 'Poor Hugh.'

'Your brother's been helping him catalogue the paintings at Greywood Hall, I understand.'

'Not just that. He's Rufus's partner.'

'They were in business together?'

'No, I mean...' She faltered, then said shyly, 'They're a couple.'

'Ah.' Lincoln paused to re-evaluate the situation. So, Hugh Buckthorn was gay. That was a bit of a surprise. 'Did you know he'd be here while your brother was away?'

'Rufus didn't say. It could've been embarrassing if Hugh wasn't expecting me to pop in.'

Yes, thought Lincoln, it certainly could have been, especially if he made a habit of strutting nearly naked round his lover's flat. 'Did Hugh spend much time over here? Was this where they worked together?'

'I don't know. He's never been in the flat when I've come round with the shopping or to tidy. But then, I'm usually here in the mornings and maybe he comes round later, when he's expecting Rufus back. We've probably always just missed each other.'

'Like ships that pass in the night. But you've met him? You've met Hugh?'

'A few times, yes, though it's all a bit awkward. Rufus was going out with a friend of mine, and I was sure they'd be getting married.

But then Rufus suddenly announced he was gay and was involved with someone. There was this huge row at home. Daddy thought Hugh had led him astray, being that much older. He was furious.' She turned away. 'So Rufus has never felt he could bring Hugh home to meet us properly.'

Lincoln nodded sympathetically. Buckthorn must have thought Rufus was coming back from Trowbridge last night. He'd donned the silk dressing gown and the nylons to stop his young lover in his tracks when he walked in, but then he'd got tired of waiting and decided to indulge in a spot of –

God, this was going to be an embarrassment for the family! *Both* families.

'How am I going to tell Rufus?' Tilly's eyes were full of tears. 'He'll be devastated! I ought to phone him.' She reached into her pocket for her mobile, but Lincoln stopped her.

'You're expecting him back this morning?'

'Yes, any time now. Maybe I shouldn't tell him over the phone, not when he might be driving. I'll wait till he gets here.'

Lincoln drew Woody aside. 'What's the betting Buckthorn thought Rufus was coming home last night and planned to surprise him?'

'Some surprise!' Woody smoothed his moustache down. 'Always thought he was more of a ladies' man.'

'Goes to show you can't believe everything you read in the papers.'

Still, Lincoln himself had thought the same, envying the youthful Hugh Buckthorn his glamorous life in the fast lane all those years ago: lissom young starlets on his arm and in his Alfa Romeo, beach parties in the south of France, and young royals on the guest list at Greywood Hall banquets.

Woody beamed. 'Reckon the media's going to love this! Who's going to talk to the press office?'

Lincoln glanced back towards Tilly, who'd returned to the warmth of the Portakabin.

'Given the nature of the situation,' he said, 'we keep this as private as possible for the family's sake. Most likely it's a stupid accident, a kinky sex act gone wrong. The less we tell the media the better.' He knew word would leak out somehow, though: an incident like this was a gift to the tabloids. 'It should be Dale Jacobs dealing with Media Relations, but since he's laid up in Presford General, DCS Youngman had better handle it.'

'So are *you* leading on this one, boss?'

Lincoln turned at the sound of the mortuary van entering the lane and creeping towards them. 'I'd better tell Youngman what's happened and let him decide. Until Jacobs is fit, though, it's going to have to be me, isn't it? Unless Youngman's got a spare DCI up his sleeve.'

Without the distraction of Hugh Buckthorn's wretchedly undignified body, Lincoln could survey the scene more thoroughly.

'Nothing to suggest this was a burglary gone wrong,' he said, taking in the orderly condition of the flat. 'No drawers pulled out, nothing in disarray – except the victim.'

'Nothing much here to steal. The foreman was telling me Rayner only uses it as a sort of base while the work's going on, doesn't keep anything of any value here. No sign of anyone going through stuff looking for items to nick.'

The flat certainly looked good – better still without the addition of a dead body. The conversion from a mill to an apartment block was being carried out sympathetically, even retaining the original leaded windows, narrow but so tall that they gave an abundance of light.

Indeed, the place looked *so* good, it was hard to imagine that anyone else had been in the flat last night, apart from Buckthorn himself. Scenes of Crime would look for anything suspicious, of course, anything that helped tell the narrative of what had happened here, but Lincoln's first thought was that this was the scene of a sad and somewhat embarrassing accident.

The kitchen was immaculately clean, with few provisions in the eye-level cabinets apart from what Trish would have called 'store cupboard staples': tea and coffee, cereal, rice, nuts and tinned beans. The fridge held several bottles of dry white wine, some milk, butter, and cheese, all unopened.

'No washing up.' Lincoln waved his gloved hand towards the drainer.

'Dishwasher.' Woody swung open a couple of cupboard doors until he located the hidden Neff. He tugged it open. 'Nothing in it.'

'Buckthorn was here all evening without having so much as a glass of water?'

Woody checked the stainless-steel swing bin for a discarded bottle or carton. 'Empty. Not even a bin liner. So when did you leave Buckthorn's cottage, boss?'

'Elevenish? He didn't say anything about coming over here last night. But then, why would he?' Lincoln gazed round the gleaming kitchen, not surprised that Rayner had proposed using it to advertise the development. 'He must have planned an intimate evening with Rayner, found he wasn't here and decided to have a bit of fun on his own.'

Woody shivered. 'Bit chilly to be messing about with no clothes on.' He strolled over to the nearest radiator – old-style, industrial, maybe one of the factory's originals – and felt it. 'Barely warm.' He chuckled at his unintended pun.

Lincoln grinned, although he didn't feel very jovial. He'd liked Hugh Buckthorn, brief as their acquaintance had been. He hadn't expected to be investigating his death within hours of sharing a pot of coffee with him.

'We need to establish Rayner's movements last night, confirm he was in Trowbridge.' He hunted around for Buckthorn's phone and keys, but they weren't in the living room or the kitchen. 'Where are his clothes?'

He followed Woody down the short hallway beyond the living room. Through the open door of the master bedroom they saw a Barbour jacket on the bed, and Woody went over and searched its many pockets.

'Keys,' he said, dropping them onto the bed: two key rings with Yale and mortice keys on them. 'Wallet. No phone. No car keys. Someone probably dropped him off, or else he got a cab.' He flipped the wallet open. 'Credit cards, debit card, business cards. Fifty, sixty, eighty-five pounds in cash. Oh, and this.' He slid a slim plastic pouch of white powder out and held it up. 'Coke?'

Lincoln nodded. 'Looks like it.' No surprise there, really: cocaine was a drug that ignored class distinctions. 'Might be prints on that pouch.'

Woody nodded as he dropped it carefully into an evidence bag.

Lincoln crossed the room, struck by the view from the window. Beyond the tall brick chimney and industrial rooftops of the oldest parts of the Old Shoddy Mill, he could see the river snaking away through the flooded water meadows, leafless trees and wintry vegetation marking its route for a good two or three miles to the west.

In the distance stood the church tower of Speldon Magna with its delicate finials – and, though out of sight, Corner Cottage.

As he turned back, his eye was caught by a strange flickering light from under the bed. He knelt down and lifted up the bedspread. A smartphone lay on the floor under the bed, its screen lit up by a notification or message. It must have tumbled off the bed and skated across the uncarpeted floor.

He reached for it and grabbed it. 'Probably fell out when he chucked his jacket down.' He pressed some buttons, brought the screen back to life. 'The battery's low.' He looked round for a charger but couldn't see one plugged in anywhere in the bedroom. 'Six missed calls from Rayner, yesterday and today.'

Scrolling back through the log, which only showed the previous forty-eight hours, he noted a call to 'Rufus mobile' at eleven on Wednesday night. On Thursday evening at three minutes past six Buckthorn had called 'Rufus home', then had rung an unidentified mobile number at six twenty. He slid the phone into a bag. 'Where are the rest of his clothes?'

Woody checked the en suite. 'Nothing in here. Is there another bedroom?'

The spare bedroom, beyond the main bathroom, was much smaller than the master. Clothes were piled on the bed: shirt, jersey, trousers, on top of a pair of black woollen socks and some cotton boxer shorts. One discarded black leather brogue lay upside down on the floor at the end of the bed.

'Where's his other shoe?' On hands and knees, Lincoln groped around until he found it in the space between the wall and the bedside cabinet. He reached in for it, pulled it out. Squatted on his haunches, puzzled.

Woody peered down at him. 'Penny for them.'

'How do *you* get undressed?'

'Er... how do most people get undressed?'

'No, I mean...' Lincoln lumbered to his feet. 'You kick your shoes off, you take off your jersey, then your shirt and your trousers. You take your socks off and drop them into your shoes or on the floor. Then you take your shorts off.'

Woody stared at him as if he were mad. 'This time of year I'd have my PJs at the ready before I took my boxers off. But I'm still not sure what you're getting at, boss.'

Lincoln pointed to the pile of clothes on the bed. 'If he'd got undressed in here, I'd expect his clothes to be lying the other way up – underwear on top, the last things he took off. But his socks and pants are underneath. He'd probably have sat on the bed to take his socks off, and yet the quilt's completely smooth. And I'd expect his shoes to be together, not chucked down any old how. Did he get undressed somewhere else in the flat and then dump his clothes in here?'

Woody shrugged. 'Reckon he didn't want his clothes cluttering up the master bedroom.'

'So let's say he undresses in the master bedroom, puts his suspender belt and stockings on. Picks up his clothes and shoes, dumps them on the bed in the spare room. He's naked except for a thin dressing gown and his Pretty Pollys. It was bloody freezing last night and yet he's wandering round the flat like that?'

'He went to boarding school, boss. He grew up at Greywood Hall. Reckon he didn't feel the cold like the rest of us.'

'Or there was someone else here. Someone else picked his clothes up and dropped them on the spare bed. Accident or not, we shouldn't assume he was on his own when things went wrong.'

'Reckon the SOCOs will look for anything out of place,' said Woody. 'Though it looks to me as if he was here on his own.'

Voices echoed in the stairwell. A commotion on the landing, an argument.

One of the uniforms stuck her head round the door. 'The owner of the flat's arrived,' she said. 'He's refusing to go back downstairs.'

Lincoln peeled his gloves off as he told Woody to carry on looking for anything that might be relevant. 'I'll go and speak to Mr Rayner.'

CHAPTER 9

'So you're an expert on Charles Lundy?' Trish looked at Stewart Hubbard over the top of his application form. The job advert had asked for a qualified librarian or archivist to assist in the cataloguing and organisation of Lundy's collection of seventeenth-century manuscripts and books. Stewart had been the only applicant.

Now here he was, pleasant and enthusiastic, if a little old-fogeyish with his horn-rimmed spectacles and neatly combed hair, tweed jacket and cords, gingham shirt and knitted tie.

'I wouldn't call myself an *expert*, but yes, he's the subject of the doctoral thesis I'm working on. I first came across him in one of my previous posts, where they had Lundy's very own copy of *Bibliotheca Hookiana*.'

Trish hoped her ignorance didn't show on her face. 'Really? His very own copy?'

She couldn't have hidden her ignorance well enough, because Stewart went on, 'Yes, it's the catalogue of Hooke's library, compiled by Millington. Very rare. Only about six copies still in existence. As you know, Lundy was a supporter of Robert Hooke, especially in his dispute with Isaac Newton. After Hooke died in 1703 there was a massive auction of his library, and Lundy went along. Quite a lot of what's here,' he added, encompassing the library with a wave of his hand, 'was probably picked up at that auction. Lundy marked various entries, though what the marks meant is a bit obscure.' A broad grin transformed his face. 'And I've actually held that catalogue in my hands, run my finger down the list of titles just as Lundy did nearly three hundred and twenty years ago. Never could I have dreamt I'd ever find myself *here*, in Lundy's library.'

'Goodness!' Trish wished her own yearning to work here had been as heartfelt. She'd simply needed an escape, an excuse to change the direction of her life. She hadn't planned to stay as the Local Studies librarian at Barbury Library forever, but she certainly hadn't wanted to move on while Kate was still at school. She'd never regret helping Linus Bonetti in his quest to expose the abuse and corruption going on in the council, but she regretted having to leave a job she loved.

This one, although interesting, was only temporary – and a long way from home.

Stewart gave a modest smile. 'I probably know almost as much about Charles Lundy as you do.'

Or an awful lot more. Trish scanned his application form again, impressed by his track record: English degree, a spell as an archivist in Oxford, museum collections development manager in Norwich, something similar in Winchester... Now, at thirty-eight, he was taking time out to do a PhD. On paper he was better qualified for her job than she was.

'And that's why you want this post, to help with your thesis?'

'I want this post because I need to earn some money. Working in Lundy's own library is the most incredible bonus. I could hardly believe my luck when I saw the advert.'

'I'd show you round, but most of the books are still in crates, so there's not a lot to see.'

'In crates? Why's that?'

'The building was refurbished last year, and the books were moved out. I've only been here a few weeks myself, and unboxing everything's taking much longer than I expected.'

Stewart grinned. 'Nothing I like better than rolling my sleeves up and getting on with it. The library I sorted out in Oxford was in a similar state.' He paused to survey the room. 'So this was Lundy's own study?'

'Apparently, though the whole house has been reconfigured over the centuries. But yes, it's the room with the most natural light.'

He stood up and crossed to the window. 'And with a superb view of the sea.'

'The interview isn't quite over,' Trish reminded him sternly. 'I have a few more questions.'

Stewart turned back from the wintry panorama of a leaden sky meeting a pewter sea. He was smiling, quite unperturbed by her tone. 'I'm hoping the next question is "okay, Stewart, when can you start?"'

CHAPTER 10

'I'm sorry, Mr Rayner, I can't let you into the flat.' Lincoln shot out onto the landing, pulling the door shut behind him so Rayner couldn't see inside. He shouldn't even have been allowed to get this far.

'I have to go in! You don't understand! I need to see—' He tried to shove Lincoln aside, but one of the uniforms caught him by the arm and held him back.

'Is there somewhere we can talk, Mr Rayner? Another flat, perhaps?' Lincoln looked back along the landing towards the far end of the building. Doors stood open, letting narrow blocks of weak winter sunlight fall across the floor.

'They're not finished.'

'Let's see.'

No, the other flats weren't finished, but the one next door to Rayner's did at least have a couple of benches and a trestle table that the builders had been using. Tungsten lamps were positioned so they cast enough light for the workmen to continue after dark, though they were turned off now.

Lincoln sat down, using the edge of his notebook to sweep away the film of sawdust that coated the table.

'What happened?' Rayner demanded, as if Lincoln had been personally responsible for the unfortunate accident that had claimed Hugh Buckthorn's life. 'How did he die?'

'We can't say at this stage.' Lincoln flipped his notebook open. 'Can you tell me where you were during the last twenty-four hours?'

'Me? You're not suggesting—? Okay, okay. I've been in Trowbridge since Wednesday morning. I've got this project, a redevelopment like this one. It's a brewery, been empty for years. Except it's taking longer than I expected to get the paperwork in place and I need to keep chasing people and the planning officer and so...' He stopped gabbling and shut his eyes, caught his breath. Opened his eyes again. 'Are you sure it's him? That it's Hugh?'

'Mr Rayner, please.' Lincoln waited, pencil poised.

'I was in a hotel last night, and the night before. The Premier Inn. I tried calling him. Couldn't understand why he wasn't answering. We always talk last thing, wherever we are.'

'And you came back here this morning because...?'

'I've got a site meeting with Austin. Austin Kendall, the foreman. Was *supposed* to have a site meeting.' He sat slumped on the bench. He was in his early thirties, Lincoln estimated, his sandy hair cut short at the back and sides, the fringe left floppy. He wore round, wire-rimmed glasses that sat neatly on his freckled nose, giving him a schoolboyish look. He was much shorter than Buckthorn – five-five, five-six, with a softness to his build, a little too much weight for his height.

'I can't believe I'm doing this.' He pulled his navy parka more tightly round him and shook his head. 'I don't understand why Hugh was here.'

'We'll come to that. So you checked out of your hotel this morning and came straight here?'

'I told you, I had to come back for a site meeting. Shit, when I turned into the lane and saw all the blue lights and the police cars...'

'When did you last speak to Mr Buckthorn?'

'The night before last. Wednesday. He rang me about eleven.'

'What did you talk about?'

'God knows! The joys of staying in a budget hotel, probably.'

'How did he seem?'

Rayner shrugged. 'Fine. He was fine.'

'He was at home?'

'I suppose so.' He took his glasses off and let them dangle from his hand.

'Did he ask when you'd be back?'

'He didn't need to. He knew I'd be in Trowbridge until this morning.'

'So he came over here last night even though you weren't going to be here?'

'Obviously.' He jammed his glasses on again, sprang up and strode across the room, sidestepping a sawhorse, a stack of plastic buckets and a gas cylinder as he headed for the window. There he gazed hopelessly out at the chilly morning before leaning his back against the wall of exposed brick and facing Lincoln once more. 'He's got keys.'

'Did he often spend the night here when you were away?'

'Not often, no. Maybe when he's been out for the evening in Barbury and had a bit too much to drink, he'll leave his car in town and crash here. Cheaper than paying for a cab to take him all the way home to the cottage. They charge the earth to drive you out to the villages after dark. Hugh says they react like you're asking them to take you over the Styx!' He laughed, but then his face fell and became sad again.

'So maybe last night was one of those nights? He had a few drinks somewhere in town, left his car there and got a taxi out here? Maybe forgetting you wouldn't be home?'

'But it's not like him to do that without letting me know. And Tilly said...' His voice shrank to a whisper. 'Tilly said he was wearing *stockings*.'

'Yes, that's right. Not easy to talk about, I know, but there's nothing wrong with dressing up, playing games, sex games. A man's private life is—'

'Hugh wouldn't *dress up*! In all the months I've known him, he's never suggested dressing up, no role play, nothing like that.'

'Maybe not when he was with you, but maybe on his own he might.'

'Then it's a side of him I didn't know.'

'And you've been seeing each other since...?'

'The end of September.'

Not even six months. No time at all, really. 'Might he have brought someone else back here?' Lincoln was still surprised that Buckthorn himself had piled his clothes on the spare bed so haphazardly.

'There's nobody else.'

'You can never be sure.'

'I'd know if he was seeing someone.' Rayner was adamant.

'Maybe it's someone he's only just met.'

'That's not how he is. That's not how we are. He'd never pick someone up and bring them back here.'

Lincoln didn't argue with him. Easy to delude yourself you're the centre of someone's universe. Easy to kid yourself they'll never be unfaithful, never stray, have a fling, do something stupid for a quick thrill.

As he knew from experience.

'If Mr Buckthorn drove here, where would he have parked? I didn't see any spaces outside.'

Rayner turned back, taking his glasses off again and wiping his eyes with the back of his wrist. 'We have to park in the market square while we've got the Portakabin here. A bit of a bind during the day, but at night it's not a problem.' He put his glasses back on. Took a deep breath. 'He drives a Jag. It's years old. Silver. Couldn't tell you the registration number.'

Lincoln remembered the silver Jaguar parked outside Corner Cottage. 'We can get the details from the DVLA.'

'Of course. Yes. The key must be here somewhere, even if he left the car in town.'

61

'We didn't find one. We'll check to see if he got a taxi out here.' That would mean trawling local cab offices, but it might also confirm that Buckthorn came to the flat alone – or not. 'Any particular company he used?'

'Abbey Cars, usually. Next to Barbury Station.'

Lincoln left another possibility unsaid: that Buckthorn had brought someone back with him last night and, when their encounter turned sour, his companion had driven off in the Jaguar. Why else was the car key nowhere to be found?

'Anywhere else he goes to in town? Restaurants, pubs? Clubs?'

'If you're asking me if he'd go to Carew's, the answer's no! Carew's is a dive, a dump. And that wasn't how he was,' Rayner insisted again. 'If Hugh went anywhere to relax, it was the country club.' He stared down at the floor, at his scuffed footprints in the sawdust. 'You think he brought someone back here for rough sex, don't you? And something went wrong.'

'Never mind what I think. I'm not here to pass judgement – just to establish what happened.'

Rayner looked up, his expression bleak. 'They'll ticket his car if he's left it in the square.'

The least of the dead man's worries. 'I'll send someone round to look for it. And there's a chance he left his car at the country club?' Maybe they should check there first, see if any staff remembered calling a cab for Buckthorn yesterday evening.

'He went to Press Vale quite a bit, so...yes. Who's going to break the news to Laurence?'

'Laurence?'

'Hugh's nephew. His next of kin.'

Lincoln didn't fancy going to Greywood Hall, unsure of the protocol for calling on earls. Would Laurence, Lord Riverbourne, even be at home? 'I'll phone and arrange to speak to him. So Mr Buckthorn never married?'

'Came close a few times, he said, but he always knew it wasn't for him.'

Acting the footloose bachelor had certainly provided a perfect smokescreen until he felt able to come out.

'Is there somewhere else you can stay until we've finished here, Mr Rayner?'

The young man ran his hand over his boyish fringe. 'Home. I mean, back to my parents' house for – well, until you've finished here. Oh God, I'll never be able to come back here, not after this.'

Lincoln couldn't help wondering how much this incident would damage the sales potential for the Old Shoddy Mill. Or would notoriety make it an even more attractive location?

There was no silver Jaguar parked in Bridgeford market square or in the public car park next to the town's Memorial Hall. A call to Press Vale Country Club confirmed that Buckthorn hadn't been there the night before: all members and guests had to sign in, and he hadn't signed in since Sunday.

Lincoln sent a couple of uniforms over to Speldon Magna to check for the car there and to make sure Corner Cottage was secure. When Dilke arrived in Jackdaw Lane, Lincoln sent him off to hunt for CCTV cameras elsewhere in the town centre, though he doubted there'd be many to find.

Back at Barley Lane, he and Woody walked into a wall of heat as they entered the CID room.

Woody hurried across to open a window. 'Reckon they got the boiler going again.'

Breeze pretended to wipe sweat from his brow. 'You could say that, yes, Sarge. Only they've ballsed up the thermostat so it's like the tropics in here now.'

Lincoln grinned, relieved to be back in the office with all its mundane irritations, none of them a matter of life or death.

'Don't look a gift horse in the mouth, Dennis,' he said. 'Sod's law it'll go off again now you've complained about it.' He looked round. 'Still no Pam?' He'd forgotten to call her yesterday.

'She rang to say she'll be in a bit late. She's been at the hospital all night.'

'At the hospital? So her grandfather—'

But he didn't get to finish, because Dilke charged in, beaming in triumph.

'I've got some footage from the camera outside the chemist's, boss. It'll have picked up Mr Buckthorn's car if he drove into the square or down Jackdaw Lane.'

Lincoln's spirits rose. 'Let's see what you've got. We know he wasn't there any earlier than half six – that's when Austin Kendall knocked off, and he said there was no one around then. So check for the Jag any time after that.'

Leaving Dilke to go through the footage on his own, Lincoln drew Woody to one side. 'Did you know about Pam's grandfather?'

Woody looked blank. 'What about him?'

'Breezy says he's in hospital. She didn't say anything to you?'

'Nope, but then she never says much about her private life, does she?'

'True. She's coming in a bit later. I'll have a word with her then.'

After nearly an hour's laborious scanning of the security camera footage, Dilke thought he'd spotted Buckthorn's car. Lincoln and Woody crowded round his screen to watch the silver car entering the market square at seven forty-eight the previous night.

'You're sure that's it?' Lincoln asked.

Breeze, who'd been studying the photos of Rayner's flat, ambled over to give his expert opinion. 'Definitely a Jag,' he said, 'and look – his number plate's reflected in the side of the bus shelter as he goes by. Bit blurred, but it looks to me like WY07 D-something-something. That'd fit with the number the DVLA gave us, wouldn't it? Blow it up, Gray. See if you can see who's driving.'

They waited while Dilke obliged, but the result was too fuzzy.

'Can't even see if it's a man or a woman driving,' Lincoln grumbled, 'or even if there's a passenger.'

Street lights had cast a shadow across the car's windscreen, blotting out the top of the driver's head and the whole of the passenger side.

'That's definitely Buckthorn's car,' said Woody, 'but where is it now? No other CCTV, Graham?'

'I'll go back and look again. Didn't expect this to be such poor resolution.'

'Check again. With any luck the car's been picked up by another camera with a better view.'

Dilke gathered up his phone and keys, grabbed his coat. He paused, troubled. 'If someone went back to the flat with him to have sex and then something went wrong, why didn't they call an ambulance?'

Breeze threw him a pitying look. 'How are you going to explain to a paramedic what you'd been getting up to, eh? Your boyfriend's got stockings on, you're in a flat that doesn't belong to either of you and you've been playing around with nooses and freezer bags. How's that gonna look, eh?'

Dilke gazed sadly across at the photos on the whiteboard. 'They could at least have taken the bag off his face.'

Lincoln held his hands up. 'Hang on, let's not get ahead of ourselves. There's no evidence that there was anyone else in the flat with him. We can't be sure of anything until the autopsy's been done and we've got the Forensics report.'

'But if you were suffocating inside a plastic bag,' Dilke persisted, 'wouldn't you try and push it off you? See, he's got one hand on his chest and the other hand's just kind of flopped down. I mean...' He turned to Lincoln for corroboration. 'Doesn't he look *too* relaxed?'

Lincoln went back to the whiteboard and regarded the photos afresh. 'Yes, if he'd over-tightened the noose and pulled the bag too tight, he'd have clawed at it, perhaps, tried to loosen it. But once he'd lost consciousness, his arms would've gone limp. Exactly like that.'

Sitting down at his desk, Breeze attempted to strike the same pose, reminding Lincoln of a postcard Trish had kept above her desk: a reproduction of the Victorian painting, *The Death of Chatterton*. Not that the burly Breeze resembled the tragic boy poet, but something about the pose...

Yes, he was sure that if you passed out with a freezer bag over your face you'd go limp, no matter how much you'd struggled while you could. Very quickly, unless you got some air, you'd die. Or you might survive, but with brain damage from oxygen starvation.

If someone else was involved in this perilous sex game, and Buckthorn had scrabbled at their hands or arms in panic, then his autopsy should uncover skin cells under his fingernails, maybe even blood. Or the skin cells and blood might only be his own.

As Dilke headed out of the door, bound for Bridgeford in pursuit of elusive security cameras, Breeze stopped playing dead and sat up again. 'So for now we don't even know if there's a crime to investigate?'

Woody shook his head. 'Not until we know if there was someone else with him.'

For the sake of Rufus Rayner and the dead man's family, Lincoln hoped the death had been the result of an error of judgement: too much pressure, a few seconds too long without air when Buckthorn was aiming for a supercharged orgasm. An accident of his own making could be dealt with discreetly, but if someone else was involved there'd be no hope of hushing it up. And if something criminal had taken place...

'There goes the Press Vale rape case,' he said, half to himself.

'Rape?' Breeze's ears pricked up.

'One of the guests at the country club sexually assaulted a member of staff on Sunday night. Buckthorn rushed to her rescue. He was due here this morning to give a statement.'

Breeze made a face. 'Well, that's all up the pictures now, isn't it?'

'Looks like it. So where did Buckthorn go last night before he went

65

to Rayner's flat? We know he didn't go to Press Vale, but did he go anywhere else?'

'Carew's?' Breeze suggested. He flapped his hand, limp-wristed. '"The only gay bar in town"?'

'Rayner insists that Carew's wasn't Buckthorn's scene, but we need to check. Volunteering, are you, Dennis?'

Not the most broadminded of men, Breeze looked momentarily perturbed. 'If I must. But they won't be open yet, will they? I'll try them a bit later.'

While Woody tucked into his sandwiches, Lincoln phoned Greywood Hall, hoping to speak to Buckthorn's nephew and next of kin, Laurence.

'Lord Riverbourne doesn't live here,' he was told. 'He and the countess have a house in Barbury, near the abbey. I'll give you his number.'

'I know about my uncle,' Laurence said curtly when Lincoln eventually got through to him. 'Rufus Rayner contacted me.'

Relieved that someone had already broken the news to him, Lincoln offered his condolences and asked if he could call on him.

'Do you really need to, Inspector? Frankly, I can't even see that this is a police matter.'

'What makes you say that, sir?' Lincoln bristled at the young man's offhand manner. 'Your uncle's death will be treated as suspicious until the cause has been established. Surely you'd expect us to investigate the circumstances fully?'

Silence on the other end of the line, then: 'I'm concerned about the press finding out. We don't want Hugh's private life plastered all over the Internet.'

'Then the sooner we can talk face to face the better. If you don't want me coming to your house, you'll need to come to Barley Lane police station.'

Another silence, then some murmuring in the background, Laurence consulting with his wife, presumably, who answered him in a soft American accent.

'I'll be there around half two,' he said at last. 'Let's get this over with.'

As Lincoln put the phone down, Pam came in, hurrying to her desk and quickly dumping her bag down as if she hoped her arrival would go unnoticed.

'How's your grandad?' he asked.

'He's had to go into hospital. We were there all night with him.'

'Sorry. I hadn't realised he was so ill.'

'I didn't like to say anything. He had a heart attack a couple of months ago and now he's had another one, more serious this time.'

'There must be something they can do to treat him.'

'They want to put a stent in if he's up to it.'

'That's a pretty routine treatment these days, isn't it?'

'I suppose so.' She pulled her shoulders back and straightened up. 'Stupid to worry, isn't it? Like you said, it's a routine operation.' She put on a brave smile. 'So what've I missed?'

'Hugh Buckthorn of Greywood Hall has been found dead in his boyfriend's flat. Looks as if he was strangling himself for...well, for increased sexual gratification. Only something went wrong, and he died.'

She looked aghast. 'God, that's going to be horrible for his family. It'll be all over social media.'

'That's why it's vital to keep the details to ourselves, at least until we know exactly what happened.'

'So sad, the brothers dying within a few months of each other.'

'Doesn't sound as if they were close.'

'No, but even so...'

'See what you can find out about the Honourable Hugh Buckthorn. Go to the library, look through their newspaper archives, whatever you can find out. His nephew's coming in a bit later.'

'The earl's coming in?' Pam ran her hands through her spiky fair hair. 'I'd have put something smarter on if I'd known.'

He couldn't tell whether or not she was being sarcastic.

Shortly after a quarter past three, when the eleventh Earl of Riverbourne had, somewhat irritably, seen himself out of Barley Lane police station, DCS Youngman phoned Lincoln for an update.

'Not sure how soon Dale Jacobs is going to be up and about again, Jeff,' he said, 'so for the time being you'll be Acting SIO. Now then, *please* tell me this Buckthorn chap died accidentally.'

'I can't say for certain, sir.' Lincoln, overdue mug of coffee in hand, was standing in front of the whiteboard, scanning its still-meagre contents and wishing he were able to deliver the news the DCS was hoping for. 'So far it looks as if he was on his own, but he may have brought someone back to the flat with him.'

He didn't mention the clothes piled upside down on the spare bed – an indication, to him at least, that Buckthorn hadn't been alone last night.

'What *can* you tell me?'

'Looks as if he drove himself to Bridgeford last night, but the car doesn't seem to be around. His boyfriend's adamant that Buckthorn wasn't into kinky sex or dressing up, but they've only been together a few months.'

'What does the earl think?'

Lincoln snorted. 'Lord Riverbourne would probably like us to stop investigating right now, but as I explained to him, until we know the cause of death—'

'And when's the autopsy?'

'Tomorrow morning, nine fifteen.'

'And no update on the Greywood bones?'

The Greywood bones? How easily the DCS dismissed the remains of a little girl! 'We're waiting to hear if Yazmin Fletcher's dental records are a match. If they confirm it *is* Yazmin—'

'Resolving the Buckthorn case is top priority, wouldn't you say? Park the Yazmin Fletcher case for now, Jeff. You can't do anything until the identity's been confirmed, and no one need know when that confirmation comes through. Assuming it does.'

'But if it *is* Yazmin we've found, her mother needs to know.'

'Of course, of course. But there's no point telling her until you're able to follow it up. For now, Hugh Buckthorn's death takes priority. Is that clear?'

What could Lincoln do but agree?

When the call was over, he reread the notes of his conversation with Laurence. The earl had arrived promptly, dressed as if for a business meeting, keen to get on with the interview. Although slimmer than his late father, he'd inherited Howard's straight brown hair and biggish nose, and probably his tendency to put on weight. Hugh, by contrast, had been tall and lean, with the dark good looks of their Italian mother's side of the family.

'This must be a lot to take in,' Lincoln had said, struck by the earl's lack of expression, and blaming it on shock. 'Losing your father so recently, and now your uncle—'

Laurence had cut across him. 'I hardly knew him. He's been abroad for most of my life, but I know from my father that Uncle Hugh was always a risk-taker. Something was going to catch up with him sooner or later – a jealous husband or a brawl in a foreign bar somewhere.' He sighed wearily. 'We'd got to know each other better the last few months since my father died, but I find it hard to forgive him for buggering off to the south of France years ago when he should've stuck around to support Dad. Greywood Hall's a monster, devouring everything, and Hugh should've stayed to help out.'

And now he'd bequeathed his nephew the embarrassment of a most undignified death.

'Can you tell me anything about his private life?'

'Dad knew Hugh was gay, even though he was always surrounded by doting females. I don't know if he was living with anyone while he was abroad. Since he's been back he's been involved with a guy called Rayner.'

'Rufus Rayner, yes. You've met him?'

Laurence had pursed his lips in disapproval. 'Briefly. Long enough to see he's not much older than I am, for Christ's sake, and didn't even go to a decent school.'

'Rufus and your uncle were working together at Greywood Hall, weren't they? On the paintings?'

'Were they? I only go over to the Hall to deal with business that can't be dealt with any other way. We've got a very efficient estate manager.'

'You don't like the Hall?' Lincoln wondered what it would be like to live in a house with a choice of twenty bedrooms, a ballroom, a banqueting hall, drawing rooms and a library – to say nothing of the acres of parkland surrounding it.

'My wife detests it. We'll never live there.'

'Did Mr Buckthorn have some independent source of income? The cottage at Speldon Magna—'

'The cottage at Speldon Magna is rented. Hugh lived off my grandfather's legacy until it ran out, about the same time my father died. He came back here because he couldn't afford to live abroad anymore. God knows how he thought he was going to earn enough to live on.'

After the earl left, Lincoln felt even more deflated, saddened that Hugh Buckthorn's death seemed little more than an irritating inconvenience for his nephew. Would tomorrow's autopsy confirm he'd died accidentally and on his own? That was what the earl must be hoping.

But suppose forensic examination of the flat, of Buckthorn's clothes, of his body, yielded traces of another individual? Suppose Ken Burges found evidence of foul play?

Until then they needed to search for the silver Jaguar, which would probably turn up, plastered in penalty notices, in Barbury's gloomy multistorey car park.

'What about keeping a watch on his cottage?' Woody asked. 'Do we still need to have anyone over there?'

'Until we've confirmed Buckthorn's death was an accident.'

'Or not.'

Lincoln noticed the time. 'Thought Graham would've been back from Bridgeford by now. There can't be many places there with security cameras.'

The door swung open and Dilke came bowling in, nose and cheeks red from the cold outside.

'Take a look at this.' The young detective sat down at his laptop without even taking his coat off, and jammed a memory stick into the socket. 'An old lady in one of the houses overlooking the market square's been losing the gnomes off her front porch. Her granddaughter rigged up a camera so she could catch whoever's been nicking them. Stone ones,' he added. 'She's lost seven in the last couple of months.'

The screen filled with a grainy image of an empty market square at seven forty-eight the previous night. After a few seconds a big, light-coloured car turned off the main street and parked in the square long enough for the camera to capture Hugh Buckthorn at the wheel of his Jaguar. No sooner had he parked than he seemed to change his mind, reversing swiftly out of the parking place and driving on down the street, past the entrance to Jackdaw Lane and out of shot.

'At least that proves he drove himself to Bridgeford,' Lincoln said. 'But where's the car now?'

'I went all through the footage,' Dilke said, 'right up till eight this morning, and the car didn't appear again.'

'You still can't see if there's anyone in the car with him,' said Woody. 'Those streetlights cast too much shadow.'

'Definitely Buckthorn at the wheel, though,' said Lincoln, 'turning into the square as if he's come from Barbury, not from Speldon Magna.'

'Nowhere else in the village he could've parked?' Woody crossed to the sketch map on the whiteboard.

'We've checked the only other car park, and the Jag's not there.'

'Reckon whoever he took back to the flat went off in his car.' Woody stroked his moustache thoughtfully. 'We didn't find the key, did we?'

'*If* someone went back to the flat with him.' Lincoln still wasn't sure what to believe. 'Good work, Graham, finding that camera. Shame about the gnomes.'

Dilke glanced across to the empty desk next to his. 'Where's Breezy?'

'I sent him to Carew's.'

'The gay bar? He won't like that!'

'It'll be an education for him. He probably hasn't been inside the place since it stopped being the Top Note Disco.'

Woody looked wistful. 'Used to go to the Top Note with Suki when we first started going out together.'

'You'll never catch me in a disco,' said Lincoln. 'Two left feet.'

'Suki had us taking lessons.'

Of course. Woody's wife always had to do things properly.

Lincoln went over to the whiteboard to take another look at the photos of Buckthorn lying indecorously on Rufus Rayner's couch.

'Where did the freezer bag come from?' He tried to ignore the grotesque outline of the dead man's gaping mouth and bulging eyes. 'Did Buckthorn find it in the kitchen?'

'How d'you mean?'

'Did he tear it off a roll or pull it out of a packet, however those bags come?'

'I don't see—'

'Did he bring a single freezer bag with him to Rayner's flat or did he find one there in the kitchen?'

Woody looked round at him. 'Does it matter?'

'Just trying to reconstruct his last few hours. Was he already planning a spot of auto-erotic asphyxiation when he arrived at the flat? Did he go round with plastic bags in his pocket in case he picked someone up who'd go along with his little sex games?'

'SOCOs will have finished processing the flat by now. There won't be anyone there we can ask.'

'Then we need to check for ourselves, see if there are plastic bags in the kitchen.'

'What, now?'

'Somewhere else you need to be?'

'Well, actually, yes,' said Woody. 'I'm looking after the boys this evening. Suki's taking Kate over to her friend's house for a sleepover.'

Lincoln sighed. Was Trish's daughter still best friends with Charlotte, or had she moved on to somebody else, the way kids do? He missed hearing all about her, even though she'd become a difficult, moody teenager in the weeks before Trish left for Essex.

'And anyway,' Woody went on, 'reckon it's only relevant if we suspect someone else was involved. And we don't, do we?'

'I'm not sure.' Lincoln stared at the photos in the vain hope of something leaping out at him. 'I'm really not sure.'

CHAPTER 11

SATURDAY 4TH FEBRUARY

'The remains are Yazmin Fletcher's,' Ken Burges told Lincoln over the phone next morning. 'The dental records confirm it.'

When the little girl went missing in 1997, her dental records had been put on file for a situation such as this: her body turning up when it was too late to use any other means to identify her.

'Anything else of interest?'

'Like cause of death?' Ken's laugh was ironic. They both knew it would be next to impossible to establish that after all this time. 'Although...' A dramatic pause.

'Yes?'

'I found a couple of fractures in her left wrist and arm. One was fully healed, the other fresher, only partially healed. Possibly, of course, the result of accidents. You know what kids are like, charging around on their scooters and their bikes. But they're the sort of injuries you also come across when a child's being treated roughly. Might be worth checking with Social Services – assuming they've still got records from that far back.'

'Nothing in the case file about Social Services getting involved. Even when Sonia accused the father of abducting the kid, she never accused him of treating her badly.'

Might something have been missed in 1997? Records were increasingly being kept on computer by then, but plenty more were still only on paper, in folders in filing cabinets.

Another complication Lincoln foresaw was that Sonia and Bruno had been living in the Southampton area until Yazmin was three or four: City of Southampton and Hampshire councils would need to be consulted as well as Wiltshire.

'There was some damage to the back of the skull,' Ken went on, 'but after all this time I can't be sure if it was the cause of death or occurred post-mortem. With all the rubbish being chucked down into that pit over the years, the damage could've been caused by building rubble landing on her – a brick or something. Not much more I can deduce, given what little there is left of her. Sorry, Jeff, I wish I could tell you more.'

'Thanks, Ken. I've been told to put the case on hold, anyway.'

'Because of the Honourable Hugh Buckthorn?'

'His case takes precedence.'

'Well, that kiddie's family have waited all this time to know what happened to her. They can wait another few days. Whereas the Honourable Hugh's family...'

'The Honourable Hugh's family want to hush the whole thing up as soon as possible.' Lincoln couldn't hide his bitterness.

'Understandable in the circumstances. See you at nine fifteen?'

'I won't say I'm looking forward to it, but yes. See you later.'

The smoky aroma of fried bacon wafted across the CID room: Breeze had picked up his breakfast at Big Ed's Butty Wagon en route from home.

'How was Carew's?' Lincoln asked, putting the phone down.

'I didn't get propositioned, if that's what you mean.'

'You sound almost disappointed.' Pam looked up from a pile of photocopies she'd made at the library yesterday. Lincoln could see she'd taken his request for information on Buckthorn all too seriously.

'I almost am.' Breeze set his bacon butty down on his desk and wiped the grease from his fingers. 'I showed them a photo of Buckthorn, but they didn't have a clue who he was. However...' He fished his mobile out of the inside pocket of his biker jacket and swiped the screen a few times. 'This is the photo I showed them.' He turned his phone round so Lincoln could see.

It was the most recent one they'd been able to find on the Internet yesterday: Buckthorn with Rufus Rayner at the Cheese Market Gallery last December, at the opening of an exhibition. The two men were sharing a joke, Buckthorn's hand cupping Rayner's elbow as if detaining him long enough to tell him the punchline.

'Yes?'

Breeze grinned. 'The bod behind the bar at Carew's didn't know Buckthorn, but he recognised Rayner. Said he wasn't such a regular these days, but our Rufus was a frequent flyer until sometime in the autumn.'

'Hmm. Maybe he stopped going there after he met Buckthorn.' Though hadn't Tilly said her brother was going out with a girlfriend of hers until he fell for Buckthorn? Maybe he'd secretly been a customer at Carew's for a while before he came out to his family. 'So if Buckthorn wasn't at Carew's and he wasn't at the country club...'

'Does it matter *where* he was if it was an accident?' Breeze picked his butty up and chomped on it. Grease trickled down his chin and onto the chest of his T-shirt.

'If the autopsy leaves us in any doubt about what happened, the more information we have about his movements that night the better. Once a few days elapse, people forget and the trail goes cold. Coffee,' Lincoln added, more brightly. 'Let's get that kettle on.'

He was gratefully savouring the first satisfying mouthfuls of his Nescafé when Dilke arrived.

'It's on the Internet,' he said, waving his phone around. 'About Hugh Buckthorn being found dead.'

Lincoln sighed in exasperation. 'How's it got out?' He guessed that Trish would have seen about it too, would wonder why he hadn't phoned her last night to confide in her.

'How could you *stop* it getting out?' Breeze dabbed ineffectually at his T-shirt. 'All the people involved, the mortuary staff, the hospital... It'd only take one idiot to recognise him and put it on Twitter, and then it's everywhere.'

Lincoln knew he was right. 'Thank God they don't seem to have the details of *how* he died. Make sure we've got a guard on the cottage so nobody tries to get in. You know what journalists are like.'

'Have we heard anything more about the bones in the rubbish tip?' Dilke asked. 'Is it that little girl that went missing?'

'Yeah,' said Breeze. 'But we can't do anything until we've got old Buckthorn's case out of the way.'

'But Sonia Fletcher needs to know!' Pam protested. 'And it could be ages before the Buckthorn case is closed.'

'Not necessarily,' said Lincoln. 'His death was most likely accidental. The autopsy's later this morning, so we should know by the end of the day.'

She wasn't reassured. 'But suppose it *wasn't* an accident?'

Lincoln didn't answer straight away. Would DCS Youngman entrust such a high-profile homicide investigation to him if DCI Jacobs wasn't fit to return to work? Would he bring someone in from elsewhere in the county? 'Then we'll need a rethink,' he said eventually. 'Exactly what are the newspapers saying?' He checked his newsfeed while he drank his coffee.

Although a number of sources were reporting the death, none of them seemed to know the exact circumstances. *Earl's uncle found dead in Bridgeford flat*, read one. *Grieving earl bereaved AGAIN*, read another.

If they bothered to look through their newspapers' archives, they'd discover that Hugh had been a celebrity in his own right once upon a time.

'What do we tell Sonia if she phones?' asked Pam.

'Stall her. Tell her we haven't confirmed the identity yet. I don't like lying to her, but we can't do anything until after Buckthorn's autopsy.'

'And if his death *wasn't* an accident?' Breeze's eyes were gleaming with anticipation.

'If it turns out that he was murdered, it may not be our case any more.' Though Lincoln was damned if he was going to let Park Street steal the investigation from him and his team! 'Now I'd better get over to Presford General.'

Lincoln had been present at plenty of autopsies, but he had never got used to the sickening sounds of flesh and bone being cut and sawn to reveal the body's secrets.

This time it was even more difficult to distance himself. He couldn't stop reflecting on how recently he'd seen Buckthorn alive. Forty-eight hours ago he had been looking into the man's face and remarking to himself how well he'd aged, how affable he seemed compared to his depiction in the media thirty years ago. He recalled the dark curls dipping onto his forehead, and the way he fidgeted with his signet ring. They'd chatted about Press Vale Country Club, had sat together in his warm kitchen with sunshine streaming in, had savoured the coffee Buckthorn had made.

Ken Burges worked methodically and with the easy rhythm of a man who'd been carrying out autopsies for the best part of three decades. He recorded his impressions as he went along, noting any anomalies and anything on which he preferred to reserve judgement until further tests had been done.

What Lincoln found most shocking was the sight of Buckthorn's face once the plastic bag was removed from around his head. If the dead man had been aiming for ecstasy, he'd fallen far short.

'Anything to suggest it was deliberate?' he asked. 'Suicide, perhaps?'

Ken pursed his lips and studied the figure laid out on the table before him. 'The dressing gown cord was looped round his neck and tied round his leg below the knee,' he said. 'Once he put the bag over his head, he could pull the cord taut by straightening his leg, and that would tighten the cord round the neck of the bag. He could control the tension in the cord by stretching or bending that leg, leaving his hands free – for obvious reasons.' He raised his eyebrows suggestively, and Lincoln half-expected him to say *Nudge, wink wink*, but he didn't.

Lincoln wanted to be sure he'd understood Ken's explanation. 'So he'd straighten his leg out, the cord would pull taut, drawing the bag tighter round his head and restricting his air supply. Is that right?'

Ken nodded. 'And when he needed to get more air, he'd bend his leg, thus slackening the cord and easing the pressure on the neck of the bag.'

'So what went wrong?'

'Take a look at the scene photos.' Ken led him across to the workbench, where his tablet lay. Finding a photo taken from above Buckthorn's body on the couch, he ran his finger down the screen, tracing the line of the silky golden cord. One end was tied round the neck of the freezer bag. The cord snaked down over Buckthorn's chest, his belly, his limp genitals, his thigh. The other end of the cord was tied below his knee.

Ken zoomed in a little, focusing on the cord drooping between the dead man's thighs. The stockings had pressed the thick hairs on Buckthorn's legs into ugly patterns that were clearly visible through the sheer black nylon.

Lincoln frowned at the photo. 'What am I missing?'

Ken tutted, as if his star pupil had disappointed him. 'The cord was much too slack. See the way it was looped round his neck and then tied below his knee? There's no way he could've created enough tension to pull the bag tight over his face like that.'

'But his leg's gone limp as he lost consciousness, hasn't it? When he was alive, he'd have been stretching his leg out to pull the cord tight.'

Ken shook his head. 'The way this cord is tied, it would have come undone as soon as he straightened his leg.' He chuckled. 'If I need to demonstrate on a human guinea pig then I will, but I trust you'll take my word for it.'

'So if the cord didn't pull the bag tight, why did he suffocate?'

'Good question.' Ken drew back from his tablet, leaned against the workbench and folded his arms. 'And there was no semen. No signs of arousal, no bodily fluids on his hands. And in most cases of fatal auto-erotic asphyxia, you see porn magazines nearby, sex toys, photos, some other sort of stimulus. Drugs, sometimes – poppers, for instance – but there was nothing like that at the scene, was there?'

'No, but then, everything about the flat was very neat and tidy.' Once more, Lincoln wondered why Buckthorn hadn't made himself a drink, poured himself a glass of water while he prepared for his self-love session. Unless someone else had been there too, and cleaned up afterwards...

'The tox results will show if he took stimulants, relaxants, or whatever. There was no evidence that he was injected with anything.'

'We found a small quantity of what looked like coke in his wallet,' Lincoln said. 'Didn't look as if he'd opened the bag, though.'

'We'll test for it anyway. There were no signs of recent sexual activity with anyone else. He died where he was found. From the lividity, it was obvious the body hadn't been moved.'

'So, all in all—?'

'Cause of death was asphyxia. With the plastic bag over his face, he gasped to take in more air, sucking the plastic tighter against his mouth and nose. He'd have lost consciousness very quickly, within seconds.'

'He definitely didn't strangle himself?'

Ken shook his head. 'This.' He tapped the tablet screen. 'This dressing gown cord was simply a prop. The dressing gown itself was brand new. The labels were still crisp, as if they'd never been through the wash. Suggesting it was bought specially for the occasion.'

If the dressing gown had been bought recently, Buckthorn might have bought it locally. The brand name could be checked to trace stockists in the area.

Lincoln sighed. Not simply a sad accident, then. 'He could've decided to kill himself by pulling a plastic bag over his head, couldn't he?'

'Of course, but why stage your suicide to look like a kinky sex act gone wrong?'

'So if it's not suicide or an accident...'

'Look at this.' Ken swiped through the images on his tablet until he found a picture of the lethal freezer bag, cut open and flattened out. The surface of the polythene looked messy, smeared with snot and saliva, but Ken was pointing at the bottom edge of the bag. 'See those white streaks there? Where the polythene's stressed?'

Lincoln looked closely at the puckered shapes in the plastic, as if fingertips had dug into it without being able to tear it. 'Is that where he pulled at the bag trying to get it off?'

'No. That's the *back* edge of the bag. Those marks were left by someone pulling hard from *behind* him.'

'He didn't put up a fight?'

'I'd say he was taken by surprise. The bag was put over his face and pulled tight, and he was out of air in seconds.' Ken paused. 'You hear what I'm saying?'

'He was murdered.' A shiver ran down Lincoln's back and made him shudder. 'And it was staged to look like he did it himself. To humiliate him? Or so it would be hushed up to save the family any embarrassment?'

Ken shrugged. 'That's for you to determine, Jeff. When you find out who did this to him.'

CHAPTER 12

The autopsy changed everything. Buckthorn's death couldn't be hushed up or played down, couldn't be kept private so only his nephew Laurence and his immediate family knew what had happened.

Lincoln called a briefing as soon as he got back to Barley Lane. Even if DCS Youngman took him off the case, it was vital to bring together everything they knew, if only for the benefit of whoever took over the role of SIO.

He parked himself on the edge of his desk and addressed his team. 'From the post-mortem on Hugh Buckthorn, it seems we're looking at foul play dressed up to look like an accident.'

Pam gasped, but Breeze grinned and sat back with folded arms.

'Dressed *down*, more like,' he sniggered.

'Thank you, Dennis.' Standing up and crossing to the whiteboard, Lincoln pointed to the photos of the body on the couch.

'We were meant to assume Buckthorn was trying a spot of self-strangulation and pulled the cord too tight round the neck of the freezer bag. However, the cord was much too slack to exert any pressure. Someone else pulled the bag from behind.' He put his fists against the back of his head to demonstrate. 'No way he could have done that to himself.'

'Reckon they knew Rayner wasn't due back that night,' said Woody, 'and that the rest of the building was empty. Didn't you say it was odd how Buckthorn hadn't even poured himself a glass of water? They must've washed up anything they touched in the kitchen and put it all away.'

Breeze snorted. 'Doesn't mean they didn't leave traces, though. If there was someone else in that flat, they're bound to have left *something* behind.'

Lincoln agreed. 'That's why we need that report from the SOCOs.'

Dilke stared at the photos. 'Is it possible he was drugged first?'

'That's what the tox screen should tell us, but we won't get the results for a few days.'

Had the whole scene been set up, Lincoln wondered? Had Buckthorn been sedated by his killer, then undressed, the dressing gown put on him, and the stockings? Did someone lay him out on the sofa and then put the bag over his head? Conscious but too doped to resist, he'd have been dead in less than a minute.

'Shame the CCTV didn't show if there was anyone in the car with him,' Woody said.

'True, but that car must be somewhere. If he had a passenger, they'll have left some sort of trace, even if it's only a stray hair or dirt off their shoes.'

'The car hasn't been picked up on any ANPR locally, though, has it?' said Breeze.

'Which suggests that it hasn't gone far from wherever Buckthorn left it.'

'Time of death?' Dilke asked.

'Between ten on Thursday night and one o'clock Friday morning. He'd eaten not long before he died. Steak and chips and a couple of glasses of wine.'

'Plenty of restaurants do steak and chips,' Woody said. 'Plenty of pubs, too.'

'Maybe Rufus Rayner can help us narrow it down a bit. He may have had a favourite restaurant or bar. We need to talk to Rayner, anyway.' Lincoln looked across at Pam. 'Anything of interest come up in your research at the library?'

She pursed her lips uncertainly. 'Nothing much recently, but Hugh certainly got plenty of coverage years ago, even when he was a little boy. His parents were quite a glamorous couple – the ninth Earl of Riverbourne and his beautiful Italian wife, throwing exotic parties at Greywood Hall. Then Hugh acquired a bit of a reputation as a playboy, the eligible bachelor being paired off with one Sloane Ranger after another.'

Breeze groaned. 'Cuh, the perils of being rich and handsome, eh?'

Pam rolled her eyes and carried on. 'He apparently fell out with his father and went off to Italy to immerse himself in art. Came back to London when he was nearly thirty and did a Fine Arts degree. Wrote books on Renaissance painting, articles for art magazines, consultant on a series for Channel 4—'

Lincoln cut in. 'What was he doing before he came back here?'

'Buyer for a private gallery in the south of France. Reading between the lines of his brother's obituaries last year, the family fortunes are rather depleted. A gossip piece in one of the tabloids implied Hugh came back to England because he was broke.'

'That's pretty much what Laurence told me,' said Lincoln. 'Hugh couldn't afford to stay away. He never married? No partner? No children?'

'Apparently not.'

'So nothing there that's an obvious motive for murder.'

'Only his financial situation,' she said. 'Did he owe someone money? Did he get into debt?'

Breeze spread his hands questioningly. 'Why kill the golden goose?'

'It was the *eggs* that were golden, not the goose,' Pam pointed out, 'but you're right, it doesn't make sense, does it? He can't pay them back if he's dead.'

'Has he got into debt through gambling?' Woody wondered. 'He was playing poker at the country club, wasn't he, the night of that incident with the waitress – what was her name?'

'Amy,' said Lincoln. 'Amy Cartland.'

Dilke tipped his chair back, his gaze on the whiteboard. 'Was he killed to shut him up about that? He was the only eyewitness to the attack, wasn't he?'

Lincoln shook his head. 'He wasn't even an eyewitness – not really. He told Amy he'd make a statement if she reported it, but all he'd seen was her rushing out of one of the bedrooms. He didn't see the man who tried to rape her.'

Breeze grinned. 'Ah, but did the man see Buckthorn?'

'You mean, the attacker might have *thought* Buckthorn was more of a threat than he was?' Lincoln turned back to the whiteboard, although there was nothing on it that would help. 'Would someone kill him to shut him up? Amy delayed reporting the attack, so there was no forensic evidence. The case was unlikely to get to court.'

'Maybe her attacker wanted to be absolutely sure it didn't.'

'But then it's *Amy* who's the bigger threat, not Buckthorn. And why the charade with the stockings and the dressing gown cord? No, there has to be something else behind it. We need to get hold of his bank statements, see if there's anything amiss. In the meantime, Woody and I will go and talk to Rufus Rayner. And then we'd better search the cottage.'

Lincoln waited while Woody gathered up his notebook and phone. He glanced across at Pam, still clutching her photocopies. 'Good work, Pam. Keep looking.'

The Rayners lived in a detached Victorian house set back from the road on the main route north-east out of Barbury. Its long front garden lent it a rustic air but did little to baffle the incessant rumble of the traffic.

When the house was built, it would have backed onto open countryside, but the last hundred years had seen road after road replace the farms and fields that had once been there.

When Mrs Rayner opened the wide front door, she glared at the two detectives as if they were door-to-door salesmen peddling a miracle cleaner for sinks. A small woman, baby-faced and gingery, she was like an older, female version of her son. She even wore wire-framed glasses like his.

'Rufus is in the study,' she said, leading them through the lofty entrance hall to a spacious room, where her son lolled miserably in a chair by the fire. 'I'll put the kettle on.' She marched off, head held high.

The study overlooked the garden, where bird feeders hung from bare branches and dead leaves lay on the sodden lawn. The warmer days of spring still seemed a long way off, and Lincoln didn't hesitate when Rayner invited him and Woody to sit down opposite him by the open coal fire.

After getting through the usual preliminaries, Lincoln sat forward, elbows on thighs, his hands clasped lightly together. 'I'm sorry, Mr Rayner, but we believe Mr Buckthorn – Hugh – was murdered. It was made to look as if he'd killed himself, by accident or on purpose.'

Rayner's brown eyes flashed with horror. 'Why would anyone want to *murder* him?'

'We don't know,' said Woody. 'We're trying to establish where he went on Thursday evening. He'd had steak and chips a few hours before he died. Any ideas where he might have gone to eat?'

'Steak and chips? How do you know that? Oh,' he gasped when he realised how. 'He'd have gone to the Sanremo. We go – we *used* to go there every week.'

'On a Thursday?'

'Yes. That's the night I usually work late at the gallery. The guy who owns the Sanremo knows some place in Italy that Hugh knows, and they reminisce about it. And the food's good.' He tried for a smile. 'We usually go – we *used* to go there about seven, ten past, after I've locked up. But this Thursday, of course, I was away.' He stared down at the faded, antique-looking hearthrug. 'We'd got into a routine. The Sanremo on a Thursday, then back to my flat.'

Lincoln wondered who else was aware of that routine. 'You drove your own cars to Bridgeford?'

Rayner nodded. 'We'd park in the market square overnight. You're okay there until nine next morning, and we'd always be out of the flat by then. Have you found his car yet?'

'No, but we believe whoever was with him that night took his keys and left in his car.' Picking up his folder, Lincoln pulled a couple of photos out and laid them on the low table in front of Rayner. 'Do you recognise this dressing gown and this cord?' Spread out on a workbench to be photographed, the two items looked sterile and unreal.

Rayner took his glasses off, picked up the photos and peered at them carefully. 'This isn't Hugh's.'

'Are you sure?'

'Of course I'm sure. He didn't keep anything like that at the flat. If he took a shower, he'd put *my* bathrobe on afterwards. And yes, he did look ridiculous because it was far too short for him, but...' He broke off, biting his lip. 'He certainly never wore a dressing gown as cheap and nasty-looking as this.' He tossed the photos down dismissively.

'You told us before that Hugh wasn't interested in casual relationships. And yet it looks as if he went back to your flat with someone on Thursday night. You were close to him for, what? A few months? Maybe he met up with someone he'd been involved with before you?'

Rayner shook his head emphatically. 'There wasn't anyone before me. Hugh only came back to England when his brother died, and we met a few days later.'

Sex, quick and anonymous, Lincoln knew, could often relieve the stress of work, hardship, grief. How could Rayner be so sure that Buckthorn, mourning his older brother and the loss of his comfortable lifestyle abroad, hadn't picked someone up one of those first nights he was back in England – and then bumped into them again more recently? Who had he phoned on Thursday evening? How could Rufus be sure of his lover's fidelity?

Woody explained about the need to take fingerprints and DNA swabs from anyone else who might have visited the flat recently.

'No one's been into *my* flat recently, although the guys are still working on the rest of the building. The only fingerprints you'll find will be Tilly's or mine or Hugh's. Or whoever...' He tailed off.

'We'll talk to Austin Kendall,' said Woody, 'start trying to eliminate anyone using the communal areas.'

Rayner clapped a hand to his forehead. 'Oh God, oh God! Everyone's going to know what happened, aren't they?'

Lincoln nodded. 'When the victim's as high-profile as Hugh, the rumours are bound to start flying around.'

'But why did they kill him? You said his wallet was there, the keys to the cottage. Would someone murder him for his *car*?'

83

Lincoln tucked the photos back into his folder. 'If he didn't bring someone back with him, his killer must have gained entry to the flat somehow. Could anyone get into the building without him knowing?'

'The entry phone's scheduled for installation next month,' Rayner said mournfully, 'and the downstairs door lock and the phone lines. Yes, I know, I know, security should've been tighter, but it's a building site, for Christ's sake! And surely, if Hugh was there alone and someone knocked on the front door of the flat, he wouldn't answer it, would he?'

'He might have thought it was a friend of yours not knowing you were away.'

Rayner nodded wearily. 'He'd have looked through the spyhole first, I suppose, and if whoever was out there looked like an ordinary guy—'

'Or he brought someone back with him,' said Woody. 'We'll have finished in your flat soon.'

Rayner leaned nearer the fire, hugging himself as if he couldn't get warm. 'You can be there as long as you like. I can't face going back there now.'

After a moment's quiet, Lincoln said, 'You go to Carew's from time to time?'

'What? No!'

'We showed the bar staff a picture of you and Mr Buckthorn,' said Woody. 'They recognised you as a regular customer.'

'Oh, well, yes, at one time maybe, but not now I've met...' He ran out of steam. 'Until I met Hugh, yes, I went to the club most weekends.'

'How *did* you meet?' Lincoln asked, wanting to sound more sympathetic than he felt he had so far.

As he'd hoped, Rayner relaxed a little. 'Hugh came into the gallery to ask about a landscape in the window. Said he'd just moved to Speldon Magna, and the painting reminded him of the downs around the village. I was having a private view for the artist the night after, and I invited Hugh along. Thought it'd be good PR. We hit it off straight away, and it went on from there.'

'And you were working together on cataloguing the paintings at Greywood Hall?'

'Hugh had made a start on his own, and I was going to help him as soon as I had some free time. Not that I have much spare time these days! He'd got an inventory someone did years ago and was trying to match the paintings up against it.'

He took his glasses off and held them up to the light as if checking them for smudges. His eyes were moist with tears.

'We'd got it all worked out,' he went on. 'Some of those paintings have been in storage for ages, and Hugh was so looking forward to bringing them out into the open again, to give people a chance to enjoy them.' He slotted his glasses back on with a sigh. 'That'll never happen now.'

Before they left, Lincoln showed Rayner a photo of the freezer bag that had been used to suffocate Buckthorn – a photo that had been edited to remove the mucus traces of his dying moments.

'Recognise this bag?'

'One freezer bag's much like another, isn't it?' He looked away. 'Best ask Tilly. She does all that sort of shopping.' He went ahead of them into the hallway and called for his sister.

Eager to help, Tilly scrutinised the photo closely as she clutched it in both hands. 'Is that "Tesco" printed on it? I never shop at Tesco.'

'So this bag didn't come from your brother's kitchen?'

She shook her head. 'I always shop at Waitrose or Sainsbury's, and Rufus never shops for anything like that himself.'

'So,' said Lincoln as he and Woody drove over to carry out a search of Buckthorn's cottage, 'it looks as if whoever killed him brought the freezer bag with him.'

'Or with *her*.'

'Quite right. No assumptions. Or with her.'

Jason Kitto, Buckthorn's landlord, middle-aged and overweight, met them outside Corner Cottage. From the smell of his breath it was apparent he'd been killing time across the road in the Two Magpies while he waited for them.

'Hard to believe anything's happened to him,' he said. 'Nice chap, Mr Buckthorn, never any trouble. I'd heard the rumours about him being a bit of a party animal, orgies and that, but—'

'Orgies?' Woody looked askance, and the man laughed awkwardly.

'Only going by what you read in the papers, all that used to go on at Greywood Hall.'

Lincoln and Woody exchanged glances as they waited for Kitto to let them into the cottage.

'The papers always like to make something out of nothing,' Lincoln said.

'True, but there's no smoke without fire.' Kitto tapped his red-veined nose. 'Lad used to work for me, he knew a thing or two about what went on. Kids brought in from children's homes. Girls *and* boys. There was talk of one kiddie getting killed, he said, and it all being covered up, as you'd expect. But Mr Buckthorn – well, I never had any problem with him.' He rubbed his hands together. 'Ooh-kay, I'll leave you to it. If you need me, I'll be over the road.'

Once Kitto had left, they worked methodically through the cottage, starting in the bigger of the two bedrooms. It was beginning to get dark now, so they had to switch lights on. The central heating came on as they worked, which made their task a little more comfortable.

In the wardrobe they found suits and sports coats, shirts and shoes from the best London tailors and shoemakers, well worn and well looked after rather than new. A tweed jacket in houndstooth check had been carefully darned where the collar had begun to wear.

'Invisible mending.' Lincoln held the jacket up to the light.

Woody chuckled. 'Can't be invisible if you can see it.'

'Ha. I mean he's thrifty, takes care of his things.'

'Reckon a repair like that would cost more than a new jacket.'

'Not this make of jacket.' Lincoln had seen the label: Gieves and Hawkes. He ran his fingers over the all-but-invisible darn, momentarily sad for the jacket, separated for ever from its owner.

He slipped his hand into each pocket in turn, finding a white cotton handkerchief, a handful of euro coins, a paper clip, an elastic band, and a receipt for an Americano and croissant bought from a Costa coffee shop in Bath in November.

In an antique tallboy they found socks, singlets, boxer shorts. No stockings or suspenders, no frilly knickers, no bras. No sex toys in the bedside cabinet, no recreational drugs. The dressing gown hanging behind the bedroom door was a sober Black Watch tartan with a tie belt.

Buckthorn didn't have an office as such but worked at a large antique desk in the living room. His laptop and printer took up most of the space, a stack of pristine notebooks beside them, with a couple of box files lined up on the deep windowsill. His fountain pen, a vintage Parker, lay on top of the notebooks.

Beside the desk was a wide bookcase laden with titles on painting, architecture, cultural history. Reference guides to art and artists took up one whole shelf, and another shelf was mostly devoted to books on life studies, the male form in art through the ages, including books by and about the American photographer Robert Mapplethorpe.

These books alone were the only possible clue to Buckthorn's sexuality. There were no gay magazines lying around, no porn.

'We can check his emails, see if he was meeting someone that night,' Lincoln said, unplugging the laptop. He unfolded an evidence bag and Woody slid the laptop into it.

They searched the desk drawers and found a spare car key, an old pocket diary with a few phone numbers scribbled in it, some letters and a recent bank statement. His current account was overdrawn by seven hundred and forty-two pounds.

'Not much in the way of personal papers here,' Woody remarked.

'Probably had to get rid of stuff when he moved back here, downsize.'

'What d'you reckon Kitto meant about "all that went on at Greywood Hall"?'

'Come on, Woody, you know the tales that were doing the rounds last year.'

'Yeah, but there was never any evidence, was there?'

'To be fair, we didn't look very hard, did we?'

'We weren't expected to.'

'Exactly.'

When Lincoln and his team were investigating the murder of teenager Lorren Walsh the previous September, they'd found a cache of items she'd secretly taken from the men who'd been routinely assaulting her: a photo she'd sneaked out of a wallet, a handkerchief embroidered with its owner's initials. Her social worker had been Linus Bonetti, and Lincoln suspected that she'd taken these items to pass on to him, to help build a case against her attackers. After his death she'd continued to gather these small trophies, presumably in the naïve hope that another social worker would complete the work he'd begun.

Lorren had told Bonetti that youngsters from a children's home were being taken to sex parties at a rich man's house. She also told him that at one of these parties a child had been killed.

A story uncomfortably close to what Jason Kitto had heard.

Last September, pursuing Lorren's killers, Lincoln had been discouraged from asking awkward questions about these alleged sex parties. People in high places might have been implicated by the answers. Still, it niggled him to this day that at least one of the men involved in Lorren's death had got away with it. Those awkward questions still needed to be asked.

But was Hugh Buckthorn involved in any of this? How could he be? He'd been in France for the last twenty-odd years.

Hands on hips, Woody stood in the middle of the living room and looked around him. 'Where's the work he's done on the Greywood Hall paintings?'

'He's probably got a database on the laptop. We'll soon find out.'

They searched the rest of the cottage, finding nothing of significance there or in the outbuildings, so they went across the road to the Two Magpies to let Kitto know they'd finished, at least for now.

'Well, look who it isn't!' Billie Wheeler flipped her tea towel over her shoulder and grinned at Lincoln and Woody, although it wasn't a welcoming grin. Billie had given shelter to a murder suspect last year and made a tricky case even trickier.

Now, in a baggy woollen dress that clung unflatteringly to her rotund figure, she folded her arms defensively under her bosom. 'You don't look as if you've dropped in for a pint.'

The pub was quiet, only one or two other drinkers there apart from Kitto. The smell of fried potato filled the air. Fried potato and scorched cabbage.

'We've got bubble and squeak if you're hungry,' she said, nodding at the specials board at the end of the bar. Today's special was bubble and squeak with Wiltshire pork bangers. 'Terrible what's happened to Hugh, isn't it?'

'Did you see much of him?' Lincoln asked.

She shrugged her big, smooth shoulders. 'He'd pop over some evenings for a bite to eat, a few drinks. Sociable sort of chap, but more the type to ask you about yourself than give much away. He had a reputation, didn't he, back in the day? I remember, see, because the Buckthorns own all the land round here, the forest, all of it. Corner Cottage was part of the estate too. Jason bought it when the old earl had to start selling things off.'

'The old earl?'

'Robert Buckthorn, Howard and Hugh's dad. Howard inherited a shedload of debt. Wouldn't be surprised if it was the stress that killed him, trying to balance the books when there's more money running out than coming in. And now I suppose it's Laurence who's got to keep it all going, though he'll struggle to save it and keep it in the family. You ask me, he ought to sell Greywood Hall off, let someone turn it into one of those posh apartment complexes you read about.'

Lest they get sidetracked by real estate, Lincoln asked her if Buckthorn had many visitors.

'You think I've got time to be spying on people, Mr Lincoln?'

'Just thought you might've noticed.'

Billie sniffed. 'Well, I didn't. He certainly never brought anyone in here.'

Lincoln's phone rang as he and Woody walked back to the car.

It was Breeze. 'Buckthorn's car's turned up,' he said. 'Parked a couple of minutes away from the Old Shoddy Mill.'

'So why didn't we find it?'

'I'll give you the address, boss, and you can see for yourself.'

Hugh Buckthorn's Jaguar Sovereign was parked next to an ivy-swaddled house in Sixpenny Lane, a stone's throw from the apartment where he'd died. The owners of the house, the Merediths, were old friends of his and had been away in Austria, skiing. When they'd arrived home that morning, they'd found the car in their carport. Hugh knew they were going to be away, they said. He'd have known they wouldn't mind him making use of their empty driveway.

'We'll get the car checked over,' Lincoln said, as he and Woody followed the route Buckthorn would have walked on Thursday night. 'Could be something in it that shouldn't be.'

They crossed Church Street and headed down Jackdaw Lane, looking in vain for a camera that might have filmed Buckthorn during that four-minute walk.

'So if the killer didn't take the Jag,' said Woody, 'they must've had their own car here.'

'Or been picked up. I'll get Graham to go through the CCTV footage again – the lady with the gnomes.'

Woody grinned. 'The lady *without* the gnomes, you mean.'

'Ha! The other possibility is that it's somebody local, someone who simply walked away from the scene. But why take his car key?'

'Reckon they expected the car to be outside or in the square. It took us long enough to find it. They probably gave up.'

'Ah well, let's hope the media coverage brings a few witnesses out of the woodwork. Do we try the restaurant next?'

They drove out of Bridgeford and back into Barbury. The Sanremo was on the corner of the street that led from the town centre to Barbury Abbey. Not surprisingly, during the day and out of the tourist season it was closed until half past six. There was a security camera over the door, but it looked dirty and poorly maintained. Had Buckthorn been on his own when he dropped in here to have steak and chips for the last time, a glass or two of wine?

A dark blue saloon car pulled up at the kerb and the driver got out, straightening up stiffly as he pulled his black overcoat tighter round him. He was shorter than average, and stocky. Completely bald, he had thick eyebrows and a five o'clock shadow, and he was staring at Lincoln incredulously.

'Mr Lincoln!' The old man seized him in a bear hug, shouting excitedly. 'How long since you were coming to eat at Bassanio's?'

'Too long, Gino, too long!' Lincoln pulled away from him and turned to Woody. 'Remember Bassanio's? Top end of Finisterre Street?'

'The *smart* end,' Gino chuckled.

Lincoln laughed too. 'Bassanio's was the *only* smart thing about Finisterre Street.'

'That restaurant's long gone,' Woody said. 'So that was yours, Mr—?'

'Gino Paolucci. Yes, but then I bought this place. Many, many years ago. So, why you here, Mr Lincoln? It's gotta be work, not pleasure. Wait, I let you in.' He rummaged through his pockets for the keys.

It was dim inside the Sanremo, and cold. Gino discarded his overcoat as he tottered towards the kitchens, flicking switches until a few lights came on and the central heating began to hum. The air smelt of paprika and rosemary, pizza dough and garlic.

The three of them sat down at one of the tables near the window. The venetian blinds were drawn halfway down, and Lincoln noticed how dusty the slats were. Indeed, as he looked round him he saw that the tablecloths had seen better days and the carpet was worn thin in places.

'You're here about Mr Buckthorn, yes? I loved this man! He dined here many times since he come back to England. With Rufus from the gallery. You know Rufus? I can't believe what has happened.'

'When did you last see Mr Buckthorn?'

'Thursday. Earlier than usual. Six thirty, a little after? We hadn't been open long, so it was still quiet.'

'He was on his own?'

'Yes. Rufus was away, he say, on a job.'

'Did he seem distracted? In a hurry to get away?'

'Not especially. Asked how business was doing, how my wife is, my girls.'

'And when did he leave?'

'I check. It's on the receipt. I got copies in the office.'

They waited while Gino fussed around in the office behind the pizza oven. Lincoln tried to work out how many years had passed since he'd last enjoyed the Italian's hospitality. It was like meeting a schoolfriend in the street, someone you'd always liked but hadn't stayed in touch with. You no longer had much in common, but it gave you a glow of satisfaction to discover you still remembered each other after all these years.

'He paid at seven thirty-three.' Gino emerged, waving a till receipt. 'Steak Sanremo and fries. Double espresso.'

'And wine.'

'No, no wine. Why you say he had wine? Not here he didn't.'

Buckthorn must have drunk wine at the flat, Lincoln thought. He'd certainly had one or two glasses before he died. If he had left the Sanremo soon after seven thirty-five, though, and was driving into Bridgeford market square less than twenty-five minutes later, he couldn't have stopped for a drink anywhere on the way. Yet if he'd drunk wine at the flat, where was the used glass? Where was the bottle?

'That camera outside—' Woody nodded towards the entrance.

'Not working,' Gino lamented. 'Not for long time.'

'You didn't happen to see if Mr Buckthorn met anyone outside when he left?'

Gino shook his head. Then: 'It wasn't heart attack?'

'Probably,' said Lincoln quickly, 'but we're just retracing his steps. Thanks, Gino. If you remember anything else...'

The restaurant owner caught him by the sleeve as he and Woody headed for the door. 'I was sorry to hear about your wife.'

'That's okay, I...' Such a stupid response. Feeble. Lincoln looked away. Gino couldn't know that the marriage had been over long before Cathy died. Presumably she and Andy Nightingale had dined at some other restaurant on their nights out together. 'Yeah, Bassanio's was one of our favourites.'

'And you will come to Sanremo some time, yes? My daughter Olivia, she runs it now, and her boy helps out. They have me here to greet the guests, to make me feel useful.'

'Some heart attack,' said Woody as they went back to the car.

'If that's what people want to believe, let them.'

'Reckon Buckthorn met someone on the way back to the flat.'

'Or they were waiting for him when he got there. We can check his phone records, see who he called—' Lincoln broke off to read the text that had come through on his phone. 'Damn. Youngman hassling me for an update for Media Relations.'

'Can't he leave them to make something up?' Woody chuckled. 'That's what they usually do, isn't it?'

CHAPTER 13

'What time will you be back?' Curtis's mother reached out to fold his collar down, but he ducked away from her.

'I won't be late, don't worry.'

She turned away and padded back into the kitchen. Why didn't she get dressed these days instead of slobbing round in her pyjamas and socks? She'd be nagging him if *he* didn't get dressed all day.

He was out of the door before she could say anything else. The bitter cold hit him full force. He should've put a thicker coat on, a longer jacket. His breath showed up as he passed beneath the street lights. Would it snow tonight? He loved the snow when it was unspoilt and glistening, but as soon as someone walked on it, it was ruined.

Marco was waiting for him on the corner, taking a drag on a cigarette. He flicked the butt into the gutter when he saw Curtis coming. 'You're late,' he said. 'Shift starts at eight.'

'I know, I know. Had things to do.'

Marco clipped him round the head – lightly, affectionately, the way Curtis used to cuff his little brother. 'Come on, man, cheer up!'

'Cheer up? You expect me to *cheer up* after what happened?'

'Stop panicking. No one's gonna know we was even there.'

'There could be cameras.'

'Trust me, there's no cameras.' Marco sounded so sure, Curtis nearly believed him, but how could he know? Someone could have seen them on Thursday night, taken a photo with a phone. 'He was there on his own, okay, jerking off over dirty pictures. They won't be looking for no one else.' He dumped his hand on Curtis's shoulder. 'Okay?'

Curtis shrugged the hand away. 'Okay.'

They got in the car and drove into town, swinging off Commercial Street and into the central car park behind the theatre and the Chinese restaurants, the Iron Man gym and Sofa Space.

The club occupied the first floor of a tall Victorian building. Curtis vaguely remembered it being a wholesale fabric warehouse when he was a kid. The ground floor was now taken up by Lola's Launderette, and the stink of washing powder hung on the stairwell, along with the ominous smell of scorched cloth.

On the first-floor landing, a neon sign shaped like a bright yellow penis pointed the way to the solid front door of Guys, a social club that wasn't exclusively for gays but might as well have been. The music wasn't loud but it had a strong beat, throbbing, insistent. When you put your hand on the wall you could feel the vibration, as if the whole building was pulsating.

Marco worked behind the bar and Curtis washed up, though he was paid to circulate too, like a fucking hostess. *Can I get you another one of those, mate? You want to try this new beer that came in today? Shall I top you up?*

And quite a few times now he'd done a bit of work in the toilets and tried not to feel like a whore with a prick. Tried not to loathe himself and the men who took advantage of him. Or was it the other way round?

Curtis hated the club, and yet he was thrilled by the rush he got from all this dirty stuff going on. Was he gay? He didn't know for sure – only knew girls didn't turn him on, not really. When he was still at school, they'd hang round him because they said he had a certain look. They'd tease him when he told them he wasn't interested, probing for the name of his secret girlfriend.

The only girl he could talk to then was Ruby. She was as uncomfortable in her skin as he was, for different reasons: she was straight, but she was black – in a school that was ninety-eight per cent white. First thing she ever said to him, back in Year 9: 'Hey, man, how come you got a black name when you ain't black?'

She didn't always talk like that – just when the other kids were picking on her, and then she'd put on the street speak, the swagger.

'It's after my grandad,' he'd told her. 'He was Mr Curtis.'

And she'd laughed at the way he'd said it, when what he meant was that his grandfather's *surname* was Curtis, but it had come out wrong, and she never let him forget it, calling him 'Mr Curtis' all the time.

She'd left Barbury during their last term at school but, despite promising to keep in touch, she'd never so much as messaged him. Still, even two, three years later, when he was stuck in a toilet cubicle with some sweaty guy, he'd call Ruby to mind, the way she'd quote philosophy at him to make them both feel better.

'Nothing really exists,' she'd keep reminding him. 'So that's why, Mr Curtis, my best buddy, nothing matters. Ever.'

That's what he told himself when his face was slammed against the toilet wall by a six-foot moron who fancied his arse.

Now he hung back as Marco rang the bell to be let into Guys – members only, everyone welcome, gay or straight.

When the door opened, the scent of weed billowed out, making his head swim, the way the incense did in the days when he used to go to church. Incense and stale cloth, the memory of that cubbyhole behind the altar where Father Anthony kept the candles and the wine. That sweet, spicy smell would coat the back of his throat so it was all he could taste for hours.

'We got a party in,' Lloyd, the club manager, bellowed across at Curtis. 'Bloody kitchen's crammed with washing-up and there's no more room in the dishwasher.'

A party at Guys was any group bigger than four. Curtis sighed and headed for the kitchen, rolling his sleeves up. He hoped there were enough dirty glasses to keep him in the kitchen all fucking night.

CHAPTER 14

'You were only talking to him that day,' Trish said when she phoned later. 'Hugh. You said you went to his house.'

Lincoln needed no reminders of how few hours had elapsed between his departure from Corner Cottage and Buckthorn's departure from this life. He was already uncomfortably aware of his own mortality and didn't need her to remind him, especially when she was a hundred and fifty miles away.

'These things happen. His brother dropped dead out shooting. Always expect the unexpected.' But if he'd thought such platitudes would blunt her curiosity, he was wrong.

'So what happened to Hugh?' she demanded. 'A heart attack? There's a thread on Twitter about it being suicide, that he hanged himself.'

'Don't believe everything you read on Twitter, or anywhere else for that matter. Whenever a celebrity's found dead, the rumour mill goes into overdrive.' He was keen to change the subject. 'You're coming back for half-term?'

'Hope so, though whether I'll have enough time to catch up with everyone...'

He sensed that 'everyone' included himself. He could see why she'd felt unable to stay in Barbury after getting involved with the scandal around Linus Bonetti, but he also suspected she'd been calling his bluff by applying for a job so far away. Had she expected him to beg her to stay, to offer her the commitment he found so hard to make? They'd both had failed marriages, had both been wary of falling in love again. He for one wasn't even sure he *could* fall in love again, even if he wanted to.

Well, if Trish had been calling his bluff, it had backfired. She'd got the Charles Lundy Library job after all. Now here was he, rattling around in his big, unfinished house, and there was she, on the other side of the country, in a flat over the library, her house in Barbury rented out to an alternative therapist, a friend of a former colleague.

'Listen,' he said, trying not to dwell on her plans for half-term and whether or not they'd include him, 'whatever you read about Hugh Buckthorn, take it with a pinch of salt. Did you ever meet him?'

'No, but I met his brother, Howard, a year or so ago, when we were doing a display on the earls of Riverbourne through the centuries. I didn't like him much. He was really encouraging to start with, but as soon as I asked for practical help – you know, a few artefacts, photos, information beyond what's in all the reference books – he backed off, lost interest. We did the display, but it would've been nice if we'd had something a bit exclusive to help us promote it, get more press coverage.'

Lincoln sighed. 'Hugh was planning an exhibition of some of the paintings at the Hall, the ones that have been shut away in the attics for decades.'

She gasped. 'Imagine the value of the paintings that have never been shown!'

'Unless someone finishes the catalogue he started, no one will ever know what's never been shown.'

'Maybe Laurence Buckthorn would rather keep it that way,' she said. 'He must be paying a fortune in insurance already. From what I've read about the family, they're pretty short of money. There was even talk of having to sell Greywood Hall not so long ago. A big exhibition could have saved it.'

Before she rang off, Trish promised to let Lincoln know what she was doing at half-term. 'But it depends on what Kate wants to do,' she cautioned. 'I feel like I owe her as much of my time as I can spare.'

'Of course,' he said, understanding completely but still feeling disappointed. 'Do what you have to. I'll be fine.'

CHAPTER 15

SUNDAY 5TH FEBRUARY

On a typical Sunday morning, Lincoln had a lie-in and a late breakfast before tackling the household chores he'd put off the rest of the week. Loading the washing machine gave him a surprising sense of achievement, although he tended to use the same programme for everything – so far without mishap.

This Sunday, though, he didn't want a lie-in – couldn't afford the time away from his desk when the investigation into Hugh Buckthorn's death was at a crucial stage. There'd been someone else in the flat that night, it was now clear – someone who had apparently staged Buckthorn's murder to look like an act of reckless self-strangulation, death by masturbation.

At his desk in the CID room, coffee steaming in a mug beside a pot of gooey instant porridge, Lincoln pulled together what he knew so far.

Buckthorn had dinner at the Sanremo restaurant the night he died, reached Bridgeford around ten to eight and parked his car in the driveway of the Merediths' house. Then he walked the short distance across Church Street and down Jackdaw Lane to Rufus Rayner's flat knowing, presumably, that Rayner was away in Trowbridge.

After he'd let himself in, he poured himself at least one glass of wine and drank it. Naked but for stockings, suspenders and a dressing gown, he got comfortable on the couch in the living room – where someone put a freezer bag over his head and killed him.

Whoever was there with him had removed all traces of their presence, even the glass and the wine, but they could well have missed something, something too small to catch their attention, something that even the SOCOs had overlooked because it didn't seem relevant or out of place.

The door of the CID room opened and Dilke came in, looking bleary and tousled, as if he'd overslept.

'Rough night, Graham?'

'Sort of.' The young detective dumped a slim can of Red Bull down beside his keyboard. 'Met a mate from school and we went out for a couple of beers.'

'Sounds more like Breezy's kind of night out!'

'You're right, and I'm not used to it. Mum wasn't too pleased when I got home.'

Lincoln grinned to himself. He'd only met Mrs Dilke once or twice, but he'd got the impression of a proud, if anxious, mother, keen for her only son to do well, as long as he didn't put himself in danger.

'I didn't get very far with that dressing gown,' Dilke went on. 'No current stockists. The company went out of business sometime last year, so the stock would've been sold off through car boots or market stalls. I'll try the market here on Tuesday, see if they recognise it as a brand they sell.' He paused. 'A bit elaborate, isn't it?'

'The dressing gown?'

'Bringing one along. And the stockings. Setting up the whole scene. It's not an impulse thing, is it?'

Lincoln leaned back in his chair. 'Assuming Rayner's telling the truth about never having seen the dressing gown before. It could've been left behind by someone else he's had staying there. We can't take anything at face value.'

Rayner had seemed plausible enough but he'd already lied to them, denigrating Carew's but then having to admit he'd once been a regular there.

'But you're right, Graham. His killer came prepared. Whoever they are, they probably parked in the square before going down the lane to the Old Shoddy Mill on foot. Check that CCTV footage again, see if you can spot any cars arriving, say, seven thirty onwards. And look out for anyone walking towards Jackdaw Lane.'

Lincoln's phone pinged: a text from Sonia Fletcher. *Have u heard anything?*

He turned his phone face down on the desk, groaned and ran his hands through his hair. Turned his phone right way up again and texted a reply: *Still waiting.*

But before he pressed *SEND*, he changed his mind and texted instead: *I was about to call you.* A lie, but less of a deceit than the one he was supposed to practise on her, letting her assume there was still doubt about the identity of 'the Greywood bones', as DCS Youngman had so casually dubbed her daughter's remains.

But should he call her? The decision was taken out of his hands by Sonia ringing him herself.

She didn't waste time with niceties. 'Is it Yazmin?'

'The dental records match, yes.' He got up and went over to the filing cabinet, where the kettle sat on a messy tray beside a sugar bowl and two jars of coffee – one with caffeine and one without. His mug sat there too, empty, stained mahogany inside. He picked it up and stared into it uselessly.

'So what happens now?' Sonia wanted to know.

Nothing, he ought to have said. *Nothing, until we've caught Hugh Buckthorn's killer.* But he couldn't say it.

'We'll go through the whole file,' he told her, 'see if there are any leads we can follow up. Your sister was so sure Yazmin went off with Bruno, very few witness statements were taken at the scene. Still, the media coverage in the last couple of days may have triggered some memories. There could be someone out there who didn't say anything at the time but who feels able to come forward now.'

The mountains of paperwork and the hours of inputting didn't bear thinking about, even assuming people *did* come forward with fresh information. How would DCS Youngman react when he learned that Lincoln was carrying on with an investigation he'd expressly been told to defer?

'Will there be a press conference?' Sonia sounded apprehensive. 'The one we had when she went missing was terrible.'

'I'm not sure,' said Lincoln. He really didn't know. 'I'll talk to the Chief Superintendent. We're short-staffed. My boss is off sick. It's not up to me.' Excuses, excuses.

'Can I talk to him, then, your superintendent? Because it sounds as if you're not going to do *anything*.'

'It's not that, Sonia, it's—'

Dilke reached round him for the kettle and, on tiptoe, took it away to fill.

'It's this Greywood Hall thing, isn't it?' she snapped. 'This earl that's been murdered. You'll have to spend all your time on that, won't you?'

'Actually it's not the earl, it's—'

'You know what I mean. His uncle or whatever. People like that get all the attention while the rest of us have to wait in line. Like when Yazmin went missing, you all thought I was some silly little cow who'd got pregnant by a Pole. "Just a domestic" – that's what I heard someone say, one of the coppers who came to see me after it happened. "Just a domestic. She should know better than to shack up with an immigrant."'

Lincoln didn't have the words to make it right. He could apologise, but it was too late for that. The irony was that Bruno Bartek, like his father before him, had lived in England all his life. He'd learned this from the case file. Bruno's grandfather was a Pole who'd served in the

RAF and stayed on after the war, raising a family in Southampton. Bruno's only visits to Poland had been to his grandfather's sister when she was approaching the end of her life, his last visit coinciding with Yazmin's disappearance.

Lincoln guessed that the police officer who'd been so dismissive of Sonia hadn't known any of that, had made a snap judgement based on Bruno's surname and the fact that Yazmin was the subject of a custody dispute.

'Sonia, we don't have the manpower,' he said now. 'Hugh Buckthorn's killer is still out there. People are in danger until we catch whoever did this to him. We have to prioritise.'

'And Yazmin's been dead all this time, so another few months won't hurt? Is that what you've all decided?'

He sighed. 'It's not down to me. And even if it were, I'd make the same choice, hard as it is. I'm sorry.'

'How long before I can give her a decent burial?'

'I'll do all I can to speed things up, I promise. I'll keep you in the loop.'

After she'd rung off, he stood staring at the kettle, his phone in his hand. He wished to God he'd lied to Sonia after all. Had anything he said really helped her? What the hell was Youngman going to say when he found out he'd disobeyed him? Supposing she went to the newspapers now?

He made coffee and stirred plenty of sugar into it.

Dilke called across to him. 'A couple of cars were parked in the square Thursday evening. One of them could be of interest.'

Lincoln hurried across to study the image frozen on the screen. 'Which one?'

'The Mini.' Dilke pressed *PLAY* and the small car parked itself on the edge of Bridgeford market square. The time stamp was *20:04*. Nobody got out, but the driver wound his window down a crack. After a few seconds, he poked his hand through the gap to tap ash from his cigarette. 'He stays there for forty minutes and then he gets out.'

Dilke whizzed the footage forward until the time stamp was *20:45*. The windows of the Mini were fogged up. The driver opened his door and got out, donning a baseball cap as he stood up. He looked as if he was in his early twenties, with an ease to his movements even though he was sturdily built. He shoved his hands deep in the pockets of his jacket as he set off, head bent, breath showing in the frosty air, towards the top of Jackdaw Lane. The shadows swallowed him whole.

Lincoln straightened up. 'Could be our man.'

'There's more.' Dilke took a final swig of his Red Bull before advancing the footage until the time stamp read *21:25*. A much younger man, skinny, not as tall, suddenly dashed out of the shadows and raced up to the Mini. He tugged impatiently at the handle of the passenger door.

Moving less hurriedly, the driver followed him out of the darkness and unlocked the car, puffs of vapour showing in the icy air in front of his face.

'The driver's shouting at the other lad,' Lincoln said. 'Something's up.'

The skinny lad had to wait for the driver to get in and unlock the passenger door, but then he dived inside. Moments later, the Mini bolted out of the parking space and out of shot.

'Could you read the vehicle reg?'

Dilke shook his head. '*R720* – that's all I could make out.'

'That's old, isn't it? 1990s? Narrows it down a bit, at least. Those two definitely look as if they've been up to something. Let's take another look at them.' He waited while Dilke ran the footage again, freezing the screen as the younger man was frantically yanking at the door handle.

'Looks teenage, doesn't he?' said Dilke. 'Sixteen? Seventeen?'

'The driver's not a lot older, is he? Can you zoom in on him when he's getting into the car?'

Dilke did his best to enhance the image, but the driver's face was obscured first by his cap and then, when he'd got behind the wheel, by shadow.

Lincoln was careful not to set too much store by this sighting. Still, the younger man certainly seemed in a hurry to leave Bridgeford around the time that Hugh Buckthorn was breathing his last. A breakthrough – or simply a coincidence?

'No other clues?'

'I'll go through it again, but I didn't see anything else that'd help identify the car.'

With his coffee mug clutched to his chest, Lincoln drifted across to the whiteboard to see what more he could add to the timeline.

'Buckthorn pulls into the square at seven forty-eight. Decides to park in the Merediths' driveway instead. That's a few minutes away. Leaves his car, walks across the street and down Jackdaw Lane. So he probably gets to Rayner's flat just before eight. Just after, this Mini is pulling into the square and sitting there for, what, forty minutes?'

'He gets out about eight forty-five, and then he's back at nine thirty with his mate.' Dilke joined him at the whiteboard. 'Maybe Buckthorn took the younger man back to his flat for sex, but things went pear-shaped and he died. So the lad calls his mate to come and help him clean up.'

'Except the Mini arrives in the square only a few minutes after Buckthorn – too soon for anything to have gone wrong. Is the Mini waiting there to pick the younger one up when he leaves?' Lincoln sipped his coffee, knowing that as soon as he'd finished this mug, he'd make himself another one. 'Is it a set-up?' He broke off as the door opened and Woody arrived.

'Is what a set-up?' he asked.

'Couple of guys driving away from the market square about the time Buckthorn died, Sarge.' Dilke showed Woody the images of the Mini in the square, the two young men hastily driving off around half past nine on Thursday night.

'You know how it works,' Lincoln said. 'A man meets up with a prostitute – male or female – and they're ambushed by someone taking pictures and demanding money. And it turns out the prostitute's in on it.'

'You mean one of them's a rent boy?' Woody looked sceptical.

'It's a theory, that's all. Those two look as if they're up to something, and the timing fits.'

'Except the purpose of a set-up like that is to get the bloke to pay out,' Woody said, 'not to kill him.'

Lincoln sighed. 'You're right.'

Another scenario presented itself: the younger man seducing Buckthorn into taking him back to the flat, where he and the other man beat him up for being gay. Queer-bashing, gay-bashing: nasty slang for a reprehensible crime. Sadly, there was still a lot of prejudice against people whose sexuality didn't fit the so-called norm.

But the dressing gown, the stockings... As Dilke had said, it was elaborate. *Too* elaborate. There was something else going on.

'We need to identify that car,' Lincoln said. 'Any other cameras that might've picked it up going out of Bridgeford?'

'If they drove back into Barbury they'd have passed several traffic cams,' said Dilke. 'I'll get onto the Traffic Management team.'

'There can't be many old Minis knocking around that time of night.' Lincoln turned to Woody. 'I've spoken to Sonia Fletcher, by the way. She phoned. I couldn't lie to her.'

Woody made a face, a soundless 'Uh-oh!'

'My mum remembers about Yazmin,' Dilke said. 'We were talking about it yesterday. Mum knew one of the teachers at her school. She said she was a funny little kid, a bit withdrawn a lot of the time. She got really upset when her mum and dad split up.'

Lincoln thought back to the fractures that Ken found. If the little girl had been the subject of physical abuse, she'd probably been affected psychologically too. But did that have any relevance to her disappearance?

'Not much more we can do, is there?' said Woody. 'Especially now we've got this Buckthorn case to deal with.'

Lincoln sighed. 'Let's hope Sonia doesn't get tired of waiting to find out what we're doing about finding Yazmin's killer.'

'Got no choice, has she?'

'No, but she's vulnerable. That night I went round to talk to her and she wasn't there, she'd gone off in her car, half a mind to drive it into a wall or the river.'

'Family Liaison Officer?' Dilke suggested.

'She wouldn't get one, not unless it's an active investigation. And it's not, is it? It was 1997. What are the chances of finding who killed that little girl now?' Lincoln shrugged, as if he could shrug the case itself off his shoulders. 'Ah well, let's concentrate on finding out who killed the Honourable Hugh Buckthorn.'

No one picked up the phone at Traffic Management, so they got nowhere with tracking the Mini on its journey to and from Bridgeford on Thursday night. As Lincoln was sifting through the printouts and photocopies Pam had brought back from the library, he realised it was a week since the attack that Hugh Buckthorn had witnessed at Press Vale Country Club, the attempted rape from which he'd rescued Amy Cartland.

Lincoln wasn't sure whether he should follow it up. Dale Jacobs had been keen to give it priority, but that was before the death of the only witness. What would DCS Youngman say? That the victim herself was reluctant to come forward and no one could now corroborate her story? No point wasting time on a case that wouldn't make it to court.

When his desk phone rang, he was surprised to hear Jacobs on the line, demanding an update.

'You're out of hospital, sir?'

'What does it sound like? Working from home today, but I'll be at my desk in the morning. I can't sit around on my arse all day or I'll go fucking mental.'

A shadow fell across Lincoln's day. Just as he was getting his teeth into the Buckthorn case... 'Are you sure Occupational Health are okay with that?'

'Bugger OH! I've cleared it with DCS Youngman, and that's all that matters. I've got my foot strapped up, so I'll be a bit limited. You'll need to step up, Lincoln.'

Step up? Bloody hell! 'Of course, sir.'

'See you in the morning. Oh, and I've got to keep this elevated, so find me a stool, can you? Padded, preferably. Cushioned.'

'I'm sure we'll be able to find something.'

Lincoln held onto the receiver for half a minute or more after Jacobs rang off. A padded stool. Cushioned. He couldn't visualise anything in the building that would be suitable.

Woody looked round at him. 'Jacobs?'

'Jacobs. Coming back to work. Needs a padded stool to rest his foot on.'

'I can bring one in from home. My recliner's got a stool I don't use much.'

'Sorted, then,' said Lincoln sourly. 'I just need to make sure I *step up* as required.' His gaze kept returning to the photo of the lad wrenching the door handle of the Mini while his older companion calmly slid behind the wheel, leaned across and let him in. 'Is it worth seeing if anyone at Carew's knows either of these two?'

'Bit of a long shot, isn't it? And you really can't see much of either of them.'

'We've got to start somewhere, Woody.'

'There won't be anyone at Carew's now, will there? Not on a Sunday. How about asking Rayner? If they're friends of Mr Buckthorn's...'

'Your sister said you'd be here.' Lincoln let the door of the Cheese Market Gallery swing shut behind him. The sign said the gallery was closed, but Tilly Rayner had assured him that was where he'd find her brother, even on a Sunday afternoon.

Rufus Rayner glared at him over the top of a tidal wave of bubble wrap in which he was encasing a painting half the size of a ping pong table. Then he slid his glasses down from the top of his head and the glare softened into a look of wistful expectancy.

'Any news?' He propped the half-wrapped painting against the wall.

'Wondering if you recognise either of these two?' Lincoln showed him the photo of the young men about to get into the Mini.

Off came the wire-rimmed glasses as Rayner scrutinised the photo. 'No, not at all.' But something in his voice said otherwise.

'Sure?'

'I'm sorry, I don't recognise either of them. Or the car. I'm hopeless with cars.'

'It's a Mini.'

'You could tell me it was a Lagonda and I'd be none the wiser.' He put his glasses back on, handed the photo back.

'Don't you want to know why I'm asking about them?'

'I was waiting for you to tell me.'

'You know where this is?'

'Of course I do! Bridgeford, the market square. I've parked there often enough.'

'It's the market square on Thursday night, around the time we think Hugh died.'

Rayner swallowed hard. 'These are the men who...who killed him?'

'We need to talk to them in case they saw something – someone arriving at the mill or leaving it that evening. We haven't traced the car yet, but if we were able to put a name to either of those faces...' Lincoln glanced across at him, noting the way he pressed his lips together as if he were trying to stop himself from saying something. 'Mr Rayner?'

'The driver. He looks a bit like one of the staff at the restaurant we go to, the Sanremo.'

'A waiter?'

'Possibly. I can't be sure. I don't want to get anyone into trouble.'

Lincoln took the photo back. 'We'll follow it up.' Someone working at the restaurant could have seen Buckthorn leave that night, could have followed him to Bridgeford. But surely a member of the kitchen staff couldn't just jack his apron in and dash off into the night?

The restaurant probably didn't open on Sundays, but he couldn't afford to wait another twenty-four hours to identify the young driver. He'd have to call on Gino Paolucci at home, ask him if this could be one of his staff.

Rayner shrugged hopelessly. 'Look, I've probably got it wrong. It's a pretty fuzzy picture, isn't it? And it's dark.'

'We found the car, by the way. The Jaguar. Parked in Sixpenny Lane.'

'But that's only round the corner! Why didn't you find it sooner?'

'It was in somebody's driveway.'

'Oh, Lord, the Merediths. He's done that before when they've been away, so he hasn't got to leave it in the square. He's so bloody precious about that car.' He caught himself. 'Or he was. Sixpenny Lane's hardly got any lights. He'd have been walking in the dark.'

Maybe that was precisely why Buckthorn parked in the Merediths' drive instead of the square: if he were with someone, they could walk together to the flat without anyone seeing them.

'You definitely don't know this young man's name?' Lincoln waved the photo at Rayner before slipping it away again.

The gallery owner shook his head. 'I'm sorry.'

'Did Hugh like going with much younger men? This lad here...' Lincoln pulled the photo out again. 'Would Hugh find him attractive?'

Rayner snatched his glasses off, but instead of looking at the photo he covered his eyes with his hand. 'Stop tormenting me like this!'

'Tormenting you? Mr Rayner, Rufus... I'm trying to find out if one or both of these men, getting into this car only a short walk from your flat the night Hugh died, had something to do with his death. With his *murder*.'

Rayner flung his glasses down on top of the bubble wrap and turned his back on Lincoln, hugging himself tightly as if trying to make himself as small as possible. 'Okay,' he said, his voice muffled. 'Yes.'

'Yes what?'

'Yes, Hugh liked younger men.' Slowly, he turned to face Lincoln once more. 'Not *boys*, nothing illegal, nothing dodgy. When we first met, he thought I was a lot younger than I am.' He smiled ruefully. 'How many men my age still get asked to show their ID in shops? A PCSO stopped me the other day when I was coming out of the wine shop, gave me the third degree.'

'Where did Hugh meet them? You say he never went to Carew's, so where else might he go to pick up partners?'

'You make it sound so sordid! He didn't need to go anywhere special. Any bar you go into, if you give off the right signals you'll get a response. Not my scene,' he added hurriedly. 'I went to Carew's, got chatted up a few times but never had the nerve to make the first move. I'm not...' He tried to find the right word. 'I'm not sufficiently *predatory*, I suppose.'

'And Hugh was?'

'He was experienced. Confident. Charming.' Rayner looked away, his weak gaze searching for the glasses he'd tossed aside earlier. 'But why did he bring someone back to the flat?'

'A bit too cold to be out of doors?' Lincoln wasn't being facetious: it was a practical consideration. 'And more convenient than driving all the way out to Speldon Magna.'

'I suppose so.' Rayner located his glasses, put them on again. 'Oh Lord, if you talk to this guy at the Sanremo, he'll know it was me who told you about him.'

'We'll keep your name out of it.' Lincoln surveyed the gallery, the chaos of packing materials, of paintings stacked on a table, waiting to be wrapped. 'I can see why you've had no time to help Hugh with his Greywood catalogue.'

'I should never have offered to help, really, but at least he made a start.'

'I assume everything's on his laptop? The work he'd done so far?'

Rayner shrugged. 'I suppose so. As I said, we didn't get as far as working on it together. I've got so much work here, I kept putting him off.' He laughed ruefully. 'He was probably starting to realise how big a task he'd taken on. Which reminds me...'

'Yes?'

'What's happened to his...to his belongings? Only, I was wondering about his diary. There must be meetings he was supposed to attend, appointments he'd made.'

Lincoln thought back to Corner Cottage and Buckthorn's makeshift office. The only diary had been several years out of date, a pocket one with a few phone numbers scribbled in it. There'd been no current desk diary, no address book, no calendar or planner. They'd assumed everything was on his mobile.

'He had an app on his phone,' Rufus went on, 'but he preferred to write things into a "proper" diary, as he called it. Helped fix it in his memory, he said. An appointments diary, that's all it was, but he'd have been lost without it. It should've been in his jacket.'

Woody had searched Buckthorn's Barbour, a process that had taken a while because he kept discovering yet another pocket he'd missed first time. But there'd been no diary.

'We didn't find it.'

'It had his contacts in, like an address book and diary in one, and you can slip the diary part out at the end of the year and put a new one in. Really quite a clever idea.' He ran out of steam, his expression one of dismay. 'I wanted to write to people, let them know what had happened, but Tilly said...' He gave up. 'Something about etiquette. It wasn't my *place* to contact people. That should be left to the *family*.

And if his diary's gone, I don't have his addresses anyway. Why would they take his diary?'

'What were his plans for the next week or so? Do you know?'

'He was going up to London this weekend, to a couple of galleries, see what was new.'

'Staying overnight somewhere?' Lincoln wondered if Buckthorn had close friends – or lovers – in the capital.

'No need. He could be there by half ten if he caught an early train, back in time for dinner.' Rufus's gaze drifted out of focus. 'He'd have phoned me when he was on the train. Stopped at the flat on his way home. Stayed the night.'

Lincoln sensed it was time to take his leave. 'We'll find who did this,' he promised. 'But if there's anything you're not telling us…'

CHAPTER 16

'Oh, my lovely, I don't know what to say.' Hester Glass showed Sonia into the kitchen of her cottage, where a log fire burned cheerfully. Her dogs – a Jack Russell and some sort of spaniel – lay stretched out on the hearthrug, baking their bellies. 'I'll make you some camomile tea.' She reached out for Sonia's coat but was shrugged off.

'Got anything stronger? Whisky? Brandy?'

Hester frowned at her. 'Alcohol's a depressant. It'll lower your mood even more.'

'My mood can't get any lower. I'm going crazy here.'

'I might have some brandy in the cupboard. Come on, let me take your coat.'

Sonia slid her arms out of her jacket and sat down by the fire while Hester padded off into the pantry. The Jack Russell kept twitching in its sleep every few minutes, but it didn't disturb the snoring spaniel. The heat of the fire and the smell of the dogs were comforting enough to calm Sonia at last.

Hester padded back with two small glasses of ruby-coloured brandy that she placed carefully on the coffee table. She sat down and settled her voluminous skirts around her. 'What have they told you?'

No matter what time of year it was, Hester wore ankle-length cotton petticoats topped with one or two skirts in different materials, depending on the weather. Today her top half was encased in several layers: a Fair Isle waistcoat over a linen shirt, an oversized cardigan to finish it off.

The summer that Sonia first met her, the summer she'd left Southampton and tried to settle in Barbury, Hester had worn sandals on her bare feet all the time, resorting to thick socks and ankle boots only when the clocks went back. Her daughter, Genevieve, Yazmin's age, looked similarly bohemian in clothes Hester made herself. It was Genevieve who'd first brought the two women together by befriending Yazmin in the park one day. Sonia and Hester had got chatting, and had soon become as close as their daughters.

Since Yazmin's disappearance, Hester's cottage had been an occasional sanctuary, even though their friendship had faded over the years.

Today was one of those days when she desperately needed Hester's company.

'They know it's Yazmin.' Sonia sipped her brandy, relishing the way it burned in her chest and set fire to her bloodstream. 'They've checked the dental records.'

'Oh, my lovely, you must feel terrible. But at least now you know.'

Sonia tasted the sickly sweetness of the brandy on her lips. 'Why did I keep going to that horrible chapel? Why did I trust someone to answer my prayers? The Church of Heaven's bloody Promise! Who was I kidding?'

'Having faith got you through those first few months, didn't it? Kept you going by giving you hope?'

'I let myself be conned, going there week after week, holding my hands up in the air and shouting for Yazmin, as if she could've heard me.'

Hester sat back in her chair, her clothes rustling round her as if she were an enormous hen on a fabric nest. That fateful summer she'd had long, henna-ed curls, thick and untamed. She'd looked like a Victorian gypsy, and Sonia had fallen a little in love with her.

Now her hair was a dreary shade of brown, limp and lifeless, damaged by too much time spent outdoors in all weathers, scorning vanity.

'I acted in good faith.' Hester crossed her hands on her bosom. 'I wouldn't have taken you there if I'd thought it was a sham. If it helped you to believe Yazmin was alive—'

Yazmin was alive. Yazmin had been alive, and then she wasn't. Sonia's head filled with the image of the light going out in her little girl's eyes. Of her pulse slowing, stopping…

'When they found her in the woods,' she said, her throat prickly from wanting to cry, 'she was wearing the clothes she was wearing that day. And those sandals, those fucking plastic sandals! She was probably dead before I even got home from the police station.'

Sonia had felt an unbearable sense of loss when Yazmin disappeared, as if a hole had opened up in her heart. Yet, at the same time, a weight had been lifted from her shoulders. Maybe she really was still alive! Someone else was going to look after Yazmin better than she could.

The Church of Heaven's Promise had seemed to fulfil her needs, giving her a place where she could concentrate on her love for Yazmin and try to reach her, where she felt close to her.

How could she have been so deluded?

'You hungry?' Hester asked.

Sonia shook her head. 'I could do with another drink, though.'

'I'll make you some tea. Ginger okay?'

No point arguing. 'Ginger's fine, thank you.' She watched as Hester put the kettle on, fetched the cups, took down the tin of ginger teabags from the shelf. 'I can't even arrange the funeral yet.'

'You want any help, you know where I am.' With a swish of petticoats, Hester was back by her side, her arm round her shoulder. 'I'll always be here for you.'

'How's Genevieve?' Sonia asked when the tea was made.

'Oh, she goes her own way, Genevieve does. Don't see much of her these days, what with the new job she's got in Andover.'

'Genevieve's the age Yaz would be now.'

'I know, my lovely, I know.'

'Don't you miss her?'

'Of course I do, but we've got our own lives to live. It's natural for a child to leave its mother.' She reached out, as if to apologise for her tactlessness, but Sonia snatched her hand away.

Yazmin had wanted Genevieve to go to the funfair with them that awful weekend, but Sonia had said no, lest her sister, Julie, turn her nose up at Yaz's funny little friend with her hippy clothes and her fair hair in beaded cornrows. How different things might have been if Sonia had said yes and taken Genevieve along.

'Does she ever talk about her? About Yazmin?'

'Not for a long time, no. She was only young when it happened. I thought it best to let her—'

'Forget? To let her forget?'

'No, no, I wasn't going to say that. To let her memories fade, was what I meant, so she'll only remember the happy times.'

'Let me know how you got her to do that,' Sonia said bitterly. 'Then tell me how I can do that, too.'

CHAPTER 17

Gino Paolucci didn't recognise the driver of the Mini.

'Why you think I know this boy?' he asked, rather more testily than Lincoln would have expected. 'How is he anything to do with Mr Buckthorn having a heart attack?'

'I can't go into that, but a witness thought they'd seen this young man working at your restaurant. I needed to follow it up as soon as I could.'

Gino shook his head, his expression dour. 'We only got a small staff these days, Mr Lincoln, all permanent, no casuals.' He handed the photo back. 'Your witness got it wrong.' And with an abrupt farewell he shut his front door, leaving Lincoln out in the cold.

Driving home, disappointed that Gino hadn't been able to put a name to the driver of the Mini, Lincoln tried not to resent the imminent return of DCI Jacobs. His new boss would, no doubt, want to do things differently, would challenge every decision and, more depressingly, would insist on stalling the investigation into little Yazmin Fletcher's death.

The Old Rectory was cold. Hadn't the heating come on when it should? Cursing under his breath, he dived into the pantry where the boiler lived. All was quiet. He checked the pressure, saw it was too low, wondered if there was a water leak somewhere.

Without even taking his coat off he trawled the house, inspecting every radiator, every water pipe he could reach. The cat looked up at him, startled, from the middle of his bed, then tucked its head back under one white paw and went back to sleep.

He found the culprit in the box room, water pooling under the radiator and spreading steadily across the bare floorboards.

'Bugger.' He shook his head at it, chastising it for letting him down. He dug out a heap of cloths from the kitchen to mop up the flow, and left it. Nothing he could do about it tonight. He'd call a plumber in the morning.

The phone rang: Trish, wondering how he was, excited about her new assistant starting the next morning.

'I couldn't have asked for anyone better,' she said. 'He knows more about Lundy and his contemporaries than I do.'

'Aren't *you* the expert?'

'I wish! I know enough to get by, but Stewart seems really knowledgeable. You okay?'

He told her about the leaking radiator and, briefly, about Dale Jacobs.

'Is he nice?' she asked.

'He's my new DCI. He doesn't need to be nice.'

'I mean, does he seem like someone you could work with?'

'Too soon to say.'

'And you've been to the library?'

He grinned in spite of himself. 'You're desperate to know what your replacement's like, aren't you? I sent Pam along to do the research for me, but I forgot to ask her to report back. You'll be a hard act to follow, Ms Whittington.' He hurried to change the subject. 'Still coming home for half-term?'

'It's awkward, what with Stewart starting work.'

'Can't you leave him in charge, since he knows so much already?'

'That wouldn't be fair, would it?'

'You couldn't get away for a long weekend?' He knew that even if she could, she'd want to spend the time with her daughter, not him.

'I'll see what I can fix up.' This time it was Trish who was quick to change the subject. 'Did you find out if the skeleton you found was that little girl? Yazmin?'

'Yes, but keep it to yourself. I shouldn't really have told her mother, but I couldn't leave her wondering any longer.'

'Poor woman. God, if anything like that happened to Kate...'

'Don't go there.'

Trish sighed heavily. 'I took this job because I thought Kate would come with me. If I'd known she was going to dig her heels in and stay in Barbury...'

'She seems happy enough, from what Woody tells me.'

'He's not going to tell you if she's miserable, is he?'

'You could give up this Essex job and come home, leave What's-His-Face in charge.'

'I could, yes, but I'm not going to.'

There was an awkward silence. He could have told her how much he missed her, but he didn't. She was already putting enough pressure on herself, without him piling emotional blackmail on top.

'Kate's fine,' he said. 'It'll be easier for you to get away once What's-His-Face can hold the fort for you.'

'His name's Stewart. And yes, I suppose you're right. I'd better go. Sleep tight.'

CHAPTER 18

Monday morning, and DCI Dale Jacobs had returned to Barley Lane.

'The pain keeps me awake at night,' he told Lincoln, 'that's the worst of it.' His left leg rested on a tweed-covered stool Woody had brought from home. A natty-looking brace encased his foot and ankle, protecting the tendons he'd strained when he crashed his car.

Lincoln nodded sympathetically, although he wished more than anything that the DCI had stayed off sick. Better still, that he'd never left Bristol.

'Any idea what made you go off the road?' he asked. 'Did you swerve to miss a badger or something?'

'A badger? Nah, some bastard drove right up my backside, dazzled me. Bloody LED lights. Couldn't see where I was going. Next thing I know, I'm upside down in a hedge between here and Presford.'

'Lucky escape,' Woody commented as he went back to his desk. 'People drive like maniacs on that road.'

Jacobs grunted. 'So...what's been happening in my absence?'

Lincoln briefed him on the progress so far. 'The nearest we've come to suspects is these two lads here.' He tapped the photo of the Mini parked in Bridgeford market square, though he wasn't sure if the DCI could see it clearly from where he was having to sit.

'We still don't know who they are?'

'The Mini could've been picked up by a camera between here and Bridgeford. I'm hoping Traffic Management can help us ID the driver.' Lincoln nodded across towards Dilke. 'Graham's been liaising with them on that.'

Dilke turned at the sound of his name. 'I'll let you know as soon as they get back to me, sir.'

Jacobs winced as he leant forward to rub the back of his damaged ankle. 'You'd never believe how fucking uncomfortable this is.' He sat back. 'But no clue as to motive?'

'Various possibilities,' said Lincoln. 'A sex game gone wrong, or photographing him in compromising positions for blackmail but taking it a step too far—'

'Killing him because he's queer, gay, whatever we're calling it this week?'

Lincoln was taken aback by Jacobs's insensitivity. The DCI was meant to be setting an example, not letting his own prejudices show. 'That's a possibility, yes.'

'So it needn't be an isolated attack.'

'Sir?'

'This could be a campaign against homosexuals, a vendetta. Yes?'

'Well, yes, but Hugh Buckthorn's the only victim we're aware of.'

'So far.'

'So far, yes.' Lincoln couldn't be sure, but he sensed the DCI rather relished the prospect of a juicy case of serial murder.

'Naturally, the kiddie in the rubbish dump goes on the back burner for now – DCS Youngman's orders. The Buckthorn case takes priority. Understood?'

'But, sir, we need to let her mother—'

'It goes on the back burner. Or isn't that a phrase you're familiar with down here?'

Lincoln was conscious of the room going quiet behind him. 'We know the phrase,' he said. 'Just not familiar with the concept of finding the remains of a missing child and not letting her mother know for certain that it's her.'

'She's waited this long. She can wait a bit longer.'

'Have you any idea how much media interest there is in this case? We can't just shunt it onto the back burner!'

'What, and the media won't be interested in an earl who's found dead in women's underwear? It's an ongoing murder investigation,' Jacobs shouted, pointing his finger at the whiteboard, 'and it fucking takes priority!'

'He wasn't an earl,' Breeze muttered.

'What? You say something?'

Breeze rolled his shoulders and spoke up. 'I was clarifying the situation, sir. Mr Buckthorn was the earl's uncle.'

'I don't care if he was his bloody maiden aunt, the case takes priority. Understood? Lincoln? Understood?'

Seething inside, Lincoln nodded. 'Understood.'

'That's settled, then.' Jacobs eased himself back in his chair, evidently in pain. 'I've got to move around at least once an hour. I'll go and take a piss while I've got the chance.'

As he hobbled off, the room seemed to let out a collective sigh.

'Isn't there anything we can do about Yazmin?' Pam asked in little more than a whisper. 'It could be months before we know who killed Hugh Buckthorn.'

Lincoln hoped Buckthorn's murderer would be caught sooner than that, but he was relieved to know he wasn't the only member of his team reluctant to consign Yazmin's case to the metaphorical back burner.

'Get hold of any Social Services reports you can find,' he told her. 'Go as far back as you can – Hampshire and Southampton, not just Wiltshire. Look for anything suspicious, any concerns raised. And then we'll look at the original investigation. But not a word to the DCI or anyone at Park Street.'

She grinned. 'For your eyes only, boss.'

When Dale Jacobs limped back into the room, he made a detour to make himself some tea, inspecting each of the mugs in turn until he found one he deemed acceptable. 'Nothing more on Press Vale, I take it?' He leaned against the filing cabinet to ease the weight on his ankle.

Lincoln headed back to his desk. 'Isn't that on the back burner too?'

'It hasn't occurred to you that there could be a connection, Buckthorn being a key witness?'

'He was the *only* witness. I'd be surprised if he was killed to shut him up.'

'Dead men can't make statements.'

'His statement would have been worthless. He didn't see who attacked the girl.'

'Would've given us a chance to turn that place upside down. There are rumours going around about criminal activity at Press Vale.'

'Rumours? What sort of rumours?'

'You know it's owned by a syndicate?'

'Press Vale Enterprises, yes.'

'I've heard at least two or three members of that syndicate operate on the wrong side of the law. Investigating the attack on the Cartland girl would've given us an excuse to go in there and take a look around. A sprat to catch a mackerel – or is that another expression you're not familiar with down here?'

Lincoln bristled, biting the inside of his cheek in an effort to keep his temper. When at last he could trust himself to speak civilly, he said, 'So what have you heard? What's going on at the country club?'

'We had a tip-off about foreign girls being brought in there as sex workers.'

'You're kidding! We'd have heard something about it before now.'

116

Jacobs pursed his lips. 'If you say so. I'm only going by what I've been told by a reliable source.'

'You're suggesting Buckthorn was killed so we wouldn't follow up Amy's allegations?'

'It's a motive, isn't it?' Jacobs made his tea and began to hobble back with it, slopping it over the floor until Lincoln, despite an urge to punch him, took it from him and set it down on the desk that had been Shauna's. 'If someone there is up to no good,' Jacobs went on, 'the last thing they'd want is for us to go in and start interviewing the staff, searching the rooms, checking the register.' He hoisted his leg up onto the stool once more. 'A name that's come up is Pete Doubleday. You've come across him, haven't you?'

Lincoln certainly had. 'He was involved with stealing high-performance cars and hiding them at his farm. And money laundering.'

'Money laundering?'

'He was putting dirty money through a local charity. Until one of the trustees realised what he was up to.'

'Good for him!'

'Her. The trustee's name was Holly Macleod. She tried to siphon the money off for herself, but didn't live long enough to enjoy it. Still, she put it out of Doubleday's reach, but nobody knows where.'

Jacobs sniggered. 'Nice to know the bad guys don't always win.'

'Doubleday got away, though. Fled to Spain. He was tipped off that we were about to raid his farm, but when we got there Mr Doubleday and the cars were nowhere to be found.'

'Tipped off?'

'By someone at Park Street.' Lincoln was pretty sure he knew who, but he'd never find out for sure, especially since the most likely culprit was dead.

Jacobs, perhaps for the sake of diplomacy, made no comment about the integrity of his colleagues at Park Street nick. 'Would Doubleday get involved in trafficking, d'you think?'

Lincoln shook his head. 'He wouldn't be that stupid. And from what little I do know of him, he'll steer clear of anything involving lengthy chains of go-betweens he can't control. If he risks coming back to the UK he'll be arrested.'

'That's the trouble with these bastards, though, isn't it? They think they're too fucking clever to get caught. So if Doubleday's stuck in Spain, who's minding the shop? Who's running things at Press Vale?'

'Not sure if any of the consortium members get involved with the day-to-day running of the country club. And there's been no trouble there since Doubleday moved abroad.'

Jacobs looked unconvinced. 'Need to dig a bit deeper into Press Vale Enterprises, find out what's *really* going on there. And before you say anything, I'm not expecting you to do that. I'll get someone at Park Street onto it.' He gulped his tea thirstily. 'As for Buckthorn's murder, we need to put names to the two lads in the Mini – especially since they're the *only* suspects you've turned up so far. How many days have you been working this case, Lincoln?' Wincing quietly, he cranked himself round so he could reach the keyboard. 'That question was rhetorical, by the way.'

Once more, Lincoln chewed the inside of his cheek rather than say something he might regret. Luckily he was distracted by Dilke bringing some welcome news.

'The Mini was picked up by traffic cams as it was going back into Barbury Thursday night, boss. Got the full index number. Registered to a Jonathan Mortimer.' He reeled off Mortimer's date of birth and address: Heath Close, on the Barbury Down Estate.

Lincoln was puzzled. 'But he must be nearly seventy! The driver was in his twenties.'

'Could be his son who was driving it?' Dilke suggested. 'Or his grandson?'

When he and Dilke arrived at Heath Close, Lincoln quickly concluded that Jonathan Mortimer wasn't at home, hadn't been home for a while. The pocket-sized front garden of his bungalow was overgrown, with empty beer cans littering the ragged lawn.

'He's in hospital,' his neighbour said, leaning over the party fence. 'Had a stroke a little while back. They need to keep him in till he can manage on his own again. Is this about the car?'

'How do you mean?' Lincoln asked. 'Has something happened to it?'

'It's been parked down the road ever since he went into hospital, but one night last week there was someone going along the close trying car doors. Next morning I saw Jon's car wasn't there any more.'

'Which night? Can you remember?'

'Wednesday. I wasn't long back from bingo. I looked out and saw him.'

She couldn't describe the would-be car thief, except he was wearing a baseball cap.

Lincoln showed her the photo of the two men getting into Mortimer's Mini in Bridgeford market square. 'Recognise either of these lads?'

'Not a very clear picture, is it, and my eyes aren't too good these days. Actually, the one driving... There's a lad comes round here gardening, odd jobs, anything needs doing. That could be him.'

'Who does he work for?'

'I've never seen him with anyone. Nice enough lad, but a bit fly-by-night, if you know what I mean, only ever wants paying in cash. Which suits me, but I bet he's not declaring it. And you're never sure, with these lads, whether they're secretly scouting you out for burglary.'

'What's his name?' asked Dilke.

The woman frowned, trying to remember. 'Mark. Marcus. No, Marco. Sounds Italian, doesn't it, but he isn't. Least, he doesn't sound it, although he does look quite Italian, now I think about it.' She smiled to herself. 'Don't know his surname, though.'

'Could be our driver,' Dilke said as they headed back to the car. 'And if he's been doing odd jobs round these bungalows, he'd know Mr Mortimer's not there to notice his car's gone.'

'Then where is it now? When did Traffic Management last pick it up?'

'On the roundabout near the Duke of York, eleven o'clock Thursday night.'

'And no sign of it since?'

'No. It probably turned off into a side road where there aren't any cameras.'

'Let's get uniforms looking out for it, then.'

Back at Barley Lane, Lincoln was relieved to see that Dale Jacobs wasn't at his desk.

'Where's the DCI?'

'He said to tell you he had to go over to Park Street,' said Breeze. 'Called a cab and hobbled away.'

'Reckon DCS Youngman wanted to see him,' Woody said. 'He took a call and left soon after. Any joy at Heath Close?'

'Might have a name for the driver. We spoke to a woman who thought she recognised him. Marco. Looks Italian, she said, and he does odd jobs around the close where the Mini was nicked.'

'Marco Ross?' Breeze looked up, his hand deep in a family-size packet of crisps.

'You know him, Dennis?'

'I know *of* him, yes. Lady friend of mine used to do his mum's hair. She's Italian.'

'Your lady friend's Italian?'

Breeze snorted. 'No, boss, Marco's mum. She's married to Frankie Ross, or was.'

The hairs on the back of Lincoln's neck stood up. That was a blast from the past! 'Frankie Ross? The Fruit Machine King?'

'Cuh, I know he made a fortune with his gaming machines back in the day, but he probably wouldn't want to be called that now.'

Frankie Ross had cornered the market locally and then farther afield, installing gaming machines in pubs and clubs. He'd gone on to offer leasing deals for music centres and security systems, TV screens and behind-the-scenes technology. While he was on his way to making his first million, Lincoln recalled, he'd married Gabriella Paolucci, Gino's younger daughter, the headstrong one. So Marco Ross must be Gabriella's son. Well, well...

'What else can you tell us about Marco, Dennis?'

Breeze shoved another handful of crisps into his mouth. 'Early twenties? He was in trouble a year or so ago, some sort of set-to with his stepdad. You want me to look him up?'

'Don't interrupt your lunch.'

'No, that's okay.' Oblivious to Lincoln's sarcasm, Breeze leaned the bag of crisps against his desk phone. 'I'll let you know if I find anything.' And, hunched over his keyboard, he attacked it as if it were a typewriter.

Lincoln turned to Woody. 'Rufus Rayner asked me about Buckthorn's diary, but we didn't find one, did we?'

Woody shook his head. 'Only that old one at the cottage.'

'This was one he always had on him, according to Rayner.'

'Nothing's turned up, not in the flat or in his car.'

'If his killer is someone Buckthorn knew, they'd want to make sure there was nothing in his diary about meeting them.'

'Wouldn't that have been in his phone?'

'Possibly, but Rayner said Buckthorn liked to write things in a "proper" diary. And if they looked for his phone, they didn't find it. *I* found it, remember, under the spare bed.'

'Gives you a bit of power, doesn't it?' Woody supposed. 'Knowing someone's plans, who their friends are.'

'Eavesdropping on someone's life.' Lincoln shuddered at the thought of Buckthorn's killer exploiting his friends, gloating over the appointments he wasn't going to keep, the planned trips on which he'd never embark.

His desk phone rang.

'Preliminary toxicology report on Hugh Buckthorn,' Ken Burges said brightly. 'Flunitrazepam in his system. Rohypnol.'

The so-called 'date rape' drug. 'Slipped into his wine?'

'Most likely, although you can't rule out the possibility that he took it knowingly, as a relaxant – though that'd be an odd thing to do if he planned to have sex.'

'How quickly would it have taken effect?'

'Within fifteen minutes, half an hour at the most.'

Dilke had been right when he observed that the body had looked almost *too* relaxed, Lincoln thought. Buckthorn had taken, or been given, a strong sedative with his wine. He'd then been stripped and dressed up while he was too woozy to resist. Laid out on the sofa, insensible, he'd been unable to defend himself when someone put a freezer bag over his head and held it tight.

And all traces of the drug, the wine, his glass, had been cleared away.

'Thanks, Ken. That puts a different perspective on it. Anything else? Cocaine, possibly?'

'Didn't find any trace in his urine. Nothing else of interest so far. I'll let you know if anything new turns up.'

Lincoln put the phone down and crossed to the whiteboard. He circled the photo of the two young men, the passenger clearly agitated, hurrying to the Mini. What had happened in the hour or so before the camera captured that image?

The young man who might be Marco Ross had parked the stolen Mini in the market square around the time Buckthorn arrived at Rayner's flat. He'd waited forty minutes before getting out and heading into the shadows at the top of Jackdaw Lane. Had he been giving the younger lad time to seduce Buckthorn and slip him some Rohypnol? Had he been waiting for a call or text telling him it was time to set the scene?

'You were right about Buckthorn, Graham,' Lincoln called across to Dilke. 'He'd been drugged, or drugged himself. Rohypnol.'

'Roofies?'

Breeze let out a low whistle. 'He's not gonna get a stiffy if he's taken roofies, is he? What's that all about?' He hammered away on his keyboard for a minute longer before relating what he'd found out about Marco Ross. 'He's twenty-two. Beat up his mum's boyfriend, January last year. Got probation on account of how he was only trying to protect his poor old mum.'

Not so old, Lincoln thought. Gabriella was a year or so younger than he was, and when he'd first seen her working at Bassanio's, her father's previous restaurant, she'd seemed more than capable of defending herself. But that was years ago now, when he and Cathy were still together, and when fantasising about the attractive waitress at their favourite Italian restaurant seemed harmless fun. Even then, though, she'd have been married to Frankie, must already have been the mother of a teenage son.

A son who could now be a murder suspect.

'Got an address for him, Dennis?'

'Barbury Park Avenue.'

'A bit more upmarket than I was expecting.'

'So, the Fruit Machine King bought himself a palace! Mind you, Marco wasn't living there at the time of the assault,' Breeze pointed out. 'He was at a house in Avalon Row. That's one of those terraces on the main road to Bridgeford.'

'Not quite as salubrious as Barbury Park Avenue. We need to find that Mini. It's the only way we can put those two lads in Bridgeford that night. The CCTV images of them aren't good enough, but we know that's the car.'

'We've got uniforms and PCSOs out looking for it,' said Dilke. 'It can't have disappeared entirely.'

'It might as well have.' Lincoln ran his hands through his hair, impatient to get on with the case while the DCI wasn't breathing down his neck. 'Did Buckthorn have the younger lad in his car with him when he arrived in Bridgeford? Where did he pick him up? We need those phone records.'

'They've just come in,' Dilke said. 'I'll start going through them.'

They concentrated on the calls Buckthorn made in the week leading up to his death. He'd phoned Rufus Rayner's mobile at least once a day. A couple of times he phoned the Cheese Market Gallery, perhaps when Rayner wasn't answering his mobile. He called Barbury Wines and the Sanremo Restaurant, Barbury Delicatessen and Press Vale Country Club. He had a five-minute conversation with his nephew Laurence, and he also rang the main office at Greywood Hall. The night of his death, about five past six, he rang Rufus Rayner's home number.

'Why would he phone Rayner's house?' Lincoln threw the question out to his team.

'Maybe he'd forgotten he was going to be away that night,' Woody suggested. 'There's no landline at the flat yet, is there? If Rayner wasn't answering his mobile, Buckthorn maybe rang the house in case there was something wrong.'

'The Rayners didn't say he'd called, did they?'

Woody shook his head. 'Maybe he changed his mind and hung up.'

'According to this, the call lasted nearly two minutes.'

'Maybe he left a message. They could've deleted it without even listening to it. Didn't Tilly say her parents disapproved of Buckthorn? Blamed him for leading Rufus astray?'

'We'd better speak to Tilly, then. She might know.'

'And then there's this mobile number,' Dilke said, 'unregistered, pay as you go. He rang it twice: late on Saturday night, and again at twenty past six on the evening he died.'

'Let's try calling it.' Lincoln dialled the number, but it rang and rang, unanswered, no voicemail, until it eventually cut out. 'Does that number ever ring Buckthorn?'

Dilke shook his head. 'Never. But then, he didn't get many incoming calls. Probably been careful about giving his number out.'

'I expect all those years of being hounded by the press taught him to guard his privacy. What about his landline?'

'Still waiting for the records from BT.'

Lincoln had an idea. 'We haven't shown this photo to the staff at Carew's, have we?' He looked across at Breeze, who shook his head in protest.

'Can't you send someone else, boss? I got a real hostile vibe off that lot when I showed them Buckthorn's photo on Saturday.'

Dilke was laughing. 'They probably picked up the hostile vibes *you* were giving off!'

Lincoln raised his hands. 'Please, just somebody, *anybody*, go to Carew's and show them the bloody photograph!'

The room went quiet. Then: 'The landline records have come in,' Dilke said meekly. 'Shall I go through them, boss?'

'Yes, yes, please.' Lincoln didn't bother to look up when Breeze grudgingly threw his biker jacket on and stomped off to Carew's.

When the report on Buckthorn's car came through an hour or so later, it added disappointingly little to the investigation. There were a few particles of gravel in the passenger footwell, but nothing more distinctive than the sort of debris the ribbed sole of any shoe or trainer would pick up from any road surface. No fibres, buttons, strands of hair, discarded chewing gum. No clear fingerprints, no bodily fluids.

A briefcase in the boot contained a notebook and pens and a couple of books. Lincoln arranged to have the bag sent over, though he wasn't sure how useful it would be.

Breeze barged into the room, lumbering towards the kettle and his box of Yorkshire teabags as soon as he'd slung his biker jacket over the back of his chair. 'Cuh, and there was me assuming Carew's was the only gay club in town. Heard of Guys? And I'm not talking about the hospital.'

'Guys? Where's that?' The sound of the kettle getting up steam made Lincoln thirsty for coffee, and he strode across to join Breeze at the filing cabinet.

'Over the launderette in Commercial Street.'

'The launderette near the car park?' Lincoln remembered it well from his bedsit days: damp machines encrusted with Daz, and dryers full of lint from other people's underwear.

Breeze nodded. 'Been there a year or so, apparently, according to my new friend, Ferdy.'

'Ferdy?'

'Bloke behind the bar at Carew's. Told me Guys is a private club, members only. More *intimate* than Carew's, from the sound of it.'

'You didn't pop round there to sample it yourself then?' Dilke was grinning broadly.

'It's evenings only, smart arse.'

Lincoln held his hands up. 'Hang on, hang on! What's this private club got to do with our lads in the Mini?'

'Marco Ross. Ferdy recognised him from that photo. Marco worked at Carew's back last summer, then handed his notice in because he'd got a job at Guys.'

'Marco's gay?'

'I didn't ask, but I wouldn't be surprised. Most men go to the pub to watch football, don't they, have a few beers, slag the wife off? Not gonna get that at a gay bar, are you?'

Lincoln sat back from his desk. 'What, you mean gay men don't watch football?'

'I mean, if you *aren't* gay, it'd probably drive you up the wall listening to a load of blokes going on about Judy Garland.'

Lincoln sighed. Had Breeze learned *nothing* from the diversity training courses he'd been on? Or was he trying to be provocative, winding Lincoln up when he knew perfectly well how outdated and outrageous his comments were? One of these days, his stupid remarks were going to get him into trouble. 'Come on, Dennis, get your jacket on. Time we called on Marco Ross at home.'

But Avalon Row was another disappointment: Marco had been thrown out of his flat there because of complaints about noise and late-night drinking. The landlord didn't know where he'd gone, and didn't care.

'Let's take a look at Guys,' Lincoln suggested as they drove away, 'at least check to see if he's still working there.'

'Do we both need to go in?' Breeze asked hopefully. 'We don't want to go in mob-handed, do we?'

'You volunteering? I can wait in the car.' Lincoln tried hard to suppress a grin.

'No, no, that's okay, boss. We'll go in together.'

CHAPTER 19

As Curtis was taking glasses out of the dishwasher, Lloyd dived through the swing door from the bar, face like thunder.

'Fucking police,' he hissed, flinging a damp cloth onto the kitchen worktop. 'That's all I need!'

Curtis had heard the downstairs buzzer but hadn't thought twice about it, hadn't even bothered to listen to what was mumbled over the entry phone. The club didn't open for another half hour, but there was always some twat who'd turn up early and expect to be let in if they leaned on the buzzer long enough.

'The police? What do they want?'

'If I knew that, sunshine, I'd be working as a fortune teller instead of running this place. I'd certainly be earning more money! Move your butt! I've gotta get past.'

Curtis shoved the drawer shut and straightened up so Lloyd could squeeze past him to reach the key safe. 'What, like in uniform?'

'Turn you on, would it, policemen in uniform? No, a detective inspector, so *not* in fucking uniform.' He flew down the stairs to unlock the front door.

Thoughts spinning, Curtis eased the drawer out again and mechanically removed the rest of the glasses, setting them carefully on the worktop as he strained to hear what was going on. Two pairs of feet trudging up the stairs behind Lloyd, who always went up and down them soundlessly, like a cat. A rumble of conversation, Marco this, Marco that...

Oh, fuck! If they were looking for Marco, they'd be looking for *him* too! Lloyd was leading them over to the bar, away from the kitchen, out of earshot.

Curtis glanced across to the key safe. Still open. The key that caught his attention was the one on the hook labelled *FIRE*. He snatched it off the hook and slipped back out onto the landing. The fire exit was up a couple of steps on the way to the gents', but he had no idea where it led.

Once he'd unlocked the heavy metal door, he took the key out again and barged his way outside. He found himself on a rusty metal landing perched a few feet above the roof of the ground-floor extension.

Detergent smells steamed out of vents beneath his feet as he paused long enough to shut the fire door and lock it behind him.

The handrail was icy-cold under his hand as he leapt down the rungs of the fire escape. He landed awkwardly on the concrete behind the rubbish skips, then scrambled to his feet. He limped towards the car park, where he could quickly lose himself in the shadows.

Why were the police looking for Marco? How soon before they came looking for *him*?

Lincoln flopped down at the kitchen table without even taking his coat off. Which was just as well, because the house felt as cold as it was outdoors. He'd forgotten to call the plumber. No heating, no hot water – and just when he could have done with a long shower or a soak in the bath. He heaved himself to his feet and made himself some coffee, rooting in the cupboard for something that would be quick to cook.

He'd spent the day chasing leads that went nowhere: Buckthorn's bank accounts, the forensic tests on the Jaguar, Marco Ross's Avalon Row address, and Guys, the club where he was said to be working.

The manager of Guys, Lloyd Beach, had been unsure about the identity of the young man photographed getting behind the wheel of the Mini in Bridgeford market square.

'Could be Marco,' he'd allowed, 'but it's a crap photo, isn't it? They all wear those caps, don't they? Wish they wouldn't. Makes their hair smell.' He'd looked up at Lincoln as he handed the photo back. 'Bad for the follicles. Hair needs air.' He'd swept his hand over his own shaven scalp.

'You don't recognise the other lad?'

'Could be anybody.'

'How about *him*?' Breeze had asked, proffering a photo of Buckthorn. 'This man ever been to your club?'

Beach had taken the photo and stared hard at it as if weighing up how best to answer. 'Been in the news, hasn't he?' he'd said at last. 'That toff they found dead.'

'"That toff",' Lincoln had told him coldly, 'is Hugh Buckthorn, and he was found dead on Friday morning. Did he ever come in here?'

'Members only.' Beach had jabbed a chapped thumb at the sign over the bar – little more than a serving hatch, really – and given Lincoln a sour smile.

'Is that a yes or a no?' Breeze's biker jacket had creaked as he folded his arms. 'We could go through your membership records, see for ourselves.'

'Not unless you've got a warrant. Data protection and all that.'

Breeze had sniffed, then nudged Lincoln's arm. 'You smell that, boss? Smell like weed to you?'

All Lincoln could smell was a faint whiff of cigarette smoke and the tang of washing powder, but he'd guessed what Breeze was up to. 'Could be, Dennis, could be.'

Lloyd Beach's resistance had quickly given way. 'Okay, he came in here a few times, but not often.'

'How recently?'

'The Saturday before last.'

The Saturday before he died.

'Did he arrive with anyone?' Lincoln had asked. 'Did he leave with anyone?'

'I don't watch all that goes on. All I ask is that the punters pay for their drinks and don't smash up the furniture.'

'Come on.' Breeze had bulked himself up as if he'd turn nasty if Beach didn't tell him what he needed to know. 'We're talking about an aristocrat, local royalty. You saying you never looked across to see who he was getting off with?'

'He came here to chat and have a drink. I never saw him leave with anyone, although it doesn't mean he didn't meet someone afterwards. But that's none of my business. If it doesn't happen on my premises, I'm not interested in what these guys get up to.'

Lincoln and Breeze still hadn't spoken to Marco, though: Monday was his night off. Beach had grudgingly scribbled an address and phone number on a Post-it note, but it was only when they'd got back to the car that Lincoln recognised the address as the flat in Avalon Row from which the young man had been evicted.

'Got his number now, though,' Breeze had said. 'That's something.'

But would Beach warn Marco that the police wanted to talk to him?

Now, sitting at home in his overcoat, a cup of packet soup congealing in front of him, Lincoln wondered why Buckthorn had frequented a place like Guys, a club with little atmosphere, its furniture and fittings looking second-hand – and not in a cool way. He suspected it was nothing more than a tarted-up pickup joint, not even pretending to celebrate the gay lifestyle in the way that Carew's did. Seedy – that was the word. Sordid.

But then, why did some men climb uncarpeted stairs to lie in filthy beds with female prostitutes? Did they punish themselves out of guilt? Was it part of the excitement, their sexual urges so strong, their manhood so potent, that they could ignore their surroundings while they screwed some empty-eyed woman old enough to be their mother? He'd never been that desperate, that driven, although he might have come close once upon a time, just for the chance of some comfort for an hour or so.

He gave up on the soup and poured it down the sink. He was kidding himself when he insisted he'd rather live on his own. What was it Sonia Fletcher had said to him? *'You're a man who needs someone, aren't you? Even if you can't admit it.'*

She was right, but why did he push people away? If he were honest, he'd even pushed Cathy away once they were married. No wonder she'd sought comfort of her own with Andy Nightingale. Was he pushing Trish away now?

The cat came slinking into the kitchen in search of food, rubbing round his legs until he doled out a few clumps of Whiskas for it.

Cupboard love, that was all it was. While the cat guzzled happily, Lincoln rang Trish, suddenly desperate for the sound of her voice.

'How's What's-His-Face doing?' he wanted to know. 'Reorganised the library yet?'

'Don't be silly. He only started this morning. It'll take him at least until the end of the week.'

He loved to hear the warmth in her smile, to imagine her taking the phone over to a cosy corner of her living room and curling up in the chair to talk to him. She'd sent him a few photos of the flat when she first moved in, but it had looked a bit unloved, her own stamp not yet imprinted on its bland decor. By now, he was sure, she'd have made it her own, brought her own unique style to it.

If *she* couldn't get away to visit Barbury, maybe *he* could take a weekend off to visit her. But not yet. Not with so much going on.

'There was lots about Hugh in the papers yesterday,' she said. 'They're all speculating about what killed him.'

'They can speculate until they're blue in the face. There'll be a press release at some point, but until then—'

'It's not straightforward, then?'

'Trish, I can't say anything about it yet, okay?'

'Have the family been sworn to secrecy too?'

'What?'

'No one at Greywood Hall was available for comment. Unquote.'

'The earl doesn't live at the Hall.'

'Don't wriggle out of answering. Why's it all so hush-hush?'

He hated having to keep her in the dark, but he had no choice. 'Let's just say it was suspicious and leave it at that.'

'You drive me up the wall sometimes!' Her voice was soft with amusement. 'Be thankful I'm too far away to throw something at you.'

CHAPTER 20

TUESDAY 7TH FEBRUARY

Lincoln was towelling himself dry after an inevitably cold shower when he heard his mobile ringing. He hurried to answer it before his caller rang off. At this time in the morning it must be urgent.

'What's the latest?' DCI Dale Jacobs made no apology for this six fifteen call.

'The latest? We might have a name for the driver of the Mini. Marco Ross. Father's a businessman called Frankie Ross—'

'Frankie Ross?'

'You've heard of him?' When would the Fruit Machine King have come to the attention of a detective from Avon and Somerset? Maybe Jacobs was familiar with a different Frankie Ross. It wasn't an uncommon name.

'I had a run-in with a guy called Ross when I was at Bristol. He was flogging security systems to pubs and clubs.'

'Sounds like the same Frankie Ross. How come you had a run-in with him?'

'I didn't like his sales technique. "Aggressive" doesn't come close. He was expecting to pick up some lucrative contracts, only I—' He broke off. 'Let's just say I put the word round, and leave it at that.'

Lincoln reached out for his bath robe and struggled into it without letting go of his phone. One-handed, he tried to tie the belt, but had to give up.

'Marco's been working in a gay club called Guys,' he told Jacobs. 'Buckthorn went there a few times, but the manager wouldn't be drawn on whether he picked anyone up. I doubt it's the sort of bar you go to for the ambient music and craft beers.'

Jacobs snorted. 'And this Marco Ross was involved in the killing?'

'All we know is that Marco and his mate were rushing back to their car in the market square around the time Buckthorn died. The younger lad looked agitated, couldn't get back in the car fast enough.'

'Sounds like he's implicated, doesn't it? Listen, I'm going into Park Street today, and I'll be working from there for the foreseeable. Can't manage the stairs at Barley Lane till this foot's a bit easier, and of course Park Street's got lifts. But that doesn't let you off keeping me informed of any developments.'

'Of course, I would always—'

'Don't make me look stupid by keeping me in the dark, okay? DCS Youngman warned me that you like to do your own thing, but you don't do that with me, okay? Is that understood? Lincoln?'

'Understood. Sir.' Lincoln slung his mobile onto the bed as soon as Jacobs rang off. So Youngman thought he 'liked to do his own thing', did he? Didn't quarrel with the results, though, did he? 'Doing his own thing' evidently paid off – most of the time.

Too wound up for breakfast, he dressed quickly, gulping down some coffee before leaving the house.

'So I brought that stool in for nothing?' Woody regarded the footstool that stood abandoned by Shauna's desk. 'How can the DCI run the investigation from Park Street?'

'He phoned me this morning, early. I'd only just got out of the shower. We mustn't keep him in the dark or he'll look stupid.'

Woody smoothed his moustache. 'Reckon he's not meant to be out in the field at his grade, but shouldn't he be a bit more hands-on than that?'

Breeze chuckled as he lifted a big mug of tea to his lips. 'Maybe that's how they do things in Avon and Somerset. Remote control.'

Lincoln went over to the whiteboard, pleased that he could add something more to it after yesterday's visit to Guys.

'The manager of the club confirmed the driver of the Mini is Marco Ross.'

'He didn't say as much,' Breeze put in, 'but you could tell from his face.'

'He couldn't put a name to the other lad,' Lincoln said, 'or wouldn't, but he did tell us Hugh Buckthorn dropped in there a few times.'

Woody's eyebrows went up. 'I've never even heard of the place.'

Lincoln began to add a few more points to the timeline. 'Significantly, Buckthorn was there the Saturday before he died – the same night he called that unidentified mobile number at nearly midnight. Thursday night, he called the same number around six twenty. Suppose it was Marco Ross he was calling, after he met him at the club? Or Marco's young buddy? The first call is maybe to arrange a date later in the week. The second call's to confirm when and where.'

'He couldn't have been meeting Marco,' Woody pointed out. 'Marco didn't get out of the Mini until quarter to nine.'

'You're right.' Lincoln prodded the CCTV image of Jonathan

132

Mortimer's car. 'So let's suppose these two – Marco and this lad – were working together to set Buckthorn up.'

Breeze tipped his chair back as he studied the whiteboard. 'You're saying Marco's a killer?'

Lincoln didn't like to believe that Gabriella Ross's son was a murderer, but he certainly seemed to be involved.

'Reckon everyone's got it in them to kill, with sufficient provocation,' said Woody.

'Have we got a mugshot of Marco?'

'Yeah, from when he was arrested last January.' Breeze hunched over his keyboard, and within seconds a face appeared on his screen.

No one could deny Marco Ross was a good-looking young man, his Italian heritage apparent in his dark eyes and glossy black hair. His mouth was full and sensuous, his olive complexion marred only by a gash on his cheek, sustained during the fight that had landed him in custody last January. When the mugshot was taken, that gash would still have been smarting.

'Gino Paolucci's grandson,' Lincoln said. 'Gabriella's son.'

Woody gasped. 'From the Sanremo? She's the one who's running it?'

'No, that's Olivia, Gino's older daughter. Gabriella's a few years younger. Rufus Rayner thought he recognised Marco from the restaurant, but I suspect it was Marco's *cousin* he's seen there, Olivia's son. The boys are about the same age, and they probably look a bit alike.'

It would also explain why Gino had been so offhand when Lincoln showed him the photograph of the two lads and the Mini: he'd recognised Marco but hadn't wanted to land his grandson in trouble.

Breeze sniffed. 'Does that help us find him, though?'

'We know where Gabriella lives,' Lincoln said. 'Even if Marco's left home, she might be able to tell us where to find him.'

Gabriella Ross's house in Barbury Park Avenue was much larger than her father's, in a modern Georgian style with a portico out of all proportion to the rest of the frontage.

Ushering Lincoln and Woody in from the sleety rain, she pointed imperiously at a mat inside the front door, where she expected them to leave their wet shoes. 'If you wouldn't mind,' she added, in case they did.

Despite its grand exterior, the house felt empty and unfinished inside, with ghostly shapes on the hall walls where paintings must once have hung. Had Frankie Ross taken his share of furniture and fittings with him when he left the marital home? Maybe Gabriella hadn't got round to rearranging what was left or replacing what she'd lost. Was her boyfriend still on the scene, the man Marco had punched and kicked to protect his mother – or so he'd claimed?

She showed them into the living room, where yet more pale rectangles decorated the walls in place of paintings.

She must have noticed the way Lincoln's gaze was drawn to these absent works of art.

'Quite the collector, my ex-husband,' she said, her voice as husky as he remembered. 'To look at him, you'd never imagine he knew the first thing about art or books, but he was a cultured bastard. The only time he took me back to Italy, he insisted we went to Florence so he could see the Uffizi Gallery.' She laughed bitterly at the memory. 'How did you find me? Don't tell me you asked my dad. I doubt if he'd remember my address.'

'This is the address on the incident report,' Lincoln said, 'from when your son and your partner had their altercation. We took a chance on you still being here.'

She sniffed and flopped down on the linen-covered sofa, folding her arms and crossing her legs.

'Don't think I haven't thought about moving out! Frankie didn't waste any time buggering off to Spain as soon as he could, and who could blame him? I'd move to Italy given half a chance. Not bloody Florence, though. I'd buy a little flat in the village where Dad came from. I hate English winters. I could have two fires going in this lounge and it wouldn't be warm enough for me.'

The room was certainly warm enough for Lincoln, and he shrugged his coat off before he sat down across from her. Maybe if she dressed more for comfort than for glamour she wouldn't feel the cold so much. Her soft jersey dress looked too flimsy to keep anyone warm on a day like today. He remembered her, years ago, swooping in and out of the kitchen at Bassanio's, her shiny dark hair piled up into an unruly bun. She'd put on weight since those days, but it suited her. Her hair, though dabbed with grey now, was still long, thick and glossy.

'You live here on your own?' asked Woody, notebook at the ready.

'What business is it of yours?' She flexed her foot, the sleek leather shoe slipping from her heel, dangling as if it were about to drop. 'Trevor's abroad at the minute, if you must know. He should've been back yesterday, but his flight was delayed. Ice on the wings. They'll use any excuse these days. If you've come to ask me about my ex-husband—'

'It's Marco we need to talk to.'

'Marco? He hasn't lived with me since he turned twenty. First, he didn't want anything to do with his father because Frankie's latest girlfriend – sorry,' she corrected herself sarcastically, 'Frankie's *fiancée* isn't much older than Marco. Some glamorous little tart from Bristol. And then Marco decides he wants nothing to do with me either. Nice reward for bringing him up virtually single-handed the last few years!'

'Okay, so he's not here, but where can we find him?'

'No idea. He thought he had the right to tell me who I should go round with. I didn't put up with that from his father and I bloody well wasn't going to put up with it from him!'

'Was that why Marco got into a fight with Trevor?' asked Lincoln. 'Because he didn't think Trevor was good enough for you?'

Her brown eyes narrowed in disgust. 'Are you naturally patronising or did they send you on a course?'

Lincoln ignored her question. 'According to his statement, Marco attacked Trevor to protect you. You told the officers who attended that Trevor had become abusive and Marco was defending you from him.'

'They'd both been drinking,' she said, looking away. 'It's not a night I care to recall.'

'What about Marco's mates?' Woody asked. 'Who does he go round with?'

She pursed her lips in distaste. 'Some lad or other. Don't know his name. There's something weird about him. He's eighteen, nineteen, but he looks a lot younger, and more like a girl than a boy. He dyes his hair stupid colours and shaves his eyebrows. Wears eyeliner.'

Woody chuckled. 'Sounds like the New Romantics!'

She stared at him coldly. 'Long before my time.'

'Take a look at this.' Lincoln slapped a photo onto the coffee table that stood between them on the shagpile rug. 'You recognise either of these two?'

Suspicious, she studied the picture of the Mini. 'Where's this?'

'Is this Marco?'

A crease appeared between her dark eyebrows. 'Could be.'

'And the lad with him? Is that his mate, the one you say's a bit weird?'

'The photo's too blurred to see his face, but yes, that's about the shape of him.'

'Any idea what his name is, where he lives?'

She sat back. 'Why do you want to talk to Marco? What's this about?'

'You've heard about Hugh Buckthorn?'

'Of course I've heard. You're not suggesting that Marco—?'

'Your son and his mate may have seen something significant that evening, that's all. Perhaps without even realising it.'

She wasn't taken in. 'You think, because he had a go at Trevor, he'd *kill* someone? That's crazy!'

'What about his mate?' Lincoln flicked the photo with his finger. 'We need his name, Gabriella. Come on.'

She folded her arms more tightly, hugging herself. 'All I know is he had a little brother who died a few years back. Glue-sniffing. Got hold of something, didn't understand the dangers. They don't, do they? You got kids?'

'I've got two boys,' Woody chipped in before Lincoln could answer. 'Still too young to get up to that sort of mischief.'

'Shame they can't stay that way!' She forced a laugh. 'Dad used to make such a fuss of Olivia's boy and my Marco. They made up for him not having a son to carry the business on. But Marco didn't want to work in the restaurant, and then Dad got upset when me and Frankie got divorced. Catholics are meant to stay together for life, like swans.' She uncrossed her legs, smoothing out the skirt of her dress. 'Such a disappointment I've been to him.'

Lincoln put the photo away. 'You know Marco works at Guys?'

'What, the hospital?'

'The club in Commercial Street.'

'Never go down that way. What sort of a club?'

'For gay people,' Woody said. 'For gay men more than, y'know, gay women. Probably.'

'You're saying my son's *gay*?' The crease between her eyebrows deepened in scorn.

'You were suggesting his mate's sexuality—'

She rounded on Lincoln. 'Don't tell me what I was suggesting! I haven't seen Marco since Christmas Eve. Another bloody awful day, that was, him not liking Trev being here. Words were said, and I haven't seen him since. He phones every now and again, but I don't know where he's living or who he's with. Except,' she finished, waving a hand in disgust at the photo on the table, 'he must still be going round with that Curtis.'

'So you *do* know his name.'

She bit her lip, caught out. 'That's not his surname. Don't know his surname.'

'What about his little brother's name, the one who died?'

'Aaron. That's all I can remember.'

Woody made a note. Lincoln hoped it might be enough to find out Curtis's surname, but he doubted it.

'Your sister's running the Sanremo now?' he said as they stood up to leave.

Gabriella stood up too, leading them towards the front door and watching while they put their shoes on again. 'And good luck to her. People don't eat out like they used to. Dad would never dream of closing it, but I bet Olivia can't afford to take a wage out of it. You seen the state of that place? People want a bit of class when they eat out, not drab and dreary like she's got it.'

While Lincoln and Woody were calling on Gabriella Ross, Graham Dilke was trawling Barbury market in search of dressing gowns like the one in which Hugh Buckthorn had been found dead.

The sky hung over the town like a leaden blanket, threatening rain but trying to snow. Not a good day to pitch your stall and display your wares, with fewer customers than usual, and even fewer inclined to spend their time browsing.

Dilke used to get dragged to the market most Tuesdays and Saturdays when he was a kid, his mum always eager for a bargain, always ready to spend ages nattering to stallholders she treated like old friends. Now he was slogging round the market because he was a detective following a lead, canvassing the clothing stalls in search of a discontinued brand of dressing gown. He had no luck at the first three, but then he approached Alex's Quality Gear. Unseasonal nylon cardigans, jumpsuits and outsized zip-up jerkins swung from hangers above his head. Icy rain was beginning to speckle the jeans stacked on Alex's sloping table, and the beanie hats were getting damp. Then, next to some cheap three-pair packs of Y-fronts and socks, Dilke spotted a familiar brand of dressing gown.

'One of these take your fancy?' Fiftyish and very overweight, with a knitted hat pulled well down on his forehead, Alex unfolded the topmost dressing gown in a single smooth movement, holding it up so Dilke could better appreciate its quality.

When Dilke flashed his warrant card, the stallholder looked wary, expecting trouble.

'Sold one of these recently, Alex? We're looking for someone who might've bought one in the last week or so.'

Alex roughly refolded the dressing gown and regarded him with hostility. 'This sort of shade?' The ones on display were the colour of full-roasted coffee beans.

'Dark blue.'

Alex turned away to sneeze, then blew his nose into a wad of tissues. He coughed, trying to clear his throat. 'Takes years off your life, a job like this. I'm out in all weathers. After I pack up here, I've got to sling everything back in my lock-up before I can go home and put my feet up. You don't want to look at my legs,' he advised, 'the varicose veins I've got!'

'I'll take your word for it. Now, have you sold any dark blue dressing gowns like this lately?'

'Well, they're not a winter garment, if I'm honest. And I am.' Alex pointed to his signboard: *Honest Bargains, No Rip-offs.* 'Young fella come round last Tuesday, bought my last Midnight Blue, medium long. I'd have said he was a large, myself, but I suppose it wasn't for him.'

'Was he on his own?'

'Yeah, far as I could tell.'

'How did he pay?'

'Cash, of course. Can't afford to take cards, what with the charges they sting you with. I'm only scraping a living here as it is, without giving Barclays a tip every time I make a sale. But I can tell you who it was.'

'You can?'

Alex leaned closer, his knitted helmet grazing Dilke's ear. 'But you didn't hear it from me, okay? You gotta promise me he won't find out who told ya.'

Pam's trawl through Social Services reports added little to what they already knew about Yazmin.

'Wiltshire Social Services first got involved not long after the family moved here,' she told Lincoln when she'd finished going through everything. 'Sonia took an overdose, possibly accidental. Then in 1996 a teacher reported some bruising on Yazmin's arm, but the social workers were satisfied it was the result of a playground accident. Bruno moved out in September '96. He and Sonia agreed access arrangements, but she kept sabotaging them, turning up late for the handover or cancelling at the last minute, saying Yazmin was ill. If she was afraid of leaving Yazmin alone with Bruno she'd have reported him, wouldn't she? If she thought he was abusing her, say?'

Lincoln agreed. 'If there'd been even a hint of abuse, he wouldn't have been left alone with her. More likely Sonia was unhappy and lonely, afraid Yazmin would choose to stay with Bruno instead of her.'

'She should've been putting Yazmin first.'

'Of course, but Sonia was in a bad place. She still seems very vulnerable. That's why I don't want to keep her in the dark any longer than we have to. She found this photo.' He reached over for the snapshot Sonia had lent him: three men and two little girls at a barbecue party. 'Scan it and stick it on the board.'

Pam took it from him. 'I recognise Yazmin, but who are the others?'

He pointed to each face in turn. 'Bruno's in the middle behind Yazmin, with two of his workmates. Lee, the tall one on the left, lived next door to them. He'd got a new job and was moving away, so he had a farewell barbecue in his back garden. The other little girl is his daughter. This was the summer of '96.'

'And the other guy?'

'Edgar something or other, known as Ned. He worked as a labourer for the council, then got a job at Bruno's garage. Sonia couldn't remember his surname, except he was Polish, or his parents were. Might be worth tracking him down if we can.'

'He'd have been interviewed and eliminated at the time, surely?'

'Worth checking through the files for his statement. He worked with Bruno, they were mates. Something might have been said that didn't seem relevant back then but could be useful now.' Though Lincoln feared it was unlikely. 'David Soloman was the SIO, wasn't he? I only remember him vaguely. He retired not long after I started here. He had a bit of a reputation: old-fashioned, did things by the book, a bit unimaginative. Any other possible leads?'

'Not really. DCI Soloman's team homed in on Bruno at the start because Julie was so sure it was Bruno she'd seen taking Yazmin away. But once they knew he was in the clear, they went through the usual suspects, the sex offenders register and so on, and got nowhere. However, there's a possible query against Harry Miller, Julie's husband,'

'What sort of query?'

'He was interviewed. Not under caution, just routine. But someone's scribbled a note on his statement, something about "a gap in his timeline", whatever that means. There's nothing obvious in his statement and they didn't interview him again, so it could be nothing. I'll check to see if he's been in trouble since.'

'Good idea. But nobody else in the frame?'

'No. All traced and eliminated.'

'Check Miller out, then, and see if you can track down those workmates of Bruno's – though how you'll find them after twenty years...'

She sighed hopelessly. 'The garage might not even be in business now.'

Lincoln stood up and stretched, his back stiff. 'Good work, Pam. I know it's hard, having to be so clandestine about this case, but we can't leave Sonia in limbo indefinitely. God knows how we crack this Buckthorn case.'

'Any developments?'

'Gabriella Ross, Marco's mother, gave us a first name for his mate, the one who was in such a hurry to get away from the market square. He's called Curtis, and she remembered he had a younger brother, Aaron, who died from sniffing glue a few years ago. Ring any bells?'

'Yes, actually.'

'It does?' He hadn't expected it to be that easy.

She nodded. 'I was only a few weeks into the job, still in uniform. Me and my partner were dispatched to a skate park behind the old paint factory on Presford Road. Some kids had been playing around with cans of butane – you know, lighter fuel. They were only eleven, twelve, and one of them had passed out and the others panicked. Turned out that he'd thrown up and then choked on his vomit. His mates didn't know what was happening to him, didn't know what to do. He died before anyone could help him.'

'And that was Aaron?'

'Aaron Starkie. We had to go round there, break the news to his mum. One of my first calls like that. She thought he was in school.'

'You remember the address?'

'No, but I remember that day so clearly, even now, that I could take you to the house.'

CHAPTER 21

Sharon Starkie's house was in sharp contrast to Gabriella Ross's. It stood on the corner of a road of older council properties, all brick and pebbledash. Some retained the hedges and front gates they were designed to have, but most used their front gardens to park cars and vans, and the occasional caravan.

Sharon's lawn was long gone, replaced by concrete so old it was crumbling like stale oatcakes. A couple of bikes leaned against the side wall, their tyres flat, and a wheelie bin stood surrounded by rubbish the refuse collectors must have declined to take: a cardboard box of broken china, a lopsided television stand, a collapsed wicker chair.

Lincoln thought back to Ploughboy's Pit on the edge of Greywood Forest, repository for rubbish such as this, year after year. Thought back to the small bundle of bones, the fragments of a summer frock, a plastic jelly shoe –

He was wrenched back to the present as the front door opened. Sharon Starkie didn't look well – hair unkempt, slight frame swamped by overlarge pyjamas, feet in unlaced pink trainers. Her face froze as if in terrible anticipation of news that no mother should have to bear – until Pam explained that they'd come to talk to Curtis.

She relaxed a little. 'Why d'you want to talk to my Curtis, then?'

'He may have witnessed an incident last week,' Pam said.

'An incident?' Sharon turned and led them into the front room, where a gas fire was going full blast. The windows streamed with condensation, and the house smelt as if she'd been cooking fish all morning. 'Not one to get into trouble, Curtis isn't. Quite the opposite. Real softie, my Curtis.'

They sat down on uncomfortable dining chairs at a cluttered table. When Pam showed her the photo of Marco Ross and the lad who might be Curtis, Sharon put her hand to her mouth, shocked.

'You're sure this is your son?' Lincoln could tell by her reaction that it was, but he needed her to confirm it. 'This is Curtis?'

She nodded. 'He promised me he wasn't going round with Marco anymore. A bad influence, that boy. Makes out he's so clever, talking like something out of *The Sopranos*. His mum and dad are Italian, see, so he acts like he knows all these tough guys. I told Curtis, this is Barbury, not the effing Bronx. If he's got my Curtis into something...' She shook her head, running out of words for what she'd do to Marco if she got her hands on him.

'His dad's Italian?' Lincoln wasn't sure he'd heard her right.

'Ross isn't his real name. Look him up. You'll see for yourself.' She held the photo up so she could read the time stamp. 'Thursday night?'

'Where was he Thursday night?' Lincoln expected her to claim that Curtis had been at home in bed or watching television with her, but Sharon handed the photo back and said, 'He was out. Went out after his tea, about seven, seven thirty. He works at this bar in town, washing up, waiting tables. Lola's.'

'Lola's is the launderette, isn't it?' said Pam. 'In Commercial Street? Do you mean the bar upstairs?'

'Isn't that Lola's?' Sharon frowned, confusion in her tired eyes. 'Sorry, I've never been there. I don't go into town much these days.'

'Has Curtis ever mentioned meeting Hugh Buckthorn?'

Now Sharon's face was full of fear as she put two and two together. 'You saying my Curtis had something to do with what happened to that man?'

'Curtis and Marco were in Bridgeford that night,' Lincoln said carefully. 'We need to talk to them to find out if they saw anyone leaving the flat where Mr Buckthorn died. That's why we need to speak to them.'

'I haven't seen him since yesterday morning. He didn't come home last night. When you turned up on my doorstep, first thing I thought – well, you can guess what I thought.' She peered at Pam with disconcerting intent. 'You were here before, weren't you? When I lost Aaron. Only you were in uniform then.'

Pam nodded sadly. 'I'll never forget having to come here and break the news to you. I wish I hadn't had to.'

Sharon set her mouth in a hard line. Lincoln expected her to come out with some sarcastic rejoinder, but she said quietly, 'Must've been rough on you, love, having to do that. Especially when you're too young to know what it's like to lose a kid.'

They sat in silence for a moment or two, then Pam said, 'Where does Curtis go when he doesn't come home overnight? Is there a friend who puts him up, a relative?'

Sharon shrugged. 'Not that I know of. We're not a big family, not close. He's all I've got and I'm all *he's* got. I don't know who his friends are any more – apart from that bloody Marco Ross.'

'Have you got your son's mobile number?' Lincoln asked.

Sharon fetched her own phone from the kitchen and reeled off Curtis's number. As he wrote it down, he recognised it as the number Buckthorn had called the night he died.

'Can we see his room?' He knew he was chancing it, but he hoped that Sharon was too worried about her son's welfare to insist on a search warrant. And he only wanted a quick look anyway, to get a sense of who her son was.

She resisted for only a moment before leading them back into the hall. 'Top of the stairs, across the landing. Not that there's much to see.'

Upstairs, Lincoln and Pam edged round each other in the crowded bedroom. Curtis obviously slept on the top level of a bunk bed, the lower level neatly made up beneath an Arsenal FC coverlet, a couple of threadbare cuddly toys sitting against the pillows. Had this been Aaron's bed?

'I'll have to look Frankie Ross up when we get back.' Lincoln put his hands on his hips and looked round him. 'Wondering if Sharon's right about him being Italian.'

'Does it matter?' Pam picked the top book off a pile of *Warhammer* paperbacks and idly flipped through the pages before putting it down again.

'Not really. Just surprised it passed me by.'

'You don't know him, do you, this Ross guy?'

'Not personally, no. Not sure our paths have ever crossed. Although the DCI has crossed swords with him in Bristol.'

'With Frankie Ross?' She looked as surprised as Lincoln had been when Jacobs had told him.

'So he says.' He paused in front of a close-up photo of a young man's face: a selfie Curtis had printed out and skewered to his wardrobe door with a dart. His hair was dappled orange and tawny, with a green stripe over one ear, a purple stripe over the other. He'd shaved his eyebrows off and accentuated his lower lashes with kohl. It was the face of someone who didn't like himself much.

Pam nodded at the posters adorning Curtis's walls. 'I'd have expected pictures out of lads' mags,' she laughed, 'not Nietzsche.'

Philosophical quotations were printed across black and white portraits of their authors, a modern take on the classic Che Guevara image Lincoln had once pinned up in his own bedroom – until his father ripped it down and tore it to shreds.

Sharon must be more tolerant, letting her son paper his walls with the sayings of Marx, of Camus, of Nietzsche. *'There are no facts, only interpretations.' 'Always go too far, because that's where you'll find the truth.'*

A Yamaha keyboard was set up against one wall, with speakers and recorders connected to it by a cat's cradle of leads and cables.

Lincoln tilted his head towards a big Nietzsche poster that read: *'Without music, life would be a mistake.'* 'Looks as if Curtis has taken that one to heart.'

'He's really into his music,' Sharon agreed, leaning in from the landing. 'He puts it up on the Internet.'

Lincoln cast an appraising eye over Curtis's electronic set-up. 'He's got some pricey kit here. You help him buy all this?'

'Me? No! He's been doing extra shifts at work. They're a barman short. He gets some generous tips.'

Lincoln nodded, though he suspected it more likely the money came from selling drugs or sex, or both. 'We really need to talk to him, Sharon. He's not in any trouble, but the sooner we talk to him the better.'

She took his card and stared at it before turning to Pam. 'You got a card, love? Only, maybe if I think of anything, it might be easier.'

Pam took Lincoln's card back and wrote her own details under his. 'Let us know as soon as you hear from Curtis, okay?'

Lincoln and Pam arrived back at Barley Lane to find Dilke looking pleased with himself.

'Marco Ross bought a dressing gown from the market last Tuesday,' he told them. 'Medium long, dark blue, exactly like the one Buckthorn was wearing.'

'And the stallholder's sure it was him?'

'Yeah, he's known Marco a while, though it doesn't sound as if he likes him very much.'

'Anyone else with him?'

Dilke shook his head. 'He was on his own.'

Lincoln stood staring at the whiteboard as his team assembled. At last they might be getting closer to proving the two young men were involved in Buckthorn's death.

'Okay,' he said, 'we now know it was Curtis Starkie that Buckthorn phoned late on Saturday night and again on Thursday. He and Marco both work at Guys, and that's where Buckthorn was on Saturday night.' He pointed to the crime scene photos. 'A possible scenario? He took a shine to Curtis, so the two lads decided to take advantage of him. They'd take some photos when he thought he was alone with Curtis, and then they'd blackmail him.'

'They wouldn't have got very much,' Pam put in. 'From what I've read, Hugh was practically broke.'

Lincoln shrugged. 'They probably thought that anyone brought up at Greywood Hall must be loaded. Saturday, they decide to target him. Tuesday, Marco buys the dressing gown. Wednesday, he steals the Mini. Thursday, Curtis gets a call from Buckthorn to say he'll pick him up and take him to Bridgeford. Marco follows them in the Mini and waits for Curtis to call him.'

'What's he waiting for?' asked Breeze, leaning back in his seat, right ankle resting on left knee.

'For the roofies to work. We know Buckthorn had a glass or two of wine shortly before he died, and that he took Rohypnol. Curtis may have slipped the roofies into the wine, or Buckthorn could've taken them voluntarily to help him relax. Either way, Marco waits in the car until he thinks Buckthorn will be out of it.'

Breeze nodded, working through the timeline. 'So as soon as Buckthorn's knocked out, Curtis phones Marco to come and help him set things up – undress him, put the stockings on him and the dressing gown, lay him on the sofa with the cord round his neck and the bag on his head—'

'No, not the bag.' Dilke chucked down the pencil he'd been chewing. 'The photos need to show his face. They can't shame him into paying up if no one can see that it's him.'

Lincoln agreed. 'You're right, Graham. So if they're not setting him up for blackmail, what's their game?'

'Queer-bashing?' Breeze uncrossed his legs, crossed them the other way.

'That's a horrible phrase, Dennis. We're talking about violent assault, men beating a man up because they don't like the way he lives his life, because he's different from them.'

'Attacking him because he's gay, then,' Breeze amended sheepishly. He tugged at the top of his fluorescent green sock and pulled it farther up his bristly shin. 'They hate gays, so they've lured Buckthorn into a date with Curtis so they can teach him a lesson, make an example of him. Only they went a bit overboard.'

'They work in a gay bar,' Dilke reminded him. 'Why would they work in a gay bar if they hate gays?'

145

'Maybe they hate posh people, then,' Breeze offered instead. 'Aristocrats, blokes with loads of money.'

'But he *didn't* have loads of money,' said Pam.

'They don't *know* that, though, do they?'

Lincoln shook his head as he stared at the whiteboard. 'Stop! We're going round in circles. Doesn't this all seem too, I don't know – too *subtle*? If this is meant to be an attack on gay men or rich blokes, why isn't it more blatant, more obvious? Why not some kind of mutilation, ritual humiliation of some sort, something that sends a clear message? This...' He waved a hand at the photos of the body laid out on Rufus Rayner's couch. 'This is so dressed up, it's in disguise!'

Nobody spoke, all eyes on the crime scene photos.

'But why kill him at all?' Pam asked at last. 'What's he done to them?'

Lincoln sat down next to her and looked back up at the whiteboard. He tried to find the answer, but instead he came up with more questions.

'Why were we meant to assume he was on his own in the flat? Why were we meant to accept it was simply an embarrassing accident?'

Dilke rolled his pencil between his palms. 'So we wouldn't investigate it.'

Lincoln snapped his fingers. 'Exactly. If the Earl of Riverbourne had had his way, the police wouldn't even have been involved.' He stood up and returned to his place in front of his team. 'What do we know about these two lads?'

He tapped the photos on the board. The mugshot of Marco had now been joined by the moody selfie that Curtis had stuck to his wardrobe door. Pam had photographed it, tidying it up in Photoshop to erase the dart sticking out of the original.

'Marco's a bit of a Jekyll and Hyde character,' Dilke remarked. 'The old people on Barbury Down talk about him helping them out with gardening and odd jobs, but the guy who sold him the dressing gown sounded scared of him – of him *and* his dad.'

Lincoln spun round in surprise. 'You mean Frankie Ross is still in Barbury? His wife – his ex-wife – said he'd moved to Spain, and that he and Marco don't have anything to do with each other these days.'

Dilke shrugged. 'The guy on the market stall talked about Frankie as if he'd seen him not that long ago, with Marco.'

'According to Curtis's mum, Frankie's actually Italian,' Pam told the others. 'I looked it up on the way back, and she's right.'

Woody pulled a doubtful face. 'Italian? With a name like Ross?'

'He's of Italian *descent*.' She paraphrased the information on her phone. 'Born Franco Rossetti, though probably no relation to Rossetti the artist. His grandfather was an Italian prisoner of war, settled here and started up an electrical engineering firm that Frankie's father later sold to some big conglomerate. "Frankie Ross rose to fame as head of leisure company F. Ross Barbury Inc, where he was dubbed the Fruit Machine King." Unquote. The joys of Wikipedia, eh?'

Even though the marriage hadn't lasted, perhaps their Italian ancestry had brought Frankie and Gabriella together in the first place. Lincoln thought back to the empty walls of the marital home.

'Well, whether or not he's related to Rossetti the artist,' he said, 'Frankie apparently has an eye for a good painting.'

Breeze scoffed. 'Cuh, and to think he started out servicing one-armed bandits!'

'Do we know anything else about Marco?' Woody asked. 'Anything in the report from his arrest?'

Breeze scrabbled through his wire tray until he found the paperwork again, the background report on Marco's attack on Trevor, Gabriella's partner. 'He hadn't been in trouble until the fight with his mum's boyfriend. He'd been smoking pot the day he went round his mum's, he says here, and it clouded his judgement.'

Lincoln could understand Marco picking a fight with his mother's partner, especially if he'd been under the influence of pot. But that was very different from murdering Hugh Buckthorn, a crime that had apparently been carefully planned and meticulously executed.

Was he wrong about Marco and Curtis being the culprits?

Woody interrupted his train of thought. 'Reckon we're back to Press Vale Country Club. Did someone want to make absolutely sure Buckthorn didn't give a statement about what he saw?'

Lincoln's patience ran out. How many more times did he need to say it? 'Buckthorn. Didn't. See. Anything. If anyone's in danger over that incident, it's Amy Cartland!'

Even as he said it, he feared he was tempting providence. But it was true: the murder of a young waitress in a country club would raise far fewer flags than the killing of a high-profile member of the aristocracy.

He strode back to his desk. 'We're getting nowhere fast, sitting here theorising. We've got enough to bring those lads in for taking Mortimer's Mini – when we can find them.'

CHAPTER 22

Trish broke off from unpacking yet another crate of books. The shelves of the library were gradually refilling, thanks to the efforts of Stewart Hubbard, her new assistant. Her original plan had been to work through the stock one crate at a time, as she'd been doing before his arrival, but he'd persuaded her to get all the books back on the shelves.

'Even if they're the *wrong* shelves,' he'd said with a grin. 'Once they're all out of their boxes, we can see what we're dealing with.'

'I'll be unpacking boxes in my sleep!' She rubbed her aching back.

Stewart carried another armful of leather-bound tomes across to the shelves. 'Did the trustees *really* expect you to do all this on your own?'

'They did indeed.' She was relieved that he was willing to roll his sleeves up and get stuck in – although she wished he'd given her time to do a risk assessment before he started opening boxes and hoisting their contents onto vacant shelves.

At the end of the morning, they sat themselves in the library's tiny work area to eat sandwiches Trish had prepared in her kitchen upstairs.

'So what's the plan?' he asked. 'Get everything catalogued and on the Internet so people know what's here?'

'Ultimately, yes, though only serious researchers are going to be able to look at the actual books.'

'What a waste! I bet Lundy didn't acquire all these works so they could be hidden away.'

'No, but you know as well as I do how rare some of these books are. Access has to be limited.'

'Of course, of course. Still a shame.'

'I'm also expected to identify anything the Trust can sell to raise funds for the library's upkeep, though I really don't know where to start.'

'But what could they sell that wouldn't destroy the integrity of the whole collection? I know dear old Lundy collected anything that took his fancy, but that's the joy of his library, isn't it? You never know what you'll find.' Stewart helped himself to another sandwich. 'They're philistines if they imagine you can cherry-pick a few high-value titles without spoiling the rest of it.'

'I know, but it's part of my brief—'

'And how are you going to know what's worth selling unless you get some dealers in? We both know what sharks *they* can be.'

She secretly agreed with him, but she was obliged to come up with some suggestions for the trustees.

'Where would I start?' she asked rhetorically. 'His books on Essex? Philosophy? Maths? Astronomy? Since I've been here, most of the enquiries have been about his books on alchemy.'

'Ah, alchemy! The art of turning base metals into gold. Wouldn't we all like to know the secrets of that one?' He laughed. 'But if that's what researchers expect to find here, all the more reason *not* to sell the books by John Dee and Arthur.'

'Arthur?'

'Arthur Dee. John Dee's son. Physician to Tsar Michael in Moscow and author of *Fasciculus Chemicus*, his writings on alchemy. Now, if we found something here by *him*...' His eyes lit up.

'I haven't so far.' She hadn't even heard of him.

'I wonder if Lundy bought anything by Newton at that Hooke auction.'

'There are one or two books here by Newton—'

'No, I mean any manuscripts. You haven't seen anything like that?'

Trish had to admit she hadn't. 'But I've barely scratched the surface of what's here. Any manuscripts would be bound up with pamphlets and other odds and ends Lundy picked up. Some of those volumes are a right old mishmash.'

'Perhaps I'll take a look at those sometime, see what's in them.' He gestured down the library to a bay of miscellaneous works they'd set aside because they defied classification: collections of political tracts and advertisements, ephemeral papers that Lundy had gathered in his long lifetime. He'd had them carefully bound, but the lettering on the spines was no longer legible.

Trish was conscious of how much work lay ahead of them, and how little time. 'Let's deal with the straightforward stuff first,' she suggested, 'and then we can concentrate on the miscellanies.'

'Fine, okay.' He dusted salt from his fingers as he finished the last Pringle. 'Changing the subject completely, I need to find somewhere else to live, somewhere a bit nearer than Chelmsford. The bus takes forever.'

'You don't drive?'

149

'Not at the moment. I'd rather be nearer. Any chance of finding somewhere to rent round here? You haven't got a spare room in your flat, have you?' He cast his gaze upwards.

'God, no! My flat's minuscule!'

In truth, she *did* have a spare room, the bedroom that would have been Kate's if she'd agreed to move to Essex. But Trish couldn't bear the thought of sharing her kitchen and bathroom with the person she worked with, no matter how amenable and pleasant Stewart might be.

'It's early days,' she said, 'and the bus service is pretty reliable usually. I'm sure you'll get used to it.'

He heaved a theatrical sigh. 'I'll have to, won't I?'

CHAPTER 23

Lincoln remembered to phone Len Painter, the plumber, towards the end of the afternoon.

'I'm booked solid till next Monday,' Len told him, 'but I'll try and fit you in. You've got your work cut out, eh, with this earl getting murdered?'

'Who told you he'd been murdered?' Lincoln tried to laugh it off despite his growing alarm that someone somewhere was revealing more than they should. 'And it isn't the earl, it's his uncle.'

'Same difference. Still one of the nobs, isn't he? Suppose they get priority treatment, eh? Not like the rest of us.'

Lincoln decided it wasn't worth having an argument with the one man who was available to fix his leaking radiator, and they agreed that Len would come round in the evening to take a look at the problem.

Dilke called across the room to announce that the Mini had been spotted by a couple of PCSOs. 'It was in a side street, not far from the roundabout where the traffic camera picked it up Thursday night.'

'Let's get it taken in, have a SOCO team go over it. It'd be good if we could find Marco and Curtis too.'

The phone rang: DCI Jacobs wanting an update.

'The Mini's turned up,' Lincoln told him.

'About time. And the lads who were in it?'

'Still looking for them.'

Jacobs grunted. 'Still looking for a motive too, yeah? Supposing somebody else paid them to kill him?'

'That's a possibility, of course, but it still doesn't tell us why.'

'Press Vale Country Club.'

Lincoln might have known that was coming. 'Buckthorn didn't see anything of the attack on the Cartland girl. Nothing he said would've been enough to take it further.'

'Doesn't matter. We'd have followed it up, taken a good look round the place, uncovered what's been going on there. With Buckthorn out of the picture and the Cartland girl afraid to pursue it, we've lost that excuse.'

Why wouldn't Jacobs let it go? Whatever intelligence he or his colleagues at Park Street had received about the country club, Lincoln doubted if sex workers were being ferried into it, trafficked from abroad. It had a reputation to maintain. Pete Doubleday had criminal connections, certainly, but he was lying low in Spain now and could have no practical role in Press Vale's management, even if he still remained a director.

'You're hoping Buckthorn's murder gives you the excuse you're looking for, sir? The sprat to catch a mackerel?'

'It's the excuse we're *all* looking for, Lincoln. This isn't a personal vendetta against Press Vale Country Club and its owners.'

'No, of course not, sir.' It merely sounded like it.

'We've just found out that one of the directors of Press Vale Enterprises is Frankie Ross. What d'you say to that, Lincoln? Marco Ross's father. Still convinced the two cases aren't connected?'

It was after seven and raining when Lincoln finished for the day. Len the plumber was due at eight, so he'd have ample time to get home. He sat in his car in the yard behind Barley Lane, wipers and heater on, waiting for the windscreen to demist and for the car to warm up before he set off.

He'd been surprised to learn from DCI Jacobs that, along with Pete Doubleday, Frankie Ross was one of Press Vale's directors. But was it so surprising? Two prosperous men of a similar age, both familiar with Barbury, both living in Spain with business interests in England. It was more than likely that they knew each other, at least slightly.

But would Ross resort to murder to prevent the country club being investigated? And if he took such drastic action, would he involve his own son?

And yet Jacobs's theory was compelling: destroy Amy's case and avoid scrutiny of the country club. Get rid of Buckthorn in a way that appears accidental.

And yet, and yet... Lincoln couldn't wholeheartedly subscribe to his boss's theory. Wouldn't it have been simpler to get rid of Amy?

He started the car and headed home, hoping that Len would be able to fix the radiator for him.

'Are you going to keep the open fire?' Trish had asked when Lincoln began to have the Old Vicarage refurbished. 'It'd be so cosy.'

'I'll keep the fireplace, of course,' he'd told her, 'but I don't know about using it. It'd mean getting the chimney swept and buying coal.

And you're the one who's always going on about fossil fuels and the environment.'

She'd punched his arm. 'But I can just imagine this living room with a lovely open fire burning in the grate.'

'I'll get one of those coal-effect electric jobbies,' he'd suggested to wind her up. 'You'll never know the difference.'

Now he wished he'd gone ahead and had the chimney swept, had stocked up on coal and kindling. Now, too, he wished Trish were ten minutes' drive away instead of a hundred and fifty miles.

He pulled into his driveway at twenty to eight. Rain slashed down, icy and sharp, and he put his head down as he ran the last few yards to the porch of the Old Vicarage. Fumbling for his keys in the dark, he sensed sudden movement away to his right. He strained to see through the rain and the sodden tendrils of his hair.

'Len?'

But it wasn't Len. A hand thrust a metal rod towards him, making him dodge away instinctively. And then a bright beam of light emerged from the metal rod, and he saw that someone was shining a torch towards the door so he could see to put his key in the lock.

He peered through the torch's glare, trying to make out who was on the other side of it. 'Sonia?'

Sonia Fletcher pulled her hood back from her face. 'Please, please let me in! I need to talk to you. Don't turn me away!'

'You'd better come in.' Lincoln got the door open, reaching round to turn lights on. 'But I warn you, I've got no heating.'

'I don't care about that. I need to know what you've found out about Yazmin.'

He eased his wet mac off and draped it over the newel post. Time to drag a couple of fan heaters out from the cupboard under the stairs.

'How did you know where I live?'

'I followed you from Barley Lane. I needed to speak to you. I couldn't wait any longer.'

'Sonia, everything I've found out I've shared with you. Right now this murder case takes priority. You can understand that, can't you?' He watched as she sank down at the bottom of the stairs, a worn out, dispirited woman trying to make sense of what had happened to her daughter. And there wasn't much more he could do to help her.

'Of course I understand, but I haven't got to like it, have I?' She put her head in her hands, her hair tumbling down loose around her face. 'I'm going mad here, not knowing whether you've found anything out.'

'I've got an officer looking into the original reports, going through the paperwork. Twenty years ago methods were different, there weren't the techniques available to us that we have now—'

'DNA testing, do you mean?'

'There was DNA testing then, but unless there was already something on file for comparison it didn't help much. And that was the whole point,' he added, opening the cupboard under the stairs – gingerly, in case everything he'd shoved into it fell out. 'If the police had found something her abductor had touched or dropped, something of Yazmin's he might have handled, they could've tested it for DNA, maybe found a match. But Yazmin vanished without a trace. Not that I have to tell you that, of course.'

He reached into the cupboard for a fan heater, wishing he could have this conversation somewhere more suitable than his chilly hallway.

'You showed me a photo of her dress.' Sonia pulled her hair back into a tight ponytail, securing it with a band from round her wrist. 'And one of her sandals. Have you found the rest of her clothes?'

He was about to explain that the rubbish from Ploughboy's Pit still needed to be sifted, but then he stopped himself. How could he tell her that her little girl had been buried under an avalanche of redundant baby buggies and decorators' rubble, fly-tipped garden waste and broken bikes?

'We're still sorting through everything around her,' he said, standing there with a fan heater in one hand, the lead in the other. He wasn't even sure if that was true: he'd heard nothing more from the team tasked with going through it, and feared DCS Youngman had ordered them to stop, at least for now.

'Did they find her knickers?'

'Her knickers?'

'Because if you could still find pieces of her cotton dress, then you should've found her knickers, which were nylon. It's true what they say about synthetics,' she added bitterly. 'They last forever.'

She was right. If the pieces of the dress were still salvageable, albeit very fragile, then Yazmin's nylon panties should still be intact – unless she hadn't been wearing them when her body was dumped. Too late now, of course, to find out if she'd been assaulted, raped. Odds on, she had been. There was a sad, immutable pattern to the murder of children by strangers: the motivation was almost always sexual.

'We haven't found her knickers, no. At least, not yet.' Lincoln thought back to the description of Yazmin at the time she disappeared, and remembered something else. 'We haven't found her cardigan either.'

'Her grandma knitted that for her. Grandma Bartek.' She dipped her head. 'Yaz used to keep her dolly in one of the pockets.' She looked up, her eyes bright. 'Did you find that? Her little doll? That was plastic too. It doesn't decompose, plastic. Lasts forever.'

Lincoln hadn't noticed a doll in among all the junk around the bones, but it could have been there somewhere. He should have chased the SOCO team, got an update. Now it was probably too late. 'Let me plug this heater in.'

Once the heater was sending out some welcome warmth, he sat down on the hall chair, a chair he rarely used except to dump things on as he came indoors. 'Yazmin broke her arm a couple of times, didn't she? What happened?'

'It wasn't Bruno, if that's what you're thinking. The first break, she fell over in the playground and landed awkwardly. She hadn't long started school when it happened, and she never really caught up. She was always a bit behind.'

'And the second time?'

Sonia shrugged. 'She was such a clumsy kid, rushing about, not looking where she was going. She could never wait for anything. She caught her arm in the kitchen door somehow. One of those silly accidents.'

'And when was this?'

'Two or three months before—' She hesitated. 'May, June. The cast made her arm itch in the hot weather.'

'And it was Presford General she went to?'

'It was an *accident*,' she insisted. 'One of those stupid accidents.'

He nodded, sighed. 'Was there anyone at the time that you thought, even for a second, might have taken Yazmin away?'

'Apart from her dad?' Her head sank down again. 'No, no one.'

'Were you and Harry close?'

The question brought her head up fast. 'Harry? Julie's Harry?'

'You never had any concerns about him?'

'Why are you asking?'

'I'm trying to think of anyone else who might have taken Yazmin away, someone she went with willingly.'

'But why ask about Harry?'

'Because I'm guessing you were all quite close, you and Bruno, your sister and Harry.'

'Not especially. Once Bruno got his new job and moved us here

155

from Southampton, me and Julie hardly saw each other. That's what I hated most – having to leave my family behind and never having time to go over to see them. That's why going to the fair with Julie and her kids was such a treat.'

'Yazmin liked seeing her cousins?'

'Oh yes.' Sonia sniffed, wiping her nose with the back of her hand. 'Yaz was so excited about going to the fair, all the rides she was going to go on, all the prizes she was going to win. She hardly slept the night before, she was so wound up.' Her gaze drifted away across the hall to where the fan heater was stirring the air, bowling dust balls along the floor. 'You not got a cleaner? Place this big, you need someone to come in, help you out.'

'I should get a cleaner, yes. Right now I'm trying to get the building work done.'

'Bet you wish you'd never taken this place on.'

'Sometimes.' More often than he'd care to admit.

'That little house I've got is all I can afford. I've never had a steady job – always done bits here, bits there. Even now I've got three or four jobs on the go, just to make ends meet. I've worked in shops, in a cab office, telesales, bars. I even did a therapy course, got a diploma and everything. But who was I kidding, trying to heal other people when I couldn't even heal myself? I'm broken.'

Headlights swept across the ceiling, and the crunch of gravel heralded the arrival of Len Painter. Lincoln cursed silently, afraid Sonia would take fright.

And she did just that, ducking out into the rain when he opened the door to let the plumber in. Exactly as she'd ducked out of answering his question about her brother-in-law, Harry Miller.

CHAPTER 24

WEDNESDAY 8TH FEBRUARY

Next morning, Lincoln took Woody back to Guys in the hope that Lloyd Beach would be there, even if none of his staff were.

'Jacobs has still got a bee in his bonnet about Press Vale,' he said as they strode along Commercial Street from the car park. A bitterly cold wind raced towards them, and walking fast was the best way to keep warm. 'He's convinced Buckthorn was killed to stop any investigation into the Cartland girl's claims.'

'What makes him so sure there's a connection?'

'Frankie Ross is one of the directors.'

'He's saying Frankie got Marco to kill Buckthorn?' Woody sounded as doubtful as Lincoln felt. 'Gabriella said he'd have nothing to do with his dad.'

'Frankie might have won him over. But would he have used Marco to kill Buckthorn? He'd have got a professional to do it if he really wanted to make it look like an accident. He'd make sure it got done properly.'

On the ground floor of the building that housed Guys, Lola's Launderette was in full swing, plastic baskets of washing backed up on top of the machines, waiting for a tumble dryer to be free.

The two detectives climbed the stairs to the first floor and followed the sign of the neon willy. Surprisingly, the door to the club was open. A dark-haired, broad-shouldered young man was vacuuming the thin carpet in a desultory way that was leaving it ruckled but not much cleaner. He switched the Hoover off and turned to shut the door – only to come face to face with Lincoln and Woody.

Lincoln's first thought was that they should have brought uniformed officers with them, but he hadn't expected Marco to be at work. He braced himself for the young man to charge past them and down the stairs, but Marco calmly unplugged the vacuum cleaner and wound the flex carefully round the handle.

'Club's shut,' he said. From his tone, Lincoln could tell he knew they weren't punters. 'Opens at six.'

Woody identified himself. 'We want to have a word with you about a car that was stolen from Heath Close.'

Marco shifted his weight, leaning away from them. 'The Mini? I didn't steal it. I borrowed it. In fact, I was giving it a run so the battery don't go flat while Mr Mortimer's in hospital.'

'Did Mr Mortimer give you permission to "give it a run"?'

'Course. Said I was welcome to drive it anytime.'

'He left the keys with you?'

'The spare key, yeah.' He nodded, looking so innocent. Maybe he didn't realise the car had been found, quite clearly hotwired.

'Got your licence on you?'

Marco made a show of patting his sweatshirt, which had no pockets in it. 'It'll be in my jacket.' He sidestepped towards the bar, where a fleece-lined denim jacket was slung over one of the pumps.

'I'll get it for you.' Woody reached across and lifted the jacket down, holding it up while Marco went through each pocket in turn.

'Must've left it at home. Since I wasn't driving today.'

'And you're insured to drive Mr Mortimer's car?' Lincoln asked.

He shrugged. 'Should've checked afore I offered to give it a run round for him, I suppose.' He grinned suddenly as if this were some huge joke. 'Not going to arrest me, are you?'

The interview room was sweltering, the boiler doing its best to keep Barley Lane police station at a steady temperature of twenty-four degrees.

'While we've got you here…' Lincoln sat down across from Marco Ross.

There was enough evidence to charge him with taking Jonathan Mortimer's car without his consent, but that wasn't all Lincoln wanted to ask him about. He laid a photo on the table: Marco and Curtis either side of the Mini in Bridgeford market square. 'What were you doing there that night?'

'I told you. Giving the car a runaround so Jon don't come home to a flat battery.'

'And Jon – Mr Mortimer – knew about that?'

'Thought it'd be a nice surprise when he come out of hospital.' Marco leaned as far back as he could in the rigid chair, one arm draped nonchalantly over the back of it. His gaze shifted calmly from Woody's face to Lincoln's, dark brown eyes watching to see what Lincoln was writing, although the notes were a scrawled shorthand anyone would find hard to read, especially upside down.

'Good friend of yours, is he, Mr Mortimer?'

'I do his garden for him, clean his bins, do his windows.'

'For free?'

'A law against *that* now, is there?' He cast a sidelong glance at his solicitor, Jean Vowles – a woman near the end of her professional career, Lincoln guessed. She'd had her hair cut since he'd last seen her, the severely tight bun replaced by a jaw-length pageboy style that wasn't a lot more flattering to her angular face.

Lincoln decided to move on. 'So you drive to Bridgeford to give the car a run. And then you stop in the market square for nearly an hour. What were you waiting for? For the engine to cool down?'

'I was waiting for my mate.'

'Which mate was that?'

Marco nodded at the photo. 'Curtis. Curtis Starkie. He don't drive. Thought he might like a lift home.'

'That was kind of you. Lift home from where?'

'Bridgeford, of course.' He grinned.

'What was he doing there?'

'No idea. Seeing friends, probably. You'd have to ask him yourself.'

'We will.' Lincoln hoped it wouldn't be long before they tracked him down. 'How did he know you were waiting for him?'

Marco swung his feet back under his chair. 'I texted him.'

Lincoln sat back, letting Woody ask the next question.

'Where did you go when you got out of the car?'

'Needed to take a leak. There's no toilets open that time of night and I didn't want to go into the pub. I walked down the street a bit, went up an alleyway.' Another exchange of glances with Jean Vowles. 'Needs must, eh?'

Woody pointed with his pencil at the time stamp on the photo. 'You were gone forty minutes. Reckon you didn't need that long to empty your bladder.'

Jean bent her head and whispered something in Marco's ear. He frowned unhappily before continuing.

'Okay, I went to meet Curtis at his mate's place. I don't know the address, don't even know the guy's name, but it was down Church Street. There's a turning opposite the butcher's, and it's down there.' He looked from Lincoln to Woody as if to check they believed him. 'I didn't tell you before because I didn't want to get no one in trouble. There was a few joints going round, yeah? A bit of grass, but that's all.'

'And that's where you were between leaving the car at eight forty-five and coming back with Curtis at nearly nine thirty?'

'Yeah. Apart from when I was "emptying my bladder".' His gaze, fixed on Woody's face, was steady and bold.

Lincoln felt sweat trickling down his back as he took over the questioning. 'Did you see anyone else while you were waiting in the car? Hugh Buckthorn, for instance?'

'Wouldn't know him from Adam, to be honest with you.' Then Marco put a finger to his lips and tutted. 'Oh, you mean that lord who's died? That one?'

'Did you see him on Thursday night?'

The young man shook his head, and the way a stray curl fell down onto his forehead reminded Lincoln of the way Buckthorn's shaggy, grey-streaked hair had misbehaved in much the same way. Both men had Italian mothers – an ironic coincidence. 'Didn't see no one,' Marco said. 'There's not many lights in Bridgeford, is there, once you're out of the market place? It's not a place to go walking round on your own after dark.'

He was baiting them, Lincoln felt sure, relishing the risky business of rousing suspicion that could be neither confirmed nor refuted.

'Your mate looks a bit frantic there,' Woody said, pointing to Curtis tugging at the car door handle in his rush to get away. 'Something put the wind up him?'

'He's sensitive. His feminine side makes him a bit hysterical sometimes. We had a bit of a falling-out – not with each other, with the guy we was chilling with. Curtis overreacted.'

'So you went the whole time without hearing this mate's name?' Woody persisted. 'Reckon someone must have spoken to him, called him by name while you were there.'

'Not that I recall.'

Lincoln suddenly saw his theory collapsing: when the two young men emerged from the shadows, heading for the Mini, they hadn't come from the Old Shoddy Mill. They hadn't come from Jackdaw Lane at all. They'd come from Church Street, which ran at right angles to it.

They weren't running from a murder scene but from an argument at a drug den! The timing was merely a coincidence! He'd got it all wrong!

Except – Marco had bought a dressing gown exactly like the one Buckthorn was wearing, and Buckthorn had rung Curtis earlier that evening, hadn't he?

Trying to quieten the doubting voice in his head, Lincoln took over again. 'Curtis knew Mr Buckthorn, though, didn't he?'

Marco's eyes narrowed. 'Dunno. Did he? You'd have to ask him yourself.'

'How did he get to Bridgeford if you didn't give him a lift there?'

A shrug. 'Not a big place, is it, but there's buses that go there from here.'

Lincoln's muscles tensed. His fists clenched, but he made a conscious effort to relax them. This was what Marco wanted, to wind him up, him and Woody.

'Reckon he caught the bus, then?' Woody, in contrast, sounded upbeat, interested. 'You know what number? It'd help us work out when he got there if we knew which number bus it was. I reckon, that time of an evening, it's probably one of those Hoppa buses, y'know, the little ones. Is it the B60 that goes out that way?' He turned to Lincoln as if he might know. 'Reckon we can check that easily enough, see which bus he caught. They've got CCTV on that route now, haven't they?'

'I don't fucking know how he got there!' Now it was Marco's turn to show tension, prompting Jean to lift her thin hand from her papers and hold it there a moment, signalling for him to calm down.

Lincoln sat up, trying unobtrusively to ease his shirt away from the sweat on his back. These interview rooms didn't even have windows you could open...

'Let's go through this again,' he said. 'How did you know Curtis was in Bridgeford that evening, and that he'd need a lift?'

'He texted me. I told you.'

Lincoln checked his notes, though he didn't need to. 'No, Marco, you said *you* texted *him* to say you'd come over to give him a lift. Is that right?'

A deep groove formed between the young man's glossy black eyebrows. 'Oh yeah. He texted me earlier on, told me he was going over to Bridgeford.'

'What time was that?' Woody asked. 'When did he text you?'

'Sevenish? No, no, later than that. More like seven thirty. Then when I was in the car I thought it'd be nice to offer him a lift back.'

'And get in on the action too?' Lincoln forced a grin as he said it. 'Chill with some mates, smoke a bit of weed? Why should *you* get left out in the cold? Because it was really cold that night, wasn't it? Look, you can see your breath.' He pointed to the photo, the white bursts of exhaled breath in the icy air. 'Looks like you're shouting at him.'

'Like I said, he got a bit...overwrought, you might say, and I was trying to calm him down.'

'What did you fall out over?' Woody asked. 'You two and his mate?'

Another shrug. 'Can't remember. Don't take much to set some people off. You're chilling and then—' He snapped his fingers. 'It all goes to shit.'

'Looks like you were angry with Curtis, though, doesn't it?'

Marco glanced at the photo. 'It's not as bad as it looks. He gets on my tits sometimes, that's all.'

'Did he tell you he'd had a phone call from Mr Buckthorn that evening?'

'Yeah? He didn't say nothing, but, like I said, I didn't know the guy, so Curtis wouldn't have bothered to tell me.'

They weren't getting anywhere. They could keep on at Marco for the rest of the day, but would he tell them anything useful?

'Are you trying to protect him, Marco? Giving us this story about Curtis hanging out with some pothead friend of his down Church Street?'

'Protect him? Why would I protect him?'

'Because he's your mate. You go round together. You're close. You've got a special relationship.'

'You saying what I think you're saying?' Marco's eyes were suddenly fierce. 'That I must be gay? Is that what you're saying?'

'You work in a gay bar. It'd be natural to assume...' Lincoln didn't finish his sentence. If Marco was gay, he didn't want to admit it. Was there some conflict there, some shame?

'Okay then, Marco,' he said, with a quick glance at Woody. 'Do you recognise this?' He drew a photo of the dressing gown from his folder and slid it across the table.

Marco made a point of peering closely at it. 'What is it?' He sounded mystified.

'It's a dressing gown. Dark blue. Bought in Barbury market. Apparently bought by you.'

He shook his head. 'Nah! Not my sorta thing. And it don't look big enough for me.' He lifted his head, fixed his gaze on Lincoln. 'Looks like a medium to me.'

A sharp intake of breath as Lincoln tried not to lose his temper. 'How do we find this place you went to with Curtis to see his mate?'

Parking in Bridgeford market square nearly an hour later, Lincoln and Woody headed down Church Street, following the directions Marco had given them. Even as they walked, Lincoln realised it was impossible to tell from the CCTV exactly where Marco had gone when he got out of the Mini on Thursday night. Had he and Curtis emerged from the shadows of Jackdaw Lane less than an hour later, or from the shadows of Church Street?

According to Marco, Curtis had texted him at about seven thirty, telling him he was going over to Bridgeford. Sharon Starkie had told them her son went out between seven and seven thirty that evening, so Marco could well be telling the truth.

'There's the butcher's,' Woody said. 'The turning must be down here.'

Opposite the butcher's they found a flagstoned passageway, cluttered with wheelie bins, leading to Riverbank Terrace. A row of four quaint but poorly maintained cottages, the terrace must have been built for the mill workers originally. Now the properties were rented by local people who probably didn't earn a lot more, relatively, than their Victorian predecessors.

From the tenant in the first house, they learned that, yes, the one at the end had become a bit of a hang-out for 'druggies'.

'I'd report him,' the woman said, 'but I don't want my front door stove in, thank you very much. Mind, it's all gone quiet the last few days. Think he spends a lot of his time asleep.'

'You know the tenant's name?'

'Hodges. James. They call him Jumbo.'

The door of number 4 now stood slightly ajar. Woody announced himself and pushed it open. Lincoln followed him into a living room that was littered with takeaway leftovers, beer cans and cola bottles. Needles and silver foil, throwaway lighters and laden ashtrays were scattered on a wrecked three-piece suite, along with bloodstained cotton wool and filthy tissues. In the kitchen, dirty mugs and dishes sat in a few inches of scummy water.

'Christ, what's that smell?' Lincoln put a hand over his nose.

Woody peeped into the downstairs bathroom at the end of the dark little hallway. 'Toilet's backed up.' He pulled the door firmly shut behind him.

Lincoln stood looking round him. 'No sign of Jumbo Hodges.'

Upstairs, in the front bedroom they found a soiled double mattress partially covered by a nylon sheet. The other bedroom, little bigger than a box room, had been used to dump a collection of supermarket carrier bags stuffed with clothes and electrical goods that had probably been salvaged from skips or charity bins.

They headed back to Barley Lane. They were running out of time to confirm one way or the other where Marco and Curtis had gone the night that Buckthorn died.

'Curtis's mate was out,' Woody said as he and Lincoln, Marco and Jean Vowles took their places across from each other once more. 'Shame we can't speak to Curtis himself. Any idea where we can find him?'

'Might be at work,' said Marco wearily, 'like *I* should be.'

'If you want to keep your job,' Lincoln snapped, 'don't go nicking cars.'

'I didn't nick it. I told you—'

'Yeah, you were driving it to charge the battery. If you had a spare key, why'd you have to hotwire it? If Mr Mortimer had said you could drive it for him, why'd you have to nick it after dark, and after you'd tried a few other car doors first?'

Marco folded his arms and scowled down at the table. He must have known it was pointless to deny the theft, even if he was sticking to his version of events in Bridgeford.

'It's only a poxy old Mini, anyway,' he said at last. 'It's not like I took something valuable. Like a Jag.'

Did he know Buckthorn drove a Jag? Was this another attempt at getting a rise out of his interviewers, wrongfooting them into accusing him of involvement in the murder?

'Whatever sort of car it was, you took it without the owner's consent,' Woody said severely. 'It's not the first time you've been in trouble. You won't get off with probation this time.'

'I'm not sure threatening my client is entirely helpful.' Jean's tone was equally severe.

'Reckon he needs a reminder of how much trouble he could be in, that's all.'

'Let's take a break,' Lincoln suggested. 'We'll stop it there for now.'

'If only we could get hold of Curtis,' Woody muttered as they walked back to the CID room. 'Or this Jumbo Hodges. How else can we be sure he's telling the truth?'

Lincoln threw his notebook and pen down on his desk. 'We can be sure Jonathan Mortimer didn't ask him to take his car out for a run! I'm worried that if we let Marco go today, we won't see him again.'

'We can keep him overnight.'

'Yes, but will we be any farther forward by tomorrow morning?'

'I couldn't find any record for James "Jumbo" Hodges,' Woody said. 'He's either been lucky or incredibly careful.'

'Or he's just started out. Though that house looked as if it had seen some action – and I don't mean the sexual kind.'

Before leaving Riverbank Terrace, they'd called on the woman they'd spoken to earlier, and tried to leave her a card.

'You expect me to put myself at risk?' she'd snapped, wrapping her cardigan tightly round herself. 'If you lot turn up, he's going to have a fair idea who tipped you off.'

'All you need do is give us a ring to say there's someone in there.'

She'd snatched the card out of Woody's hand. 'No promises, mind.'

CHAPTER 25

'She hasn't said a word about them finding Yaz, has she? You saw it on the news, didn't you, Harry, or was it on Facebook?' Julie Miller, Sonia Fletcher's sister, was perched sideways on the edge of her sofa while husband Harry lolled back in his armchair, hands folded on his chest.

Pam had come to Southampton to talk to the Millers, to see if Julie could remember anything more, and also to gain an impression of Harry – the only other man, apart from Bruno Bartek, who seemed to have spent much time with Sonia and her daughter.

'Facebook, yeah,' Harry agreed. 'On the Barbury page, but someone'd shared it to the Southampton one I look at.'

'We've been expecting reporters to come round any minute,' Julie went on, 'but we moved a few years ago. Just hoping our old neighbours don't give the game away.'

'It's old news,' her husband told her as if she were worrying about nothing. 'No one's gonna want to talk to us now.'

'So you haven't spoken to your sister yet?' Pam had assumed that the women were close and that Yazmin's disappearance would have brought them even closer.

'No, but she texted me.' Julie lifted her phone up and dropped it back into her lap.

'She can't have been surprised,' Harry said lugubriously. 'She must've known.'

Julie, plump and energetic, her short brown hair highlighted and shiny, glared at him. 'Yeah, but it's different when you get proof, isn't it? You go on hoping, don't you, kidding yourself? But seeing the body—' She broke off and turned to Pam. 'Did Sonia have to identify her?'

'Wouldn't have been a body, would it, you daft sod?' Harry cut in. 'It'd be a skeleton, wouldn't it, after all this time?' He looked to Pam for corroboration.

'We had her dental records,' Pam said, and left it at that. For a man who might have been implicated, he was remarkably unfazed.

No one spoke for a minute or two. The Millers' long-haired tabby cat stretched itself out on the windowsill above the radiator, and they all watched it until it let out a long sigh and fell asleep again.

Pam smoothed down a fresh page in her notebook. 'So you thought it was Mr Bartek who'd taken Yazmin?'

Julie glanced across at her husband. 'I only saw the back of him, but yes, yes I did. I was sure it was Bruno. Same sort of light brown hair, same blue polo shirt he had for work.'

'We were expecting it, though, weren't we?' Harry put in. 'After all the trouble they were having. That's why you were so sure it was him.'

'What sort of trouble?'

'You must've read the reports.' Still lolling back, Harry's only animation was the shifting of his folded hands on his flabby chest. 'They couldn't agree on when Bartek could have Yaz over to stay with him, so you can imagine the rows! Bartek had quite a temper on him!'

'And so does our Sonia!' Julie rolled her eyes. 'You were asking about what I saw, but I was looking at Yaz as much as at the fella, the way she was hopping and skipping along beside him. And by the time I'd got hold of my two so I could go after her, she was out of sight.'

Pam studied her notes for a minute and a half, letting the tension build in the silence, a trick she'd learned from Lincoln.

'Was there anyone else Yazmin might have gone off with so willingly? Anyone else she'd have been so comfortable with?' She was looking at Julie, but in her peripheral vision she noted the way Harry shifted in his chair.

'Can't think of anyone,' the Millers said, not quite in unison.

'But then,' Julie added, 'we didn't see them much after they moved to Barbury, did we?'

Harry shook his head. 'No idea who they took up with once they moved. And *she* took up with some weirdos, didn't she?'

Pam caught the scornful look Julie aimed at him. 'Weirdos, Mr Miller?'

'Some New Age-y lot. Believed in reincarnation, communicating with the dead – you name it!' He laughed wryly. 'She got right taken in, didn't she?'

He must have expected his wife to agree, but Julie sighed and said hopelessly, 'She was lost, Sonia was, even before Bruno left her. And then, after Yaz went missing, she turned to anyone she thought could help. Some of them were only too quick to take advantage.'

'In what way?'

'Trying to receive messages from beyond the grave,' said Harry in a wobbly voice that was meant to sound ghostly. 'For a price.'

'Beyond the grave?' Pam turned to Julie.

167

'She went to some weird spiritualist church for a while, met some medium who tried to make contact with Yaz.'

'Church of the Promised Land,' said Harry.

His wife flung him another warning look. 'The Church of Heaven's Promise, it was called, in a little place called Bridgeford. But the medium said she couldn't locate Yazmin "on the Other Side" so she must still be alive.'

'And your stupid sister believed her!' Harry sounded more amused than anything. 'Those people took her in good and proper!'

'She wasn't well, Harry. She wasn't herself.'

'Sonia was *always* herself,' he said, as if they'd had this debate many times over the years. 'That was half the trouble. Didn't want to put anyone else first.'

'And the day of the funfair...' Pam again glanced at her notes. 'Where were you, Mr Miller?'

'Me? Working.'

'On the bank holiday weekend?'

'That's the busiest time! I'm a coach driver. Was. I've chucked it in now.'

'So where were you that weekend?'

'You'll have it in your records.' He nodded at Pam's notebook as if she'd got his original statement folded up inside it. Indeed, she'd written down a few points from it, but she was hoping to hear it from him now.

'Was it Bournemouth? Sorry, I should have—'

'Beaulieu. It was Beaulieu, then on to Lymington and back.' He scowled at her, no doubt seeing through her attempt to catch him out. 'Beautiful Beaulieu, that's where I was, with a party of fifty pensioners wanting to stop for the toilet every ten minutes.'

Pam recalled the scribbled note in the files: a gap in Miller's timeline, but no detail of when the gap occurred. 'Can you remember when you left home and when you got back?'

'It was twenty bloody years ago, love. How do you expect me to remember that?'

Julie glanced across at him. 'You always left in good time, didn't you? You were always there ages before you needed to be in case the traffic was bad.'

'Which it would've been, the bank holiday weekend. I had to get to the coach station for nine because they were boarding from half past and leaving at ten. That was the usual routine. Stopping at Beaulieu for lunch and the Motor Museum. You ever been? It's very nice. But then,

I'm into transport. May not be your sort of thing. On to Lymington for a cream tea, back at the coach station about six. Nice leisurely outing,' he said sourly. 'But exact times I can't give you.'

Pam drew a couple of dots in her notebook. Joined them up. How long would it take to drive from Beaulieu to Presford? Forty minutes, not allowing for traffic? Abduct Yazmin – half an hour. A third dot. Drive to Bridgeford – half an hour. Dispose of her body, drive back – two more hours...

But Miller was driving a coach. Where would he have parked at the funfair? How would he have known where to find Yazmin? And he surely couldn't have driven a fifty-six-seater coach up to Greywood Forest! No, it didn't add up.

His wife said crossly, interrupting Pam's train of thought, 'I'm sure she blamed me, Sonia did, because I said it was Bruno, but I said it in good faith. How was I to know he wasn't even in the country that weekend?'

'You're not gonna find out who did it after all this time, are you?' Harry sounded very certain. 'Not after twenty years.'

'You'd be surprised,' said Pam. 'People remember things, or they come forward because something's been on their conscience, or they're no longer afraid to name names. And, of course, there's DNA nowadays.' Although she knew that wasn't going to be much help in Yazmin's case.

'The wonders of science,' said Harry. 'Never ceases to amaze me what they can find out these days. But if she's been there all that time, you're not going to find anything useful, are you? Not after twenty years.'

Julie bit her lip and looked away across the room, gazing sadly at the cat sleeping, oblivious, on the windowsill. 'I don't know where the time goes,' she said, turning back to Pam. 'Our first grandchild's due in a few weeks, but I don't know how I'm going to tell our Sonia.'

CHAPTER 26

Curtis Starkie longed to go home, have a shower, eat a proper meal. But he couldn't. Not until he'd spoken to Marco and made sure they weren't in any trouble. Until he knew the police weren't looking for him, he *daren't* go home. It would be dark soon and the temperature would drop. He didn't like the cold.

He'd found his way into an empty house down Gas Lane. Gasholders used to tower over the street, but they'd been dismantled a few years ago. He wished he'd watched them doing that. The best way to find out how things are put together is to take them apart.

There was no electricity, no heating in the house, but he'd grabbed a couple of duvets someone had stuffed halfway into a charity bin outside Sainsbury's. Better than nothing.

Camping out like this reminded him of when he was a kid and Aaron wasn't much more than a toddler. Their Auntie Sue had taken them to the seaside to stay in a caravan. They'd had to use communal showers and washing-up points, find their way to the toilets in the dark, hoping no one had used up all the paper. It'd been fun then, an adventure, but this, now, on his own, was no fun at all. No laptop, no music, nothing to read.

What would he do when he needed to wash his clothes? How would he dry them? He could try Lola's, downstairs from the club. Could you use a launderette if you'd only got a few things to wash?

He needed to eat, and soon. All he'd got were a few crisps and some cheese strings. His stomach ached with hunger.

He ventured out, scooting down the overgrown garden to the footpath that ran along the backs of the houses, ducking down so the neighbours couldn't see him. He tried Marco again as he hurried along, but there was still no answer.

In the paper shop down the road, he stood in front of the chill cabinet trying to choose between cheese and tomato or tuna mayonnaise sandwiches. Decided on cheese and tomato and queued to pay.

His gaze fell on the *Southern Evening Echo*, piled up next to the counter. A headline shouted at him above a photo of Hugh Buckthorn: *IT'S MURDER Earl's gay uncle in suspicious death probe.*

He dumped the sandwiches on a shelf and rushed out. Shit shit shit! He stopped dead, traffic noise spinning round him as if he were in the middle of a manic carousel. He pulled his phone out. *Battery level critical.*

Fuck! He'd have to go to Guys tonight to charge it, scrounge some food, a couple of cans of something. Maybe Marco would be back. Why wasn't he answering his phone?

Lloyd had called him from the club earlier, wanting to know where he was, wanting to know why Marco had run off this morning with the cleaning half-done.

'And he's not answering his bloody phone,' he'd grumbled. 'Fucking waste of space, the pair of you. If it wasn't for who his dad is—'

'I'll be there tonight, okay? I'll cover for him if he's not in.'

'You better had, or I'll fire the both of you.'

Curtis pulled the bag of white powder from his pocket. If he struck lucky, it could make him a tidy profit over the next couple of nights. He'd rather be peddling coke than selling himself.

CHAPTER 27

'Traces of cocaine found in Mortimer's Mini,' Woody said, reading the forensics report that had just come in. 'Prints matching Marco Ross, plus unidentified ones which, I expect, belong to our Mr Starkie.'

Lincoln took the report from him. 'I doubt if the coke was Jonathan Mortimer's. So the lads were snorting coke in the car?'

'The traces were on the floor between the nearside door pillar and the front passenger seat. Reckon a few grains fell out of Curtis's pocket? If it's true that he was meeting his mate to buy drugs—'

'I was rather hoping Marco made that up.' Lincoln sat down heavily at his desk and glowered at his screen, angry with himself for jumping to the wrong conclusion about the young men's movements on Thursday night. He'd seen Marco get out of the Mini and assumed he'd gone down Jackdaw Lane to the mill. He'd seen Curtis tear out of the darkness, desperate to get into the car, and he'd assumed he and Marco were fleeing the crime scene.

The DCI had been more than happy to accept that Marco, directed by his father, was involved in Buckthorn's death, but what would he say when Lincoln told him that the young men were actually in Church Street, visiting Jumbo Hodges to score drugs?

'Reckon the coke could've been for Buckthorn?' Woody wondered. 'He'd got an unopened bag in his wallet, remember?'

'If the prints on the bag match the unidentified ones in the Mini, the coke in his wallet could've come from Curtis.'

'Could be that's why Buckthorn phoned him that evening. Putting in an order.' Woody grinned. 'That's who's fuelling the market these days – the ruling classes snorting coke after their dinner parties. You ever taken anything like that, boss?'

Lincoln shrugged. 'Smoked a few joints when I was younger. Didn't we all?'

Woody shook his head. 'I didn't, no.'

No, of course not: Woody had probably been born strait-laced.

'There was no coke in Buckthorn's system, but he could've been planning to take some later that evening.' Lincoln's phone buzzed with a text. 'Pam's on her way back from talking to Sonia's sister and

172

brother-in-law. Not a word to the DCI, remember!'

'How long are we supposed to put off talking to Sonia?' Dilke asked. 'She might decide to go to the newspapers if she feels we're giving her the runaround.'

'Let's hope it doesn't come to that.' Lincoln stared at the whiteboard, disconsolate. 'I'm worried we've got this case all wrong. Marco and Curtis could be in the clear and the killer's already slipped through the net.'

He'd hoped to hear one of his team contradicting him, assuring him that they were still on the right track, but there was quiet in the room.

Then Breeze piped up. 'If we rule out blackmail gone wrong, and attacking him because he's gay or because he's run up debts through gambling, what are we left with, motive-wise?'

Lincoln perched himself on the edge of the nearest desk. 'The attempted rape at Press Vale? And yes, I know the Cartland case would never have made it to court, with or without Buckthorn, but the DCI's convinced something's going on there, and that Frankie Ross, as one of the directors, is desperate to stop us turning the place upside down. God knows what Jacobs expects to find there – sex workers, drug traffickers...' He sighed heavily, gazing at the whiteboard without really seeing it. He implored it to shout the answer out to him, but it stayed silent.

'So if it's nothing to do with the attack on Amy Cartland, what other motive is there?' Dilke asked. 'Jealous lover? Partner of one of his lovers?'

'Field's wide open,' said Breeze. 'According to the papers, the Honourable Hugh had loads of affairs with women over the years.'

'Yes, when he was younger,' Lincoln agreed, 'but according to Rufus Rayner—'

'Rayner's bound to make out he was the love of Buckthorn's life, isn't he?' Breeze ransacked his pockets for chewing gum. 'Maybe Rufus isn't such a victim as he makes out.'

'His alibi checks out,' said Woody. 'He was having a meal in a pub near his hotel, table booked for eight thirty. He paid the bill at nine fifty-five.'

'Table for two?' Breeze waggled his eyebrows suggestively.

'No, he was on his own. I spoke to the manager myself. He and Rayner had a long chat about the old brewery he's hoping to turn into flats.'

'If there'd been someone else in Buckthorn's life, someone who might have posed a threat, surely Rayner would have said something to us?' Lincoln recalled how distraught the young man had been when he arrived at the Old Shoddy Mill and learned of his lover's death. He'd appeared baffled, uncomprehending, unable to explain why anyone might have taken Buckthorn's life.

'Yeah, but how long had him and Buckthorn been together?' Breeze went on. 'Six months? I've gone longer than that between haircuts!'

'We're getting nowhere fast.' Lincoln turned away from the board. 'And we're running out of time to hold Marco. We'll have to charge him with taking the car without Mortimer's consent and then let him go. Unless anyone's got a better idea?'

'No, but seriously,' Dilke persisted, sounding unusually earnest. 'We don't know who else Buckthorn was seeing, do we?'

'Nothing obvious in his phone records or his emails,' said Lincoln. 'He didn't seem much interested in social media. No dating apps.'

'Or none that you recognised,' Breeze grinned.

Lincoln thought how envious Rayner had sounded, describing the ease with which Buckthorn could pick up partners. 'Any bar you go into,' he'd said, 'if you give off the right signals you'll get a response.'

Had Buckthorn simply picked someone up in a bar or club and brought them back to the flat for a one-night stand? Someone who happened to be a sadistic killer?

But why the staging, the dressing gown, the stockings?

One step forward and two steps back. If only they could get a lucky break!

Pam appeared in the doorway, looking flustered. She hurried across to her desk and dumped her shoulder bag down.

'Well, that was fun,' she said. 'The M27 was bad enough, but then I get back to Barbury and the road to the Green Dragon's at a standstill.'

'How did you get on with the Millers?'

She turned her computer on and pushed her sleeves up. 'Sonia's sister blames herself for assuming it was Bruno with Yazmin, naturally enough. But there's something a bit off about her husband, Harry. He was so sure there was no chance of catching whoever took her away. I'd say he's given it a lot of thought. I'll bet he's looked up what happens to dead bodies after twenty years.'

That sounded promising. 'Alibi?'

'A coach trip to Beaulieu and Lymington, a party of pensioners. He was driving. We could check, I suppose, if we can find out who he was working for.'

'Wouldn't the Park Street team have checked at the time? Okay, they concentrated too much on Bruno Bartek at the start, but their next trace-and-eliminate interviews would've been the immediate family.'

'Well, yes, they interviewed Harry Miller, but I found that note about a gap in his timeline, d'you remember? I've gone over and over it, though, and I can't see how he could have left fifty old dears toddling round the Motor Museum while he drove from Beaulieu to Presford to abduct Yazmin. And in a coach.'

'See what more you can find out about him. But you're right, his alibi sounds pretty solid. Anything else strike you?'

'Only that Sonia got involved in some sort of spiritualist church, got taken in by a medium. Harry Miller doesn't seem to have much time for her.'

Lincoln recalled what Sonia had told him about going to the chapel in Bridgeford – how she'd sought answers and been taken in by people all too ready to take advantage of her grief. 'You really think Miller could be a suspect?'

'Not really, but I'll keep digging.'

'How's your grandad?'

Her face clouded. 'We're waiting to hear whether they can operate or not. All a bit nerve-wracking.'

'It must be. If you need time off—'

'No, it's fine. *I'm* fine.' She turned back to her screen. 'I'll see if I can find out who Miller worked for.'

'But discreetly.'

'Of course. Oh, and I found a contact number for ex-DCI David Soloman, the Senior Investigator. It's a Bournemouth number. He must've moved to the coast when he retired.'

'I don't blame him.'

She grinned. 'I'll call him later.'

Lincoln arrived home to a warm house. Len had been able to fix the leak last night and the boiler was working again.

'That radiator's going to need replacing before long, though,' he'd warned.

Like so much else in the Old Vicarage.

Where had Sonia fled to when Len arrived last night? Lincoln had tried phoning her, texting her, but she hadn't responded. She was so vulnerable, and yet in other ways so tough. Knowing her daughter's fate must have brought some relief, but he doubted if it brought closure.

He sat in his kitchen with a glass of Jameson's whiskey, the lights low, a CD of early Miles Davis playing quietly. He liked his own company, always had, but sometimes on a night like this, cold and bitter outside, at the end of a frustrating day, he craved something more. Maybe if he and Trish moved in together – big 'if' – he could still have his own space. He'd moved into her house for several months last year while the Old Vicarage was being made habitable, but their working hours meant they'd spent little time together. Even when they were both off duty they'd often spent weekends apart, when Trish took Kate to visit ex-husband Vic or his parents.

'Don't you have any interests apart from work?' Trish had laughed. 'You should get out and about more when you're here on your own. You could keep fit at the same time. Walk whenever you can. Get a bike.'

He certainly wasn't getting a bike, but during those months he was living with her and Kate he'd got into the habit of going for long walks when he could. Once he moved into the Old Vicarage, though, fiddly repair jobs and decorating took up most of his free time, and long walks had become a rarity. Maybe in the spring…

Now, revelling in the comfort of warm radiators, he phoned Trish, guessing she'd be curled up with a book or, like him, listening to music.

She didn't answer.

He texted her, telling her he'd call her when he was in bed.

She didn't answer his text either.

He went to bed, rang her again. Texted her again: *You OK? Try you again later.*

But, despite his best efforts, he drifted off to sleep soon after his head touched the pillow, his phone lying on his chest.

Perhaps because he'd been musing about the pros and cons of living with someone, he dreamed about Cathy for the first time in a while. He dreamed they were travelling to the coast for a few days away. Halfway there he realised they hadn't packed anything: no clothes, no toiletries, no bank cards, no cash.

You always do this! the dream Cathy complained. *Now what are we going to do?*

And with the logic of dreams, he found himself calling on George and Kay, Cathy's parents, his former in-laws. Just as he was about to ask them if they could put them up for the night, he stepped into their hallway and fell down, down –

He woke, his heart pounding. He hadn't thought about George and Kay for weeks, not since December, when he noticed they hadn't sent their customary Christmas card. Had they lost his new address, or quietly decided it was time to stop keeping in touch?

He rolled out of bed, irritated that the dream had brought back memories not only of Cathy's parents but also of Andy Nightingale.

He'd hated Andy for stealing Cathy away from him and wrecking their marriage. He'd blamed him, too, for her death – quite unreasonably, of course, but he'd needed to blame someone, and Andy had been an easy target.

But had he ever been angry or jealous enough to consider *killing* him?

At the time, yes.

In his mind's eye he saw Hugh Buckthorn laid out, exposed, on Rayner's couch. Since his return to England, how many other lovers had there been? Even in the last weeks of his life, he'd visited Guys at least twice, most likely looking for sex without strings, although Lloyd Beach had insisted he hadn't seen Buckthorn leave with anyone the few nights he dropped in.

Yet he'd called Curtis Starkie on the night he died. Because he hoped to seduce the young man or because he wanted to buy coke?

Where was Curtis now? Lacking his buddy Marco's bravado, he'd be scared to come forward, but he couldn't stay in hiding for ever.

Two o'clock in the morning and rain began to rattle onto the tarpaulin stretched tight across the roof of the Old Vicarage. Lincoln resisted the temptation to pour himself an unhealthily generous measure of whiskey, and made himself some coffee instead. Then, listening to the World Service, he dropped off to sleep during a repeat of *From Our Own Correspondent*.

CHAPTER 28

THURSDAY 9TH FEBRUARY

Next morning, Lincoln woke to steady rain and thick mist. He wondered if Trish was enjoying better weather in Essex or if it was raining pretty much everywhere across the south of England.

He blundered around in the kitchen, making coffee and checking his phone for messages, although his eyes were too bleary to read his screen. He showered and shaved, dressed, made more coffee, then picked up his phone again.

Two missed calls from DCI Dale Jacobs within the last half hour.

What could be so urgent at this time in the morning? He was afraid his boss had discovered he hadn't shoved the Yazmin Fletcher case onto the back burner after all.

'Go and talk to the Cartland girl,' Jacobs told him when Lincoln eventually got through to him. 'Could be our only chance to find out what's going on at the country club. Let's get to the bottom of where all these girls are coming from.'

'All *what* girls, sir? You still think something dodgy is going on at Press Vale?'

'We've picked up some very credible intel. Still not enough to go in there with a warrant, but if this Cartland kid can give us a few pointers—'

'She'd be putting herself at risk if she did. As it is, they'll probably find some excuse to fire her.'

'So what's she got to lose? Go and see her, find out what you can. See if she's remembered anything else from that night. Use your people skills. Anything new on Buckthorn? DCS Youngman wants to be able to tell the press something.'

'We've got Marco Ross in custody, but we can't hold him much longer. We can charge him with taking and driving away, but that's all.' Lincoln braced himself to deliver the bad news. 'Trouble is, sir, we can't be sure from the CCTV exactly where he went when he got out of the car that night. He could have gone down Jackdaw Lane to Rayner's flat, or he could've gone down Church Street.'

There was a pause heavy with dissatisfaction. Then, 'You sounded fucking sure up till now. What's changed?'

'His account of where he went that night. He told us he was there to collect Curtis from a mate's house, and so far his account checks out.'

'Fuck! What about this Curtis? Any sign of him yet?'

'Not so far.'

'Then look harder! It's too much of a coincidence that Frankie Ross is involved in the country club and his boy's caught up in this murder. Talk to the Cartland kid, use your powers of persuasion. Still not convinced Buckthorn was killed to shut him up, are you?'

'No, sir, I'm not. If someone wanted to make sure the rape allegation wasn't investigated, why kill the only witness, and in such a sensational way? It'd make more sense to shut Amy up.'

At last Jacobs sounded as if he might be taking Lincoln's opinion seriously. 'Yeah, you're right. That would make more sense, wouldn't it?'

Exasperated by his boss's stubborn insistence on digging into Press Vale's affairs, Lincoln drove over to the Cartlands' house. If Jacobs had some score to settle from his time in Bristol, why let his pursuit of Ross jeopardise this investigation? Who'd passed him 'very credible intel' about criminal activities at the country club?

The Cartlands lived on the outskirts of Barbury, in a red-brick cottage that overlooked bleak winter fields and lines of leafless trees.

Mrs Cartland opened the door and invited him in, fussing straight away about making him a hot drink and finding some biscuits, or would he like a scone?

'Black coffee's fine,' he told her, 'a couple of sugars.'

'Mr Lincoln?' Her husband appeared in the doorway of the living room, a hand held out in greeting. He was short with a muscular frame, his shoulder-length greying hair swept back from a weather-beaten face. 'Thanks for coming over. Amy still doesn't want to talk about what happened, especially now.'

'I understand how she feels, but we don't believe Mr Buckthorn's death has anything to do with the incident at Press Vale.'

'So what...?' Cartland's hands were spread as if he were inviting Lincoln to share the details of the case with him.

'The investigation is ongoing,' was all Lincoln could tell him. 'Now, is Amy here?'

Lincoln looked back over the brief notes he'd taken while Amy was talking, though she'd said little that added to her original statement, given at Park Street, that Jacobs had shared with him.

'And you've been working at the country club since December? Is that right?'

The young girl shook back the curtains of shiny blonde hair that framed her face. 'Since the middle of December, yeah.' With restless fingers she pleated the hem of her jersey top. Released it and gathered up another stretch of the bright blue material to pleat and release. 'I was only going to be there, like, temporary, but they kept me on.'

'Tell me again what you were required to do.'

She lifted her chin and stared out of the conservatory window to where magpies were quarrelling on the lawn, marching about as if they owned it. 'I was bar staff officially, but I was supposed to do whatever needed doing to keep the customers happy. Within reason.' She tutted crossly. 'I told Dad I didn't want to take this any further. I wish he'd listen.'

'This probably won't be going any further, but I need to hear your version of events in case anything like this happens there again.'

'That Buckthorn man shouldn't have said anything. He only made things worse.'

Lincoln held himself in check lest he said something he'd regret. 'Mr Buckthorn was prepared to back you up by making a statement,' he said, his jaw tight. 'You should be glad someone was willing to stick their neck out for you.'

'Why are you having a go at *me*? I never asked for his help!'

'No, but he gave it willingly.'

She pouted like a petulant five-year-old. 'Is that why he was killed? Because of me?' Her round face, heavily made up even this early in the day, filled with fear. 'I want to forget that it ever happened. I just want to get on with my life.'

'I'm sure you do, but I need to ask you a few more questions. Are there any foreign-speaking girls working at the country club? Girls brought in from elsewhere?'

'One of the other girls in the bar is from Eastern Europe somewhere. Romania, I think she said. But what's this got to do with what happened to me?'

'Did she say how she came to be working here in Barbury?'

'Came over with her boyfriend, only he went off with some other girl as soon as they got here. But the rest of the girls there are local, as far as I know.'

'Were you expected to let the guests chat you up, buy you drinks, that sort of thing?'

180

'You mean, were we expected to have sex with them?' Her tone was brash, but Lincoln sensed that, underneath this display of bravado, Amy Cartland was scared. She was nineteen years old, still living at home with parents who seemed protective and caring. Yet a man who'd rescued her from her would-be attacker was dead. Lincoln wasn't convinced there was a connection, but Amy couldn't be sure of that. And, ultimately, neither could he.

'And *were* you expected to have sex with the customers?'

She pouted again. 'No one came out and said it, like, but you kind of knew, if someone asked you, you couldn't refuse.'

'You mind if I run through things again? I need to be sure I've got the details right.' He held her gaze, aware of her discomfort but needing her to put up with it a little while longer. 'You were working in the bar, yes? A guest in the Abbey Suite phoned down to order some drinks to be sent up. Can you remember what the drinks were?'

'I'm not sure. Brandy? I can't remember.'

'Just the one drink? Was he on his own?'

'Um...' Amy glanced out of the window. 'Maybe it was two drinks. I'm not sure now.'

'But there was definitely no one else in the room when you got there, as far as you could see?'

'I didn't see anyone else, but they could've been in the bathroom.'

'You put the tray down and he grabbed hold of you. Is that right? From behind?'

Her blonde hair shimmered as she nodded quickly. 'I thought he was going to kill me. Pulling at my shirt, ripping the buttons off. And then he threw me on the bed, undid his zip and got on top of me. He kept trying to push my skirt up, only I managed to roll out from under him. I ran out of the door and Mr Buckthorn was there.'

'What happened to the clothes you were wearing that evening?'

'The clothes?'

'It might not be too late to have them examined in case—'

'I threw them away. I put them in the bin the next day, I was so upset.'

'Oh. That's a shame.' Any hope of making a case against her assailant, or indeed of even identifying him, flew out of the window. Not that Lincoln had expected anyone to be charged, given the lack of an eyewitness and Amy's hesitancy, but even so, with Dale Jacobs being so keen to pursue it...

The clothes would be in landfill by now.

'You said you didn't really see the man, but can you remember *anything* about him? What did he look like?'

'Much bigger than me.' Amy wasn't much more than five feet tall, so that didn't really help much. 'And a bit overweight. Forty-something. Brown hair, kind of going grey at the sides.'

She could be describing *me*, Lincoln thought. 'Did he have an accent? Was there anything special about the way he spoke?'

'Can't remember. I'm sorry,' she said, sounding flustered now. 'Look, I just want to let this whole thing go.'

Lincoln got back to find an unwieldy brown paper sack on his desk. Inside was the leather briefcase from the boot of Buckthorn's Jaguar, his initials stencilled on the flap.

He opened the briefcase and took out all it contained: two books, a spiral-bound notebook, a pencil and three ballpoint pens.

The books were both on art: a paperback on the Renaissance and a slim hardback, published in 1950, on the Italian painter Paolo Uccello, by John Pope-Hennessy.

The notebook appeared unused, though Lincoln flipped back and forth through it to make sure. 'So where are his notes on the paintings he was cataloguing?' he wondered.

'He must have a workspace at the Hall,' Woody suggested, 'somewhere he can leave his stuff. Rayner should know.'

When Lincoln rang the Cheese Market Gallery, it was Tilly Rayner who answered.

'My brother's with a customer,' she said. 'Can I help?'

'Do you know where Hugh Buckthorn was working while he was cataloguing the paintings at Greywood Hall? Did he have an office there?'

'He was using a little room next to the Long Gallery, though I don't know how he could get anything done there. It's absolutely freezing.'

'Sounds as if you've tried working there yourself.'

'I have, actually. When Hugh started, he was writing the entries out in longhand and passing them to me to put on the laptop. But my hands started seizing up with the cold and I couldn't bear it any longer. I gave up after a few days.'

'While I've got you there, can I ask you something? Hugh called your house the night he died. Did you or your parents speak to him, do you remember?'

'Why would he have called the house? He knew Ru was away.'

'If Rufus wasn't answering his mobile, he might've called to make sure he was okay?'

'Then he'd have rung *my* mobile. And he didn't.'

'He didn't leave a message, perhaps?'

'Not as far as I know. Does it matter now?'

'Probably not.' It niggled Lincoln, though: Buckthorn had made a two-minute call to the Rayners' house the night he died. If he didn't speak to any of the family, he must have left a message. Had one of the Rayners deleted it?

Lincoln's next call was to Greywood Hall, where a much older woman answered with rather less affability than Tilly had. Why did he want to visit the Hall? Mr Hugh (as she called him) had hardly ever been there.

At last he persuaded her that a visit was essential, and with great reluctance she agreed to admit him next morning.

'Come to the front gate at nine sharp and ring the bell,' she told him in tones that suggested she'd rather he used the tradesman's entrance. 'Someone will bring you through.'

CHAPTER 29

Curtis was polishing glasses and shelving them behind the cramped bar when Marco walked in, minutes before their shift was due to start. He looked like shit. He'd been at the police station, he said, and they'd charged him with taking the Mini without old Mortimer's consent.

'He'd have let you borrow it,' Curtis said. 'I'm sure he would.'

'Yeah, I'm sure too, but that's not the point. They was asking me about the murder.'

'So Hugh *was* murdered!' He'd been hoping the newspapers had got it wrong, exaggerating the way they do, but the police must know. 'What were they asking you?'

'Where we were that night.'

'Where *we* were?'

'Keep your voice down! If Lloyd finds out, we'll never hear the last of it.'

'Did you tell them what happened? Did you tell them he was like that when we found him?'

'You fucking mad? I told them we wasn't even there. You went down those old cottages to see your mate, and I come over to give you a lift home. They got no proof we was anywhere near that flat. We come up Church Street to get back to the car, okay? That's what I told them. You was with your mate all evening and then I come to pick you up. Stick to that and they got nothing.'

'Why can't we tell them the truth?' Curtis was scared he'd forget what he was supposed to say. Why lie when they'd done nothing wrong? They couldn't have saved Hugh. No point calling the police when he was already dead.

'They'll use any chance they get to dump me in the shit,' Marco hissed. 'They can't find who really done it, so they'll make scapegoats of us, you and me.'

'But Marco—'

'Supposing it was that coke he got off of you? Supposing that's what killed him? How you gonna explain that, eh?'

'You can't put this onto me!'

'No, but the cops will, you wait! You're in this as deep as I am.'

Curtis polished the glass until it squeaked against the cloth. Then he put it carefully up onto the shelf, his head swimming with terrible thoughts of the police and prison and upsetting his mother and never having the future he thought he was going to have.

'Do what I tell you and it'll be okay,' said Marco, clapping him on the shoulder. 'Stick with me, kid, and I'll make you famous.'

Famous for what, though? Curtis's stomach was churning. He flung the glass cloth down and rushed into the lavatories through the door labelled *Hommes*.

CHAPTER 30

The wind was getting up again by the time Lincoln left Barley Lane that evening. Although the sky was noticeably lighter than it had been even a week ago, it was still winter and there was still a chance of snow.

When he got home, he found the boiler had turned itself off again. He swore a few times, turned round and went back out again, pausing only to feed the cat.

In a corner of the bar at the King's Head he rang Trish, one hand pressed against his ear to cut out the noise.

'You didn't answer my text,' he said. 'I was worried.'

'I was with Stewart. We had a working supper.'

'A working *supper*? That's a new one!'

'We'd spent all day lugging books around. We'd earned it.'

Why did he feel so ridiculously jealous? This was a work colleague she was talking about, probably a geeky-looking bibliographer who collected stamps or plastic figurines from *Lord of the Rings*.

She laughed. 'Sounds as if you're having a party yourself!'

'I'm in the pub. My heating's packed up again.' He didn't mean to sound as if he was whining. She had enough to cope with, far away from her family. He couldn't begin to tell her how much he missed being with her, sleeping beside her, waking up with her arm across his belly, her face pressed into his shoulder. 'Are you still coming home for half-term? You said you—'

'Probably not. Kate's going to her father's, which she'll hate after a couple of days, but she's adamant, so there's not much point. I can't face staying with Suki and Mike if Kate isn't there.'

'Stay with me.'

'With no floorboards down, and no heating or hot water?'

'We could go to a nice hotel.'

'Your idea of a nice hotel is a Travelodge on the A303.'

'That was an emergency.' A few months earlier, he'd returned from interviewing a key witness to find police swarming all over the Old Vicarage, pursuing allegations – false, of course – that he'd been up to no good. The nearest Travelodge had been a welcome sanctuary.

She tutted. 'To be honest, it's not worth driving all the way from Essex for just a few days.'

'*I* could come to *you*.'

'Jeff, you're in the middle of a murder investigation. *Two* murder investigations.'

'One and a half. Yazmin's case is meant to be on hold.'

'But it isn't?'

'It isn't.' His hand tightened round his glass. *Say it, say it! Tell her how you feel!* But the words wouldn't come. 'You're right,' he said instead. 'It's a long way to drive, and I really need to be here.'

'I'll call you. What are you doing about the boiler?'

'I'll get Len to look at it again.'

'Len Painter the plumber?' She was grinning. Even over the racket from the bar, he could hear her grinning.

'Yes, Painter the plumber. Maybe he's got a mate called Plummer who does decorating.'

'You were mad to buy that house.'

'I know. I tell myself that every day.'

A long pause, then Trish said quickly, 'I'll call you, then. Saturday?'

'Saturday.' He nearly asked her if she was planning a working breakfast with Stewart, but thought better of it and rang off.

A woman walked in, a bit younger than him, casually dressed, lightly made up. She glanced across at him and he knew they'd met before, had a drink here, gone on somewhere else.

'Hello,' she said, as if she'd been hoping to meet him again but hadn't expected to. 'Want some company?'

CHAPTER 31

FRIDAY 10TH FEBRUARY

Lincoln took Pam along with him to Greywood Hall next morning. Woody was off to Bridgeford too with Breezy, on the lookout for any other CCTV cameras in Church Street that might corroborate – or undermine – Marco and Curtis's alibi for the night Hugh Buckthorn died.

On the way to Greywood Hall, Pam chattered about her grandfather's operation, scheduled for that morning. Lincoln let her talk, guessing it helped soothe her nerves.

'I've been reading up about the Buckthorns,' she said as they came within sight of the Hall's impressive entrance gates. 'The ninth earl, Hugh Buckthorn's father, made himself awfully unpopular. He lost thousands at the gaming tables and treated his tenants appallingly. They welcomed Howard with open arms when he inherited the estate.'

'And now Laurence has blown it by proposing to turn Greywood Hall into a Wiltshire version of Thorpe Park.'

'It's only a zip wire and a woodland assault course, boss. Sounds like good fun to me.'

He didn't bother to argue with her.

Before long, they were driving into the cobbled courtyard and parking beside a tall fountain adorned with cavorting cherubs. Today, though, the fountain was turned off and the cherub-ringed bowl was empty, except for abundant splashes of bird shit.

'We've got to ask for the estate manager,' he said. 'Mrs Pinfold.'

The estate office was housed in what must once have been a stable block. He leaned in over the half-door and called out. A short, dumpy woman popped up from the dim interior and, without saying much, led them through an unassuming side entrance into the main building.

They climbed stairs and strode along corridors and climbed more stairs until they arrived at the Long Gallery, where watery light seeped through a succession of tall diamond-leaded windows onto the faded carpet. Grecian busts on marble pedestals punctuated the opposite wall, staring sightlessly towards the courtyard below. The woman halted abruptly at a door halfway along, produced a key and unlocked the room where Hugh Buckthorn had been working.

They followed her inside. The air felt so chilly, Lincoln wasn't surprised that he could see his breath when he spoke. No wonder Tilly Rayner's hands had got too cold to use a keyboard when she'd tried to help Buckthorn with his catalogue.

'So this is where Mr Buckthorn was cataloguing the paintings?'

'Yes, when he wasn't ferreting about in the attics. That's where most of the paintings are stored, of course – the ones that aren't actually on the walls.'

'Are there many in storage?' Pam asked.

'Only a few hundred.' The woman's lip curled. Was she being sarcastic or trying to make a joke? Hard to tell. 'Of course, they aren't attics as you and I might understand them. They're rooms at the far end of this floor, where it's been blocked off to create storage areas for artworks and furniture that aren't in use all the time. No rickety ladders or stairs to climb!' Even when she was trying to be humorous, her expression remained dour.

'If you'd like to leave us to take a look around...?' Lincoln gestured as if to show the woman out, but she didn't budge until Pam started very gently to push the door shut. Only then did she retreat.

With the door closed and the estate manager safely outside in the Long Gallery, Lincoln and Pam looked at each other.

'Not sure she thought much of Hugh,' said Pam. '"Ferreting about"? For goodness' sake, it's his *home*! They're paintings that belong to *his* family!'

Lincoln looked round the sparsely furnished room Buckthorn had been using as a workroom. Spotting a two-bar electric fire in the corner, he switched it on, watching with satisfaction as the ash-grey elements began slowly to glow dull red and then bright orange.

'He'd be making more work for her, "ferreting about" after paintings that haven't seen the light of day for decades.' He began to search the desk while Pam sifted through papers piled on a bookshelf next to three chunky volumes listing art auction prices.

'I've found the old inventory, at least,' he said. With gloved hands he lifted up an old exercise book. Its cover proclaimed, in large and flamboyant handwriting: *Artworks at Greywood Hall, Summer 1976*. 'That was the year of the great drought. Must've been bliss working in this room during the heatwave.'

Pam took the book from him and turned the pages carefully. 'Who did this list?'

'One of Buckthorn's aunts.'

'There are ticks against some of the entries. Ones he's checked himself?'

'Possibly. Tilly started to type up a database for him, but she got so cold she gave up. I'm guessing Buckthorn carried on writing it out longhand, maybe on cards or in a notebook.'

Pam perused the old inventory. 'There are prices against some of these. Hmm, pretty impressive.'

Lincoln took the exercise book back. '£140,000? £72,000? These don't look like prices from forty years ago – more like now.'

'Was Hugh was putting a current value on them as he went along? For insurance purposes, perhaps?'

'Or to see what they'd fetch at auction if the earl decided to sell them?'

'Or if *he* did? He's got no money, the earl is never here, and no one knows exactly what paintings are in the attics. Supposing Hugh was planning on selling some of them – privately, perhaps, so he wouldn't attract attention? Who's to know what *should* be here? No proper inventory, no record, no trace.'

Lincoln had to admit it was a compelling reason to salvage the unseen works from the attics, to catalogue and photograph them, checking their prices against auction records. Hugh Buckthorn was an expert on Renaissance art, so who better to value and, indeed, market some of the paintings that had been in his family for generations?

But might that lead to murder?

'Let's think who knew he was going through the paintings,' he said. 'Rufus and Tilly Rayner, and the estate manager who showed us in.'

'The earl?'

Lincoln shook his head. 'Laurence didn't seem to know what I was talking about when I mentioned it to him.'

Looking round the small room, he noticed a picture leaning against the wall, wrapped in sacking. It was about two feet by three, and when he peeled the sacking away he saw it was a familiar landscape in an ugly frame. 'That looks like the abbey.'

Pam agreed. 'But a very long time ago. Not a house in sight.'

He lifted the label attached to the metal eye on the back of the picture. '"By Benjamin Osgood *c*.1760. Prior Hill." Where's that?'

'It's not a where, it's a who. Prior and Hill are the auctioneers in Presford. Maybe this painting's one he's decided to sell. We could ask Mrs Ray-of-Sunshine if she knows what he was up to.'

190

The nickname made him smile. The estate manager, Mrs Pinfold, certainly wasn't the cheeriest of individuals. 'Apart from "ferreting about", you mean?'

He carried on searching the desk drawers, finding little more than a few pencils, a metal tape measure and a dog-eared address book. The addresses were mostly art suppliers, framers and so on, but they'd been written in the book some time ago: the London phone numbers had the *01* prefix that had gone out of use in the 1990s. He assumed the address book was Buckthorn's, dating from before he spent most of his time abroad. It might even have belonged to the woman who'd done the original inventory.

'So are we going to explore the attics?' Pam asked eagerly.

'We'll need to summon Mrs Ray-of-Sunshine to show us the way.' Lincoln stooped to switch off the electric fire. Cold air seemed to rush in the moment he did so.

As they let themselves out of the room, Pam's mobile rang. Lincoln waited with his hand on the door as she stepped slowly across the Long Gallery to the windows. She leaned against the window frame, staring out at the rainy courtyard as she listened to her caller.

'Yes,' she said, her voice dull. 'Of course.' Then, 'But can't I—? But won't he—? No. Okay. Yes. Yes.' She bowed her head as she slipped her phone away.

'Bad news?' He let the door go. 'What's happened?'

'He's had a stroke. My grandfather. Something went wrong during the operation.'

'Then you need to get over to the hospital. Now. Come on, let's find a way out of here.'

Lincoln dropped Pam off at Presford General, with strict orders not to worry about work.

'Just let me know how things are going,' he said, and watched her run across the concourse and through the sliding doors.

Driving back alone to Barley Lane, he had time to weigh up the possibility that Hugh Buckthorn was selling off some of Greywood Hall's artworks, perhaps illicitly. Huge sums of money could be involved. Suppose he'd been working with someone else and they'd fallen out?

Dilke looked up. 'You're back early, boss. Thought you'd be gone all day.'

'Pam had to go to the hospital. Her grandad's had a stroke.'

'Oh no! Is he—?'

'Listen, can you read through the transcript of Buckthorn's emails again? We may have missed something.'

'Such as?'

'Was he trying to sell off some of the Greywood Hall paintings? Who was he selling to? He may have gone behind Laurence's back.'

'You can't really put a Picasso on eBay, can you? Not even a lesser known one. He'd need a dealer, wouldn't he – a middleman? Especially if he wanted to keep it quiet.'

'I don't know about a Picasso, but when I met him he told me he was trying to track down a Caravaggio that had been hidden away for a long time. See what you can find out.' Lincoln wheeled round as the door opened and Woody and Breeze came barrelling in.

'Gawd, it's bloody freezing out there!' Breeze rubbed his hands together and pressed them against the radiator. 'Ouch! And now I've burned myself!'

'Any luck in Bridgeford?'

Woody dropped a DVD onto his desk before hanging his coat up and sitting down.

'Some CCTV footage from a jeweller's halfway down Church Street,' he said. 'The camera's over the shop door, but it should pick up anyone walking along Church Street. I'll fast forward to Thursday evening. What time did Marco say Curtis went to his mate Jumbo's place?'

'About seven thirty.'

Lincoln came over to watch the footage on Woody's screen as the seconds ticked by on the counter.

'How did you get on at Greywood Hall?' Woody asked.

'Fine, until we had to drive to the hospital. Pam's grandad. Something went wrong when they were operating. He's had a stroke.'

'Oh Lord!'

'She'll ring when she's got some news.'

They carried on staring at the screen, realising how quiet Bridgeford must be after the shops had shut.

And then, at nearly twenty-five to eight, a scrawny youth scurried by. Badly cut hair badly dyed. He glanced quickly at his reflection in the shop window before turning his collar up and hunching himself inside a jacket too thin for the time of year.

'That's Curtis Starkie. Go back! Let's look at him again.'

Woody restarted the DVD a few seconds before the young man appeared. 'I'll zoom in on his face if I can.'

The moment the youth turned to check how he looked, Woody froze the screen and zoomed in. Curtis looked a bit strange because his eyebrows were missing, making his eyes look wide with surprise. Kohl underlined his lower lashes.

'And this is definitely the same lad that got into the Mini?' Lincoln was confident it was, but he needed to be sure.

'Same build,' said Dilke, who'd come across to look too. 'And that little jacket. He must've been freezing.'

Lincoln could have wept: Curtis was exactly where Marco had said he was, heading down Church Street *away* from the market square and Jackdaw Lane. He was off to buy some drugs from a mate, and that's where he must have been coming from when the CCTV picked him and Marco up nearly two hours later.

'Are we back to square one?' Woody asked carefully, no doubt sensing Lincoln's dismay. Doubt had set in earlier, but this CCTV seemed to confirm they'd got it wrong, that the two young men had come up Church Street to the Mini, not up Jackdaw Lane.

'There's still the dressing gown,' said Dilke. 'And Buckthorn phoning Curtis earlier. There has to be a connection.'

Lincoln nodded unhappily. 'Let's look at the rest of the footage. We should see Marco going past on his way to collect Curtis from Riverbank Terrace.'

Lincoln watched the CCTV footage all the way through, but there was no sign of Marco Ross going down Church Street as he'd said he had. That much of his story was untrue.

However, the alibi he'd given Curtis seemed solid: at a few minutes after nine, Curtis was scurrying back up Church Street towards the market square, pausing outside the jeweller's to admire his reflection in the window. He'd smoothed a fingertip over his shaven eyebrows and run a hand through his multicoloured hair.

He evidently wasn't in Rayner's flat helping Marco set the scene for an apparently accidental death.

And yet, less than thirty minutes later he was haring from the shadows towards the stolen Mini, agitated and in a panic because Marco hadn't opened the car door quickly enough.

It didn't add up. What had happened between him pausing to check his reflection outside the jeweller's and his dash to the car? Where had he gone to in those crucial twenty minutes or so?

'I hoped this footage would show us where Curtis was, one way or the other,' Lincoln had to admit, 'but it just adds to the uncertainty.'

Woody didn't say anything, but Breeze puffed his cheeks out and said sullenly, 'It's the only camera we could find, boss. Don't blame us because it doesn't show what you want it to.'

Lincoln chucked the marker pen onto his desk and shoved his hands through his hair. What a bloody useless day!

'If we could track down this drug dealer mate of Curtis's,' Dilke said, 'he might be able to tell us where he was off to when he left there.'

Breeze hooted. 'What, you're saying Curtis went, "Right, now I'm off up the road to kill this earl!"'

Lincoln's patience ran out. 'Right now, it's *Curtis* we should be looking for, not his druggie mate. I'll ring Sharon Starkie, see if she's heard from him.'

But Sharon hadn't seen her son since Monday morning, and sounded genuinely worried. 'He's never stayed away this long,' she told Lincoln. 'I'm scared that Marco's got him into trouble somehow.'

'What makes you say that?'

'Now his dad's back, who knows what Marco's getting up to?'

'But I heard they don't get on.'

'Oh, they've had their ups and downs, but now he's getting married again, Frankie's all over him and Marco's lapping it up. It upsets Curtis, the way Marco brags about him. Best thing that could happen is that Frankie takes his boy back to Spain with him, though I don't suppose Curtis would want that.'

And neither would Gabriella, Lincoln guessed.

'Whyever he looks up to Marco, I don't know,' Sharon went on. 'But that lad's a charmer like his dad, and I'm scared he's talked my Curtis into doing something stupid.'

So maybe Jacobs was right about Frankie Ross and his son being involved together in Buckthorn's death. Had Curtis merely been a pawn in this game of murder, disposed of by more powerful players once he'd served his purpose? Lincoln hoped not.

As soon as he put the phone down, Dilke called him over.

'Buckthorn emailed Stoakley's auction house in December,' he said, highlighting the relevant lines of the transcript, 'asking about a Caravaggio, wanting to know when it was sold.'

'And what's the answer?'

'They can't say. A private sale.'

'Maybe he was trying to *buy* it,' Woody suggested.

Breeze chortled from behind his screen. 'You any idea how much you'd have to pay for a Caravaggio, Sarge? Even *I* know you're talking loads of money. The guy was hard up!'

Woody shrugged. 'Reckon maybe he had one tucked away, then, and wanted to know what it was worth.'

Lincoln recalled his last conversation with Buckthorn. 'He told me there was a Caravaggio somewhere in storage at Greywood Hall. He wanted to exhibit it next year, try to bring the crowds in.'

'How do you know what something's worth if it's never been on sale before?' Woody wondered.

Dilke shrugged. 'And how do you prove it's what you say it is?'

'You turn to the experts to help you establish the provenance,' said Lincoln. 'There were plenty of experts listed in the address book we found at the Hall, though it looked a bit out of date. But come on, why would someone kill him over this?'

Woody shook his head. Dilke stared at his screen.

Breeze leaned back in his chair, tilting it at a risky angle. 'Who's got most to lose if Buckthorn's selling the paintings off?'

'The earl,' Lincoln said. 'But he didn't even seem to know Buckthorn was cataloguing them, let alone trying to make some money out of them.'

'There wasn't anything out of the ordinary in his bank accounts,' said Dilke.

'But if Buckthorn wants to flog some paintings for big money,' said Breeze, 'he won't want the dosh coming into his bank account, will he? He'll want to hide it from the taxman.'

'A numbered Swiss bank account? Can you still get those?'

Lincoln shook his head. 'They're a thing of the past, Woody. You'd have to set up a company and hide behind that. We've found nothing to suggest Buckthorn's ever had that kind of money, or that he's actually sold any of the paintings. All we found – all *Graham* found – was some tentative email approaches to auction houses.'

Woody sighed in frustration. 'So what are we left with? Why was he killed?'

The room went quiet again. Breeze's jacket squeaked as he reached into his pocket for his nicotine gum and posted another piece into his mouth.

'Hatred,' he said, his breath spicy. 'Someone wanted him dead, but they wanted to humiliate him too.'

'So now you're saying it's personal, Dennis?' Lincoln got up and slowly paced about. 'Not a warning to other gay men or rich men or rich, gay men, or people with gambling debts?'

'I know that's what I thought before,' Breeze admitted sheepishly, 'but like you said, they nearly got away with making it look like an accident, and that doesn't send a message to anyone.'

'Who hated Buckthorn so much that he – or she – wanted him dead? Who's he crossed in the six months he's been back home?' Lincoln threw the question out, but he wasn't expecting an answer. 'Is his killing simply random?' he asked at last. 'Did he pick someone up that night and take them back to the flat for kinky sex and they attacked him? Could it be as simple as that?'

'So Marco buying a dressing gown like his was just a coincidence?' Dilke sounded sceptical.

'That crime scene didn't look random,' said Woody. 'A pickup that's gone wrong would've looked chaotic. They'd have run out of there like greased lightning.'

Lincoln agreed. 'Someone took time to tidy everything away, clean up. Buckthorn was drinking wine before he died, so what happened to the bottle and the glass, or glasses? We found nothing in that flat that shouldn't have been there, nothing left behind by a killer in a panic. So no, *not* a random pickup gone wrong.'

'Maybe Marco's involved, but not Curtis,' Dilke suggested. 'Maybe the two lads *aren't* in this together.'

Lincoln didn't know what to believe. Gambling debts, a lovers' quarrel, rough sex gone wrong, the Press Vale incident: none of those motives was compelling enough to justify a murder so sadistic and theatrical.

'We've set a lot of store by what Rufus Rayner has told us about Buckthorn,' said Woody. 'But as you said yourself, boss, they'd only known each other six months. We haven't talked to anyone else who might've known Buckthorn better.'

Woody was right, but who was there to ask? Laurence, Lord Riverbourne, had dismissed his uncle as a risk-taker who should have done more to help his brother. The estate manager, Mrs Ray-of-Sunshine, had regarded him as a nuisance. Who else could they ask?

'What about those friends of his in Sixpenny Lane, where he parked his car?'

'The Merediths?'

Dilke phoned them. The person who answered was a house-sitter, looking after the place while they were in Norway. 'They like to ski,' she told him. 'And Norway's one of their favourite places.'

Another dead end.

'It's been a week since we first went to that flat,' Lincoln said wearily, 'and we're not getting anywhere. What are we missing?'

CHAPTER 32

Frankie was doing his cuffs up as he came into the room.

'You want me to come with you?' Donna asked. She saw he'd fastened the left one but was struggling with the right. 'Let me.' She knelt up on the sofa cushion as he offered her his right cuff. 'You must be one of the few men I know who still wear these.' She slipped the cufflinks into place and took his hand in both hers.

'Me, your dad and who else?' He lifted one eyebrow, teasing.

Probably someone even older than her father. 'It's nice. Adds a bit of class.'

He pulled away from her, grinning. 'What, and I don't have enough class without them?'

'Course you do. You know what I mean. They're sophisticated. So you don't want me to come this evening?'

He checked himself in the big mirror, smoothing his tie down, tweaking his collar. 'No. It'll be all business talk tonight. You'd be bored shitless.'

She'd be bored shitless here in the hotel, waiting for him to come back, but she could tell by his tone of voice that he didn't want her there. It'd be all boys together at the country club, drinking, telling dirty jokes, hatching plans. No place for a woman.

His mobile vibrated on the coffee table. She could see *Marco* flashing up on the screen. Frankie grabbed the phone, then quickly rejected the call.

'You should have answered it,' she said. 'I wouldn't have minded. He'll wonder why you don't want to speak to him.'

'I'll call him back when I'm in the car. And I don't need you to tell me when I should answer my own fucking phone.'

'I only meant...' She didn't want to seem jealous of Marco, resentful of the attention Frankie gave him. There'd been friction between them, she knew, trouble stoked up by his bitch of a wife poisoning the boy's mind against his dad. But Frankie was trying to heal that rift now, and Marco sounded keen to make amends too, for father and son to spend more time together.

'When do I get to meet him?' Still kneeling on the seat, Donna leaned over the back of the sofa, resting her chin on her arms. She was going to be a stepmother. She still couldn't get her head round the idea, but maybe once she'd met Marco it'd be easier. He was only twelve years younger than her so it was going to be strange, but she'd do anything to please Frankie, to make their marriage work out better than his first one had.

'You'll meet him when I'm ready for you to meet him. Don't keep on at me!'

She slid down on to the sofa, hugging her knees. 'You'd better go or you'll be late.'

He dropped a kiss on the top of her head and left the room. She heard him lifting his overcoat off the coat rack, his scarf, his trilby. She imagined him arriving at the country club, handing his hat and coat to the guy on reception, smoothing his hair back and striding into the meeting room. He'd be the most stylish man there. Commanding. Who else knew what a softie he could be in private? She smiled to herself.

When she heard the front door slam, she crossed to the marble fireplace and gazed at her reflection in the big mirror above it. Ash-blonde hair, grey eyes. Diamond ear studs he'd given her as an engagement present. Even her father had been impressed.

She'd known Frankie since she was a teenager, when her father first became one of his clients. A client, and then later a friend, a golfing buddy. She'd been involved with one or two men her own age, nearly married one of them, but once she'd fallen for Frankie there was no going back.

Donna was pleased that Frankie and his son had patched things up. Would Marco approve of her? The wedding was set for Easter, and then Frankie planned for them to return to Spain as soon as they were back from their honeymoon. Marco could stay with them for a few weeks in the summer. She couldn't wait to fly out there, get away from this bloody awful weather, to recover from this long, dreary winter.

The phone rang, and she picked it up without thinking.

'Is Frankie there?' A gruff voice. 'It's Marco.'

'Marco? Hi. No, he's had to go out. It's Donna here. Can I take a message?'

'I don't leave fucking messages!' He rang off.

She put the receiver down gently, as if that would soften the blow of his anger. Glancing in the mirror, she saw a bright spot of colour in each cheek. Marco was going to be more of a challenge than she'd anticipated.

CHAPTER 33

'Well, that was quite a week!' Trish stood, hands on hips, as she surveyed the library shelves that were filled once more with Charles Lundy's extensive collection, thanks mainly to Stewart's efforts.

Stewart beamed with pride. 'At least we can see the wood for the trees at last. We can start the cataloguing now.'

She shoved her fringe back from her forehead. 'Let's call it a day and come back to it refreshed on Monday. I don't know about you but I'm knackered.'

He grinned slowly. 'Sorry. I'm just impatient to get to work on the collection.'

She grinned back. 'It'll still be here on Monday. We can come back rested and raring to go!'

He picked his jacket and coat up, grabbed his bag. Checked his watch. Tutted.

She glanced at her own watch. 'Oh no, I haven't made you miss your bus, have I?'

He slipped his jacket on. 'No worries. There'll be another one around seven.'

'But look—' She waved towards the big windows that overlooked the water. 'It's snowing or sleeting or something. You can't wait around in that. I'll give you a lift home.'

'No, I really can't ask you to do that.'

'It's my fault you've missed the bus.'

'If you're sure...?'

'I'm sure.' She locked the library door, crossed the hall and ran up the stairs to her flat. As she keyed in the entry code a shadow fell across the door, making her mis-key the last digit. She turned quickly.

'Sorry,' said Stewart. He reached out and pressed the push-button timer that turned the landing light on.

She caught the tang of his aftershave or body spray, a faint scent of sweat beneath it. 'Thanks.' The second time she entered the code, the door opened. 'Won't be a sec.'

She dived into her flat, shutting the door very decisively behind her. The place was a mess, apart from anything else, but even if it had been pristine she wouldn't have wanted Stewart coming in here this evening. She was tired, in need of time on her own. It had been a hectic week and she felt physically and mentally drained.

And she hardly knew him.

She put her coat on and stuffed a woolly hat in the pocket. Picked up her bag, making sure she'd got her phone. This time of year, in this bleak, unforgiving landscape, she dreaded her car breaking down.

When she opened the door again the landing light had gone off, leaving her in total darkness. Her heart thudded. She couldn't see Stewart, but then she heard the swish of his coat as he swiftly punched the timer switch again. Her pulse settled.

'These can be adjusted, you know.' He banged his fist against the switch. 'It hardly stays on long enough for you to get all the way up the stairs.'

'Adjusted?'

'There are switches inside, controlling how long it stays on for. I can fix it for you tomorrow.'

'Tomorrow's Saturday.'

'So?'

'Monday's soon enough. I've managed okay so far. Thank you anyway.'

She drove him to Chelmsford through rain and occasional squalls of sleet.

'Where shall I drop you?' If she drove him to his door, he might invite her in and she'd have to make some excuse.

'Here's fine.' He pointed to a row of late-night shops and takeaways, all lit up, plastic crates stacked outside one of them, wheelie bins lined up outside another.

She pulled up alongside the kerb. 'See you on Monday.'

'Thanks for the lift. You're sure I can't fix that light for you tomorrow?'

'No! Enjoy your weekend!'

He clambered out and slammed the door, then began to walk along the pavement past the garish shopfronts. Did he live in a flat over one of these shops? She'd imagined him somewhere smarter.

Before she pulled out from the kerb, she glanced in her rear-view mirror and saw he'd stopped outside the Asian grocery shop. Rather than drive any deeper into the town itself, she reversed into a side road to turn around. Frost was beginning to form on the tops of cars. It'd be a cold night.

As she drove back the way she'd come, she saw Stewart waiting at a bus stop farther up the street from where she'd dropped him off. She was tempted to stop and ask him if he needed a lift all the way home, but then decided it would embarrass both of them.

Less than half an hour later she was back in the flat, tidying up while she waited for some pasta to cook. It reminded her of life in the bedsit she'd had to share when she started at university, before Vic rescued her and they'd escaped together into a rented two-bed house. If only their marriage had worked out! But at least they'd had Kate, so it had been worth it.

Should she have let Stewart come over tomorrow to adjust the light switch? He wasn't a qualified electrician, though, and she could be in trouble if he messed it up. He was certainly more personable than she'd expected, and not as irritating, even though he did know so much more about Lundy and his books than she did. Why hadn't *he* applied for the job she got?

When the pasta was cooked, she tipped it into a dish and shook some ketchup over it. So much for healthy eating, she thought, forking spaghetti into her mouth without really tasting it, glancing at her phone the way she was always telling Kate not to.

She flopped onto the sofa, a novel open on her lap. She'd spend a few minutes reading and then she'd ring Jeff. She knew he was disappointed she wouldn't be in Barbury at half-term, but she couldn't face staying with Suki and Mike. She could stay at the Old Vicarage – but supposing Jeff still hadn't got the boiler sorted out?

She missed him. She hadn't expected to land the Essex job, not really. She'd longed for him to beg her to stay, but he hadn't. Had he thought this job was what she wanted? Yes, it was a challenge, and she needed to leave her post at Barbury Library, but if he'd told her he wanted her to stay, she could probably have found something nearer.

Too late now. By the time her contract ran out, he might have met someone else and settled down, given up on her and Kate.

She'd phone him in a minute. She'd read a chapter or two and then she'd phone.

But she'd fallen asleep before she'd even read a couple of pages.

CHAPTER 34

'My grandad's died.' Pam's voice on the phone was so quiet, Lincoln could hardly catch her words. 'He didn't regain consciousness.'

What could he say that wouldn't sound banal? 'I'm so sorry, Pam. Is there anything I can do?'

'I need a couple of days off, that's all. Mum's in a bit of a state and I don't like to leave her. But what about Harry Miller? I was trying to track down the company he worked for.'

'The details will be in the file, won't they? I'll get Graham to follow it up.'

'I'm sorry.'

'Don't be. You need to look after your mum.'

When Pam rang off, Lincoln looked round the deserted CID room. Friday evening, late, and he'd sent everyone else home after an intensive few days trying to solve Hugh Buckthorn's murder. He was in no rush to leave: he'd be without central heating another night, since Len Painter the plumber couldn't get to him until tomorrow evening.

Poor Pam! She was close to her family, and losing her grandfather must be a huge wrench. He guessed she would also berate herself for needing to take time off in the middle of an investigation.

He sighed, trying to sort out in his own mind the link between the incident at Press Vale and Buckthorn's death. Assuming there was a link.

Dale Jacobs was convinced someone at the country club had had Buckthorn killed so Amy Cartland's allegations wouldn't be investigated. He kept dropping hints about reliable tip-offs to do with criminal activity at Press Vale, but he'd never come up with anything concrete or specific. It was as if he were looking for an excuse to undermine the place – and to have a go at Frankie Ross.

And now Lincoln had to admit that Marco may not have been at Rayner's flat after all, demolishing Jacobs's theory that he killed Buckthorn on Frankie's orders. Yes, Marco had bought that dressing gown, and yes, Buckthorn had phoned Curtis earlier that evening, but the CCTV footage of the two young men emerging into the brightly lit market square couldn't show for sure where they'd come from: Jackdaw Lane or Church Street.

Sitting at Pam's desk, Lincoln leafed through her neat piles of paperwork. He opened the folder of press articles about Hugh Buckthorn and reread news stories he could recall from thirty-odd years ago when he was an impressionable Worcestershire teenager. Photos of young Hugh making the most of London's nightlife had made him yearn for the glamour and excitement of the capital. When he'd moved to London himself only a few years later, though, he'd soon found the glamour was fake, the excitement short-lived.

Now, he turned a page and saw a piece Pam had photocopied about Howard Buckthorn's sudden death last year. Howard had a widow, of course: Laurence's mother. She must know at least a little more about her brother-in-law than her son did. The Dowager Countess of Riverbourne, Lady Adelaide Buckthorn.

But where did she live? Somewhere on the estate?

Back at his desk, he searched for her on the Internet and discovered she'd stayed on at Greywood Hall after her husband's death. In the few photos he found of her she looked imposing, with a fondness for headscarves and Barbours. Like the Queen, only taller.

He'd call the estate office in the morning and ask to speak to her. Maybe at last someone would be able to throw some light on what her brother-in-law had been up to.

CHAPTER 35

SATURDAY 11TH FEBRUARY

Lincoln was halfway to Barley Lane next morning when Dale Jacobs phoned him.

'The Cartland girl's gone missing.'

His mouth went dry. 'Missing? Since when?'

'Didn't come home last night. Went out to meet some mates in Presford, left them around ten, hasn't been seen since.'

'Where did they meet up?'

'Some bar called the Cadillac.'

Lincoln could visualise it – the old Coach and Horses, gutted and refurbished, popular with young drinkers. 'Who's dealing with it?'

'My team here. Come in and tell them what you know.'

As he was led through Park Street's incident room, Lincoln marvelled at how much more up to date the equipment and the furniture were. The CID room at Barley Lane resembled something out of the Dark Ages in comparison.

Jacobs was already waiting in the conference room, seated at the head of a huge, highly polished table. On either side sat an officer: a dark-haired woman Lincoln recognised from some training course or other, who introduced herself as DS Orla Cook; and DI Rick Nevin, with whom Lincoln had worked a while ago, a similar age to himself, overweight and nearly bald.

'Rick and Orla here need all you've got on Amy Cartland.' Jacobs pitched forward, hands folded on top of a pile of paperwork. He moved awkwardly because, Lincoln realised, his injured foot was elevated on a stool beneath the table.

Lincoln told them all he knew: that Amy had run into Hugh Buckthorn's arms in her escape from the Abbey Suite after she'd been attacked by one of the guests. The country club manager, Olly Powell, hadn't felt it necessary to involve the police, and Amy herself had been anxious to let it drop.

'She didn't even tell her parents what had happened until a day or two later,' he explained, 'by which time the rooms had been cleaned. Unfortunately she's thrown away the clothes she was wearing that night.'

'All of them?' asked Orla in disbelief. 'Why would she throw all of them away?'

'She was traumatised, not thinking straight.'

Nevin ran a hand over his polished scalp. 'Doesn't help us much. We might've been able to get something off them.'

Lincoln snorted. 'Helping the police wouldn't have been uppermost in her mind at the time. She wanted to get rid of any reminders that someone tried to rape her.'

Jacobs patted the air between himself and Lincoln. 'Let's calm down, shall we? Either way, we need to find her. Let's start with her workplace, talk to other staff at Press Vale, see if she was close to any of them.'

And have a poke around the country club for foreign girls who shouldn't be there, Lincoln thought bitterly.

He watched as Dale shoved a sheet of paper at Nevin and at Orla: some sort of briefing note about Press Vale.

'Could something have happened to her because of this attack, sir?' Orla asked. 'Someone's tried to shut her up?'

'Let's treat this as a missing persons case for now. No jumping to conclusions. But yes, it's something we'll have to consider if she doesn't turn up.' Jacobs glanced across at Lincoln as if expecting a challenge, but Lincoln had nothing to say. He could only recall what he'd said so blithely a few days earlier: that if Amy's attacker wanted to avoid investigation he should have eliminated Amy, not Buckthorn.

And it looked as if someone had decided to get rid of them both.

'Are we reading too much into this?' Nevin sat back in his seat. 'She's a young girl, out for a night on the town, goes to a bar, leaves without her friends... It's copybook, isn't it?'

'What, so she was fair game?' Orla threw him a sharp look.

'No, I'm saying it's most likely someone's spotted her coming away from the Cadillac a bit the worse for wear and he's followed her, taken advantage. We need to look at CCTV round the club, follow her as far as we can, see if anyone's tailing her.'

'And any boyfriend she might've broken up with,' Orla put in, 'any guy who might bear her a grudge.'

'We can find that out from the people she works with.' Jacobs sounded energised as the list of actions grew.

'Ask her friends first,' said Orla. 'They're the ones who'll know.'

'And talk to her parents,' Lincoln urged. 'She seems to be close to them.'

206

Orla sneered at the suggestion. 'They're the *last* people she'll have confided in!'

He felt like quietly sneaking away.

Jacobs let him off the hook. 'Not sure there's much more you can do to help us at this stage, Lincoln. Thanks for your input. Keep me posted, yeah?'

'Amy Cartland's disappeared.' Lincoln pulled his chair out and turned his laptop on. Got up again and headed for the kettle. 'Park Street's dealing with it.'

Woody looked shocked. 'Is this connected to the incident at Press Vale?'

Lincoln shrugged. 'It's handed the DCI the excuse he was looking for. Now he can go in there and turn the country club upside down on the pretext of looking for her.'

'Has anyone spoken to the manager there?' It was Dilke who spoke up. 'Buckthorn took Amy to his office, didn't he? Who did the manager tell?'

'Buckthorn didn't feel he took Amy's allegations seriously, didn't expect him to act on them.'

'Doesn't mean he didn't tell his bosses,' Woody said. 'He'd want to warn them there could be trouble coming their way.'

Lincoln held his hands up. 'Not our concern now. Let's leave it to Park Street.'

The kettle boiled and a round of hot drinks got made. There was none of the usual chatter.

'She could've gone home with a boyfriend,' Breeze offered as he went back to his desk, 'someone her mum and dad don't know about. Girls do that.'

An incoming text made Woody's phone ping. 'Hey, it's from that lady in Riverbank Terrace. Jumbo's back at number 4.'

The little row of cottages was quiet and dank. A ginger tomcat sauntered along the path ahead of Lincoln and Woody, pausing to pee on number 3's wheelie bin before trotting off towards the river.

Woody chuckled. 'Charming! Let's hope Jumbo Hodges gives us a nicer welcome.'

Lincoln shivered and turned his collar up. 'God, these houses must be hellishly damp.'

'Mills need water,' said Woody, who knew about such things.

'Bridgeford relied on the mills for work. That's where most of its wealth came from.'

'Not much evidence of wealth here.' Lincoln pushed against the door of number 4 and it juddered open. The distinctive scent of marijuana hung in the air, underpinned by the pondweed tang of sodden brickwork and the stench of a blocked toilet.

A halogen heater had been installed in the living room since their last visit to the cottage, and it had certainly warmed the place up. Something, or someone, stirred in the shadows on the far side of the room.

'What the fuck you want?' The gruff voice of a young man barely awake.

Woody made the necessary introductions. 'We're looking for James Hodges. Is that you?'

'Bastard coppers! I done nothing.'

'We didn't say you had. Listen, James, we need your help.'

Lincoln studied the young man who'd emerged from the tangle of duvets and blankets that lay, an untidy nest, against the far wall. When he stood up it was obvious that, however he'd come by his nickname, it wasn't because of his size.

Jumbo Hodges wasn't much over five feet four, and looked unhealthily thin, his jeans and sweatshirt hanging off him. His short hair was patchy, as if he'd pulled it out in clumps, and a similarly patchy beard shadowed his bony cheeks and chin. Had he let the beard grow so he looked less like an anaemic ten-year-old?

Lincoln tried the light switch and was surprised to find it worked, a low-wattage bulb coating the filthy room in phlegm-coloured gloom. 'We're looking for a mate of yours. Curtis Starkie. Ring any bells?'

'Haven't seen him in a while.'

'How long a while? This week? Last week?'

'Last week sometime. Thursday? The night that Buckthorn guy killed hisself.'

Lincoln didn't waste time putting him right. 'You're saying Curtis was here that evening? What time?'

'Seven thirty? A bit after. He come off the bus.'

That agreed with the time Curtis had passed the jeweller's shop. 'Remember what time he left?'

Jumbo shrugged his bony shoulders. 'About nine? He was shitting hisself about missing the last bus back into town.'

'The last bus goes at twenty-five to ten,' said Woody, who must have made a point of checking. 'He'd have caught it easily if he left here at nine.'

'Yeah, but he had to see someone first.'

'Who was that, then?'

'Didn't say.'

Lincoln cheered inwardly. The CCTV footage had picked Curtis up at a few minutes after nine, pausing to check his reflection in the jeweller's shop window. That gave him nearly half an hour before the bus left the market square.

Long enough to call on Hugh Buckthorn in Rufus Rayner's flat. Long enough to sell him some coke, but long enough to seduce him? To slip him Rohypnol and assist in his murder?

'Did he say *who* he was going to see before he caught the bus?' Woody went over and tugged the curtains open, letting weak sunlight dribble in over the sofa, the floor, the messy armchairs.

'Can't remember. We were having a few drinks, a few smokes. Kind of messes with your head, y'know?'

'You sell him any coke?' Lincoln asked as he picked his way to the kitchen through the rubbish on the floor.

'Not me, no.' Of course not.

In the kitchen, Lincoln hooked the fridge open with his little finger. Someone had refreshed its contents since he and Woody had been here last, though it was still dotted with black mould. He suddenly thought of Tilly Rayner restocking her brother's immaculate fridge, oblivious to the presence of Buckthorn's dead body only a few feet away. What a shock that must have been for her!

He shut the fridge and stepped back into the living room. 'You remember him getting a text while he was here?'

'No idea. Might have.' The lad's face contorted with anxiety, as if he was worried that wasn't the right answer.

Woody squatted down and warmed his hands on the heater. 'What did you fall out over?'

'Don't look into that heater,' Jumbo warned him. 'You'll go blind.' Then: 'We didn't fall out. Who said we did?'

'Sure you didn't argue, have a row?'

'Why would we? We're mates, me and Curtis. We was in the same class at school. Both freaks,' he added with a laugh that turned into an ugly-sounding cough.

'You know where we can find him?'

'Lives with his mum up Barbury Down.'

'Yeah, we've tried there,' said Woody. 'He hasn't been home.'

'He goes round with an arsehole called Marco Ross, but I don't know where he lives. In town somewhere.'

'Was Marco here that night? Did he come to pick Curtis up?'

'Marco? Haven't seen that nutter in months.'

'So much for Marco's version of events,' said Woody.

They were driving back to Barley Lane, the weather deteriorating as they left Bridgeford behind.

'We knew he was lying when we saw the CCTV footage from the jeweller's. He didn't go down Church Street like he said he did, and Curtis walked back towards the market square on his own.' Lincoln switched the wipers on, but the sleety rain smeared itself across the windscreen faster than the wipers could sweep it away. 'But was it Buckthorn that Curtis was going to see? To sell him some coke? Or meet him for sex?'

'Reckon whatever he was planning, things didn't work out, or he wouldn't have been racing up to the Mini in the market square twenty minutes later.'

Lincoln sighed, exasperated. 'We're not going to find out until we speak to Curtis himself.'

Back at his desk, he learned there was no news of Amy Cartland.

'The DCI's been trying to get hold of you, Boss,' Dilke told him. 'Your phone must be switched off.'

Coffee took priority over phoning Jacobs back. Lincoln could still taste the stagnant air of Riverbank Terrace.

'Who owns those cottages?' he asked Woody while the kettle came to the boil.

'The Riverbourne Estate, most likely. Why?'

'Doesn't seem right, Greywood Hall standing empty and people like Jumbo Hodges living in their own shit.'

'Reckon lads like Jumbo would live in their own shit if you gave them a mansion on Barbury Park Avenue.'

'Which reminds me. What address did Marco Ross give when we let him go on Thursday? I should've checked sooner.'

'I'll find out.' Woody settled down at his desk.

Coffee in hand, Lincoln rang his boss. 'Sorry, sir, my phone must've been off.'

'I should be able to get hold of you 24/7, Lincoln, not when you deign to turn your fucking phone on. We're going into Press Vale tonight.'

Was he talking about *raiding* the place? 'Not till tonight?'

'More chance of finding out what's going on there if we leave it till then.'

'But if Amy's there...if she's in danger...'

'A few more hours isn't going to hurt.'

Lincoln's fingers clenched round the phone. 'You don't know that.'

There was an empty pause. 'Questioning my tactics, Lincoln?'

'I'm questioning your priorities.'

The next pause was even emptier. Then, 'Well, don't! I may have come in from Avon and Somerset, and I may be a good fifteen years younger than you, but I'm your senior officer, okay? Understood?'

'Understood. But I still think—'

'Well, don't bloody think! Just follow orders, okay?'

Lincoln took a deep breath. 'Did the CCTV outside the Cadillac give you anything useful?' he asked, as levelly as he could. 'Could you see where Amy went when she left?'

'Still checking. None of the cab companies remember her.'

Lincoln had reassured her father that Buckthorn's murder was nothing to do with the attack on Amy, but had he got it wrong?

'Can you track her mobile? Maybe—'

'Park Street's got this, Lincoln. Your job is to find Buckthorn's killers. And talking of phones, fucking keep yours on, okay?' He rang off.

Lincoln drank his coffee, resisting the urge to hurl it at the whiteboard. He was suddenly aware of Dilke hovering by his desk.

'Was that the DCI, boss?'

'How did you guess? Not sure Jacobs and I have really hit it off.'

'He's from Bristol,' Breeze called across. 'They do things differently there.'

'I've been going over Hugh Buckthorn's murder,' said Dilke, still hovering.

Breeze snorted. 'Like the rest of us haven't been!'

'What about it?' Lincoln left his desk and went over to the whiteboard, glad that the timeline could be updated since the conversation, such as it was, with Jumbo Hodges.

'We've been working on the theory that Marco and Curtis went into the flat, slipped him some roofies, got everything set up when he was unconscious, yeah?'

Lincoln nodded, wondering where this was going.

'But now we've seen the CCTV from the jeweller's, we know Curtis could only have been with Marco for maybe twenty minutes after he came back from seeing his mate.'

Lincoln nodded again, running his gaze along the timeline as he listened.

'So who was helping Marco set things up in the flat?' Dilke came up to the whiteboard too. 'He couldn't have done it all on his own, could he? He got out of the Mini at quarter to nine, while Curtis was still with his mate. How long do roofies take to work?'

'Fifteen minutes, half an hour?'

'So if Marco doesn't even reach the flat until, say, ten to nine, allow fifteen minutes until Buckthorn's out of it...'

'How could Marco get everything set up on his own in half an hour? That's what you're saying, Graham?'

Lincoln tried to visualise Marco struggling to undress Buckthorn, who, if not insensible, would have been very drowsy. Stripping him and then putting the dressing gown onto him, the stockings and suspender belt, laying him out on the couch –

'Buckthorn's a good six foot,' he said. 'Must weigh about eighty kilos. Marco's a strong-looking lad, but you're right, how's he going to manage all that on his own?'

'If Marco's involved at all,' Dilke said, 'there must have been someone else in the flat helping him.'

In Lincoln's head, Dale Jacobs's voice was yelling a name at him: *Frankie Ross*.

'No one else came into the market square after Marco and Curtis, though, did they?' he said.

'No, boss, but we kind of stopped looking once those two appeared, didn't we?'

He was right. Lincoln had that sinking feeling again, knowing he'd overlooked something elementary. What was he always telling his team? *Never assume* – advice he himself had ignored.

'Okay, Graham, look at the CCTV again—'

'Gnome cam?' Breeze chuckled.

'Yes, Dennis, gnome cam. See if anyone else emerges from Jackdaw Lane – as far as you can tell, given how shadowy it is – in the hour or so after the Mini drove off.'

Woody leaned back in his chair, eyeing the whiteboard. 'The other end of the lane's a dead end, isn't it? Could someone have gone out that way, though?'

Lincoln shook his head. 'It's blocked off because of the building work, and no way of getting round the barriers by the old chapel.'

Woody and Lincoln scrutinised the network of narrow lanes and streets that made up Bridgeford's centre, searching for some other escape route Buckthorn's killer or killers might have taken. But no – the only way out was back up the lane to Church Street and the market square.

'Can't we question Marco again?' Woody sounded as frustrated as Lincoln felt.

'Not until we've got something new to put to him.'

'We have. We know he lied about going down Church Street to pick Curtis up from Jumbo's.'

'It's not enough.' And if his father really was involved, Marco would be unlikely to risk incriminating him. Contrary to what Gabriella Ross had told them, her son and his father had clearly reached some sort of reconciliation.

'You asked what address Marco gave when he was bailed,' said Woody. 'It's 84 Commercial Street.'

Lincoln frowned. 'Commercial Street? Isn't that where Guys is?'

A quick Internet search confirmed that 84 Commercial Street was the address of Lola's Launderette and Guys Club.

'Reckon there's staff accommodation upstairs?' Woody wondered. 'It's a three-storey building. He works there, so maybe he's been sleeping there as well since he got chucked out of Avalon Row.'

'Or he's using it as an accommodation address while he's sofa surfing. I don't suppose he wants to go home to his mum now he's patched things up with Frankie.'

'Where's the Fruit Machine King living when he's not abroad?' asked Breeze. 'Maybe Marco's moved in with him.'

Lincoln rang Gabriella to ask, braced for a chilly response.

'I have no idea where Marco is,' she said dismissively. 'He wants to suck up to his father, he's welcome. They deserve each other.'

'Where's Frankie staying while he's over here?'

'He's taken a suite at the Black Swan.' She put on a posh voice to say it, audibly unimpressed by her ex's pretension. 'And yes, it's expensive, but he'll have sussed out some way to claim the costs back through the business. Frankie Ross didn't get rich by paying his way.'

As soon as Lincoln put the phone down, he picked it up again and dialled the number for Greywood Hall. When he was put through to Adelaide Buckthorn, he explained that he was hoping to talk to her about her late brother-in-law.

She sounded less than delighted to hear from him.

'I really can't tell you anything more than you can learn from the newspapers and the Internet, Inspector. Hugh was abroad for most of the past twenty years, even when his father was dying – which put a massive burden on my husband's shoulders. I would describe our relationship as estranged.'

'You must have spoken to him—'

But before Lincoln could finish his sentence, the Dowager Countess of Riverbourne had very firmly put the phone down.

CHAPTER 36

Barbara Trent looked out of her sitting room window and saw a slightly built woman walking up the road towards the forest, her strides long and slow as she tackled the slope, a woman who didn't seem used to country walks. She wore a sort of patchwork coat and lace-up boots, with her hair in a ponytail. She wasn't local.

'Come on, Corky. Walkies.'

While Barbara fought her way into her mackintosh, the little terrier scrabbled at the door, eager to get outside even though it was cold and damp and sleety.

Where the metalled lane petered out and became the chalky track into Greywood Forest, blue and white police tape still encircled the tree trunks, inadequately blocking access to Ploughboy's Pit. The tent and the other paraphernalia from ten days ago had been whisked away, but Barbara tutted to see all the takeaway trays and paper coffee cups still littering the area – rubbish left behind by the police and the journalists, gawpers and ghouls.

Ploughboy's Pit was now sealed with fresh steel plates, shiny and heavy, laid flat across from wall to wall and padlocked in place.

The woman had reached it and stopped. She was scowling down at the sparkling metal expanse as if she found it offensive.

Barbara knew who she was, had suspected that was who it was as soon as she saw her loping past her window, heading for the woods.

'Sonia?'

The woman spun round at the sound of her name. Her eyes were huge, her face pale, hollowed out by grief. 'Yes?'

At Barbara's feet, Corky was investigating a takeaway wrapper, snuffling and scuffling. 'I'm the one who...' She halted, watching her dog while she searched for the right way to say it. 'We were the ones who found your little girl.'

Ten minutes later, the two women were sharing a pot of tea in Barbara's sitting room.

'I guessed it was Yazmin,' Barbara said, passing shortbread to Sonia, who politely waved it away. 'Because of the timing.'

'Timing?'

'She was lying on some bags of cement left over from when the council were up there.' She tried to be as delicate as she could. Sonia might've been upset that Ploughboy's Pit had been covered up, but she'd have been horrified if she'd seen the state of the place where her daughter's bones had been lying all these years.

'What were the council doing up there?'

'Filling it in – or that was what they were supposed to be doing. My neighbours' boy – they've moved away now – it was his first job after he left school, so I remembered it was '96 they were doing it, pumping cement in, the mixer going for days on end. He tramped mucky boot prints all up the path and into the house. His mother was livid, although at least it meant she had him home for his lunch.'

She laughed, but she should've known Sonia wouldn't see the funny side. Life had seemed simpler then, Barbara reflected. She'd still been working for the earl, her parents were still alive, although her father's health had already begun to fail.

She glanced across at Sonia. Such a wan little face! 'You'll want to arrange a funeral, won't you?' she said. 'To celebrate her life.'

'Did you see her? Did you see Yazmin?'

Barbara hesitated, but then, prompted by the way Corky had settled himself on the rug, she said, 'She was curled up as if she'd put her head down and gone to sleep.' Would that console this poor woman? Could anything?

'I wanted to look for her cardigan – the one her grandma knitted her.'

'They put that steel cover on, closed it up. Unless the police have already taken things away...?'

Sonia's mouth was set in a tight line. 'They won't tell me anything. It's killing me, not knowing.'

'Your husband? Yazmin's father?'

'He died.' Sonia hung her head, her ponytail sliding round, exposing a neck that looked too fragile to hold her head up. 'I didn't even know. He'd been dead for months before they found me to tell me.'

'That must've been awful.'

'Have you got kids?'

Barbara shook her head. 'I was a career woman,' she said, brightly enough to dispel any sympathy Sonia might have felt obliged to offer. 'And I was looking after Mum and Dad.' Though any thoughts of marriage and children had been put out of her mind long before she was forced to assume the role of carer. 'I worked at Greywood Hall,' she added, so Sonia would realise what a wise choice she'd made. 'Personal assistant to the earl.'

This didn't seem to impress Sonia much. 'Did you see a white cardigan there, near Yazmin?' she asked. 'Or a doll?'

'I couldn't see much. It was quite early. We'd had that terrible gale and now I've still got a load of scrap metal in my garden I can't get rid of. Aren't the police going on looking for clues?'

'They've given up. Because of this man that was murdered. Did you know him? You must've done, working for the earl.'

Barbara pushed her hair back from her forehead. 'Yes, the earl I worked for first was Hugh's father, Robert, and then I worked for his brother, Howard.'

'Aren't you scared?' When Sonia looked up, her eyes were full of terror, the pupils dilated.

'Scared? Why should I be scared?'

'Living on your own when there's a murderer at large.'

Barbara's thoughts flew back to her childhood fear of the forest, the banshee-wailing of the wind in the firs towering over Greywood Terrace.

'I've got Corky. He won't let anything happen to me, will you, boy?' The little dog's ears pricked up, but he didn't open his eyes.

'Why's it called Ploughboy's Pit if it was the army that dug that hole in the first place?'

'There was a well there long before the army took it over and enlarged it. I suppose the farm workers used it to fill the water troughs in the field. There was some legend about a ploughboy reaching into the well to grab a gold sovereign he saw in the water one evening. He reached in to grab hold of it, lost his balance and fell into the well and was drowned. Of course, what he'd really seen was the reflection of the moon.'

Sonia's eyes widened in horror. 'Did that really happen?'

Barbara wished she hadn't said anything, but it was too late now. 'Parents make up stories to scare their children away from danger, don't they? Cautionary tales.'

'I suppose so. Did you say it was the council that filled the hole in?'

'Yes. Well, half-filled it in and then gave up. I don't suppose anyone came to inspect their handiwork. Even then it wasn't like the old days, when a supervisor would come round to check.'

Sonia pushed her cup aside. 'Thank you for the tea. I need to get back now.'

CHAPTER 37

After half an hour's scrolling through the CCTV recorded by the gnome cam, Dilke spotted someone else emerging from the shadows on the edge of Bridgeford market square the night Hugh Buckthorn died – only this time it was clear from his position that he was exiting Jackdaw Lane, not Church Street.

'What time's this?' Lincoln craned forward to read the time stamp.

'Twenty-two sixteen.' Dilke paused the image as the man strode briefly into the glare of the street lamps.

'That hat's casting too much shadow over his face,' said Lincoln. Could that be Frankie Ross?

No sooner had the man stepped into the market square than he had disappeared again, moving out of range of the gnome cam's lens.

'Did the chemist's CCTV pick him up?' Woody wondered.

'That's even worse quality than the gnome cam, but I'll check it anyway.'

Woody opened his lunchbox and extracted a foil parcel that he carefully opened on his desk, paper napkin at the ready in case of spills. 'What was the DCI so mad about?' he asked, prising a cheese and pickle sandwich out of its wrapper.

'I asked him why he was waiting till tonight to go into Press Vale. He didn't like me questioning his tactics, as he put it. But he should be talking to Amy Cartland's colleagues *now*.'

'Why the delay?'

'He must be hoping the team will see more activity if they wait till tonight. More of these "illegal sex workers" – should they even exist.'

'Seems to have it in for Frankie, doesn't he, the DCI?' Woody bit into his sandwich. 'Can't believe Press Vale would get into that sort of thing. It's got a respectable reputation to protect.'

'True, but Pete Doubleday's still one of the owners, and look at the criminal connections *he's* got!'

'The original Teflon Man – nothing sticks.' Woody dabbed at a blob of Branston pickle clinging to his moustache. 'Reckon they've got some history?'

'History? Ross and Jacobs? There was some sort of clash when

218

Jacobs was in Bristol, something to do with Ross's aggressive sales pitch. But you don't get to be the Fruit Machine King without being a bit pushy.'

'Are we talking protection, though, d'you think? Putting pressure on pubs and clubs to take his systems?'

'Maybe, but he's never been charged with anything. I'm pretty sure he's clean.'

'I'll look him up.' Woody finished his sandwich and wiped his fingers carefully. 'I'll let you know if I find anything.'

Dilke came over with a printout from the chemist's shop camera.

'He's only visible for a couple of seconds,' he said as Lincoln took the printout from him. 'And not much clearer.'

They studied it together. 'That's not a baseball cap, is it?' said Lincoln. 'More like a trilby.'

'Is he trying to hide his face from any cameras?'

'Possibly.' Would Frankie Ross wear a trilby? 'And that's the only appearance he makes?'

Dilke nodded. 'Doesn't help much, does it? He could be anybody.'

'Except there's nowhere else he could have come from but the Old Shoddy Mill. Where Hugh Buckthorn was lying dead. Stick it on the board, Graham. We need to find out who he is. Check the jeweller's CCTV, see if he went down Church Street after that.'

'Nothing on record about Frankie Ross,' Woody said, coming across, 'but under his real name, Franco Rossetti, he was convicted of common assault in 2000. He chased after a couple of lads he thought had keyed his car, and got into a set-to with their father.'

Lincoln was taken aback. 'Not quite so squeaky clean, then.'

'And there was something else, wasn't there, a few years ago?' Breeze ambled over to join the discussion, builder's brew in hand. 'Can't remember the details, but it got in the papers. Bloke called Carrick, Garrick, Garrett, something like that. Same line of business as Frankie. They were going after the same contracts and then this bloke was found dead.'

'So?' Lincoln had to coax the punchline out of him.

'There were rumours it was down to Frankie.'

CHAPTER 38

'Did you speak to an Inspector Lincoln, Laurie?' Adelaide Buckthorn was drinking tea with her son in his house overlooking Abbey Green. The upstairs drawing room was cosy – unlike most of Greywood Hall – and she was charmed by the view. Through the sleety rain, the bare branches looked like wild black scribbles on the ancient grey walls of Barbury Abbey, and she relished the warm homeliness of Laurence's house. 'Did you talk to him about Hugh?'

'Briefly. Why do they assume Hugh was murdered? I should've thought it was obvious he was messing around with someone and they slipped up. Why make it worse for us, turning it into some huge mystery?'

Laurence stood up and paced restlessly across to the big windows, staring out unhappily at the dreary afternoon. Adelaide felt terribly sorry for him. People kept phoning to offer their condolences, no doubt hoping to find out more than the newspapers could say about the circumstances of Hugh's death.

She still couldn't believe he was gone. She'd never say anything – goodness, it was no secret at the time – but she and Hugh had been an item years ago, when she was trying to choose between going to university and working in Switzerland as an au pair for friends of her parents.

She was twenty-one and Hugh twenty-three. He'd fallen out with his father because he wanted to get a job in an art gallery instead of going into the army.

'We could get married,' he'd said to her, 'run away to London, live in a garret.'

'You can't be serious.'

He'd laughed: that gorgeous laugh, the handsome face, film star good looks, his mother's colouring – and, perhaps, her Italian temperament, impulsive, passionate, romantic. 'Let's just run away together, then,' he'd begged, 'if you won't marry me.'

For a few short months she'd been tempted, drawn to him far more strongly than to his older brother. But, even then, there was something about him… She'd sensed already that he'd never settle down to married life, too much the adventurer, too addicted to the adulation he'd enjoyed all his life. He had girlfriends everywhere.

Instead of university Adelaide had chosen Switzerland, putting herself beyond Hugh's reach, far enough away for her to get over their silly romance. Within months, though, her father had died, she'd returned home, and Hugh's father had invited her to stay at Greywood Hall. Had he decided she'd make an ideal wife for Howard, his son and heir, already turned thirty and still single? Whatever his intentions, he'd brought her and Howard together for good, their marriage lasting nearly thirty years.

'I want to do the right thing by Laurie,' Hugh had told her after Howard's funeral, when he'd decided to give up his home in France, move back to England, to this corner of Wiltshire if not to Greywood Hall. 'This is his heritage, after all.'

Yes, the future of the Riverbourne title depended on Laurence now. Howard and Adelaide's first son, Thomas, had died in a riding accident as a child, when Laurence was still only a baby. The old advice about producing 'an heir and a spare' became painfully apposite, especially when she was warned against having another baby after Laurence's difficult birth.

She glanced across at her son, now twenty-five and due to become a father himself in the summer. Of course, he'd naturally prefer this elegant house to the Hall, but how she longed to have him closer to her! Would she ever be able to persuade him to move back there?

He crossed to the fireplace, leaning his arm along the mantelshelf as he bent to poke the fire. 'We should make plans for the funeral.'

'We can't do anything until the police release the...' She bit her lip, sought other words but failed. 'We can at least talk to the funeral director, start to make arrangements.'

'Did he make a will?'

'Of course. Your grandfather insisted your father and Hugh both made wills. Why do you ask?'

'God, Ma, imagine how we'd feel if he'd left anything to that Rayner fellow!'

She groaned. She'd met Rufus at an exhibition to which Hugh had invited her. She'd spent the evening trying to imagine what life might have been like if she'd run away with Hugh instead of settling down with his brother. It would have been less comfortable, certainly, but a lot more fun. She was sure if he'd found the right woman he wouldn't have felt the need to seek out men.

Why on earth had he been attracted to Rufus, who was pudgy and gingery, with fair skin and freckles? It wouldn't have lasted. Hugh loved the sun, but that horrid little Rufus must have to hide from it.

'We must arrange to see Hugh's solicitor,' she said wearily. 'The sooner we get things moving the better.'

'The police said something about the paintings.' Laurence rested the poker against the hearth and straightened up.

'What about them?'

'That Hugh was cataloguing them.'

A prickle of alarm made her stiffen. 'He didn't need to do that. Your Aunt Dodo did an inventory years ago.'

'Hugh said something to me about bringing out pictures that have been in storage for years. He thought we could work towards an exhibition, bring the public in.'

'Those paintings are in storage because they're not worth displaying.' She thought of the attics at the end of the Long Gallery, room after room of dreary pictures swaddled in sacking. She hadn't been entirely honest with Laurence: his great-aunt Dorothy had certainly started to catalogue the paintings decades ago, but she'd fallen from her horse out hunting and never fully recovered. The work had been left unfinished.

Trust Hugh to want to interfere! She'd seen him coming and going from the Hall, but hadn't realised what he was up to. It saddened her now to think they could have spent some time together, even though she feared he was no longer the man with whom she'd once been in love.

'Did you tell anyone he was going through the paintings?' she asked cautiously. 'Did you mention it to anyone?'

'No, why would I?'

'I'd hate to disappoint anyone who might be expecting some sort of treasures to be unearthed.'

'God, you don't think...?' He looked round at her sharply.

'What?'

'Could something really valuable be tucked away up there? If we could find a painting that might turn things around—'

'I doubt that very much, my darling,' she said. To signal the end of the matter, she reached for her phone and tapped on the calendar. 'Now, let's see when we're both free to speak to the solicitor.'

CHAPTER 39

Gerry Garrick had been found dead in his warehouse in Presford fifteen years ago, apparently killed by tripping over a cable and hitting his head against a workbench when he was in pursuit of an intruder. No one had been arrested in connection with the break-in, although Breeze was right: there had been a fierce, if short-lived, newspaper campaign waged by his widow, who was adamant that his business rival was responsible.

That business rival was Frankie Ross.

Lincoln skimmed the newspaper articles Dilke had printed off. A chill ran through him when he read what Lisa Garrick had said.

'He made it look like it was Gerry's fault. He made it look like an accident.'

'Thanks for this, Dennis,' he said. 'Shame you didn't remember it sooner.'

'It's a long time ago.' Breeze chewed his nicotine gum, unapologetic. 'I'd forgotten until you put that picture up.' He nodded at the shadowy photo of the man in the trilby. 'He was always a smart dresser, Frankie. Just reminded me of the photos of him in the papers when it all kicked off. But nobody *really* thought it was down to him. I mean, he'd won awards, Businessman of the Year and all sorts.'

Lincoln picked up the phone to call his boss, but then changed his mind. Jacobs already thought Frankie Ross was responsible for Buckthorn's death. Why give him the satisfaction of knowing he could be right?

As he dropped the receiver back into its cradle the phone rang, making him jump. He felt foolish, and hoped no one had noticed.

DCS Youngman didn't bother with niceties. 'I've had Dave Soloman on the phone,' he barked. 'Weren't you told to park the Fletcher girl's case?'

'I was, sir, yes, but that was after we reached out to DCI Soloman.'

'*Ex*-DCI Soloman. And DC Smyth left him a message this Wednesday, but I gave you clear instructions—'

'I'm sorry, sir, she was simply following up an action I'd given her—'

'Monday, I gave you that order, via DCI Jacobs. *Monday.* Yet on Wednesday—'

'I didn't want to miss the opportunity to find out from DCI – *ex*-DCI Soloman – if there was any other paperwork we could be requesting while—'

'You went against my orders! Or was it DC Smyth who took it into her head to—?'

'No, sir, I take full responsibility.'

'So I should hope.'

'I didn't want Sonia Fletcher to turn to the media for support because we didn't seem to be doing anything. We shouldn't be keeping her in the dark day in, day out. I don't even know if the SOCOs are still going through what we found in the pit. I can't even tell her—'

'They've been told to stop. We don't have the resources to comb through bucketloads of stinking rubbish in search of – well, what the hell are we going to find after twenty years, hmm?'

Lincoln turned back towards the room, towards the faces of his team. He knew Youngman was right: the DCS was the senior officer setting priorities, having to justify this expenditure here, that cutback there. But that didn't make it any easier to accept.

'Can I ask what David Soloman said to you, sir? I was hoping to get his own impressions, anything else he could point us towards. I didn't expect him to react this way.'

DCS Youngman sighed heavily, as if he'd run out of steam. 'He didn't phone to complain. He assumed DC Smyth was at Park Street, so that's where he phoned. Staff on the desk referred him to me. Do you ever follow orders, Jeff? Or just the ones that suit you?'

Before Lincoln could reply, Youngman said sharply, 'I've told David to contact you direct. I should bloody suspend you, but I'm giving you another chance. Don't waste it.'

CHAPTER 40

Sharon Starkie emerged from the outhouse, where she'd been stacking newspapers and cans for recycling. She had a terrible headache, could hardly hold her head up for the pain, wanted nothing more than to go back indoors and lie down for an hour or so – except she was terrified of missing a phone call, a text. Scared of not being awake when Curtis rang.

The outhouse door always swelled in the damp, so she had to tug it hard to close it. As she finally got it shut, she heard a strange sound from the outside lavatory next to it. She listened, holding her breath, and her headache thumped in her temples like something trying to hatch from her skull.

'Mum?' Curtis's voice came quiet and echoey from behind the door. Then he opened it slowly and stepped out. He looked like a ghost, thin and dirty, his hair greasy, clothes crumpled.

She was so relieved to see him, she clouted him round the head before bundling him indoors with a ferocity that surprised them both.

'Have you *any* idea what you've put me through?' she yelled once they were in the kitchen. 'I haven't slept a bloody *wink*. You didn't answer my calls, my texts. I don't even have a number I can reach you on at work. I've been going out of my mind with worry.'

He pulled a chair out and slumped down at the table, putting his head down on his folded arms. 'I couldn't help it!' he sobbed into the table. 'The police are looking for me.'

'I bloody know they are! How d'you imagine I felt, knowing my son was wanted for *murder*?'

He lifted his head up, his face streaked with tears. 'What? They're saying *I* did it?'

'The police were asking me about Marco. What the fuck's he got you into?'

'He hasn't! We haven't got into anything! We just found him, that's all! He was already dead!'

She stared at him. He'd found a dead body. Never mind that he should have stuck around and called someone, but he'd seen that Buckthorn man dead. It wasn't right that he'd had to see that.

'What were you doing there, Curtis? Why did you go there?'

He wouldn't look at her.

'Curtis! Why were you there?'

He put his head back down onto his folded arms. 'I can't tell you!' he moaned. 'I can't tell you!'

CHAPTER 41

While Lincoln was looking through Pam's paperwork in search of the coach firm that had employed Harry Miller, Dale Jacobs rang.

'No joy at the country club,' he said flatly. 'No sign of the Cartland girl.'

'Wasn't the plan to go there tonight, sir?' It was still only a little after four.

'Change of plan. Decided not to wait any longer in case the kid was in danger.'

Hard not to say *I told you so*. 'Did they turn up anything else of interest?' Like a cellarful of Eastern European sex workers.

'Nope. Ross wasn't there either. Spoke to the manager, Olly Powell, though why you'd put a little tosser like that in charge of somewhere charging two hundred quid a night for a spa retreat, I don't know! Says there was no one staying in the Abbey Suite that night, so can't give us the name of the man who attacked her.'

'But Amy went up to the suite because he ordered drinks. There must be some sort of record.'

'If there ever was, he's wiped it – probably on Ross's orders.'

Lincoln's patience with his boss was wearing thin. 'Ross might be a director, but what makes you think he's hands-on? And he's abroad most of the time.'

'Yeah, well, he's not abroad now, is he?' The DCI sounded dejected, but Lincoln had little sympathy for him. If something dodgy really was going on at Press Vale, then going in there mob-handed, as he'd originally intended, would have been disastrous.

'But no sightings of Amy?'

'Nothing. She went out of range of the cameras outside the Cadillac and that's the last anyone's seen of her. Where are you on Buckthorn?'

'A man came out of Jackdaw Lane, much later than Marco and Curtis. We don't know where he went after that. He wasn't picked up on the camera in Church Street.'

'Shit! Any idea who he is? Description?'

'Tall, well built, wearing a trilby.'

'A trilby?' Jacobs's dejection turned to glee. 'Frankie Ross wears

227

a trilby. Snappy dresser, Frankie. What did I tell you, Lincoln? Frankie Ross and his son killed Buckthorn together.'

'But why?'

'To shut him up about the attack on the Cartland kid, of course!' His self-satisfaction was audible. He was probably smirking. 'We need to bring him in, get him to tell us where he was the night of the murder. If that CCTV puts him near the scene—'

'It could be some old boy in a trilby walking his dog.'

'What sort of dog?'

'Couldn't see it.'

'Because the guy in the trilby was Frankie Ross. There was no dog. Bet you anything.'

'So now what?'

'Time someone talked to him about Amy.' Jacobs abruptly ended the call.

Lincoln turned to Woody. 'The bloke in the trilby's Frankie Ross. So says the DCI, so who am I to argue?'

'What, no bollocking for carrying on with the Yazmin case?'

'Doesn't sound as if Youngman's told him.'

'Reckon David Soloman can tell us anything we don't already know?'

'Probably not, but it's worth a try. As the SIO, he should've had oversight of everything to do with Yazmin's case. If *he* can't add anything, I don't know who can.' Lincoln turned his laptop off. 'I need to get home. The plumber's coming round to look at the boiler.'

'There's one thing we still haven't worked out,' said Woody as Lincoln put his mac on and picked up his keys. 'Why did Buckthorn go to the flat that night?'

'Rufus said he sometimes crashed there if he'd been out on the town.' Lincoln edged towards the door.

'Yes, and if he hadn't got his car. But he drove to Bridgeford that night. He didn't have a drink until he got to the flat.'

'He'd arranged to buy coke from Curtis.'

'But why go to the flat?' Woody persisted. 'They could've met in the market square before Curtis caught his bus. Buckthorn could've handed Curtis his money and got his coke without even getting out of the Jag.'

'If we ever find Curtis, we can ask him.'

On the way home, though, Lincoln reflected on Woody's question. Why *had* Buckthorn gone to the flat? He'd had nothing with him to suggest he'd planned to stay there overnight. And wasn't it bad manners to have casual sex in your lover's apartment?

Was he meeting someone for some other reason? Was he there to meet Frankie Ross? But why? Did they even know each other?

He turned into the driveway, pleased to see Len drawing up too. They went into the house together, the plumber nattering about what he thought could be the root cause of Lincoln's central heating problems.

'It's all to do with the condensate pipe,' he was saying, but much of what he said was lost on Lincoln, whose mind was still circulating thoughts about Hugh Buckthorn.

He made coffee for himself, tea for Len, and sat at the kitchen table while the plumber got on with sorting out the problem pipework. He didn't take a daily newspaper, but he picked up *The Guardian* on a Saturday sometimes, if only to catch up on current affairs that otherwise passed him by. After ten minutes or so, Len stuck his head round the door.

'Gotta pop out to the van for a couple of things, Mr Lincoln, okay?'

'Fine.'

Lincoln had spent several fruitless minutes on the crossword when he heard the door open. He turned, expecting to see Len, but someone else was there instead: a man in an expensive-looking coat over an expensive-looking suit. And holding a trilby.

Lincoln leapt up, sweeping the newspaper onto the floor in his haste. Len must have left the door on the latch while he slipped out to his van.

'Inspector Lincoln?' The man was as tall as him but broader, heavier. A man with greying dark hair, black eyebrows, a swarthy complexion. 'Frankie Ross.' He held his hand out, but Lincoln ignored it. Ross jerked his head back towards the hall. 'The door was on the latch.'

'Didn't mean you could walk in.'

'I'd like a word.'

'Not sure that's appropriate.'

'No, Inspector, but it's necessary. You arrested my son.'

'Your son took a car without the owner's consent. That's against the law.'

'You interrogated him about Hugh Buckthorn's death while you were at it, didn't you?'

'I don't need to justify my actions to you. I was doing my job. Your son was in the vicinity of a crime scene. I needed to eliminate him from our enquiries.'

'And did you?' Ross took another step farther into the kitchen.

'Not entirely.'

'No?' A quizzical frown. Ross dropped his hat onto the table. 'What d'you mean?'

'What I said. We haven't entirely eliminated Marco from our enquiries into the murder of Hugh Buckthorn.'

'How can you be sure it's murder? From what I've heard, Buckthorn was a risk-taker, into bondage and all that kinky stuff.'

'Who did you hear that from? Because if you've got evidence that could help the investigation—'

'We obviously don't read the same newspapers, you and me.' Ross bent down, an agile man despite his sturdy build, and retrieved the *Guardian* from where it had fallen on the floor. 'No, we certainly don't.' He laughed softly as he held the folded paper out to Lincoln, who took it grudgingly. 'Beautiful house, this, Inspector,' he went on, his gaze roaming calmly over the high ceiling, the original tall cupboards that Lincoln had retained, the old range he'd had adapted. 'Must be costing a fortune to do up. How can you afford it on an inspector's salary?'

'You shouldn't be here. If you think you can intimidate me—'

'Intimidate you? I promise you, Inspector, if I wanted to intimidate you, you'd know about it. Not that I would, of course.'

He pulled a chair out and sat down at the other end of the table, waiting for Lincoln to sit down too before continuing. 'The police came swarming over the country club this afternoon. Makes me feel like a criminal, having you lot turn up unannounced like that.'

Lincoln noted the possessive way Ross spoke about Press Vale. Had he been there after all but lying low? 'We're trying to trace Amy Cartland, Mr Ross. The officers were hoping her colleagues could help us find her.'

'You'd be better off asking her friends about her, asking her family. No, you came to the club because you were fishing.' Before Lincoln could put him right, he went on, 'And I know it's not your team, but it's *your* boss. Dale Jacobs has got a bug up his arse about me, and I don't like it – especially when his obsession extends to my son.'

'You make it sound personal. I'm sure—'

'Because it fucking is. It fucking *is* personal. Ask him why he left Bristol.'

The sound of the front door opening startled both of them, but Ross recovered quickly, pushing his chair back and standing up.

'Got 'em!' Len held his fist up. 'Took me a minute to find the right olives.'

'Olives?' Lincoln queried.

'Ferrules,' Ross said. 'For a tighter seal.'

Len beamed at him. 'You a plumber?'

'Mechanic. Jack of all trades, really.' Ross grabbed his trilby and, smoothing back the wings of steely grey hair at his temples, put it on. He tapped the crown. 'Nice talking to you, Inspector. Do remember to ask Dale next time you see him. Ask him why he left Bristol.'

Ross had turned on his heel and marched out of the front door before Lincoln could dodge round Len to follow him. By the time he'd rushed down the drive to reach the gate, Ross's tail lights were already disappearing down the road.

CHAPTER 42

SUNDAY 12TH FEBRUARY

Pam gently lifted her grandfather's tweed jacket up from his bed and hugged it to her. The smell of his Old Spice aftershave still clung to it, as well as the bay rum he used on his hair.

'It's too soon, Mum,' she said. 'We don't need to go through his things yet.'

'I need to find his best suit, though, and that nice blue shirt he liked.' Her mother's voice was muffled as she turned back to the suits and jackets and coats hanging neatly inside the wardrobe.

For the funeral, of course. The undertakers would need to know what to dress him in.

'And there's nothing else we can do today,' her mother went on. 'We can't get the certificates or start ringing round until tomorrow, and I need to be doing something.'

'Let's have a cup of tea before we do anything else.' Pam stroked the jacket and laid it down lovingly on her grandfather's bed, trying not to let her gaze linger on the dent in the pillow, the spectacle case on the bedside table. The new Ian Rankin novel she'd bought him for his birthday a month ago lay face down where he'd left it, not quite finished when he'd been taken ill. Now he'd never know how it ended.

The tears welled up again and she hurried down the stairs to make the tea.

The weather had changed dramatically in the last few hours, the sun appearing, the wind dropping, the air losing its chill. Any other Sunday like this she'd be out on her bike, exploring the back roads, stopping to photograph houses or churches or farms that appealed to her. She might have cycled through Greywood Forest this weekend if...

If none of this had happened. Standing in her grandfather's pantry a few minutes later, staring round at all the tins and packets of food he'd bought and would now never open, never finish, Pam felt an emptiness so wretched she couldn't imagine how she'd live with it, get through the next few days, the next week, the next month...

'Where's that cuppa?' Her mother's voice was bright, but her face told another story.

As they sipped their tea, Pam's mum leafed through her father's copy of *The Messenger*, which she'd forgotten to cancel.

'Look, Pam, there's a bit about that little girl being found.' She pointed to a short paragraph beside a blurry photo of Ploughboy's Pit. 'Used to hate going past that when Dad and I used to cycle up that way.'

Pam sat back. 'I didn't know you and Grandad used to cycle up through Greywood.'

'Long time ago, love. Probably when I was thirteen, fourteen? Gave your gran a break from having us around all the time in the holidays. We'd take a flask, sandwiches, go off for the day. But that place...' She turned the page quickly. 'Must've been someone local, mustn't it?'

'How d'you mean?'

'Dumped her there. Who'd know about it otherwise?'

'*You* knew about it and so did Grandad, and neither of you is really local to Bridgeford.'

'We used to push our bikes past it, yes, but we didn't know you could hide a body there.' Her mother licked her finger and turned back to the piece about Yazmin. 'I had this idea it was a great big hole going down miles and miles, like a mine shaft. You couldn't see in. These sheets of corrugated iron used to sit on top like a sort of shallow cone.' She made the shape with her hands. 'The hole can't be that deep, though, if you found her skeleton.'

Pam thought back to the scene photos: the child's bones, a few scraps of material, a sandal. 'It had been filled in, partly. They'd kind of laid her down on a concrete ledge inside.'

'Hadn't just chucked her over the wall and run away, then.' Her mother's tone was bitter. She had no time for anyone who hurt a child or let it suffer.

Pam cradled her cup in her hands, resting the rim against her lips as she thought about what her mother had said. Yes, whoever had hidden Yazmin's body there must have known about that platform of cement bags inside. Must have seen it with the roof off, maybe when it was being filled in.

'Nice if we could cycle somewhere together when the weather's better, Pam. Ages since I got my bike out. It'll need a good overhaul, but—'

'Mum, I need to make a phone call, okay?' Pam set her cup down on the saucer and leapt up from the table. 'Sorry. Won't be long.'

*

She stood in her grandfather's garden and rang Lincoln. 'The council workers,' she said without preamble. 'One of the council workers would've known about Ploughboy's Pit – how it was inside.'

He sounded as if he wasn't quite awake. Had he been having a lie-in? It was nearly lunchtime, but maybe on a Sunday... She visualised him blundering round in search of his phone, his hair on end, his pyjamas crumpled.

'Yes, but plenty of other people have been throwing stuff away in there for years, shoving it through gaps where the roof was rusting away.'

'But Yazmin *wasn't* thrown away, was she? From the photos, it looks as if she was laid down carefully on those cement sacks rather than dumped. Who else knew there was that ledge inside where the cement bags had hardened? Who else knew how to lift part of the roof off and put it back again? My mum remembers going past that pit years ago, and she says you couldn't see inside. Yet whoever left Yazmin there *knew* they could get into it without falling down into some deep black hole.'

He didn't answer straight away. She checked her phone screen to make sure she hadn't lost the signal, which was a bit iffy in her grandad's part of Barbury.

'Nothing we can do about it today, Pam. There won't be anyone we can contact at the council on a Sunday.'

She'd expected him to be as excited as she was about a possible breakthrough, even pleased with *her*, but instead he sounded flat and dismissive. 'But it's a lead, isn't it?' she persisted, desperate for him to respond with a bit more enthusiasm. 'It's a place to start.'

Then she found out why he sounded so down. 'DCS Youngman knows we didn't entirely halt the investigation,' he said. 'David Soloman phoned Park Street asking for you and got referred to him.'

Oh Lord! She'd turned her mobile off after she'd rung Lincoln from the hospital on Friday. When Soloman couldn't get through to her number, he must have tried Park Street instead. Her stomach churned at the thought of the trouble she'd got them both into. 'What did he say? The DCS?'

'He wasn't exactly pleased, but I talked him round.'

'So we can follow this up?' She silently begged him to say yes, though she was afraid he'd say no.

'Only if it doesn't get in the way of finding whoever killed Buckthorn.'

A silent *thank you*. 'Any progress on that?'

'It's possible Frankie Ross was there that night, but we don't know why, and the only evidence we've got is some pretty fuzzy CCTV.'

'And now Amy's gone missing, hasn't she?' She turned back towards her grandfather's house. Sunlight sparkled on the roof and the bare branches of the apple trees, and she wanted to cry. 'Could it be the man who attacked her?'

'Press Vale don't know, or won't say, who called her up to that suite. Jacobs suspects they've wiped the records, so we'll never know. But never mind that – how about *you*? How are you holding up? How's your mum?'

'She's holding up better than I am.' She laughed as she brushed her tears away, as if he could see them. 'I'll be in tomorrow. Mum's got lots to sort out, which'll keep her busy.'

'We could certainly do with your help here if you feel up to it.'

'It'll take my mind off things.' She sniffed. 'See you tomorrow.'

Lincoln had been at his desk when Pam called, but now he sprang up and went over to her files of paperwork. Her mention of the council reminded him of the photo Sonia had retrieved from a dresser drawer when he last called at her house. He'd asked Pam to scan it and put it on the whiteboard, but she hadn't got that far before events had overtaken her.

He found the photo in her file. The snapshot showed Bruno flanked by two of his workmates: the neighbour, Lee, dark and lanky, hosting a barbecue in his garden before moving away to a new job; and Edgar, known as Ned, the same height as Bruno, with mid-brown hair.

'He was funny, though, Ned,' Sonia had told him, 'always clowning around. He had the girls in stitches that day. He knew a lot of the kiddies' programmes off the television and was doing all the voices, making them laugh.'

And what else had she told him? That Ned had started working with Bruno because he was fed up with working for the council. Labouring, she said he'd done, and repairs.

Like filling in a dangerous and derelict well?

But how to find him? That was the problem. Sonia couldn't even remember his surname, except his family was Polish and his surname wasn't.

Which reminded Lincoln of Franco Rossetti, aka Frankie Ross. Why had Ross dared to come to the Old Vicarage yesterday? And what did he know about Dale Jacobs's reasons for leaving Bristol?

Breeze arrived looking the worse for wear and smelling as if he'd been on the booze and curry last night.

'You seen today's papers?' he asked, knowing full well that Lincoln probably hadn't. 'Some reporter's doorstepped the Millers.' He flung his favourite Sunday tabloid down on Lincoln's desk, snatching it open at a full-page story about Yazmin Fletcher's disappearance in 1997. The headline read: *Lost and forgotten – and all because of Princess Di.*

'What's this bilge?' Lincoln was tempted to shove the newspaper out of the way, but he needed to know what was being written about the case. Did the journalist know something about Sonia's sister and brother-in-law that the police had failed to discover?

The article was accompanied by an iconic, if irrelevant, shot of Princess Diana and Dodi Fayed on the night they died – and the irate face of Harry Miller. He must have unwittingly opened his front door to the tabloid's eager reporter and her photographer.

'Someone's been digging around in his background,' Breeze said. He banged himself in the chest with his fist as he let out a belch, for which he apologised.

Lincoln looked away. Lager and curry really didn't go together. 'And? Anything crawl out of the woodwork?'

'He was a bus driver in Southampton. Had a bit of a barney with a fare-dodger on the late bus. His bosses blamed him instead of backing him up. He jacked it in and didn't work for a year. The way the journalist's written it, and the way Miller looks when he opens the door to the photographer, they've made him out to be a bit of a psycho.'

'Pam found a note on the original file about a gap in his timeline. She thought it referred to his alibi on the day Yazmin disappeared, but perhaps it was to do with the break in his employment. Why are the newspapers going after Harry Miller now?'

'Trying to make a story where there isn't one.' Breeze belched again and plodded across to put the kettle on. 'They must've talked to their old neighbours.'

'Pam's got an idea that whoever left Yazmin in Ploughboy's Pit worked for the council, was one of the men filling it in. That's how they knew it would be a good place to hide her body.'

Breeze nodded. 'Makes sense. Not a place you'd come upon by chance, is it? But how are we going to find out who worked on it after all this time?'

CHAPTER 43

Like Lincoln, if for different reasons, Sonia Fletcher didn't read the Sunday papers, and hadn't read them for years. When her sister phoned her she was still in bed, sleepy and fuddled, her mouth dry and her eyes watery.

'What've you been saying?' Julie demanded. 'Do you know how much damage you've done? Nearly twenty years we've been trying to put that behind us, and then you say something and—'

'What the hell are you on about? I haven't said anything to anyone.'

'All over the *Express*. Branding my husband as unstable, virtually accusing him of killing Yazmin.'

Sonia slumped back against her pillows. 'What? But why?'

'All because he had that fight on the bus that time. "Unemployable", this reporter calls him. He was out of work for one fucking year. That doesn't make him unemployable! He's slogged his guts out all these years and then you go to the newspapers and—'

'I haven't gone to the newspapers!'

'Well, someone has, and now they're all over our bloody front garden.' Julie rang off, leaving Sonia shaking and panicked. If the newspapers had tracked Harry and Julie down, how long before they laid siege to her own house? She crawled out of bed and peeped out, but Brewery Court was empty. Now the case was in the headlines, it wouldn't be long before her life was turned upside down. Again.

She showered and dressed, peeping out through the curtains while she made some tea. She checked the news on her phone while the tea was brewing, and sure enough there was far too much about Yazmin and Bruno and herself, along with a photo of Harry looking angry and aggressive, overweight, a bit of a perv. She'd never thought much of him – it was mutual, she knew – but she didn't wish this on Julie, her husband being demonised for the sake of a trashy story.

Should she warn Joan Best next door that the story was in the papers? No, better to make a quick getaway, hurry to her car and drive off before she lost her nerve.

Sonia knew now who had taken her little girl. Maybe she'd always had her suspicions but had never wanted to act on them. Now, though, it was time. Now she knew the truth.

She put the box in the passenger footwell of the car. The box Bruno had asked the solicitor to give to her after his death. She drove away without looking back.

CHAPTER 44

The fire at Lola's started in one of the tumble dryers about thirty minutes after the last of the launderette's customers left on Sunday evening. A loose wire close to the power socket caused a short circuit, igniting the blanket of lint that had been allowed to form over the vent at the back. It smouldered for a while before the flames took hold.

The club upstairs didn't open on Sundays, so there was no one there when smoke began to fill the stairwell. When the flames started to run along the landing, fuelled by the cheap floor covering and the varnish on the walls, Guys was empty. Up a few stairs from the sign of the neon willy was a fire door that should, by rights, have been left unlocked when the building was occupied.

A few nights ago, though, Curtis Starkie had let himself out that way to avoid the police who'd come asking for Marco. He'd let himself out and locked the door behind him. The key lay on his bedroom windowsill in a wooden box that contained various other keys he'd picked up, magpie-like, over the years.

The fire door should have been left unlocked because, although Lola's Launderette and Guys Club were empty, there was someone living on the top floor of the building, lying low after he'd been evicted from his flat in Avalon Row.

Marco Ross had been sleeping until the choking smell of the smoke dragged him awake. He snatched the top blanket from his bed and covered his nose and mouth with it before rushing out onto the landing. He could see nothing through the smoke, but felt his way down to the first floor, trying not to breathe until he could reach some fresh air. He tripped on the trailing blanket as he tried to find the little half-landing where the fire door was, and banged his head hard against the wall.

When he staggered to his feet, disoriented, he set off in the wrong direction, stepping out into nothingness where there should have been stairs.

By the time the fire service arrived, it was too late.

Lincoln heard the sirens while he was fixing himself something to eat, the klaxons echoing in the wintry night air. He was making coffee when his mobile rang: Dennis Breeze.

'Dennis?'

'Someone's set fire to Guys. My mate at Park Street called me soon as he heard.'

'Much damage?' Lincoln visualised the tall building on Commercial Street – originally some sort of warehouse or store, he dimly recalled.

'Gutted. And the best bit? It belongs to Frankie Ross.'

'What?'

'No, really.'

When Breeze had rung off, Lincoln kept checking the local news feed on his laptop. Someone had filmed the fire when it was raging, and it looked pretty ferocious. Had it been set on fire to get at Ross? To attack a club for gay men? For the simple pleasure of setting a building on fire and watching it burn?

Around midnight came news that there had been a casualty, as yet unidentified. That was when Lincoln remembered the address Marco Ross had given when he was released on bail, Woody wondering if the lad had simply used it as an accommodation address.

Supposing Marco really had been living there? No matter what other feelings he had towards the Fruit Machine King, Lincoln's heart went out to Frankie Ross. Now was hardly the time to interrogate him about his whereabouts the night Buckthorn was killed, though the question had to be asked – just not right now.

Nothing he could do this evening. Park Street would be looking into what had happened, with the assistance of the fire service. Better get some sleep.

Except he couldn't sleep, seeing not only Marco's father in his mind's eye but also his mother, Gabriella.

At half past five, he got up, showered – oh, the joy of a working boiler! – and got ready for work. He feared it was going to be a long day.

CHAPTER 45

MONDAY 13TH FEBRUARY

DCI Dale Jacobs turned up at Barley Lane soon after seven thirty. He hobbled in, leaning on a walking stick rather than the pair of crutches he'd needed a week earlier.

'Bloody Ross,' he said, throwing himself down onto the chair that had been Shauna Hartlake's. 'They found a body.'

'So I saw.' Lincoln nodded at his mobile. 'Do they know who it is?'

'Marco. They got him out before the fire reached him, but he was already dead. Smoke inhalation. He could've been making for the fire door. Which was locked,' he added grimly.

Lincoln nodded, feeling as grim as his boss looked. 'Did anyone even know the lad was living there?'

Jacobs shrugged. 'Did someone torch it to get at Frankie or Marco or the club? Was it an insurance fiddle?'

'They're sure it's arson?'

Jacobs reached across for the footstool that Woody had yet to take back home. 'What else is it likely to be, with all that's been going on?'

Lincoln's turn to shrug, stuck for an answer. Then: 'You know he came to see me?'

'Who? Frankie Ross? *You* were supposed to go and see *him.*' Jacobs swung his leg up onto the stool, flexing his foot a few times, wincing with the pain.

'Turned up at my house Saturday evening. He told me to ask you why you left Bristol.'

Jacobs shifted his gaze from his foot to Lincoln's face. 'What else did he say?'

'Not much. Our conversation was interrupted by my plumber.'

'Your what?'

Lincoln told him briefly what Ross had said to him before Len Painter killed the conversation by barging in with a fistful of brass olives.

'Sounds like we rattled Ross's cage, then,' Jacobs said gleefully, 'going into Press Vale.'

'You'd have rattled his cage going in there whether or not he had anything to hide.'

'He wasn't even there.'

'Or he chose not to show himself. Why are you so sure he's up to no good, sir? All that's on his record is an assault charge.'

'Bastards like him are always up to no good. Ross brought his business to Bristol, and before you know it he's got the monopoly on gaming machines in the pubs and clubs round the Harbourside, and people are getting beaten up if they don't buy their security systems from him. He's a nasty guy. He knew I was onto him, but he was always one step ahead. Complained to my boss that I was harassing him.'

'And were you?'

Jacobs gave a cockeyed smile. 'I was doing my job, putting the word out about him. Not my fault if some of his business associates got to hear about his tactics and decided against further investment. That's probably what inclined him towards moving to Spain when he did.'

'And inclined you towards leaving Bristol?'

'I left Bristol for *personal* reasons. That's all you need to know.'

'But he's still out to get you?'

'This accident—' Jacobs pointed at his damaged ankle. 'This was Frankie Ross, trying to run me off the road, driving up behind me, headlights flashing. What maniac drives like that unless they're *trying* to cause an accident?'

'Was there any damage on your car that could—?'

'Didn't touch me. He made sure he didn't make contact, didn't leave a trace. And if he wasn't driving that car himself, then he had one of his guys go after me. That's what he'll have done with the records of whoever was in the Abbey Suite that night: made sure there's no trace, wiped the booking details.'

Lincoln nodded, though he was doubtful about Ross's part in Jacobs's car crash. Still, someone had gone to great lengths to protect the man who tried to rape Amy Cartland: murdering the only person who might have witnessed anything – even though he hadn't – and now making the victim herself disappear.

Might it even have been Ross himself in that country club bedroom?

'If he thinks he knows who torched that place and killed his son,' said Jacobs, 'he's gonna want to take care of it himself.'

'You mean he won't co-operate with us?'

'He'll do whatever it takes. See, Lincoln, you're kidding yourself if you think you know how bastards like that operate. They'll always surprise you. And not in a good way.'

So much for Ross being one of Barbury's success stories – apart from his first marriage. A prominent businessman with an interest in art. The scion of an Italian immigrant family made good.

Lincoln turned back to his laptop. 'So now what?'

'We need to get the details from the fire people, find out what started it. Get the autopsy done, confirm how the Ross kid died.'

Lincoln dreaded the awful ramifications if Marco had been hurt before the fire started. Any chance of finding Hugh Buckthorn's killer was even more remote now that one of the suspects was dead – and where was Curtis Starkie in all this?

'And now the Yazmin Fletcher case has kicked off again,' Jacobs added wearily. 'You seen yesterday's papers?'

'I saw there's a lot of media interest.'

His boss gave him a long-suffering look that said Lincoln had been right to keep the investigation alive, but he was buggered if he was going to admit it.

'Let's hope someone comes up with something useful.' Jacobs lifted his leg from the stool and levered himself upright. 'Need to get back to Park Street. Soon as you can, find out where Frankie Ross was the night Buckthorn died. Because it looks to me as if your "old bloke in a trilby walking his dog" was definitely our guy. Keep me posted, yeah? And leave your bloody phone on.'

CHAPTER 46

'Good weekend?' Trish looked up as Stewart arrived, bringing the cold air in with him on his coat and hair and skin. She was so lucky, being able to leave her flat and simply run downstairs to her workplace, but poor Stewart had been travelling for at least half an hour on a chilly bus, with a frosty walk from the stop to the library.

'So-so. Reading, mostly. I don't much like watching television.' He pulled his scarf off and draped it across the radiator.

'You're as bad as Jeff. He won't even *have* a television. I keep telling him how much he's missing out on, but he won't be persuaded.'

'Who's Jeff?'

She was unsure how to describe him. 'Friend' sounded vague, 'boyfriend' was a bit twee, and 'partner' was, well, wrong. 'Oh, we were together for a while last year.'

'But not now?'

'I left him behind in Wiltshire.' She said it in a mock-tragic way as she got up and went over to the first bay of shelving. 'Right then, let's get these books on the database!'

She and Stewart spent the morning quietly working their way through the first dozen or so books, cataloguing them properly and checking their condition. As they worked, he regaled her with tales of other collections he'd worked on.

'I once found some seventeenth-century love letters bound in with a copy of *Foxe's Book of Martyrs*,' he said. 'That was when I was at the museum in Winchester.'

'Wow, that must've been a surprise!'

'It was. I don't suppose we'll discover anything as exciting here.'

'You never know.'

The phone rang: someone asking about Lundy's family history, of which she knew little. She'd have handed the enquiry to Stewart – he might well have been able to answer it better than she could – but pride stopped her. She refused to accept that she wasn't up to the job, even though she suspected she wasn't. But then, as the saying goes, pay peanuts and you get monkeys.

'You must've worked with Archie Gormley, then, at Winchester,' she said, when the phone call was over and she was back at her desk.

He peered over the top of his laptop screen. 'Who?'

'Archie Gormley. We were on the same library course, only he went into museum work, like my husband. Archie's been at Winchester for years.'

He shook his head. 'No, I don't remember him.'

Trish was surprised. Maybe Archie had moved on, or – heaven forbid – had been made redundant. Had she misremembered which museum he was at? Next time she spoke to Vic, she'd ask him if he and Archie were still in touch.

When they broke for lunch, Stewart asked again about adjusting the timer switch on the stairs up to her flat.

'Thank you for offering,' she said, trying not to offend him, 'but I should really only let a qualified electrician change it. Health and safety and all that.'

He shrugged, disappointed. 'I'd have thought going up and down those stairs in the dark was pretty dangerous myself, but you're the boss.'

'For my sins.' She laughed, hoping he'd understand why she'd had to reject his offer of help. 'I could do with some fresh air,' she said, when he didn't reply. 'I'll be back by two.'

And despite a sky that threatened rain, she set off down to the harbour, needing to blow away the cobwebs before she went back to work.

CHAPTER 47

No one in the local council offices could tell Lincoln who might have been employed on the filling-in of Ploughboy's Pit in 1996.

'The county council would've taken over that sort of work by then,' he was told by a man who sounded as if the end of the afternoon couldn't come soon enough. 'We haven't had our own workforce since...well, since a long while before that.'

No one at County Hall could help, either. Employee records were indexed by surname, and if Lincoln couldn't give them that, there was nothing they could do.

From reading Pam's notes, he knew that the garage where Bruno, his neighbour and Ned used to work had closed down years ago, so there was little point in pursuing that line of enquiry. When she texted him that she was on her way in, he decided he should shift his attention back to finding out who killed Hugh Buckthorn.

As soon as Woody, Breeze and Dilke arrived, though, the talk in the CID room was all about the fire at Guys, the shock of Marco Ross's death.

'He was a cocky little bastard,' Breeze said, 'but you wouldn't wish that on anyone, would you?'

Woody shook his head. 'Arson, do they reckon?'

'Too soon to say,' said Lincoln. 'I feel bad for Frankie, and for Gabriella.'

'And for Curtis,' Dilke put in. 'They must've been close.'

'Reckon he'll come forward now?'

Lincoln shrugged. 'I don't know, Woody. We don't even know if he's still alive.' He told him about Frankie Ross turning up at his house.

'That's a bit out of order, isn't it?'

'Yes, and he's a more dangerous character than I took him for at first. Mind you, Jacobs seems a bit *too* eager to pin everything on him. He's convinced Ross had him run off the road. To be honest, listening to him earlier on, he sounded a bit paranoid.'

'Frankie Ross?'

'Jacobs. He spread the word round Bristol that Ross was crooked, so his investors pulled out of some deal or other.'

Woody chuckled. 'Reckon it'd take more than a bad word from a skinny DCI to kill off a business deal!'

'My thoughts exactly, but there's obviously something going on between them.'

Lincoln and Woody drifted across to the whiteboard.

'What's this say?' Woody peered at a note pinned beside Buckthorn's photo. 'Prior Hill?'

'Prior *and* Hill. Auctioneers in Presford. Pam and I found a painting at Greywood Hall that looked ready to be sent off to them. She was going to follow it up, but then—'

'I'll do it. And I'll ask them about their dealings with the Honourable Hugh.'

Pam arrived, taking her cycle helmet off and ruffling her hair back into shape. 'I always seem to miss the fun,' she said breathlessly. 'Did you get anywhere with the council?'

'Why don't you sit down and have a cup of tea before you dive into work?'

'Thanks, boss, but I'd rather get stuck in.'

The best therapy, as he knew from experience.

'No joy with the council,' he told her, 'not without Ned's surname. Of course, we could be barking up completely the wrong tree.'

'Except that Julie thought it was Bruno at the fair because, from the back, the guy with Yazmin looked so like him: same colouring and the sort of blue polo shirt that Bruno wore for work. Yazmin would've felt safe with Ned because she'd met him at least once, at that barbecue.' She pointed to the photograph that was now pinned up on the whiteboard.

Lincoln had to agree that Ned had become a strong suspect. 'He'd know her name, which would put her at her ease. And maybe he'd put on one of his funny voices to make her laugh.' He stared at the photo, at the unassuming young man standing behind Yazmin and the neighbour's little girl. 'How did the original investigating team miss all that?'

'We have the benefit of knowing where he dumped her body. We know from Sonia he worked for the council before he got a job at the garage, but that wouldn't have seemed significant at the time. It's only when we wondered who would know what Ploughboy's Pit was like inside—'

'When *you* thought—'

'Actually, it's my mum who should take the credit.' Pam's cheeks glowed. 'We were talking about it and she got me thinking: who would know about the bags of cement being left behind in there and hardening into that little platform? It had to be someone who'd seen it with the roof off, who'd been there when they were filling it in and knew how the roof fitted on.'

'I'm still surprised the original team didn't interview him.'

'Maybe they did but the paperwork got lost. Maybe Bruno and Sonia persuaded them it couldn't be him.'

'Or somebody just screwed up.' Lincoln sighed hopelessly. 'So how do we follow it up now? How do we find him?'

'I thought about that on the way here.' She turned her computer on and pushed her sleeves up. 'Polish groups.'

'Are there any?'

'There's one in Presford, and someone there might know what Edgar or Ned's surname was. Worth a try?'

'Definitely.'

Leaving Pam to get in touch with the Polish community group, Lincoln went back over the timeline for the night of the murder at the Old Shoddy Mill.

If Buckthorn wasn't planning to spend the night in Rufus's flat – and he'd got nothing with him to suggest he was – why was he going there? The most obvious answer: to meet someone, someone he didn't want to invite to Corner Cottage. But meeting for what? Sex? To buy drugs? To talk?

'You think Frankie Ross arranged to meet Buckthorn at the flat? Why would he want to do that?' Lincoln wondered.

'To find out what Buckthorn had seen at Press Vale?' Breeze offered.

'Bit blatant. He'd be making it obvious he was worried about what Buckthorn might say.'

Woody came across, a big grin on his face. 'Prior and Hill have been in communication with Hugh Buckthorn quite a lot over the last few months. He's asked them to value some of the paintings from Greywood Hall. He's been taking some of the smaller ones to them.'

'Instead of inviting the valuers to the Hall? That suggests he's wanted to keep it quiet. Did they say what the valuations were?'

'They'd prefer to discuss the matter in person,' said Woody, imitating a snooty accent. 'I said we'd be along later today.'

An hour or so later, Dale Jacobs called to say the fire at 84 Commercial Street hadn't been arson after all.

'Preliminary findings? Electrical fault in the launderette.' He sounded disappointed. 'Poor maintenance, the fire investigator's saying, and the fire door was locked.'

'And Marco? Nothing suspicious?'

'They're guessing he got disoriented when he was trying to reach the fire door. Died from smoke inhalation.'

'Who owns the launderette?'

'Our friend Frankie. This is all down to him.' Jacobs sounded suddenly much brighter. 'Let's hope he was insured.'

Breeze found a local news bulletin that showed Ross standing in Commercial Street, staring glumly into the charred ruins of his building. A young woman stood beside him, presumably the fiancée of whom his ex-wife, Gabriella, had been so disparaging.

'Bloody lucky the fire didn't spread to the buildings next door,' Breeze commented. 'Could've been a lot worse.'

'It's bad enough,' said Lincoln. 'He's lost a son and we've lost a key suspect. And we can hardly question him about Buckthorn today. He'll have other things on his mind.'

When Pam announced that she was off to see someone from the local Polish centre, Lincoln decided he, too, needed to get outside. He turned to Woody. 'Let's go and see Prior and Hill.'

CHAPTER 48

The Presford salerooms of Prior and Hill were ranged round three sides of a cobbled courtyard. The auctioneers had probably sold cattle and other livestock on those cobbles in days of yore, but now the commodities they bought and sold were art and antiques.

Lincoln had expected to be greeted by some fusty old boy in a tweed suit, so the glamorous young woman in a fluffy polo neck and red cords was a surprise. Her hair was the colour of butterscotch, shoulder-length and shiny. She introduced herself as Penelope Hill, then led them into a small office that was dominated by a dark mahogany table and chairs, with a coffee machine on a matching sideboard.

'Yes, Mr Buckthorn came to us for valuations of some paintings,' she confirmed, 'though of course I'm under no obligation to reveal those valuations to you.' She smiled.

Lincoln was annoyed as much by the smile as by the obstructiveness. 'If you can't tell us the actual figures, can you at least indicate the range of values you estimated these paintings might fetch?'

Penelope seemed reluctant to divulge that information. 'I must stress, he was asking only for valuations. He wasn't attempting to sell anything.'

'But that might have been his next move, depending on those valuations?'

'Possibly. Or he needed the valuation for insurance purposes.' Another pleasant, if still cool, smile.

Lincoln thought back to the oil painting of Barbury Abbey that he'd found in Buckthorn's little workroom, waiting to be sent here. 'Do you still have any of the paintings he asked you to look at?'

'No, he took them away with him.' She looked uncomfortable all of a sudden, tossing her hair back over her shoulder, not allowing her gaze to linger long on either Lincoln's face or Woody's.

'Was there something else?' Lincoln asked carefully. 'Did something strike you as...not right?' He guessed Buckthorn had been insistent about keeping the valuations quiet, not wanting his nephew, the earl, to know he'd requested them.

'They were all copies.'

Woody's eyebrows shot up. 'He was trying to pass them off as originals?'

'Oh no,' she said. 'I sensed that he *suspected* they were copies but didn't have the resources himself to establish that for certain. That's why he came to us. They were very good,' she was quick to emphasise. 'Whoever painted them knew what they were doing.'

'Reckon this is a stupid question,' said Woody, 'but do copies have much value, compared to the real thing?'

Penelope smiled politely. 'Well, of course, it depends on the age of the copy. Centuries ago it was common to make copies of important works, often done by the artists themselves, or by their assistants. Contemporary copies can have nearly as high a value as the original.'

'And in the case of the paintings Hugh Buckthorn brought to you?'

'Our experts identified them as relatively modern copies, so relatively worthless.'

'Maybe for display while the originals were kept safely locked away?' Lincoln suggested, trying to find an honourable motive for the deception.

Penelope shook her head. 'I understood from Mr Buckthorn that they were the only version he had.' Another tossing back of her glossy, golden locks. 'Confidentially, I'd say he was trying to find out if Prior and Hill had handled the sale of the originals at some point in the past.'

'And had you?'

Her colour rose very subtly. 'Yes, but at least twenty-five years ago. I wasn't able to tell him exactly.'

'That would be when his father was Lord Riverbourne.'

'That's right,' she said. 'And when my *grand*father was in charge of this auction house.'

'She could've offered us a cup of tea,' Woody grumbled as they got back into the car. He started the engine. 'Or even a coffee out of that machine.'

'You're getting to sound like Breezy!'

'Just thought a posh firm like Prior and Hill would offer a bit of hospitality.' He sniffed. 'What do you reckon was going on, then, with these paintings? Was Buckthorn making sure he'd got the real McCoy before he tried selling them? Or testing the waters to see if he could pass fakes off as the real thing?'

'Posh Penelope wasn't giving much away—'

'Not even a cup of tea.'

'It sounds to me as if Buckthorn suspected Prior and Hill had sold the originals years ago, and that his father and his brother had copies made to replace them.'

'Why bother?'

'If people roll up expecting to see a particular view of Bridgeford or a portrait of the sixth Countess of Riverbourne, you can't show them an empty space on the wall.' Lincoln thought back to Gabriella Ross's house in Barbury Park Avenue, the pale rectangles left when Frankie walked out on her, taking his art collection with him.

Penelope had told them she had no way of knowing to whom her grandfather had sold Lord Riverbourne's paintings a quarter of a century ago.

'The sales were to a select few buyers,' she'd said, 'that's all I can tell you. He was very proud of his relationship with Greywood Hall.'

She wouldn't be drawn on whether Prior and Hill had since handled sales for Howard Buckthorn, or the present Lord Riverbourne – Howard's son, Laurence – but it didn't sound like it.

'Doesn't amount to a motive for murder, though, does it?' Lincoln said now, as he and Woody drove back to Barbury. 'So what if a lot of the paintings at Greywood Hall are fakes? If you've done the tour and suspect the Gainsborough was a forgery, you ask for your ten quid back, don't you?'

'Ten quid? Is it really ten quid to go round Greywood Hall?'

'I've got a leaflet somewhere.' The leaflet Hugh Buckthorn had given him when Lincoln called on him at Corner Cottage, shared that delicious pot of coffee...

His mobile rang.

'Pam? Any luck with—?'

'Sharon Starkie rang me. Curtis wants to talk.'

'He's home?'

'Yes, but that's not where I'm meeting him. I said I'd—'

'Pam? Pam!' Lincoln glared at his phone. 'I've lost her. Bloody signal. She's going to meet Curtis Starkie somewhere.'

Woody glanced across at him. 'On her own?' They'd hit the inevitable traffic snarl-up near the Green Dragon roundabout and were at a standstill.

'She knows she's not supposed to.' Lincoln sighed. What was the point? He tried calling her back, but he only got her voicemail.

He rang Sharon Starkie.

'Yes, he's back, but he's terribly upset about that Ross boy,' Sharon said. 'God knows why! He's been nothing but trouble. Curtis seems to blame himself for what happened, but I said to him, I said, how can that fire be *your* fault? Don't be silly. But he won't listen.'

She didn't know where he'd arranged to meet Pam Smyth, though.

'Pam can't bring the lad in,' said Woody as Lincoln ended the call. 'She was on her bike.'

'I wonder...'

'What?'

'Take a left onto Presford Road at the roundabout.'

'Left? But—' Woody indicated and moved across to the left-hand lane.

'The skate park,' Lincoln said, pointing through the trees that bordered the ring road. 'I could be wrong, but—'

Pam leaned her bike against the chain-link fencing at the edge of the skate park. It was quiet today, apart from the incessant rumble of traffic on the nearby ring road. Fluorescent graffiti decorated the walls, the shelter, even the obstacles themselves, though on this gloomy winter's day the whole place looked a bit sad.

Curtis pushed himself away from the wall of the shelter when he saw her. She recognised him from the CCTV and from the selfie he'd attached to his wardrobe door with a dart. None of that had prepared her for how nervy and fragile he was in person, edgy as an addict needing a fix, even though his mother had insisted he didn't take drugs.

Not after what had happened to his little brother.

'Used to love coming here with my board,' Curtis said. 'We'd spend all day here, me and Aaron. He was getting good, y'know? He could've been as good as me in time. This was where you found him, yeah?' He wiped his nose with the heel of his hand.

Pam nodded, wrenched back to that summer's day when she was still in uniform. The half-dozen pre-teen boys with Aaron had been blank with fear, one or two in tears, the rest uncomprehending. And the boy lying blue-lipped and lifeless on the tarmac, vomit trailing from his mouth and down his *Transformers* T-shirt.

'That's right,' she said to his big brother now. 'I wish I could have got to him sooner, but his mates didn't know what was happening to him, didn't know what to do.'

'He was a good kid, but when he was with his mates...' He bent his head, staring at the ground, his hands thrust into the pockets of his inadequate jacket.

'What did you want to talk to me about, Curtis?'

He looked up at her now, his gaunt face pale, made strange by his shaved-off eyebrows. 'It was my fault – what happened to Marco.'

'What happened to Marco was an accident. They know that now. It was on the news. One of the launderette machines caught fire. How could that be your fault?'

'But if I—'

'You can't blame yourself, Curtis. You mustn't.'

He still looked on edge, fidgety with nervous energy. Did he blame himself for Aaron's death, too? Did he feel he should have looked after his baby brother better?

'I'm scared I'm in trouble,' he said, shifting from foot to foot. 'And now Marco's gone you'll pin all of it onto me, won't you?'

'All what?'

'What happened to Mr Buckthorn.'

Out of the corner of her eye, Pam glimpsed a car pulling up at the entrance to the skate park. The boss and the sarge.

'Curtis, listen.' She moved so the lad wouldn't see them. 'Come to the station and tell us what really happened that night. It'll be better if you tell us, won't it? You'll feel better getting it off your chest. The longer you put it off...' She shrugged. 'Well, it'll just get harder and harder, won't it?'

He looked away across the deserted skatepark, the blaring colours of the graffiti muted by the dismal light of the afternoon.

'I just want to go home,' he said, on the verge of tears. 'I want it all to be over.'

CHAPTER 49

Sonia had been hanging around outside his house for hours, waiting for him to return. She'd seen him emerge at half past eight that morning and get into his car, an old Volvo that hadn't been cleaned in ages. He'd reversed out of his yard, then climbed the steep hill to the main part of the town, the Volvo's engine labouring on the incline.

She didn't mind waiting. She had plenty of time. She'd waited years for this. She'd left Barbury yesterday and driven west as far as Frome, just over the border into Somerset. After a sleepless night at a budget hotel, she'd driven a few more miles to reach Shepton Mallet, arriving as the sky was beginning to get light. If only she had time to go to Glastonbury! But even though it was just a few miles farther on, she needed to stop here, to do what she'd come to do.

It took her a while to find his house, an old and run-down place overlooked by the forbidding walls of the former prison. Did he live here on his own? Was he married with a family? The outside of the house gave no clue, apart from a plastic recycling crate at the front of his yard, filling up with lager cans.

She walked back up into the town and then back down again, scared of missing him. She did this a dozen times until, at not quite five, the Volvo rumbled down the hill and swung into the yard. He got out. He was twenty years older, but she'd have known him anywhere.

She stepped forward, level with the side of the car. 'Hello,' she said, her voice cracking. 'Hello, Ned.'

CHAPTER 50

Curtis Starkie sat across the table from Lincoln and Pam, with solicitor Jean Vowles beside him. He looked in need of a decent meal, and smelled as if he needed a shower too. He was eighteen, nearly nineteen, but looked much younger.

'Where have you been staying?' Lincoln asked him before the interview got officially under way.

'Gas Lane. Empty house down the end there. Bloody freezing. No electricity.'

Unlike his friend Marco Ross, Curtis wasn't cocky, didn't try to play games with his interviewers. When Pam asked him what had happened the night Hugh Buckthorn died, he told them, evidently relieved to get it off his conscience.

'Mr Buckthorn phoned me that evening when I was having my tea,' he said, his hands clamped between his knees, his chin not far above the surface of the table. 'He wanted some coke for the weekend.' A quick glance at Jean Vowles. 'He got some off me at the club the weekend before, but when he phoned he said he was going up to London the next Saturday and wouldn't be around.'

'What time did he phone you?'

'Must have been about quarter past six or just after. Told him I'd have to go over to Bridgeford to get some off Jumbo, and he said that was fine cos he was going to be in Bridgeford too, at his mate's flat. I knew where he meant. He told me about it when we had a chat at the club.'

'At Guys?'

Curtis nodded.

'How did you get to Bridgeford?' Pam asked.

'Got the bus. I don't drive. So I got some more stuff off of Jumbo and we chilled for a bit and then I went down the lane to the flat.'

'What time was that?'

'Left Jumbo's about nine. Needed time to drop the stuff off at the flat before I caught the bus. It's the last one, you see,' he told them earnestly, 'nine thirty-five. I didn't want to miss it. So I went up to the flat, knocked on the door and—'

He shut his eyes and took a deep breath before opening them again.

'Marco came rushing out,' he went on. 'Nearly knocked me over. I couldn't work out why he was there. And then he says, "Look what I've found! He asked me to come round, and when I got here the door was on the latch, and I walked in and found him like this." And I went into the living room and he was there on the sofa. Mr Buckthorn. I wouldn't have known it was him if Marco hadn't said.'

'Tell us exactly what you saw,' said Lincoln, 'as far as you can remember.'

Curtis sighed unhappily, then did as he was told. 'He was lying back on the sofa with a rope round his neck and plastic over his face. He had stockings on and, like, a dressing gown or something. And there were magazines and photos all over the floor. Must've needed them to get him going, I s'pose.'

'Magazines?' Pam asked. 'What sort of magazines?'

'*Gay* magazines. The sort they put on the top shelf in the paper shop. There's always some lying around at Guys. Gay porn. I didn't look too closely. I nearly threw up, seeing him like that.' He reached out for the plastic cup of water and drank thirstily.

Lincoln read the notes he'd made, taking his time before asking the next question. 'Did Marco say why he'd gone there?'

'He said Mr Buckthorn took a fancy to him, wanted him to come round for an hour or so.'

'Did he say what time he'd arranged to go there?'

Curtis shook his head. 'But he must've got there about nine, not long before me.'

'Would Mr Buckthorn have asked you to come round at the same time?'

A shrug. 'He could've forgotten. Or else he wanted us both to be there.'

'A threesome?'

Another shrug. 'Some of the men at Guys... It kinda sickens me what they get up to, y'know? I only went to work there because I needed the money and because Marco was there and he vouched for me. And the men there, they didn't make me feel like a freak. But it's not really my scene, y'know?' He dipped his head. 'Can't believe it's gone. That Marco's gone.' Tears glistened on his cheeks.

'Why didn't you come forward sooner?' asked Pam gently. 'If you'd come and told us what happened... Why did you think you'd be in trouble?'

'How was it gonna look? Someone could've seen us. And Marco—'
He broke off.

'Yes?' Lincoln leaned in. 'What about Marco?'

'He said maybe it was my fault Mr Buckthorn died. That there was something wrong with the coke he had off me. I was fucked whatever I did.'

Lincoln could imagine the lad's terror, wanting to call for help when he saw Buckthorn's dead body but fearing he was implicated. Marco had manipulated him, the way he'd tried to manipulate Lincoln and Woody when they'd interviewed him.

'Did you see or hear anyone else around when you went to the flat?' Pam asked. 'You're sure Marco was there on his own?'

'He must've been. Looked like that flat was the only one that was finished.'

'Were you arguing with Marco when you left?' Lincoln took the CCTV images out of his folder, pointed to the one which showed Curtis's agitation, Marco's breath in angry clouds between them.

'That was about the car,' said Curtis. 'The key to Mr Buckthorn's Jag was lying on the counter in the kitchen. He must've dropped it there when he came in. Marco wanted to take it, take the Jag. I told him not to, how was it gonna look, we can't take his car and then say we weren't there. But he wouldn't listen. When we got to the square, all that was there was the Mini he nicked in Heath Close. No sign of the Jag. I was glad. It would've been wrong, taking that car.' He hung his head. 'I liked Hugh. I could talk to him about stuff, and he listened, y'know?'

Curtis left Barley Lane with his mother, along with a neighbour who'd given her a lift. As soon as they'd departed, Lincoln turned to Woody.

'That explains the missing car key. Marco picked it up, planned to take the Jag but couldn't find where it was parked.'

He remembered the way the young man had taunted them when they'd interviewed him about the stolen Mini: *It's not like I took something valuable, like a Jag.*

The car key was now most likely in the smouldering ruins of his attic hideout over Guys.

'Anything else we didn't know about?' asked Woody.

'Curtis said there were gay porn magazines and nude photos on the floor by the couch, but we didn't see anything, did we?'

They surveyed the crime scene photographs. No magazines on the floor, no nude pictures.

'Reckon someone must've taken them away,' said Woody.

That was the only explanation. 'That's something Ken Burges mentioned when we were discussing auto-erotic asphyxiation—'

'As you do,' Breeze put in with a chuckle.

Lincoln ignored him. 'That he'd have expected to see photos around, sex toys, some sort of stimulus. Yet there was nothing.'

'Marco could've cleared them away,' Breeze suggested, his leather jacket squeaking as he folded his arms.

Pam shook her head. 'No, Curtis said he and Marco left at the same time, went back to the Mini together – as we know from the CCTV.'

Lincoln thought back to that first Friday morning and his conversation with Tilly Rayner. She'd been at the flat to restock her brother's fridge and pantry, and yet –

'I tripped over the Rayner woman's carrier bag when I went into the Portakabin to talk to her,' he remembered. 'How come it was still full if she'd already put Rufus's shopping away?'

'Reckon *she* cleaned up,' said Woody. 'Put away all the rude photos, anything that'd make her brother look bad.'

Breeze snorted. 'What, like a naked dead aristocrat on the sofa wouldn't make him look bad?'

Even if Tilly had phoned the emergency services as soon as she found the body, she'd still have had time to tidy away anything she thought might incriminate Rufus. She'd also unwittingly spoiled the solo sex scene the killer had created.

'She could still have them,' said Pam, 'the magazines and photos. There could be forensic evidence on them. They'd be no use in court, but—'

'Whoever set things up was careful not to leave any prints anywhere in the flat,' said Lincoln. 'They'll have worn gloves.'

She looked disappointed. 'Do you believe what Marco told Curtis? That Buckthorn had invited him to the flat?'

Lincoln pointed to the timeline. 'He made out he'd only just got there himself, but we know he left the Mini at quarter to nine and would have got to the flat by ten to nine at the latest. My theory? When Curtis knocked on the door, Marco was helping someone set the scene. He saw Curtis through the spyhole and had to think fast, told him Buckthorn had asked him round and that's how he'd found him. Whoever else was there, they kept themselves out of the way until Marco shoved Curtis out of the door and they rushed back to the car.'

'Frankie Ross came up Jackdaw Lane at quarter past ten,' Breeze said. 'You're thinking he's the "someone" Marco was working with?

Once the two lads had gone, he hung around to put the finishing touches, clean up, wipe everything down?'

Lincoln nodded. 'Yes, except now Marco's dead, how do we get his father to admit any of it? We need evidence that Ross was inside the flat, but Forensics found nothing.'

'And we still don't know *why* he wanted Buckthorn dead.' Woody tugged at the hairs in his moustache as he studied the whiteboard.

Pam, too, looked deep in thought as she stared at the photos of Buckthorn and Frankie Ross. 'Buckthorn must've known Frankie already,' she said. 'He wouldn't have opened the door of the flat to a total stranger, would he? He wouldn't have invited Frankie in and had a glass of wine with him unless he thought he could trust him.'

Lincoln could see what she was getting at. 'But Ross wasn't in his phone contacts.'

'Didn't you say his diary was missing? Maybe he'd got contacts in there that weren't in his phone. And if he'd arranged to meet Frankie that evening, he might've put that in his diary too.'

'Which is why it was taken out of his jacket.'

'But where would those two have met?' Woody asked, sceptical. 'They'd be like chalk and cheese.'

'Opposites attract,' said Pam.

'Or maybe,' said Lincoln, 'they go back farther than we realise. They're about the same age, aren't they? They both grew up here. They could've hung out at the same clubs when they were teenagers, gone to the same concerts. And there's the Italian connection – Frankie's family and Buckthorn's mother.'

Woody still wasn't convinced. 'You're saying Frankie Ross could kill a man he's known since they were kids?'

'Yes, if the stakes were high enough. We need to talk to Ross.' Lincoln turned away from the whiteboard, impatient with its refusal to shout out the answers. 'I know he's got all this to deal with, losing Marco, his building going up in flames, but even so... Where was he the night of Buckthorn's murder? I assume he's still staying at the—'

His desk phone rang before he could finish, and he snatched it up.

'There's a Mr Soloman to see you, sir,' the uniform on the front desk told him. 'Shall I send him up?'

Ex-DCI David Soloman looked less than well. Lincoln only vaguely remembered him from their few encounters, Soloman about to leave Wiltshire, Lincoln only recently arrived. Now, all these years on, the older man's skin was deeply lined, and a little too yellow to be healthy. His head jutted forward from his stooped frame.

'You didn't need to come all the way up here, sir,' Lincoln told him as Dilke brought mugs of coffee in. 'But I'm grateful that you have.'

'Thought I'd see how much the old place has changed.'

'You were based here at Barley Lane?'

'Started off here before they expanded Park Street, then I moved across. Nicer atmosphere here,' he added. 'Expect you feel the same.'

'We're just waiting for the merger.'

'Good luck with that.' He took a sip of his coffee. 'Get out while you can.'

Lincoln pulled his mug towards him. After a few preliminaries he asked him if, as Senior Investigating Officer on the Yazmin Fletcher case, he'd had his own suspicions about anyone.

'The mother was a bit of a weirdo,' Soloman said without hesitation. 'All sorts of batty ideas about reincarnation and the afterlife. Mad as a box of frogs!' He chuckled and took another slurp of coffee. 'The father seemed straight enough, but you can never tell – Eastern Europeans, inclined to be sly.'

Lincoln leaned away from him. He talked like someone from the days of the Empire. He'd most certainly have voted for Brexit. 'Bruno Bartek was born and brought up here,' he said, 'and so was his father.'

Soloman looked mildly surprised. 'It's a long time ago. I forget the details.'

'Was one of his workmates ever in the frame? A young chap called Edgar or Ned? We don't have a surname, but he may have been from Poland originally.'

Soloman shook his head slowly, then: 'There *was* a fella we wanted to talk to, but he'd gone abroad on holiday. Not sure if we ever did get round to talking to him. Can't remember his name, though. It wasn't a foreign name.'

'No, he'd changed it.'

'You said you didn't know his name.'

'We don't. Only that he changed it to sound English. You can't even remember what letter it began with?'

'Come on, it was twenty years ago! As far as I know, every likely suspect we had was traced, interviewed and eliminated. If we didn't pursue him, it was because something told us he wasn't a viable suspect. You know as well as I do, you go with your instinct.' Soloman sat back, rubbing his thighs as if to signal his imminent departure. 'Not sure

261

why you thought I'd have anything to add. I've come all this way but, frankly, we could've had this chat over the phone.'

Lincoln could have reminded him that it was Soloman who'd chosen to come here in person, but instead he said, 'It didn't seem suspicious that a man you wanted to interview had left the country soon after that little girl went missing?'

The eyes that stared back at him were brown and inexpressive, the whites tinged yellow. 'The logistics of dealing with police forces abroad... All the bloody paperwork. Resources were as strapped then as they are now. We thought the culprit was closer to home. Bartek couldn't have taken her himself because he was in Poland, but we did wonder if he'd put someone else up to it.'

'The girl's mother was sure he hadn't.'

A nasty smile. 'Afraid I didn't set much store by anything that lassie told me. She was crazy. I even considered whether—' He stopped himself, shaking his head.

'Whether what? That Sonia herself was in some way responsible?'

'Take it from me, that lassie wasn't right in the head. Chasing this religion, then that one, going to fortune tellers and quacks and mediums. She got in with some sect or other, Church of the Promised Land or some such, used to meet in an old chapel in Bridgeford. Kept trying to make contact, talk to the kiddie beyond the grave.' He gave a bark of a laugh. 'She was unstable. Even before the kiddie went missing she was scuppering Bartek's access visits, going against what they'd agreed. Women like that shouldn't have kids if they can't look after them.'

After David Soloman had left, Lincoln took deep breaths, trying to bring his blood pressure down and keep his temper. Thank God he'd never had to work with the man!

Was Ned the suspect who'd gone on holiday? Why hadn't Soloman's team followed it up? Lincoln had a good idea why not: a combination of penny-pinching, over-reliance on gut instinct, and poor teamwork. That fateful combination had allowed Ned to escape detention.

Now, all these years later, there'd be no chance of identifying him.

CHAPTER 51

'Tell me what happened.' Sonia faced Ned Adams across his kitchen table. As soon as she'd walked in she'd known he was living on his own, no woman around, no children, the worktop crowded with six-packs of Tyskie lager and unwashed crockery. The units could've done with a coat of paint, or at the very least a good clean, and the floor tiles were tacky and broken. Everything reeked of nicotine.

When she looked at Ned, she could imagine how Bruno would look now. They were of similar colouring, similar build – something she hadn't noticed before. No wonder Julie had mistaken him for Bruno when she saw him walking away with Yazmin. They could've been brothers. His hair was a dull greyish brown now, his face haggard, his body slight but out of condition, a beer belly pushing against the grey fabric of his sweatshirt.

'What happened to Yazmin, Ned?'

He peeled the ring pull off a can of lager, grabbed a packet of cigarettes. He took his time swigging from the can, banging it down, lighting a cigarette, drawing on it a few times. She noticed a tremor in his hands. Was he nervous or was he sick?

'How did you find me?' he asked. 'Did Bruno tell you where to find me?'

'Bruno's dead. But yes, I got your address off him.'

Less than forty-eight hours ago she'd dragged out the box of papers that Bruno's solicitor had passed on to her after his death. More out of desperation than in hope, she'd searched through the contents and found, among a collection of old letters and postcards, his tattered address book. There, on the first page: *Adams, Ned*, with his Presford address crossed through and this one, in Shepton Mallet, written underneath. She remembered then: Bruno had told her the name had originally been Adamski, but Ned's father had changed it so the family would fit in better.

'It was an accident,' Ned said now, 'what happened. I didn't mean for that to happen to her.'

'An accident? You could've reported an accident, couldn't you? Taken Yazmin to hospital, called someone. Not left me wondering for

263

twenty fucking years where she was, not knowing if she was dead or alive!'

He couldn't look at her. She didn't want him to, didn't want to meet those sad grey eyes. She didn't want to feel pity for him.

He'd only gone to the fair because he had nothing better to do, he said.

'I saw your little girl. She was on her own, no one looking after her. Bruno was always wanting to see her, so I thought I'd take her to him. I didn't know he was away. She recognised me, asked me if her daddy was at the fair too.'

'Recognised you?'

'Remember? That barbecue party Lee threw when he got a new job and was moving away. We were all there – Lee and Bruno, Lee's lady, you, the little girls.'

His silly voices, mimicking the characters off kids' TV like he was a human parrot. Lee's little girl and Yazmin had been enchanted.

His prominent front teeth were bad, she noticed as he took the cigarette out of his mouth and tapped the ash into a grimy saucer. He looked unwholesome. She struggled to hide her revulsion so she could stay here long enough to learn the truth about her daughter.

'So she went with you because you said you were taking her to her daddy?'

He nodded. 'And I was going to. Me and Bruno had a bit of a bust-up at the garage, and I thought if I brought his little girl to him we'd be mates again.' He crushed his cigarette butt into the saucer, scattering ash. 'I'd got my little van and she hopped in and off we went, only—' He broke off, raking his fingers through his hair. 'She changed her mind about going to see her dad. I tried to persuade her, but she started shouting and screaming.'

Ned got up abruptly. Fearing he was about to strike her, Sonia reeled back, but he was simply in need of fresh air. He shoved the sash window up and leaned out. It was still light even as the day was fading, and birds were calling from the trees overhanging his yard.

'So you had to shut her up.' She could scarcely imagine the horror her daughter had had to endure.

'No,' he said, turning back into the room. 'No, it wasn't like that.'

Sonia couldn't breathe. The walls of the kitchen seemed to tower over her. 'How was it, then?'

'We pulled into this side road. It was like a dead end where there were lock-up garages, a bit of a building site, right on the edge of the town. I told her I'd turn the van around and go back, but she opened the door and jumped down. I got out to go after her but the van started to roll back, and it knocked her over before I could get the handbrake on.'

'You ran her over?' Getting the words out was painful, as if they were barbed, scratching her throat as she uttered them. 'You drove over my little girl?'

'No, no!' His eyes were full of anguish. 'She hit the back of her head when she fell. There was, like, a concrete post lying there, and she cracked her head on it. I didn't know what to do. I picked her up and put her in the van and—' He turned back to the window. 'I drove round with her in the van for a bit, trying to work out what to do.'

'You could've taken her to hospital! You could've dialled 999. You could've saved her!'

'No.' He was adamant about that. 'I could see she was gone.'

The walls were slanting in towards her, like the sides of a tent. The ceiling was coming down. 'And then what?'

Still staring out of the window, he told her. He'd done a job for the council once, filled in this hole in the ground under the trees at the edge of some woods. He decided he'd put her there.

'I parked up, took her out of the van. She'd wet herself,' he added awkwardly, 'so I took her panties off her. And then I carried her up to this place where I'd worked the year before and I laid her down carefully and...' He started to sob, perhaps with relief that he was shedding himself of the guilt that had burdened him for twenty years. Shedding it and loading the pain onto Sonia instead.

She stood up, her legs trembling. 'You killed her.'

'It was an accident! An accident!' His eyes were red. His lips were wet. He put his fist against his mouth and gulped back a howl.

'All these years...' Everything ground to a halt. This was where her life stopped. Everything came to an end.

'I wanted to tell you,' he sobbed, 'I wanted to say something. You used to go to that church in Bridgeford, that chapel place—'

'Heaven's Promise? In Jackdaw Lane? You followed me?'

'I didn't know how else to get to talk to you. And I'd go and wait outside until you came out, but you were always so upset, and you were always with someone and then...' He shook his head. Spittle shone in the corners of his mouth. 'You stopped going and I didn't see the point.'

He had no idea of the depths into which he'd thrown her. No idea at all. 'You bastard!' she hissed at him. 'You complete and fucking *bastard!*'

'What are you going to do?' He was whimpering. She was surprised he wasn't already on his knees.

She could hardly breathe, she was so angry. 'I don't know.'

'I kept her little coat.'

'Coat?'

'Her white coat.'

'Her cardigan, you mean?'

'She left it in the van when she jumped out. I kept it safe. I was going to give it back to you but...' He crossed the room to a corner dresser. From a cubbyhole at the top, he took down a brown paper bag. The white cuffs of the sleeves peeped out, though even in the half-light she could see they'd yellowed over the years. He proffered the bag with something approaching tenderness.

Sonia stared at the cardigan. Last time she'd seen it, Yazmin had been wearing it, her plastic doll in one of the pockets, spoiling the shape of it.

She reached out and took the bag, hugging it to her as if she were hugging her little girl. She wanted to be able to smell Yazmin again, but the bag and the cardigan inside it smelled musty, kept too long in a damp cupboard. He'd ruined even that much!

There was a knife on the worktop, in amongst the beer and the food packets, the unwashed dishes and the ash trays, the filth of his existence.

When he moved towards her, Sonia took hold of the knife, letting the paper bag slip to the floor unheeded. Did she ram the knife into him or did he run onto it? She couldn't tell, only that it didn't take as much force as she would have expected. She wrestled the blade out of him, the handle slippery with blood – his blood or hers, she couldn't be sure. Gripping the knife awkwardly, she stabbed him again, the walls pressing in, the ceiling pressing down, nothing quite real any more.

Then she let go.

And that was how she left him, Edgar Adamski, Ned. She walked out of his house, closing the door quietly behind her.

The blackbirds were calling out as she walked back to her car. Spring wasn't far away now. How long before anyone went looking for him? Long enough.

It was only when she'd driven away and was halfway back to Barbury that she realised she'd left the brown paper bag behind, the white woollen cardigan. Too late now. She couldn't go back.

CHAPTER 52

Lincoln looked round at the faces of his team, grateful for the continued existence of Barley Lane as a separate entity from Park Street, even though its days were, inevitably, numbered. God help him if he ever started to turn into the type of man David Soloman had become!

'We've made some progress on the Buckthorn case at least,' he said. 'Curtis Starkie was only in Rayner's flat a few minutes, but he remembers there were magazines and photos lying around on the floor. My guess is that Tilly Rayner got rid of them when she arrived with her brother's groceries on Friday morning. She may even have removed the wine glass Buckthorn drank from, in case Rufus's fingerprints were on it. He was supposed to be in Trowbridge, but maybe she was afraid he'd changed his plans and come back. I bet she picked up anything she thought might incriminate him and stuffed it into her shopping bag. Which I nearly fell over not long afterwards.'

He wished it had occurred to him then that the bag should have been empty. Ah well...

Woody took over. 'Marco was already inside the flat when Curtis got there. He made out he'd only just arrived, but we know he got out of the Mini and went down Jackdaw Lane about eight forty-five. He told Curtis that Buckthorn had invited him round for a quickie, and he'd found him dead when he got there. The two lads left together, and Marco drove them back into town in the Mini.'

'Why didn't Curtis report it?' Dilke asked, horrified.

'Marco told him the coke he sold Buckthorn could've been what killed him. Best if they pretended they hadn't been near the place.'

'But Curtis saw no sign of Frankie?' Breeze asked.

Lincoln shook his head. 'The only evidence we have that Frankie was anywhere near the flat is those few seconds of CCTV, a man in a trilby turning the corner out of Jackdaw Lane and into Church Street about ten fifteen.'

'Unless there's anything in the stuff that Tilly took away with her.'

'It wouldn't be admissible in court, but if we had something that proved to ourselves that he was there...'

'Can we arrest Tilly Rayner?' asked Dilke. 'She removed evidence that could've led us to Buckthorn's killer. We could arrest her for perverting the course of justice.'

Lincoln knew he was right. He thought back to the mild-mannered young woman cowering inside her coat while site foreman Austin Kendall tried to comfort her. She may have acted in haste, panicking that her brother might be implicated in a serious crime, but she'd interfered with a crime scene. She'd attempted to cover up what she feared might be Rufus's involvement in his lover's death.

Even if she'd acted on impulse, she could have come clean once she'd calmed down, when she was sure Rufus was in the clear.

And what about Buckthorn's two-minute phone call to the Rayners' house the night he died? She'd claimed to know nothing about it, but had she lied about that, too?

'We need to bring her in,' said Lincoln, 'and find out what else she's been keeping from us.'

After a brief phone call to tell Dale Jacobs his plans, Lincoln took Pam with him to the Rayners' house.

'They'll be sitting down to dinner, won't they?' said Pam as she buckled up. 'It's nearly seven.'

'Then we'll have a captive audience. We need to bring her in now, before any other evidence goes missing.'

Rufus came to the door. 'You've got some news?' His voice was cautiously hopeful.

'No, but there have been some developments. May we come in?'

They followed him into the study, where Lincoln and Woody had interviewed him previously. The fire had burned low in the grate and the curtains hadn't yet been drawn shut. It wasn't the cosy room it had been on Lincoln's last visit.

'Is your sister here?' Pam asked.

'Tilly? Of course she's here. Shall I call her?' He took a step towards the door.

'Wait.' Lincoln put a hand out to delay him. 'Did you know Hugh phoned here the evening he was killed?'

Rufus looked puzzled. 'Why would he? He knew I was away. He'd never call here.'

'He phoned here at about five past six. Maybe he left a message. Is there any way of checking?'

Rufus took his glasses off, put them back on again. 'I'll see.'

Pam followed him out into the hall, watching as he pressed buttons on the rather dated-looking machine. '*You have NO saved messages,*' the answerphone told him sternly.

A man emerged from the back room, tugging a napkin from his shirt front. Shorter than average, with a halo of white hair that grew back from a domed forehead, he emitted a powerful energy despite his size.

'What is this?' he demanded. 'Rufus?'

'It's okay, Dad. They...the police...were asking about a message that...might have been left.'

'What message?' Cornelius Rayner's tone was indignant.

'Hugh phoned here the night he died,' said Rufus, suddenly firm in response to his father's anger. 'Apparently he left a message.'

'Or spoke to someone here,' Lincoln put in. 'It was a two-minute call.'

'We need to speak to Tilly,' said Pam.

'What's this got to do with Tilly?' Confused, Rufus looked round at his father for clarification, but Cornelius avoided his gaze.

Lincoln sensed that Rufus had no idea what his sister had done to protect him. He was less sure about how much Cornelius knew.

Without anyone having to call her, Tilly crept down the stairs like a little girl who'd been put to bed but didn't want to miss the excitement of the grownups' dinner party. Pam ushered her into the study while Lincoln made it clear to her father and brother that they should stay where they were. Then he followed Pam and Tilly into the study and shut the door.

Tilly sank down in the chair by the dying fire.

'Do you know why we're here?' Lincoln asked her.

'Because of what I did when I found Hugh's body.' She appeared to have no idea how much damage she'd done.

'What happened to the items you removed from your brother's flat?'

'Everything's still in my bag. I haven't touched it since I brought it all back. Shall I go up and get it?'

'DC Smyth will go with you. And then you'll have to come back to Barley Lane with us.'

They went back out into the hall, and Pam went upstairs with Tilly to fetch the hessian shopping bag. By the time they came down again, Mrs Rayner had appeared. She reached out to her daughter but Tilly shrugged her off, taking her coat off the peg at the bottom of the stairs.

'Did you know about this?' Rufus turned on his father, standing his ground, furious.

'Come on, Rufus,' said Cornelius, with one eye on Lincoln. 'Don't make this any more difficult than it is.'

Tilly touched her brother on the arm. 'I won't be long. You mustn't worry.'

The contents of Tilly's bag comprised half a dozen gay porn magazines and various photos – probably bought on the Internet – of teenage boys in the nude. A couple of the photos might have been of Rufus, but a combination of dim lighting and soft focus made it impossible to be sure.

Wrapped in a tea towel was a very sticky glass and an empty bottle of red wine, its cork loose in the bottom of the bag. No tell-tale sediment was visible in the glass, but maybe the Rohypnol had been slipped into the bottle. Would any of these items yield forensic evidence placing Frankie Ross at the scene? Lincoln didn't hold out much hope.

The Rayners' family lawyer, Bernard Fisher, was quietly attentive as Tilly settled herself in the interview room across from Lincoln and Pam, but, as she'd shrugged her mother off at home, she shrugged Fisher off now, though more subtly.

'Why did you remove items from around Hugh Buckthorn's body?' Lincoln asked her. 'By which I mean the magazines and photos we found in your shopping bag, and a wine glass and a wine bottle.'

'I thought Rufus must have come home early and they'd had a row or something. The photographs were horrible, and the magazines. I dreaded the thought of people going in there and jumping to the conclusion that my brother was...' She shuddered. 'That he was a pervert. Or that Hugh was, for that matter. I liked Hugh. He was a good man.'

'Why did you take the wine glass away?'

'Rufus might have been drinking out of it and you'd find his prints on it, and on the bottle too. You'd know he'd been there.'

'But *you* knew he hadn't.'

She shook her head. 'I couldn't be sure. He could have driven over from Trowbridge and then driven back again. I panicked. I didn't want to give Dad an excuse to make Ru give up his dream of doing up places like the Old Shoddy Mill. Dad's afraid Ru will sell the gallery to concentrate on property, and that'd break his heart.'

'Why would that break your father's heart?' Pam asked.

Tilly seemed surprised she needed to ask. 'Dad set up the Cheese Market Gallery over forty years ago. It would kill him if it closed down or had to be sold to someone outside the family.'

'So your father's an art expert too?'

'Yes, of course. He's been a dealer ever since he left Prior and Hill – you know, the auctioneers – and started up on his own.'

A lightbulb lit up in Lincoln's brain. Could Cornelius Rayner be the dealer with whom Hugh Buckthorn had been negotiating the sale of the Greywood Hall paintings?

'Did you touch or remove anything else at the crime scene, Tilly? This is crucial.'

'No,' she said, shaking her head sadly. 'I picked up the magazines and the photos, and then I saw the wine glass on the floor near Hugh's hand. I was going to wash it up, but then I thought it'd be safer to take it away, and the bottle. I tipped the rest of the wine down the sink, which seemed an awful waste but I didn't know what else to do. I wrapped the bottle and the glass in a tea towel and put it all in my bag with the magazines. I was on autopilot, really. Whatever it took to protect my brother.'

CHAPTER 53

TUESDAY 14TH FEBRUARY

In the immediate aftermath of the fire that killed Marco, the media response had been sympathetic. Frankie was shown standing alone outside the charred shell of 84 Commercial Street on Monday morning, head bowed. Local people took to the *Messenger* website to offer their condolences to the young man's parents, and to the much-loved restaurateur Gino Paolucci on the loss of his grandson.

Frankie Ross's fiancée didn't seem to have much more than a walk-on part in the drama, while Marco's mother, Gabriella, maintained a discreet silence.

By Tuesday, though, questions were being asked about where to lay the blame for the tragedy. A senior fire officer cast doubt on whether anyone should have been living on the top floor of the building in what was, essentially, an attic space. The poor maintenance of the launderette's wiring and equipment was also mentioned in passing, as was the unfortunate – and illegal – locking of the only fire exit.

Responsibility for all these faults fell to the owner of the building: Frankie Ross.

As well as these misgivings, the *Messenger* website carried photos of 'missing barmaid' Amy Cartland and a sketch map of her last known movements, a dotted line tracing her route from the Cadillac bar along the street to the next junction, where CCTV cameras lost sight of her. *The Messenger* described her as 'fun-loving and bubbly'.

'Media-speak for "irresponsible and asking for it",' Lincoln commented sourly to Woody as he read the screen. 'They've even used a selfie that makes her look like a flirty show-off.' The photo showed Amy looking over her naked shoulder and pouting suggestively. He hadn't established much of a rapport with the young woman when he interviewed her at her parents' house, but he didn't feel she deserved to be portrayed so coarsely.

Regrettable, too, was the mention of Hugh Buckthorn. Mrs Cartland had let slip to a reporter that her daughter had been rescued by 'a knight in shining armour' after 'an incident while she was working'.

'Lord Buckthorn was the perfect gentleman,' she was quoted as saying. 'But we're in bits in case whoever killed him has gone after our little girl.'

Lincoln was left with a nasty taste in his mouth after reading that – and not just because Amy's mother couldn't even get Hugh's title right.

'Good result with the Rayner girl, though,' said Woody as he settled down at his own keyboard. 'Gives Media Relations something to do.' He read aloud from the *Messenger* website: '"A woman has been arrested in connection with the murder of Hugh Buckthorn. She has been released on bail pending further enquiries."'

Lincoln tutted. 'I bet there'll be plenty of speculation about the role she's played in all this.' He shoved himself away from his desk and headed for the filing cabinet. The kettle sat there, still warm from his last mug of coffee, but he felt in need of extra caffeine this morning.

Yesterday evening, when he and Pam had gone to bring Tilly Rayner in for questioning, he'd seen something flash between Rufus and his father that looked a lot like hatred. Had Rufus realised that one of his family had spoken to Buckthorn the night he died and not told him? Or had deleted a message he left? Had he found out that Cornelius had colluded with Tilly to erase any evidence that Rufus might have been involved in his lover's death?

'Did we know Cornelius Rayner was an art dealer?'

'What, the father? No. Could he be the middleman Buckthorn was using to sell the paintings?'

'Or attempting to sell. We've no evidence that he actually sold anything.'

'How does that square with what he thought about Buckthorn being gay, seducing his darling son?'

'Business is business.'

'Rayner senior wasn't in his contacts, though, was he?'

'No, but...' Lincoln had a sudden thought that was interrupted by the kettle coming to the boil. When he'd made his coffee (two spoonfuls, with three sugars), he rummaged through the envelopes on his desk until he found what he was looking for. 'The old address book Pam and I found at Greywood Hall.' He flipped through it but found nothing under 'Rayner'. Disappointed, he started at A and went through it until he reached C and – 'Look! "Cornelius. Presford 7822."'

Woody peered over his shoulder. 'That's not Buckthorn's handwriting, is it?' The address book script was rounded and upright. From Buckthorn's notebook they knew his writing was confident and spiky, impatiently charging off to the right.

'And it's not the same as the writing in the old inventory.'

'Is it Howard's writing?' Woody wondered.

273

The door opened and Dale Jacobs shouldered his way in, still walking with a stick but obviously on the mend. Today's suit had a rich red lining that matched his tie. He and Frankie Ross were running neck and neck in the Snappy Dresser stakes.

The door opened again and DS Orla Cook came in behind him.

'Orla is acting as chauffeur,' Jacobs said. 'Or do I mean chauffeuse?'

'I'm your *driver*,' Orla said, unamused. 'Sir.'

He lowered himself awkwardly into Shauna's chair. 'Seen the *Messenger* website, Lincoln? Fucking media seem to know more than we do.'

'Nothing new on Amy?'

Jacobs shook his head, looking glum. 'It's time we brought Ross in for questioning, find out where he was the night she disappeared. I know you were holding off interviewing him because of what happened to his son, but we've shown him as much compassion as he deserves. He's got motive for having the Cartland kid disappear. He wants her to drop the rape allegations, so he's had one of his henchmen kidnap her to teach her a lesson, give her a warning.'

Only a few days ago Lincoln would have protested that such an act was hardly Ross's style, but now...

'Where are we with Buckthorn, anyway?' Jacobs demanded.

'The items recovered from Tilly Rayner have been sent off to the lab. I'm hoping the forensics—'

'Won't be admissible, though, will it?' said Orla, a beat ahead of Jacobs.

'No,' Lincoln admitted, 'but it'll be hard for Ross to keep denying his involvement if his fingerprints turn up on the wine glass.' Though he doubted the Fruit Machine King would have been that careless.

'His solicitor's been onto the DCS about me harassing him,' said Jacobs, apparently unperturbed. 'The same stunt he pulled in Bristol. They say attack is the best form of defence. My team at Park Street will bring him in, get some answers. You'll let me know what the forensics tell us, yeah?'

'Of course, but it'll be a few—'

'And keep your bloody phone on.' He hoisted himself up and limped away. Orla could have opened the door for him, but she hung back until he'd done it himself. As she followed him out, she turned and cast Lincoln and Woody a long-suffering look.

'Nice to see he's popular with his Park Street team too,' said Woody wryly.

Lincoln's desk phone was ringing, a call transferred from the front desk. 'A gentleman from London,' the uniform said. 'To do with Mr Buckthorn.'

The caller was Kingsley Shaw – an old friend of Hugh's, he said, and owner of an art gallery in Central London. 'Hugh and I did the same Fine Arts course, only he was doing it about ten years later than the rest of us.' His laugh was warm and affectionate. 'We'd arranged to meet at my gallery the Saturday after he…after he was killed.'

'You didn't consider coming forward sooner, Mr Shaw?'

'Everyone seemed to be saying it was an accident, and by the time I heard he'd been *murdered* I was, frankly, afraid to say anything. Look, I'd rather not discuss this over the phone. Can we meet?'

'In *London*?'

'No, no, I'm staying with my sister in Amesbury. I'll give you the address.'

Kingsley Shaw's sister lived a few miles out of Amesbury, in a big old house in the Woodford Valley overlooking the Avon. Lincoln had brought Dilke with him, and once the introductions were out of the way they sat with Shaw in the Edwardian conservatory. Watery sunshine had ventured out from behind the clouds, and there was a hint of spring in the snowdrops and daffodils that dotted the spreading lawns below them.

'Beautiful house,' said Dilke.

'It is, it is. And there's a superb walk up across the fields to Stonehenge. Not that I ever get round to doing it,' he added ruefully.

Kingsley Shaw could have been Hugh Buckthorn's younger brother, so similar was he in looks and style. But where Buckthorn had been relaxed and urbane, Shaw seemed on edge and uncomfortable.

Lincoln let Dilke take notes as Shaw explained how he knew Buckthorn and what their plans had been for the weekend – the weekend Buckthorn hadn't lived to see.

'Every few weeks he came up to London to see what I'd got in the gallery, and we might go to the National or one of the smaller galleries – whatever took his fancy.'

Shaw paused to take a sip of his coffee. His gaze wandered to the view down the lawn to the tree-lined river, the rooks in the skeletal treetops. 'He wrote to me—' He put his cup down and reached for an envelope on the table. 'One of the few men I know who still write letters rather than sending you texts or emails!' Another laugh. 'He'd been cataloguing the paintings at the Hall and he'd come across...anomalies, shall we say?'

Lincoln leaned forward, intrigued. 'Anomalies?'

'He was working from an old inventory someone in the family did years ago. He was alarmed to find that quite a few of the paintings had been sold since the inventory was done – paintings he felt should have stayed in the family. But then, when he was going through the storerooms, he discovered that some of those paintings were still there.'

'We understand a number of original paintings were sold some years ago,' Lincoln said cautiously. 'Copies were made to put in their place. Was it the copies that Hugh had found in the storerooms?'

Shaw shook his head emphatically. 'What was left was *definitely* the original. Hugh knew what he was talking about – the Renaissance was his area of expertise. He was horrified to think his father had been selling copies as genuine originals. He'd have understood him selling the originals to make a bit of money, but to sell modern *copies...*'

'Forgeries,' said Lincoln.

'Well, yes. Here, read the letter. Hugh managed to track down sales records for quite a few of the paintings that his father sold. He estimated that about forty paintings had been sold in the last fifteen years, and twenty-eight of them were genuine originals. But that still means twelve of them weren't. Most of them were copies of lesser-known works by well-known artists, but we're still talking about a lot of money.'

Lincoln skimmed through Buckthorn's letter, noting the artists whose works were among the twelve copies sold: Brueghel, Van Dyck, Dürer, Gainsborough.

'Hold on. Some of these were sold in the last three years, after Hugh's father died. So *Howard* was selling them off too?'

'Yes,' said Shaw. 'That's what surprised Hugh most, I think.'

'How would you convince a dealer or a buyer that an artwork was genuine,' Lincoln asked, 'especially if it'd never come onto the market before?'

'Good question. How do you provide provenance for a painting that's been in the same family for decades, if not centuries?'

'So what's the answer?' asked Dilke.

'You approach an expert,' said Shaw. 'Someone who knows the artist's work inside out.'

'Would you have been able to recommend someone to him?'

'That was the point of us meeting up that weekend. He was going to tell me which paintings he was concerned about so I could approach the appropriate expert. He needed to be sure the versions still at Greywood Hall were the originals.'

'If the copies, forgeries, whatever you want to call them, had been sold on,' said Lincoln, 'where would the blame lie? With the dealer or with the seller? Isn't it a matter of *caveat emptor*? Buyer beware?'

Shaw shook his head. 'A reputable dealer or auction house will have asked for documents of authenticity showing the painting's provenance. If those aren't provided and the buyer still wants to proceed, even if there's no proof he's getting an original artwork, then on his own head be it. However, if the seller provides documents which have been manufactured—'

'Faked,' said Dilke.

'Manufactured with intent to deceive—' Shaw shrugged eloquently.

'Then that's a criminal offence,' said Lincoln. And Buckthorn's cataloguing of the paintings would eventually have uncovered the deception. 'What kind of money are we talking about here, Mr Shaw?'

'Given the reputation of the artists involved, the lowest price would be in the region of fifty thousand – though, of course, at auction there are always surprises.'

'And the highest?'

'More like five hundred thousand.'

Dilke let out a low whistle. 'Wow!'

'Did Hugh know who'd handled the sales of these copies?' asked Lincoln.

'A local dealer, he thought. That's why he wanted me to recommend someone well away from Wiltshire, someone who could take a look and confirm that the paintings at the Hall were the originals.'

'How come these forgeries haven't come to light yet?' Lincoln asked. 'Have the Buckthorns simply been lucky not to get found out?'

Shaw shrugged. 'Until the buyer decides to sell a painting on, it'll hang on his wall looking as good as the original. It could be ten or twenty years before it comes back onto the market, if not longer. That's when an auction house or potential buyer might spot a weakness or flaw, something that doesn't look right. Even then, they might only examine it closely if it's a high-profile, high-value picture. A fake is a bit of a ticking time bomb, really. Whoever sold those Greywood Hall copies must've hoped the bomb had a very long fuse!'

'Was Buckthorn about to expose what was going on?' Dilke asked eagerly as he and Lincoln drove back to Barley Lane.

Lincoln slowed to pass a string of riders on horses. 'I got him all wrong, didn't I? I assumed he was the one who was up to no good, when it was his father and his brother who were flogging copies as originals.'

'But they're not around anymore. Who else would be in trouble if all this came to light? The present earl? The dealer?'

Admittedly, Laurence Buckthorn had been keen to have his uncle's death dealt with as swiftly as possible, but he was probably driven by embarrassment and the need to protect the Riverbourne reputation. If he'd had any idea of the scale of the deception his father and grandfather had pulled off, he'd have surely shown more concern when Lincoln told him that Hugh had been cataloguing the paintings in storage at the Hall.

'I'm guessing the dealer knew exactly what he was doing, but who was he? Cornelius Rayner?'

'There must've been paperwork.'

'We're talking years ago.'

'Two earls ago.' Dilke grinned. 'Do we have an art fraud section?'

'You're joking! Not even the Met can afford one of those all the time. It's the first thing to go when the budget's tight.'

'Maybe Rufus Rayner knows more than he's saying.'

Lincoln thought back to the ugly looks exchanged between father and son the night Tilly was arrested. 'I'd say there's no love lost between him and Cornelius. Let's get back and work out where we go from here.'

CHAPTER 54

Halfway through Tuesday morning, Trish got a text from Vic, her ex-husband.

What's the plan for h/term?

She texted back: *U know what the plan is. K coming to U.*

Was that defo?

Bloody hell! She could see Stewart down the far end of the library, leafing through a bound volume of pamphlets. How many times did she have to tell him? They'd agreed to leave the miscellanies till the rest of the books had been done. She called out to him that she had to make a phone call, and slipped outside.

It was icy-cold, a biting wind coming in off the water, but she was so cross with Vic she hardly noticed it.

'What d'you mean, was that definite?' she snapped as soon as Vic answered. 'You invited Kate to stay with you and she's *so* looking forward to it. You can't change your mind now.'

'Whoa, whoa! I didn't say I had.' Even now, the sound of her ex-husband's voice was comfortingly familiar. 'I just asked if it was definite, in case she'd changed her mind.'

'Of course she hasn't changed her mind!'

'Like she isn't a typical teenager?'

'She's only thirteen.'

'Nearly fourteen.'

'Don't remind me! So she's coming to you next week?'

'Yes, yes. I'll pick her up on Saturday. Check with your sister and let me know what time suits her.'

'Vic, while I've got you there...'

'Ye-es?' He sounded suspicious.

'Archie Gormley.'

'Ye-es?' Even more suspicious.

'Is he still at Winchester?'

'He was last week. I was on the phone to him about the King Arthur exhibition he's putting together. Why d'you ask?'

'I've got a new assistant. One of his last posts was as a museums officer in Winchester, but he's never heard of Archie. I was afraid

Archie'd been given the chop.'

'Like so many of us.' Vic's laugh was rueful. 'There's more than one museum in Winchester, Trish.'

'I know that, but the reference was from the same one Archie's at. You're sure he's still there?'

'Of course I'm sure! Your guy couldn't have worked there and *not* known Archie – he's been chief curator for the last five years. Are you sure your guy's on the level?'

'Absolutely! I'm probably getting muddled over which museum he was at.'

'What's his name? I may have heard of him. It's a small world.'

'Stewart. Stewart Hubbard.'

There was a pause. Was he writing it down? Then: 'No, never heard of him. You want me to ask around?'

'No, no!' She laughed him off. 'I'll get back to you about picking Kate up.'

'Fine. You okay? Not fed up with Essex yet?'

'No! I've got to go. Work to do.' She ended the call. As she went back up to the library, she told herself she'd misremembered which museum had provided that glowing reference for Stewart.

Back at her desk, she worked on another of the many science books Lundy had collected. She examined it carefully for ownership marks or any other clues as to its provenance. Many of the titles were also in libraries elsewhere in the world, but every copy was unique, distinguished by its binding or plates, or pages that had been slipped in later as corrections. What she always loved to see were the handwritten annotations made by a previous owner.

Unlike the antiquarians and unqualified custodians who'd looked after Lundy's books during the last hundred years, Trish was determined to catalogue each item as fully as she could – as long as the software could cope with that level of detail.

Stewart came and sat across from her, a copy of Hobbes's *Leviathan* in front of him. 'Everything okay?'

'Yes, yes. Just fixing things up for my daughter's half-term holiday.'

'You're going to be away?'

'No, she'll be staying with her dad.' Trish hoped she sounded more cheerful about it than she felt. 'So I'll be here, don't worry!'

While Stewart went out after lunch for some fresh air, Trish dug out the folder containing his references. Her heart sank when she saw that his most recent post, held for four years until last November, had indeed allegedly been at the same museum as Archie Gormley.

The signature on the covering letter was 'Margaret Skipwith, Curator', but a quick Internet search revealed that Ms Skipwith had retired from the museum in 2012. And had since passed away.

Trish glanced at the other two references. Were they also unreliable? He'd been vetted, ostensibly, by the recruitment agency the Trust had used, but how thoroughly had they checked him out?

Yet he was clearly well qualified for the job. Why had he felt the need to fabricate a reference?

When she heard him coming up the stairs, she slipped the references away and returned to her desk, where a copy of Robert Hooke's *Micrographia* lay awaiting her attention.

Stewart plumped himself down, one of Lundy's own publications in front of him. 'Have you worked out how long it'll take us to catalogue everything, based on our average so far?'

'No, but it sounds as if you have. And please don't tell me. I already feel as if I'm working against the clock.' Against the calendar, more like: her contract would run out at the end of November, assuming the trustees didn't cut it again.

'Yes ma'am.' He gave her a jokey salute, making her smile.

She tried to put aside her concerns about his reference from Winchester, and pored over the stunning illustrations in Hooke's *Micrographia* instead.

'Fancy going for a drink after work?' he suggested. 'We've earned it, wouldn't you say?'

She thought about it. Maybe she'd be able to get him to open up a bit, come clean about that testimonial, explain why he'd felt the need to fake it.

'Yes,' she said, 'I rather think we have.'

CHAPTER 55

Lincoln called a briefing towards the end of that afternoon. Standing in front of the whiteboard, he summed up what was gradually coming to light.

'Hugh Buckthorn's death may be linked to the sale of paintings from Greywood Hall,' he said. 'He approached Prior and Hill, the auctioneers in Presford, for valuations of a number of artworks which turned out to be modern copies – as he seemed to have guessed already. He was also trying to find out when the originals had been sold, and if Prior and Hill had handled the sales. They wouldn't tell him, or couldn't, because the sales would have been back in his father's time.'

Breeze snorted in disgust. 'Cuh, so it's all fakes on the walls at Greywood Hall?'

'A few, not all. And nobody seems to have noticed. But something else has been going on. Graham?'

Dilke looked surprised to be given the floor, but then relayed what he and Lincoln had found out from Kingsley Shaw.

'Buckthorn found out that about forty paintings have been sold more recently, in the last ten to fifteen years,' he said. 'But when he checked what was in storage at the Hall, he found twelve of the paintings were still there – the originals. Which means twelve of the forty sold were forgeries. As soon as one of those paintings is put up for auction again, the Buckthorns and whoever handled the sales and forged the documents of authenticity are likely to be found out.'

'Hugh Buckthorn wrote to Shaw, who's an old friend of his, outlining his suspicions,' Lincoln added. 'They were going to meet up that weekend. Shaw estimates the value of the forgeries as over a million quid.'

Breeze hooted. 'A bloody nice commission for somebody!'

'There must be paperwork,' said Pam.

'Buckthorn couldn't find it. The phoney documentation's probably been hidden away.'

'You know who might have paperwork?' Dilke had that schoolboy grin on his face again. 'Remember that lady who found the skeleton in Ploughboy's Pit?'

'Barbara Trent?' Lincoln hadn't actually met her, but he remembered the name. 'What about her?'

'She worked for Lord Riverbourne. Not this one, the one before, and possibly the one before that. His right-hand woman, she said she was.'

'Actually,' said Pam, 'I need to ask her about her neighbour, the one who worked for the council and helped fill Ploughboy's Pit in. He might remember the name of the guy that worked with Bruno Bartek – Ned something.'

'You two go together,' Lincoln suggested, 'see what she knows – though I doubt if she'll be able to tell you much.'

It was growing dark by the time Pam and Dilke arrived on the doorstep of the last house in Greywood Terrace, the last house before the forest began.

'Should we have phoned ahead?' Pam wondered.

'Too late now.' Dilke pressed the doorbell, setting off a volley of yaps and barks from within. 'She's got a dog.'

'Yes, Gray, I know. It was the dog that found the bones.'

The door opened and Barbara stood there, the Cairn tucked under her arm.

'Oh, hello,' she said, as if she'd been expecting them. 'Don't mind Corky. Do come in.'

Giving in to her insistent offers of tea and biscuits, Dilke and Pam sat in her sitting room, the electric log-effect fire glowing cheerfully.

'I've still got that scrap metal on my lawn,' she told them as she handed round the Waitrose Duchy shortbreads. 'I've got a man coming on Thursday to take it away.'

Pam had seen Barbara on the news after she'd found the child's skeleton, but this was the first time she'd seen her in person. Her style was country tweeds and lace-up brogues, as if she were the wife of a gentleman farmer or a minor aristocrat.

In reality she was living on a pension in a former council house.

'When I spoke to you before,' said Dilke, breaking into Pam's thoughts, 'you told me your next-door neighbour's son had a job with the council, filling Ploughboy's Pit in. We're trying to trace one of the other men who worked on that job, and we were wondering if—'

'Randall,' Barbara said. 'Randall Jones. They moved away.'

'You wouldn't have an address for him?' Pam asked hopefully.

'Randall died. Thrown off his moped. Hadn't long passed his test.

Broke his mother's heart. They moved away after that. He was only seventeen.'

Pam's heart didn't break at this news, but it certainly sank a little. She'd been hoping Randall could supply a surname for the elusive Ned.

'I'm sorry,' Barbara said. She had thick, wavy hair, and kept pushing it back off her forehead. 'You've had a wasted journey.'

Dilke put his cup down. 'Actually, there's something else. To do with your time at Greywood Hall.'

Another sweep of her hand to push her hair back. 'Oh yes?'

'Do you remember Lord Riverbourne selling some paintings?'

Pam watched the woman's face, noticing the way her eyes darted from one to the other of them. At last, Barbara said, 'Which Lord Riverbourne? I worked for Mr Howard and for his father, Mr Robert.'

'Probably both of them sent paintings to auction at different times,' said Dilke. 'It was the paperwork we were after.'

'Paperwork?' Her face flushed. 'That would've been kept in the strongroom.'

'Whereabouts is that?'

'In the attics. Of course, they're not attics as you and I would envisage attics—'

Was it a script the earls' assistants learned? 'I know,' said Pam, cutting across her. 'They're at the end of the Long Gallery.' She tried not to think about the phone call she'd taken there, her mother telling her about her grandfather's stroke.

'That's right. Yes. Why do you need the paperwork now? Those paintings were sold years ago, mostly in Mr Robert's time.'

'We're investigating the possibility that some of those paintings were forgeries,' Pam told her. 'We need the paperwork to help us find out if that's true or not.'

Barbara looked a bit blank. It was impossible to tell if she knew anything.

'Who has access to the strongroom?' Dilke asked. 'Who should we speak to at the Hall?'

'The estate manager,' she said, wriggling her shoulders as if the mention of her successor were distasteful. 'Veronica Pinfold.'

Mrs Ray-of-Sunshine. Pam glanced upward, wondering if she could bear to return to the Long Gallery now. As she lifted her gaze, she spotted something she recognised: an oil painting of Barbury Abbey long before the town itself grew up around it. An oil painting she'd last seen in Hugh Buckthorn's office. It had been wrapped in sacking and was destined for Prior and Hill – or had it recently returned from there? Except it couldn't be the *same* painting. Which was the original and which the copy?

Barbara saw her looking at the picture. 'Delightful, isn't it?'

Pam surprised herself by remembering what the label had said, but that afternoon was etched on her memory now. 'Benjamin Osgood? About 1760?'

'I'm not sure about the date. It was a present from the earl, from Mr Howard, when I retired.'

Pam stood up and went over to the painting. 'It must be worth quite a bit. Have you had it valued?' Behind her, she imagined Dilke watching her in bewilderment.

'Well, no.' Barbara got up and came over.

Pam turned back. 'A painting like this is a rather extravagant retirement present, isn't it? People usually get gardening vouchers or book tokens, don't they?'

Barbara backed away. 'Are you suggesting—?' Her hands went up to her face. 'There was never anything *improper* between Mr Howard and me! He often gave me a painting or a drawing. He knew how much I appreciated nice pictures. I was a trusted employee, and he wanted to reward me for—' She halted, her mouth setting itself in a tight line.

'For what, Miss Trent? What did he want to reward you for?'

She pulled herself up to her full height and gave a little toss of her head. 'I'd rather not say anything more until I've spoken to my solicitor.'

'The first thing I want you to understand is this: I've done nothing wrong. Whatever I did, I did in good faith. If I've been taken advantage of, then...'

Barbara Trent shuddered, as if she couldn't understand how she came to be here in an interview room at Barley Lane police station, her solicitor by her side and her dog on her lap.

Lincoln had been on the point of wrapping up for the day when Pam phoned to say she and Dilke were bringing Barbara Trent in to be interviewed.

'Interviewed? You only went to ask her a couple of questions.'

'Yes, but the walls of her living room are plastered with paintings. Valuable paintings, I'd say. I expect she wants to get something off her chest.'

Now here she was, across the table from Pam and himself, a plump lady in her sixties, a tweed topcoat over a thick-knit jumper, a paisley scarf tucked into the neckline. No jewellery, her only make-up a light dusting of powder on her kindly-looking face.

'Maybe if you start from the beginning...?' He was unsure what questions to put to her – it wasn't as if she was accused of anything – but she evidently wanted to talk.

She'd worked for the Riverbourne Estate since she left secretarial college, she explained. Her father had put in a good word for her. He'd been working for the estate too, as one of their surveyors, checking up on the condition of buildings and structures and...

'Well, anyway, he got me a job in the office,' she said. 'I worked my way up to be Mr Robert's personal assistant—'

Lincoln interrupted her. 'Mr Robert?'

'The ninth Earl of Riverbourne. I was very close to the family,' she went on, preening a little, brushing her hand through her hair. 'And then I became Mr Howard's right-hand woman. That's what he called me.'

She stopped talking. Lincoln held his breath. Had she lost her nerve now she found herself in the formal setting of an interview room? When he looked at her closely, though, he saw tears wobbling on her lashes.

'What can you tell us about the sale of paintings from Greywood Hall?' he asked gently.

She sniffed, discreetly searching her cuff for a hankie, finding one instead in her coat pocket. She blew her nose delicately, then tucked the hankie into her sleeve.

'There was never enough money,' she said at last. 'Mr Robert was always having to sell something – a painting, a marble bust, furniture. He sold some Chippendale pieces, years ago. They'd fetch a king's ransom now if he'd held onto them. The paintings...' She sighed. 'He had some copies made to put on display to replace the originals he'd decided to sell. They weren't terribly good. They wouldn't have fooled an expert, but they were good enough. Visitors aren't allowed to get close to the pictures, anyway, so...'

She broke off to smooth the top of her dog's head.

'When Mr Howard inherited,' she went on, 'he was desperate for money. Death duties – you know how it is. And listen, I'm sure it was a genuine mistake to start with, but he sent several of these copies to auction, through Prior and Hill. And they sold, all of them, no questions asked. Only...'

Another pause that made Lincoln catch his breath again. 'Only what?'

'One of the buyers realised they'd been sold a pup, as it were, and approached him directly. He was mortified. He was a very honourable man, Mr Howard. This buyer made a deal with him: he'd keep quiet about being sold the copy if he could have the original.'

'The buyer didn't take it up with the auction house? With Prior and Hill?'

She gave a funny little half-smile. 'He knew he was onto a good thing. He had Mr Howard where he wanted him. If it had got out that Greywood Hall was selling forgeries...'

Lincoln could appreciate Howard Buckthorn's quandary: with one forgery exposed, every other sale he attempted would be scrutinised in detail. Previous buyers might even get their earlier purchases examined and found to be fakes. The consequences could be embarrassing and hugely expensive.

'So this buyer – he came back for more paintings?'

Barbara nodded. 'He was a keen collector – Renaissance artists in particular, though he had quite broad tastes. Mr Hugh would've been furious if he'd found out, but of course he was abroad.'

'Let me get this right.' Lincoln tried to get his head round it. 'Howard was giving these paintings away to this man so he'd keep quiet?'

'Oh no. This chap was *buying* them, but without having to bid for them at auction. It was all done through a dealer, not Prior and Hill. They came up with an acceptable price between them and everyone was happy.'

Happy? Lincoln guessed the 'acceptable price' was rather less than each painting might have fetched at auction, but Howard didn't have much choice.

'Can I ask who this dealer was?' Although he could guess...

'Cornelius,' she said. 'Cornelius Rayner. He has that place in town – the Cheese Market Gallery.'

'His son's running it now.'

'Oh, I didn't realise.' She stroked the little dog's rough gingery coat. 'Mr Hugh came to see me the night I found that child's remains. He'd seen me on the news, knew where to find me. He was working his way through the art collection, checking the paintings against Lady Dorothy's old inventory. A lot seemed to be missing, he said. Where was the little Raphael? What had happened to the Joshua Reynolds? Where was the Scrabini? He was especially upset about the Scrabini. He was counting on them for an exhibition next year, he said, an exhibition that could save the Hall, and now they were gone. He couldn't find any record of them being sold, of course, because it was all done on the quiet. He was afraid they'd been stolen and Mr Howard had hushed it up.'

'Hugh came to see you? At Greywood Terrace?'

'Yes, that Wednesday. He must've thought that if anyone knew what had gone on at Greywood Hall it would be me.'

What must Buckthorn have thought, walking into Barbara's modest home to find her walls decorated with paintings he'd have recognised from the rather grander walls of Greywood Hall? His late brother had rewarded her handsomely.

'And you told him what you've just told us?'

'More or less. He wasn't very pleased.'

Understatement. Lincoln thought back to his chat with Buckthorn on the Thursday morning – his enthusiasm for bringing unseen paintings into the light, his hopes for an exhibition that might make all the difference to Greywood Hall's fortunes. He must have been optimistic about reaching some sort of resolution.

'And the buyer who was blackmailing Howard? What was his name?' In his mind's eye Lincoln could see the empty walls of Gabriella Ross's house, the phantom outlines where her ex-husband's paintings had hung.

'A man called Ross,' said Barbara. 'Frankie Ross.'

He sat back as another piece of the puzzle dropped into place. 'Go on.'

'Mr Hugh said he'd have to talk to him, reach some agreement. He couldn't just let it go.'

After the visit from Mr Hugh, Barbara thought it wise to let Cornelius Rayner know she'd given the game away, she said.

'Why did you do that?' Pam asked, puzzled. 'To warn him Hugh might come round and have it out with him? To give him time to enlist Mr Ross's help?'

'To protect Mr Howard's memory, and his father's. If it came out that they'd sold forged pictures—' She shook her head, at a loss. 'And it would reflect on Laurence, too, and he had no part in it.'

'Neither did Hugh.'

Barbara cast Pam an angry look. 'No, and why not? Because he was swanning round the south of France when he should have been here helping Howard. Off with his supermodels and his sports cars, leaving Howard to cope with Mr Robert on his own. It wasn't fair,' she declared, her voice rising. 'And then he comes back here, wanting to know where his precious paintings are, as if it's *my* fault!'

Lincoln noticed the way 'Mr Howard' had become 'Howard'. All she'd cared about was protecting the reputation of her employer, a man she'd perhaps been more than a little in love with. 'So you called Cornelius Rayner—'

'I called Cornelius and I told him Mr Hugh was on the warpath. The silly thing is...' She stroked the fur between the dog's ears as tears spilled down her face. 'Hugh and Frank were best friends when they were boys. It's such a shame they fell out over a few pictures.'

A few pictures worth in the region of a million quid, Lincoln thought to himself. Maybe it wasn't a question of money for either man, though, more of ownership – on whose walls the Caravaggio hung, or the Scrabini.

Barbara put her elbows on the table and sank her head into her hands. 'What have I done?' she sobbed, as Corky slid off her lap and landed quietly on the floor. 'What have I done?'

Lincoln could have waited till morning to update DCI Jacobs, but he decided to phone him straight away.

'Hugh Buckthorn was killed because he wanted to get his paintings back,' he told him.

'He was murdered for some fucking paintings?' Jacobs couldn't believe it. 'Where d'you get that from?'

Lincoln explained, as briefly as he could, what Barbara Trent had said. 'I think Buckthorn went to Bridgeford that night to meet Cornelius Rayner, to find out what was going on and to see what he could salvage.'

'You're saying Rayner set him up? That *Rayner* murdered him?'

'No, I'm suggesting he expected to meet Rayner there, but Frankie Ross turned up too. When's Park Street bringing Ross in for questioning?'

'Ah, well, we're holding fire on that. Someone's used the Cartland girl's card in a cash machine in Warminster. We're waiting for the CCTV images from the bank, to see if it's anyone we recognise.'

'If Ross had anything to do with her disappearance, he wouldn't be stupid enough to let someone use her card. Sounds more like—'

'Leave it to Park Street, Lincoln. Stick to the Buckthorn case. Bring Cornelius Rayner in asap, yeah? And let's hope he gives us Ross.'

Lincoln rang Trish when he got home, but she wasn't answering. It was too late for a working supper with What's-His-Face, so where could she be?

When his phone rang he grabbed it with relief, but it wasn't Trish.

'Mr Lincoln? Joe Gibson. Len Painter asked me to call you. You've been let down by your flooring guys, I hear.'

They discussed what needed doing, and Joe sounded positive. 'I'll be round tomorrow,' he said, 'take a look, give you a quote. It'll be after work, so is sevenish okay?'

When he rang off, Lincoln saw that Trish had sent him a text: *Sorry I missed you. Catch you tomorrow.*

He called her back, but her phone was off. They were playing telephone tennis again.

Tomorrow, Cornelius Rayner would be brought in for questioning about his movements the night Buckthorn died. He'd have known the flat was empty, with Rufus away in Trowbridge. If he didn't have his own keys he could have borrowed Tilly's. He'd have waited there, knowing Buckthorn would want answers about the paintings Howard had sold, with Rayner's collusion – the fakes and the originals. Waited there with Frankie Ross.

Lincoln poured himself a measure of Jameson's and drank it down quickly. Poured himself another one. Stared at the empty glass on the kitchen counter.

An idea began to take shape in his head. He needed to get back into that flat.

CHAPTER 56

WEDNESDAY 15TH FEBRUARY

First thing next morning, Cornelius Rayner was brought in to Barley Lane.

'He wasn't very happy,' said Dilke, who had gone with Pam to arrest him. 'Tilly hung onto him like we were dragging him off to the scaffold.'

'How did Rufus react?' Lincoln watched as Rayner and his solicitor were shown into an interview room.

'Wasn't there. Back in Trowbridge, apparently.'

Did he even suspect his own father might have had his lover killed? 'I can think of worse places to be right now.'

Lincoln and Woody sat opposite Rayner and Bernard Fisher.

'I don't know why I'm here,' Rayner said, his frizz of white hair trembling slightly as he moved. 'Whatever my daughter did, she did out of foolish loyalty to her brother, but it was nothing to do with me.'

'This isn't about your daughter.' Lincoln had a thumping headache after drinking too late last night on an empty stomach, but he forced himself to concentrate. 'This is about your role in a conspiracy to murder Hugh Buckthorn.'

'A conspiracy to *what*?' Rayner reared up in his seat.

'You arranged to meet Mr Buckthorn at your son's flat in the Old Shoddy Mill on the night of February 2nd. Is that right?'

'I didn't meet anyone at Rufus's flat, not then or at any other time. This whole thing's preposterous!' He turned quickly to Fisher but the solicitor ignored him, head bent over his notepad.

'On the evening of February 2nd, at approximately six o'clock, you took a phone call from Hugh Buckthorn.' Lincoln watched Rayner's face, noticing a flicker in his eyes. 'What was that about?'

'There was no phone call.'

'We know there was. We've got the records to prove it. He phoned your landline number. If *you* didn't take the call, someone else in your house did. A call lasting nearly two minutes. Or he left a message, although most answerphones would cut out within a minute and a half, I'd have thought. So who did he speak to?' Lincoln left the question metaphorically on the table. 'The night before, the Wednesday, you took a call from Barbara Trent.'

'I don't know who you mean.'

'Oh yes you do. Barbara used to work at Greywood Hall as personal assistant to Howard, the previous Earl of Riverbourne. She's told us quite a bit about the sale of paintings from Greywood Hall – paintings for which you provided documents of authenticity, even though you knew those paintings were forgeries. Would you like to tell us about that, Mr Rayner?'

'I've nothing to say.'

'That's a shame. We were hoping you could explain to us how, while Howard Buckthorn was Earl of Riverbourne, Frankie Ross was able to purchase Greywood Hall artworks without them being offered on the open market. For rare paintings that's quite an unusual arrangement, isn't it?' Lincoln was winging it, but he wanted to get Rayner talking, wanted him to give Frankie up.

'Mr Ross is a valued customer,' said Rayner. 'The arrangement was unusual, yes, but it was an amicable one, agreed between all parties.'

Lincoln grinned. 'I bet.' He shuffled his papers for a minute or two, noticing out of the corner of his eye the way Rayner's hands tensed on the edge of the table. 'Can you describe the proposal Hugh Buckthorn put to you?'

'Proposal? It wasn't a proposal, it was a bloody—'

Lincoln met his gaze. Cold grey eyes, tiny pupils. 'It was a what, Mr Rayner? It was a bloody what? Ultimatum? Threat?'

Bernard Fisher took his glasses off and laid them on his document wallet. 'What are you saying my client has done, exactly?'

Before Lincoln could respond, though, Rayner leapt in. 'Hugh was going to go public about the copies Howard sold. He didn't care if it made Howard look bad, or their father. He didn't care if he showed me up, discredited me, destroyed the reputation I've built over *decades* as a dealer.'

'What did he want from you to stop him going public?'

'He wanted to get the originals back, the ones Howard sold to Frankie. He was prepared to pay whatever Frankie paid for them, if only he could restore them to Greywood Hall.'

'All of them?'

'Pah! He couldn't possibly have afforded to buy all of them back. But Frankie didn't want to part with them, not at any price. And why should he? He bought them at a price agreed with Howard.'

'A price far lower than the market value, because he was blackmailing Howard over the forgery he'd sold him earlier.'

292

'You can't prove that.'

The room grew warm. Lincoln's headache grew more insistent, a steam hammer in his head.

'The documents in the strongroom at Greywood Hall will give us all the proof we need, Mr Rayner,' he said. 'Paperwork Howard Buckthorn kept, along with copies of the documentation you concocted when you sold forgeries for him and for his father before him. Decades as a dealer? More like decades as a fraudster!'

There was quiet in the room. At last Bernard Fisher suggested that he should have a word in private with his client, and Lincoln suspended the interview.

'What documents?' Woody hissed as he and Lincoln waited in the corridor outside. 'We haven't been to the strongroom yet.'

'Not yet, no. But I'm confident we'll find everything that Barbara Trent said we would. After all, she was the one who dealt with all the paperwork, as Mr Howard's right-hand woman.'

A moment later, Bernard Fisher opened the door.

'My client would like to make a statement,' he said. 'He'd like to co-operate.'

Some aspirin and sweet, strong coffee eased the headache, but Lincoln was still fuming as he watched Rayner and his solicitor leave a little later. Rayner had confessed to playing a part in the sale of forged artworks, but he denied any involvement in Buckthorn's murder.

'Actually,' Rayner had said, his halo of hair bobbing, 'I remember now that Hugh *did* phone me that evening. He couldn't accept that Frankie refused to sell back the paintings. I'm afraid I gave him short shrift. But I was at home all evening. My wife and Tilly will back me up on that.'

I bet they will, thought Lincoln as he watched Rayner depart. He'd been released on bail, but his reputation in the art world would take a battering as soon as news of his arrest got out.

Woody, too, watched him leave. 'Reckon he confessed to selling the forgeries to distract us from the murder?'

'What do *you* think? I was hoping he'd give us Ross.'

'He wouldn't dare.'

'Ross doesn't know that, though, does he?'

'You hoping Ross'll find out and do something stupid?'

'Is that too much to hope for? Somehow we've got to be able to put Ross in that flat with Buckthorn. We know he was there but we can't prove it. But last night I had an idea. Fancy going back to the scene of the crime? I think we may have missed something when we thought Buckthorn's death was an accident.'

'Can't believe it's half-term next week,' said Woody as he drove them towards Bridgeford. 'Kate's going off to her dad's.'

'That'll give you and Suki a break.'

'Kate's no trouble – well, no more than you'd expect from a teenager. She's good with the boys. Reckon she'd like a brother or sister of her own, but that's not going to happen now, is it?'

'Isn't it?' Lincoln wondered what he was getting at. Trish certainly wasn't too old to have another child – assuming she wanted to.

'Can't see her giving up her career the way Suki did, not now she's landing jobs like the one in Essex.'

He kept quiet. Woody and Suki had clearly assumed the post at the Charles Lundy Library was a big step up for Trish, and not the refuge Lincoln knew it was. She hadn't even felt able to confide in Suki that she was the 'anonymous source' who'd talked to a journalist last year about the council's failings.

They parked in the market square and walked down Jackdaw Lane. Mist hovered over the stream that ran beside the mill, and the sky was a thick grey blanket of cloud. At the bend in the lane the old chapel loomed up, sad and redundant, condemned.

Nearly a fortnight after the murder, work had resumed on the Old Shoddy Mill, though Rufus's flat remained sealed off. While Woody had a quick word with Austin Kendall, the site foreman, to explain why they were there, Lincoln peeled back the police tape and unlocked the door of the flat, though he didn't go in straight away.

'I've been wondering about the wine,' he said when Woody caught up with him. 'About Buckthorn and Ross having a drink together that night.'

'Ye-es.' Woody looked at him uncertainly.

'Bear with me.'

With gloves on, they went inside. Lincoln went straight to the fridge and opened it. 'What do you see?'

Woody peered in. 'Not much food, and most of it'll be past its sell-by date by now. And four bottles of wine.'

'What sort of wine?'

Woody checked the labels. 'Dry white. German.'

'Exactly.' Lincoln shut the fridge again. 'The bottle Tilly Rayner emptied down the sink and took away with her was a South American red.'

'So?'

'How was Buckthorn drugged?'

'Rohypnol in his drink.'

'And the only alcohol he had that evening was the wine he had here, with Ross – from the bottle Tilly removed because she was afraid Rufus's prints might be on it.'

Woody still looked puzzled. 'He'd have been careful to wipe that, though, wouldn't he? He wasn't expecting Tilly to come in and clean up after him.'

Lincoln agreed. 'I'm guessing Ross brought that bottle with him. He had to make certain there was something he could drop some roofies into. The only way to be sure was to provide the wine himself.'

Woody began to cotton on. 'And he'd need to pour it himself, too, while Buckthorn was in the living room and couldn't see what he was doing.'

'Exactly. But even if he's in here and Buckthorn's in the other room, he can hardly whip out his latex gloves without looking suspicious, so we can assume he opened the bottle and poured the wine—'

'And spiked Buckthorn's—'

'—Without any gloves on. That bottle of red had a cork in it. It was still rolling around in the bottom of Tilly's shopping bag when we arrested her. Ross must've used a corkscrew to open the wine. Now, he could've brought one with him, but what's the betting...?'

Lincoln opened the cutlery drawer. Knives, forks, and spoons of different sizes were filed in compartments in a steel basket. In a section at the side lay a metal, heavy-duty combination corkscrew and bottle opener.

'Eureka!' He got his phone out and photographed the implement *in situ*. 'And once he'd used it, he probably dropped it back into the drawer without thinking. With any luck,' Lincoln went on as he carefully lifted the corkscrew out of the drawer and dropped it into an evidence bag, 'Frankie left at least a partial print somewhere on this.'

As they were leaving, he stuck his head round the door of the Portakabin to tell Austin Kendall they'd finished in the flat for now.

'Not sure Rufus is going to want to live there after all this,' Kendall said. 'But you'd be surprised how much interest there's been in the last week or so! They'll have no trouble selling the apartments when they're ready to.'

'Who actually owns the mill? Rufus and who else?'

'The other owner's a group called Press Vale Enterprises,' he said. 'Something to do with the country club.'

CHAPTER 57

By early afternoon, Trish was feeling better than she had when she got up. She'd woken with a headache, which she blamed on going to the pub with Stewart after work the evening before. Still, a headache had been a small price to pay. After a couple of glasses of wine, and in the convivial atmosphere of the Drum and Monkey, she'd felt emboldened enough to broach the issue of his apparently falsified reference.

'Did you ever actually work at that museum in Winchester?' she'd asked, toying with a glass of the house rosé.

'No, and I feel an absolute idiot,' he'd admitted. 'When I applied for this job I had to provide three testimonials from past employers, but the third one I approached didn't get back to me. I didn't know what to do. I was interviewed for a job at Winchester a few years ago, and I still had the letter from Miss Skipwith, rejecting me. I simply changed it a bit.'

'You could've explained what really happened. That would've been more honest than making something up.'

He'd bowed his head, contrite. 'I realise that now, and it was incredibly stupid. You want me to hand my notice in? Because I will, like a shot, if you'd rather I did, if you feel you can't work with me.'

'Don't be silly.' Yes, he'd undermined her trust in him, but he'd been so desperate for the job – and she was so desperate for his help – that she thought it best to say nothing. The agency handling his appointment had been at fault, too, for not checking more thoroughly.

Now, feeling more human after hungrily devouring a toasted cheese sandwich at lunchtime, Trish was back at her desk, cataloguing another of Lundy's several books about his travels in the East of England.

Stewart, meanwhile, was working on an illustrated book on alchemy which, from her viewpoint, looked far more exciting than Essex.

He broke off and sat back from his laptop. 'We still haven't found any Isaac Newton manuscripts, have we?'

'I wasn't expecting to, but it'd be quite a coup if we did, wouldn't it?'

'Imagine finding his early work on gravity! *De Motu Corporum In Gyrum.*' He gazed across the room, his eyes shining. '*On The Motion Of Bodies In An Orbit.* A long-lost manuscript.'

'The one he fell out with Hooke over?'

Stewart nodded. 'Hooke thought Newton owed him credit for giving him the idea in the first place, but Newton refused.'

'And Lundy sided with Hooke.' A spat among seventeenth-century scientists. She could imagine quill-penned letters flying back and forth. 'How much would that be worth?'

'For the manuscript of *De Motu*? Christ! You could name your price!'

'The trustees would pounce on that if they thought there was a copy here.' She sighed. 'But I'm sure if Lundy had a copy, previous curators would've found it.'

'If they'd recognised it for what it was.'

Trish wasn't sure *she* would recognise *De Motu* for what it was, but she didn't say as much. And they really didn't have time for a treasure hunt, with so many other books to get through. 'We'll have to choose something else that can be sold without spoiling the collection as a whole.'

Stewart tutted in disgust. 'The trustees haven't got the first idea, have they? Why don't you suggest launching a crowdfunding appeal on Facebook, or instigate the Charles Lundy Charity Walk?'

'God, no! If I suggested it, they'd expect me to organise it! And yes, I know you weren't serious, but even so...' She enjoyed his company, was grateful that he felt an even greater loyalty to Lundy's library than she did herself. And he made her laugh, and she needed that.

Towards the end of the afternoon she stood up and stretched, her back aching from too much sitting at the laptop. She paced around, taking deep breaths, rolling her shoulders and reaching her hands above her head, thankful that Stewart had disappeared into the cloakroom and couldn't witness her impromptu exercise routine.

When she paused by his desk to admire the magnificent atlas he was in the process of cataloguing, she saw a sheet of paper poking out from beneath his laptop: a photocopy of a page from what looked like an old auction catalogue, annotated in Lundy's own distinctive hand.

The photocopy itself had pencil scribbles on it, ticks and crosses, a couple of question marks – made, presumably, by Stewart. One of those titles he'd queried was *De Motu*.

Did he *know* there was a copy of Newton's manuscript here somewhere? Was that why he kept asking about it?

She heard the loo flush and hurried back to her desk, ready with a smile when he reappeared.

'I love these old atlases,' he said, carrying on where he'd left off. 'Fantasy geography for the most part, but a joy to browse. So you're not flying off anywhere exotic for half-term?'

'Sadly, no. And these books aren't going to catalogue themselves, are they? Let's crack on.'

CHAPTER 58

Dale Jacobs was waiting in the CID room, his foot up on the tweed footstool, when Lincoln and Woody returned from Bridgeford.

'Good work on Cornelius Rayner,' he said. 'Shame he hasn't given Ross up.'

'We've been taking another look at the flat,' said Lincoln, 'and we may have something that puts Ross there that night.'

He told the DCI about the corkscrew Ross must have used. 'His prints are on file, so let's hope there's a match.'

'Nice one! Soon as the warrant comes through, go to Greywood Hall and look for that paperwork you're after.'

'Any news on Amy Cartland?'

Jacobs gave him a strange smile. 'The bank's sent us the CCTV from the cash machine in Warminster where her card was used. It was the Cartland girl who was using it.'

Lincoln gasped. He hadn't been expecting that.

Woody looked equally surprised. 'Reckon she's gone into hiding, afraid she'll be next?'

'There'd have been simpler ways of doing that than scaring her mum and dad,' Jacobs snapped, 'not to mention taking up all our bloody time and manpower. Either she's a missing person or she's not. The Warminster lot are following it up, checking other CCTV, asking around.'

'She's not much more than a kid,' said Lincoln, 'and she's scared.'

Jacobs snorted. 'You're too soft, Lincoln. You've gotta be tough to get on.'

'We should be glad she's not been abducted or killed.'

'We should, yes.' Jacobs swung his foot off the stool. 'And when she's arrested for wasting police time, that's the first thing I'll tell her.' He stood up, lurching slightly, his bad ankle still not strong enough to support him without his stick. 'I want to get Frankie Ross. I want that bastard brought down.'

The CID room seemed ominously quiet after he'd gone.

Lincoln guessed Jacobs was afraid to bring Ross in too soon, especially since he'd already been accused of harassment. He couldn't question him until he could throw some real evidence at him – and that's what they hadn't got. Still, if the lab confirmed that Ross's prints were on the corkscrew...

Lincoln got home to find Joe Gibson waiting for him.

'I'll take a look at your floor and give you a quote, okay?'

'Fine, great.'

They went inside together, and Lincoln showed him where the living room floor ought to have been if his previous contractors hadn't buggered off.

'Cowboys, that lot,' said Joe when he heard the name. 'Bloody cowboys.'

After he'd gone, Lincoln rang Trish. She couldn't believe he'd got round to sorting the floorboards out – well, taken the first steps towards doing so.

'Cautious steps, I hope,' she'd said with a chuckle.

'Very funny. He could make a start the middle of next week.'

'That's half-term week.'

'Yes, but if you're not even leaving Essex... How's things at the library?'

'There's so much to do,' she groaned, 'and I'm never going to get it all finished.'

'Not even with Superman at your side?'

'Not even if I change my name to Lois Lane, no.'

'What's up, then?'

'Just something... I don't know. Something about him's a bit off. He faked one of his testimonials. Maybe I'm overreacting.'

'If you're worried about him—'

'I'm just tired. How's the case going?'

'Which one?' He managed a laugh, even though what she'd just told him about Stewart had unsettled him. 'I can't say much. It's all at a critical stage, but we're making progress.'

She yawned. 'Sorry. I need an early night. I'm pleased about your floor, though. Will you ring me tomorrow?'

CHAPTER 59

THURSDAY 16TH FEBRUARY

Next morning, even before Lincoln had hung his coat up, Pam had sprung out of her chair and hurried across to his desk.

'I've got a name for Edgar or Ned, the guy who worked with Bruno. The woman from the Polish community group remembers his family. They changed their surname from Adamski to Adams. She said Ned moved to Somerset a while ago, to where his uncle lived, but she can't remember where.'

'At least we've got a name now, though Adams is pretty common. But well done.'

'I tried phoning Sonia, but she's not answering.'

'Probably afraid the newspapers are trying to track her down, after the way they doorstepped her brother-in-law. Text her instead.'

When the search warrant came through a little later, Lincoln had to decide who to take with him to Greywood Hall to look for the evidence they needed.

'You want to come back to the Hall with me?' he asked Pam. 'I'll understand if you'd rather not.'

'Of course,' she said after the briefest of hesitations. 'I can't wait to meet Mrs Ray-of-Sunshine again.'

He'd phoned ahead, so Mrs Pinfold was expecting them, and they went through the same wordless performance as before, up flights of stairs and along corridors to the Long Gallery. They chased her past the chilly little room where Buckthorn had worked, until they reached double doors that she had to unlock.

'The attics,' she said, letting them step ahead of her into a dimly lit space that reminded Lincoln of being backstage in a theatre. The slightly musty, uncarpeted storeroom, where paintings were lined up in special frames away from the light, was in sharp contrast to the bright and colourful Long Gallery.

A door to the left opened into a windowless room only a little bigger than one of the interview rooms at Barley Lane. A vast safe took up most of its floorspace.

'What was it you wanted to look at, exactly?' Mrs Pinfold wanted to know.

Lincoln hadn't told her beforehand in case she took it upon herself to hide it before they got there. She might be as aware of the previous earls' dodgy dealings as Barbara Trent was, even if she hadn't been complicit in them.

'Paperwork relating to the sale of artworks,' he said. 'We were told it was kept here.'

She inhaled sharply. 'That material hasn't been kept here for years. It's been filed away in my office. My predecessor must have had time on her hands if she could shuttle back and forth between here and there.'

'I'll come back with you to get the paperwork,' Pam offered. 'Save you having to make another journey.'

On his own while the two women went back to the estate office, Lincoln left the strongroom and ambled up and down among the paintings that had been in the Buckthorn family for generations. Some artists he recognised but most he didn't, and he really couldn't tell which might have been copies and which were originals. What did the Giacomo Scrabini look like? Would he recognise a Caravaggio?

The door to the attics opened and he turned to greet Pam – only to find it was Frankie Ross standing there, his trilby in his hand.

'Inspector Lincoln. How fortunate that your visit here coincides with mine. I was hoping to meet up with you again.'

'I'm sorry about what happened to Marco.'

'I bet you are! One more little thug off the streets, eh?' He threw his hat down on a side table. 'I wasn't expecting to find anyone else here.'

'Neither was I. Here to choose your next Canaletto?'

'Can't stand Canaletto. He's bloodless and cold. No, actually, I came to measure up a picture that Howard sold me this time last year, but which I've been unable to collect until now. And you are here because—?'

'I'm here to collect proof that you bought paintings from Howard at rock bottom prices.'

Ross sneered. 'So? They were private sales. If he wasn't happy with my offer, he could have turned me down.'

'And if he had, you'd have gone public about the fake he sold you.'

'Would you blame me?' Ross strolled across to the first bay of paintings. 'I made money by working hard, not by accident of birth.'

'You and Hugh were friends, weren't you, when you were younger?'

He spun round, surprised that Lincoln knew this. 'Yes. My mother worked for the estate, so the park was my playground for years. Hugh and I were pals for a while, until he rejoined his tribe – the aristocracy. I was soon cast aside for his posh chums.'

'That must've hurt.'

'I'm thick-skinned now and I was thick-skinned then. What would hurt *you*, Inspector? Is there no girlfriend, boyfriend, lover, partner? You must get lonely in that great big house.'

Lincoln's pulse quickened. 'Not especially. I've never been a great one for company.'

'Not even the company of Ms Whittington? Patricia, is it?' Ross persisted. 'I met her once. Here, actually. She was trying to wring a nice artwork out of Howard, something to make her exhibition at the library a bit special, but she'd have been better off trying to wring blood out of a stone. And Kate, is it, her little girl? Not so little now, of course.'

'You must've been asking around about me. Why would you do that?' Lincoln refused to let him see how much he'd unnerved him by mentioning Trish and Kate.

'Did you ask your boss why he left Bristol? Didn't dare, did you?'

'I keep meaning to, but the moment's never quite right. Why don't you tell me yourself?'

Ross grinned. 'Another time, perhaps. You know, if you hadn't arrested my son, he wouldn't have been obliged to stay in the flat over Guys. He wouldn't have died.'

'Where else would he have gone? He'd been thrown out of his previous place, and he didn't want to go back to live with his mother. If you'd looked after that building, it wouldn't have caught fire. Marco died because *you* didn't do your job properly.'

Ross started towards him but checked himself. 'And your own house is in order, is it, Inspector? Because it didn't look that way when I dropped in the other evening.'

'You're not the first man who's threatened me or threatened my home. I don't have a lot to lose, Mr Ross, no matter how it looks.'

'Apart from Ms Whittington. Apart from young Kate.'

Lincoln swallowed hard. 'Why did you kill Hugh?'

'Who says I did?'

'The evidence says you did. He was prepared to risk exposing his own brother, wasn't he, if it meant he could get those paintings back? You had it all sewn up while Howard was alive. He'd do anything to cover up the forgeries he'd sold. But Hugh wasn't scared, was he? He called your bluff. He just wanted the paintings returned to Greywood Hall, where they belonged.'

'If he'd exposed Howard, he'd have exposed Laurence too.'

Lincoln stepped back. 'Laurence was involved?'

'No, but everyone would assume he was. The Riverbourne name would be tainted forever. Hugh wouldn't have risked that.'

'So he was going to appeal to your better nature? Try to reach some amicable agreement for old times' sake? You were going to sit down to discuss it over a few glasses of wine?'

A broad smile spread over Ross's face, but there was no warmth in it. 'I don't know what you're talking about, Inspector,' he said, though he clearly knew full well. 'I'm not much of a drinker myself.'

The door swung open behind him, and Pam came in, a red box file in her arms. She retreated a little, glancing from Ross to Lincoln, unsure what to do.

'Come in, DC Smyth.' With a flourish, Ross gestured for her to enter the room. 'I was so sorry to hear about your grandfather.'

'Thank you, I... Did you know him?'

'Sadly, no. Now, I won't keep you. You look as if you're going to be busy.'

And with that he picked up his hat and put it on, tapped the crown and swept out.

'Frankie Ross?' Pam guessed. 'How did he know my name? How did he know about my grandad?'

'He's playing mind games, trying to intimidate you.' Lincoln cast a last look round the shadowy depths of the attics. 'Let's get back. I've had enough culture for one day.'

CHAPTER 60

'Let's go for a walk after lunch,' said Hester. 'You haven't been outdoors since you got here, and you need some fresh air. We both do.'

Sonia reluctantly consented to being shunted out of Hester's cottage and along the muddy lane that ran past it. After she'd driven back from Somerset she'd headed straight here, telling her friend she was running away from the tabloid press and needed somewhere to lie low until the fuss was over.

'What's that on your coat?' Hester had held her away from her. 'Is that blood?'

Sonia had looked down. Her coat, her cuffs, her skirt, all were soiled.

'I saw a dog by the side of the road,' she'd said, 'and I stopped the car to check on it. It was dead, but I didn't like to leave it there, so I picked it up and moved it. It must have bled over me. I'm sorry.'

And Hester had made her strip off and dress in some old clothes of Genevieve's while she put Sonia's things in the wash. She hadn't questioned the story beyond saying how sad it was that someone had knocked the dog down, but then, some people shouldn't be allowed to get behind the wheel of a car.

Sonia had slept most of Tuesday and Wednesday, utterly drained, as if she were recovering from flu. On Thursday, though, she let Hester persuade her to go for a walk, even though it was windy and bitterly cold.

The two women tramped along the lane, sidestepping puddles and pushing against the wind. Sonia missed living by the sea, even though the Solent at Southampton was nothing like the seaside. It was the vista she missed, being able to look and look and never see an end to it – scary and comforting at the same time.

Gazing up at the bare branches now, she thought of the trees overlooking Ned's yard, thought of him staring out of the window as he told her what had happened to Yazmin.

She'd left him there and not said anything to anyone. His death would be a mystery forever. His family – if he still had one – would never know what had become of him.

305

And then, as she and Hester walked over the river, pausing on the bridge to watch the fast-flowing Press hurrying beneath them, she decided his family didn't deserve to go through what she'd been through – the years of not knowing.

'I have to go back,' she said, grabbing hold of Hester's sleeve to stop her walking on any farther. 'I have to go back and talk to someone.'

CHAPTER 61

Lincoln had thought the paperwork from Greywood Hall would be enough to incriminate Frankie Ross, but he was dismayed to find it recorded only the sale of paintings through Prior and Hill.

Exasperated, Pam dropped a sheaf of receipts back onto her desk. 'Where's the paperwork for the paintings Howard sold through Cornelius Rayner?'

'Someone must have taken it out before you got there,' Dilke suggested.

'There wouldn't have been time. Mrs Pinfold didn't know what we were looking for until we arrived. Maybe someone in the family hid that paperwork after Howard died, so his executors wouldn't ask awkward questions.'

'But who would've done that?' asked Dilke.

Lincoln took a guess. 'Adelaide, Howard's widow. What's the betting she knew what her husband was up to all along?'

Why hadn't he considered the Dowager Countess of Riverbourne sooner? He was kicking himself now, although, in his defence, the only time he'd spoken to her she'd sounded remote and uninvolved, and he'd still been working on the theory that it was Hugh who'd been up to no good, not his brother.

'It would make sense,' said Pam. 'She must have free run of the Hall, and she'd want to protect her husband's reputation, and her son's. Frankie Ross strolled in,' she told Dilke. 'Offered me his condolences.'

'That's a bit creepy! What was he doing there?'

'Measuring up a painting Howard sold him last year, apparently,' said Lincoln. 'Probably getting ready to ship it over to Spain to adorn the walls of his villa.' Again he thought of those empty spaces on the walls of Gabriella's house and wondered how she was bearing up under the loss of Marco. Had she any idea what her ex-husband and son had got into?

Pam's mobile beeped. 'Hey, the woman from the Polish community group's texted me. *Ned found stabbed in Shepton. BBC news just now.*'

They crowded round her computer screen as she brought up the BBC news page which announced that the man found stabbed in a house in

Shepton Mallet two days earlier had been named as Edgar Adams, forty-four and unmarried. Avon and Somerset Police were investigating.

'Must be the same man,' said Lincoln. 'But whether he's the one who abducted Yazmin... Pam, get in touch with whoever's leading the investigation there, tell them he could be a murder suspect. I wonder if Sonia's seen the news.'

Only a few minutes later Sonia herself arrived in the CID room, accompanied by a large woman of about the same age who was dressed in several layers of skirts, an overlarge Fair Isle sweater and cherry-red Doc Martens. Beside her, Sonia looked elfin and tiny.

'I found Ned,' Sonia said even before Lincoln had greeted her. 'I wasn't going to say anything but—'

'She found his address in Bruno's things,' the other woman put in. 'He lived in Shepton Mallet. She went there on Sunday and—'

'He told me it was an accident,' Sonia went on, talking over her. 'He said Yazmin jumped out of his van and banged her head when the van knocked her down, but—'

'He shouldn't have taken her in the first place, though, should he?' her friend said.

'He was taking her to Bruno, he said, and she wanted to go at first but then—'

'Wait,' said Lincoln, holding his hands up. 'Don't say another word, either of you. Sonia Fletcher, you're under arrest...'

Lincoln phoned Trish when he got home, relieved that the mystery of Yazmin Fletcher's death had been solved, but sad that the little girl's mother had taken the law into her own hands.

'How are things with you?' Trish wanted to know.

'I had to arrest Sonia Fletcher today,' he said, prodding a bowl of microwaved rice he no longer fancied. 'Yazmin's mother.'

'It wasn't her who—?'

'No, it was a bloke who worked with Bruno, Yazmin's dad. She tracked him down and stabbed him, left him for dead. Luckily a neighbour noticed one of his windows was wide open, which seemed odd this time of year, and found him in time. He'll live.'

Ned Adams would be in court when he was fit enough, charged with manslaughter, most likely, since there was no way of proving he intended to kill the child.

'What about Sonia?'

'Apparently he's saying she stabbed him by accident. She's been released on bail, so we'll have to wait and see.' Tiredness descended on him, as if someone had dropped a blanket over his head. 'How's Superman?'

'Still flying through the shelves, cataloguing everything with the utmost efficiency. If I left here tomorrow no one would notice.'

'Then why don't you?'

'I can't leave. I've got a contract. And I'm in charge. And I love it here, despite the cold and the sea fog.'

Phone call over, Lincoln flavoured the rice with a generous dollop of HP sauce and a blob of butter. Thought how much better he was eating these days, compared to his bedsit days. Or not.

Suppose the Trust offered to extend Trish's contract after all? Would she accept it?

He planned to call on the Dowager Countess of Riverbourne tomorrow. Trish would be impressed by that. He should have told her.

He picked up the Jameson's, surprised by how little was left in the bottle. Poured what was left and took it up to bed with him.

CHAPTER 62

Next morning, Lincoln and Woody called on Lady Adelaide at Laurence's home in Barbury.

'And what am I supposed to have done, exactly?' She gestured for them to sit down. The upstairs sitting room of her son's townhouse was elegant and warm, a good fire going, and everything about it sparkling and tasteful. Across the green, the abbey stood stately and grey, as it had for centuries.

Lincoln perched himself on the unyielding edge of the earl's antique couch.

'We're trying to trace some papers detailing the sale of artworks by your husband,' he explained. 'In particular, sales brokered by Cornelius Rayner.'

Lady Adelaide pouted and turned away. She had thick grey hair, simply styled, held back by a velvet hairband. Her broad face, handsome rather than pretty, bore the fine lines of someone who enjoyed the outdoor life. She wore the collar of her gingham shirt turned up, and her tailored jeans and leather boots were more Bond Street than Barbury.

'And what makes you think I'd have them? They must be in the estate manager's office.'

'Actually,' said Woody, 'we spoke to Mrs Pinfold this morning when we were trying to get hold of you. She said you took some of those documents out of the filing cabinet a few days ago, and as far as she knows you still have them.'

Lady Adelaide must have realised there was no point denying it, because she got up and marched out of the room. Woody and Lincoln looked at each other, wondering what would happen next.

She returned with a leather wallet the size of a laptop and thrust it at Woody. 'I suppose now everyone will find out what a fool my husband was,' she said savagely. 'I'd be the first to admit he was no art expert, but to be stupid enough to sell forgeries... That Ross man was blackmailing him, in effect. Howard was trapped – you must see that! And then he died, and Hugh came back and wanted to know where all the good stuff had gone. I knew he'd never let it rest.'

'Who decided Hugh had to die?'

Light glanced off her pearl stud earrings as she shook her head emphatically. 'It wasn't me,' she said. 'I promise you it wasn't me.'

'The DCI phoned while you were out,' said Breeze when they got back. 'The lab results came through. The fingerprints on the corkscrew were a good match for Franco Rossetti, aka Frankie Ross, aka the Fruit Machine King.'

Woody punched the air, and Lincoln felt an enormous sense of relief – but it was short-lived.

'The DCI's sending someone to the Black Swan to arrest him,' Breeze went on. 'Someone from his team at Park Street.'

'That should've been us!' said Woody. 'It's our case.'

Lincoln said nothing, but he was fuming. Just when they'd got enough on Frankie Ross to charge him, it would be Jacobs's team from Park Street who'd have the privilege of arresting him!

'Let's go through what Adelaide Buckthorn gave us,' said Lincoln, trying not to let his resentment show. 'See if any of these documents can help build the case against him.'

With Woody's help, it took him a couple of hours to check the prices Ross paid against the prices similar works had fetched at auction.

'He was ripping Howard off,' said Woody. 'Reckon some of those paintings would've fetched twice as much as he paid.'

'Still, I bet Howard didn't declare any of it for taxes. Look, here's the receipt for Ross buying the Caravaggio, but have you seen anything about the Scrabini that Buckthorn was so keen on finding?'

Woody shook his head. 'Howard can't have sold it. It must still be at Greywood Hall.'

Lincoln sighed, exasperated, still smarting over the Park Street team arresting Ross when the privilege should have been Barley Lane's. 'Why do I even care? Rich people buying and selling paintings like they're – I don't know what they're like, but it doesn't seem right that only the rich get to see these pictures.'

'But they were mostly painted for rich people in the first place, weren't they?' Dilke chipped in. 'Artists needed patrons who could pay for them to paint. They didn't paint just because they felt like it.'

'Still feels wrong.' Lincoln glanced at his mobile. He'd missed a call when he and Woody had been with Lady Adelaide. Unknown caller. He checked his voicemail and was surprised to hear a husky voice he recognised instantly.

'Gabriella here. Mrs Ross. Can you come to the house this evening? I need to talk to someone.'

The house in Barbury Park Avenue looked sad in the failing light. Lincoln parked in front of the imposing portico and wondered what would happen to Gabriella now her ex-husband was in custody. She must have been allowed to keep the house as part of the divorce settlement, but a place this grand must be expensive to maintain – or was Trevor, her partner, earning enough to keep her in the manner to which she'd been accustomed when she was still married to Frankie?

She led him into the kitchen-diner, where a few downlighters were the only illumination. Coffee was percolating on the breakfast bar, and she offered him a cup.

'Or something stronger, Inspector?'

'Coffee's fine, thanks.'

'Of course – you're on duty.' She looked unhappy and worn out, with shadows beneath her big, dark eyes.

He was off duty technically, but he let it go. 'I'm sorry about Marco.'

'I haven't really processed it yet. We're having to sort out the funeral and everything.' She hitched herself onto a stool at the breakfast bar. 'It's difficult with the way things were between Marco and Trevor and me and Frankie.'

He sat on the stool across from her. 'You wanted to see me?'

'It's about Hugh Buckthorn.' She reached across to lift the coffee pot from the hotplate. 'He came to see me the night before he died.'

'He did?'

She poured coffee and pushed his cup towards him. 'He didn't know Frankie had taken all his pictures with him when he left here. He was after one or two in particular he thought Frankie had bought off Howard a few years ago.'

'A Caravaggio and a Scrabini?'

She looked up, shocked. 'How did you know?'

'I saw him the day after, and he happened to mention them. You knew your husband was buying paintings from Greywood Hall?'

'Oh yes. He used to boast about how little he'd paid. I hated every last one of those paintings. Ugly great things. Hugh said he was going to talk to the guy who handled the sales. He thought he could work something out with him. He was friends with his son, he said, so it would be okay.' She bit her lip. 'He was wrong, wasn't he? That's why he was killed.'

'We still don't—'

'Hugh and I were together for a while before I met Frankie. Didn't know that, did you?'

Lincoln shook his head.

'I met Hugh at a party at the Hall. I didn't know who he was at first. He was a lot older than me, nearly thirty, but he was funny and clever, and so handsome! And he spoke Italian, because his mum was Italian, and he knew the little town Dad came from. We had some fun, but it didn't last – how could it? Dad was only an immigrant with a restaurant in town. Hugh was off to London to study, and I met Frankie. But before Hugh left, we'd—' She broke off, her eyes filling with tears.

'If it's too difficult to talk about—'

'Marco was Hugh's son,' she said simply. 'I never told Frankie, and I never will. I wasn't in love with Hugh, but now I've lost him *and* Marco. It makes me wonder what's the point of anything, if you can lose it all in the space of a few days.'

Without thinking, Lincoln reached out and put his hand over hers, and she didn't pull away.

'How touching.' The voice that boomed from the doorway took both of them by surprise. Frankie Ross strode into the kitchen, flinging his trilby hat onto the counter. 'Don't worry, Inspector, I won't tell your Ms Whittington.'

'What are you doing here?' Gabriella stepped down from her stool.

Ross ignored her, helping himself to coffee and shoving the pot back onto the hotplate. 'Surprised to see me, Inspector? *I* was just as surprised to see Dale Jacobs hobbling across the foyer at the Black Swan a few hours ago. Luckily I saw him in time to take evasive action. You still haven't asked him why he left Bristol, have you?'

'No, but now you can tell me yourself.' Lincoln sipped his coffee as calmly as he could, even though his pulse was racing.

Gabriella turned on her ex-husband. 'Isn't your *girlfriend* from Bristol?'

'You know she is. And Donna's my *fiancée*. But a while ago she and that moron Dale Jacobs were together, only he can't get over the fact that she'd rather be with me in Spain than with him in fucking Keynsham.'

'Was it you who ran him off the road?' asked Lincoln.

Ross looked incredulous. 'Why would I run him off the road? Why would I need to? He drives like a bloody maniac. He's been out to get

313

me ever since Donna moved in with me. He fucked up my business in Bristol, then came down here and tried to do the same. Did he give you some bullshit about Press Vale being used as a brothel? Yeah? And you want to know the truth about Amy Cartland? When that little bitch decides it's safe to show her face again, ask her what she was *really* doing in the Abbey Suite the night Hugh Buckthorn "rescued" her!'

'If you've done anything to that kid—'

'An old friend of yours sends his regards, by the way, Inspector. Pete Doubleday.'

'Doubleday?'

'I'll tell him you haven't forgotten him.' Ross took a deep breath and turned to Gabriella. 'Did I hear you right just now? Were you telling the inspector that Marco wasn't my son?' He said it pleasantly enough, but there was a dark undertone of menace. 'You really think I didn't know?'

She stared at him. 'You knew?'

'Not until he was ten or so, but then I could see he was the spit of Hugh at the same age, when the two of us were running round Greywood Hall together. I did the sums and worked it out. Still a good father to him, though, wasn't I? Wasn't I?'

'Yes, Frankie,' she said. 'You were. But why did you have to kill Hugh? Because you were jealous of him?'

'Jealous of that pervert? I didn't want anything that bastard had.'

'Except his paintings.' Lincoln stood up. 'Did he have any idea what you'd forced his brother into?'

'Howard sold me a fake and thought he'd got away with it. Only I wasn't the pushover he took me for.'

'You certainly made him pay for his mistake – over and over again.'

Ross picked up his cup, guzzling his coffee as if he were in a hurry. 'You ever hear about the sex parties Howard used to host at Greywood Hall? Kids bussed in, kids from children's homes in town. You hear about that? Howard was used to buying people's silence – punters, staff, social workers. But I didn't want money. I wanted his paintings – an arrangement that worked beautifully until the bastard dropped dead shooting pheasants. And then Hugh came back, and he wanted those paintings as badly as I did.'

He banged his cup down hard on the counter, making Gabriella jump. And then he plunged his hand into his overcoat pocket and pulled out a pistol.

Lincoln froze. 'How are you going to make this look like an accident, Frankie?'

'I'll come up with something.' He pointed the gun at his ex-wife. 'You asked this guy round this evening, Gabby?'

'No,' Lincoln cut in. 'I called here to ask about your paintings, but I see you've taken them all away.' He took a step towards Gabriella. 'What was so special about the Scrabini?'

'The Scrabini?'

Another step. 'Hugh seemed obsessed by it. I'd never even heard of Giacomo Scrabini until he told me he wanted to make the painting the centrepiece of an exhibition at the Hall. You've never seen it?'

Ross frowned, puzzled. 'What painting?'

Lincoln turned to Gabriella. 'Hugh asked you about it, didn't he? He thought Frankie must have it already.'

She nodded dumbly.

'So where is it?' Ross snapped. 'Where is this fucking painting?'

Lincoln shrugged. 'No idea. At Greywood Hall, I suppose. In fact, this morning when you walked in I thought that's why you were there. Looking for the Scrabini.' He was winging it, desperate to divert Ross's attention away from Gabriella, to get him to put the gun down.

But Ross saw through him. 'Giacomo Scrabini's in the Third Division,' he said with a sneer. 'I could pick up a Scrabini for a couple of thousand.'

'This particular one,' said Lincoln, frantically trying to summon up the names of Renaissance painters, 'could actually be by Raphael.'

'You're joking! Raphael?'

'That's what Hugh thought. And he's the expert. Was.'

'Frankie, please.' Gabriella reached out towards him.

Lincoln heard the ominous sound of the gun being cocked. The linseed smell of the gun oil made his mouth water. His pulse thundered.

'Hugh went to the flat to meet Cornelius, didn't he, Frankie? But you were there instead. Still, you'd got a nice bottle of red, you'd have a drink together, talk about the old days. Couple of roofies in his wine, give him time to get drowsy. He'd be so out of it he wouldn't know what was happening. Marco arrives to help you set the scene for a spot of kinky sex in stockings and suspenders, make it look as if Hugh died a humiliating but accidental death, a death his family will want to hush up—'

Gabriella turned on Ross as if she couldn't believe what she was hearing. 'You got Marco to help you?'

Ross shrugged. 'Twenty years we were together, Gabby,' he said, 'and you never once told me the truth about you and Buckthorn – not once. I brought that boy up as my own and I loved him, but never once did you tell me the truth. And you wonder why I left you.'

She stood her ground. 'And you loved Marco so much you got him to kill his own father!'

The sound of the shot rolled in great waves, drowning out everything else. Lincoln turned his head in time to see Gabriella drop to the floor, a smudge on her forehead. Without a second thought, without caring if he'd be shot next, he knelt down beside her body, taking her hands in his as her life slipped away.

Not Raphael, he remembered as he squeezed her hands. Uccello, that's who it was. The Scrabini could be by Uccello. When she opened her eyes again he'd tell her.

Blue light swept the living room, strobing the empty spaces on the wall where Ross's paintings had hung. Blue light reached into the kitchen, flitting over Ross and Gabriella and Lincoln.

Ross laid his gun down on the counter and held his hands up as the team from Park Street came barging in to arrest him.

CHAPTER 63

'This could be the end of your career, Lincoln. You know that, don't you?'

In a cell at Park Street, Lincoln changed out of the clothes he'd been wearing when Gabriella was shot, and dropped them into a plastic sack. He felt stupid in the sweatpants and top he'd been given in exchange. He hadn't worn plimsolls since he was at Hendon, and these weren't quite big enough and squashed his toes.

Meanwhile, Dale Jacobs kept up his admonitions from the corridor outside the open cell door. 'What the fuck were you doing there? In the home of a man we were trying to arrest? On your own. Were you involved with this wife of his?'

'Ex-wife,' said Lincoln, emerging from the cell and handing his sack of clothes to the uniform who was waiting for them. 'And no, I wasn't involved with her, and as far as I knew you already had him in custody.'

Jacobs tutted. 'We missed him at the hotel by a couple of minutes. It was like someone had told him we were on our way.'

'It wasn't me. He said he saw you coming in so he went out a different way. Why didn't you tell me about you and Donna?'

'Orla will take your statement when you're ready.' The DCI staggered a little, then limped off down the corridor, thwacking his stick against a row of lockers as he went.

Sitting in an interview room at Park Street – like everything else about the place, much more comfortable than Barley Lane – Lincoln wasn't sure if he felt numb or on fire. His whole body was buzzing as if he'd been swimming in an icy sea, every nerve ending recovering at the same time. When he looked down at his hands and his thighs, he was surprised they weren't vibrating.

DS Orla Cook put a cup of coffee in front of him before sitting down to take his statement.

He didn't admit that he'd gone round to see Gabriella simply because she'd asked him to. Yes, he'd hoped she'd have more information about Ross and his bloody paintings, but he'd have stayed to talk even if she'd just wanted to share her grief about Marco.

'I went to the house to offer my condolences because she'd lost her son,' he told Orla. 'I was off duty, and as far as I knew, Ross was in custody.'

'Had he gone there to kill her?'

'Why else turn up there with a Beretta?'

Orla tutted. 'The DCI shouldn't have taken this case on, the stupid twat. He's the one who should be in trouble, not you.'

'*Am* I in trouble?'

She shrugged. 'I need to write down your account of what happened and get you to sign it. Then it's up to DCS Youngman, I guess.'

When he got home, Lincoln sat for a while at the foot of the stairs, trying to get his head round all that had happened during the day. What had Frankie Ross planned to do after he'd dodged Jacobs and his team at the hotel? Had he hoped to hide at Gabriella's until he could escape back to Spain? Or was he going to kill Gabriella and then himself?

No, suicide wasn't Frankie's style.

He kicked off the stupid plimsolls and stomped upstairs to change his clothes. He heard his mobile ringing in the carrier bag he'd dumped on the chair in the hall. Ignored it, wanting only to shower and change, have a drink, go to bed.

The cat looked up at him from its nest in the duvet. He ruffled its head, knowing it would be desperate for food now he was home.

'Ten minutes,' he told it, and headed for the shower.

Twelve minutes later, Tux the cat was scoffing Whiskas. Lincoln, showered and changed, was staring, disappointed, at an empty bottle of Jameson's. His mobile was ringing again. He didn't recognise the number, another mobile, but he answered anyway.

'Jeff? This is Vic, Trish's husband. Have you heard from her?'

It took a moment to process the fact that her ex had his number. And that he sounded anxious. 'Not since last night. Why? Is there a problem?'

'Did she tell you about her assistant, this Stewart guy? Because I've done a bit of digging, and he should never have got that job. I've been calling her all evening and she's not answering.'

CHAPTER 64

Trish and Stewart had spent all Friday morning cataloguing books, labelling shelves and answering enquiries. At lunchtime, while Stewart sat reading the latest issue of *The London Review of Books*, Trish went for a walk, an apple and some peanuts in her coat pocket.

Much as she liked him, could she bear to be closeted with him till the end of her contract? She couldn't deny that he was good at his job, knowledgeable and hard-working, but working with him and him alone was becoming a strain.

Maybe he'd decide he'd had enough of her too, and leave early. But then how would she get everything done?

The weekend was coming up, two days off. She just needed a break.

The rest of the day dragged, but eventually Stewart went off to catch his bus. It was nearly ten o'clock when Trish remembered she'd meant to phone Kate, to wish her well for her trip to her father's the next day.

But where was her phone?

She went back downstairs, keys in hand – only to find the library door wasn't locked. She chided herself for her carelessness and stepped inside.

Down at the far end of the library a single light shone, illuminating the piles and piles of books stacked on the floor. A man on his knees was thumbing his way through the pages of book after book in search of something.

Trish switched the main lights on. Startled, the man sprang up, dropping the tome he'd been in the process of examining.

'Stewart! What the hell are you doing here at this time of night?'

His eyes were wild with terror. 'It must be here,' he said, over and over again. 'He said he had it. He wrote it in the catalogue. "I have *De Motu*." But where is it? I've been through all these volumes, but I can't find it. It must be here! It must be!'

'What must be here?'

'Newton's *De Motu*. Lundy bought Hooke's copy at the auction.'

'That doesn't mean it's still here. He could've lent it to someone who didn't give it back.'

'No! No! It must be here.' He ran his hands through his hair, looking round him frantically.

'How did you get in? I locked up.' Then she remembered that night on the landing outside her flat, his shadow falling across her as she keyed in the door code. Had he been into her flat when she wasn't there, to make copies of the library keys?

Without warning, he charged down the room towards her. She turned and ran back into the hallway, banging the switch to activate the stair light.

But it didn't come on. The switch didn't work. In darkness, Trish rushed up the narrow staircase to the flat, only to miss her footing two stairs from the top. She felt herself tumbling, arms flailing, unable to grab hold of the handrail in the dark. She banged her head, her hip, her knee, landing in a heap at the foot of the stairs.

The cold blew in from outside, a draught up the main stairs from the open door to the street. She was left alone in the dark, consciousness ebbing away. Before she slipped into oblivion, she heard her mobile ringing.

CHAPTER 65

'Have you got an emergency contact number for Trish?' Vic asked Lincoln urgently. 'I've called Suki, but the only number she's got is mine.'

'What do you know about this Stewart bloke that's got you so worried?'

'He's a book thief. He's been all over the place, walking out of libraries with priceless works. Trish had a few doubts about him so I asked around, found out he's a professional. Changes his name slightly each time, changes his look, his address... I'm worried she might challenge him. You know what she's like.'

It seemed strange to be discussing Trish in this way, two men familiar with her recklessness, her tendency to jump in with both feet.

'I'll contact the local police there,' said Lincoln, 'get them to look in on her.'

'And I'll keep ringing her mobile. She could've gone out for the evening, left her phone behind. It's the sort of thing she's always doing.'

Where could she go out for the evening, stuck where she was? Wherever she'd gone, she should be back by now. 'Vic, I can be there in under three hours,' he said before he could stop himself. 'Call me if you hear from her.'

'But you can't... Are you sure? I mean, I'd go myself, but—'

'No, it's fine,' said Lincoln, hunting round for another jacket, his only other raincoat, a pair of shoes and socks.

Twenty minutes later he was on the A303 heading for the motorway, wishing he could be making this journey any night but the Friday before half-term. Headlights on the opposite carriageway dazzled him. His stomach was growling with hunger. He was thirsty. And he was worried sick about Trish.

He'd instructed Woody to contact the local police in Essex, but it wasn't until he was on the M25, not far from the turn-off for Brentwood, that Woody called back.

'She's okay, boss,' he said. 'She's in hospital in Chelmsford. She fell down the stairs and broke her wrist, and they're keeping her in overnight in case she's got concussion.'

When he eventually found the hospital and drove into the car park, Lincoln felt like weeping with relief that Trish was safe and he was here. He was told to come back in the morning because she was sleeping, but he waited instead, dozing on a rigid plastic seat in the corridor.

At last he was at her bedside and she was surfacing from sleep.

'God, Jeff, you look even worse than I feel,' she said groggily, 'and I feel like shit. Why are you wearing that awful raincoat? You were going to throw it away.'

'Long story. At least I'm not still in plimsolls.'

'Plimsolls?'

'Never mind.' He grinned at her. 'Didn't I say I'd come to you for half-term?'

She lifted her arm in its bright blue cast. 'And didn't I say I could do with a break?'

'Come back with me. You can't work with a broken wrist.'

'I need to sort things out first. God, it gives me the creeps to think of Stewart going into my flat and looking for the keys while I was out. What else did he take or copy? I'll never know. He'd fiddled with the light switch. I was running up the stairs in the dark trying to get away from him and I fell.'

'Vic tells me he's well known on the rare book circuit. Claims to be doing research. Different name, different look, fake address.'

'You've spoken to Vic?'

'He rang me when he couldn't get hold of you.'

Her eyes lit up. 'He did? That was nice of him. But that awful Stewart could be anywhere now.'

'Don't worry about Stewart. Rest. We'll sort something out.'

CHAPTER 66

SATURDAY 18TH FEBRUARY

Lincoln drove back from Chelmsford, stopping at South Mimms services on the M25 for a late breakfast. He arrived at Barley Lane just as Cornelius Rayner was getting out of his solicitor's car.

Although he felt exhausted and could've done with a shower and a shave, Lincoln didn't want to miss the opportunity to interview him again. Had he decided at last to set the record straight? With Frankie Ross's arrest all over the news, Rayner wouldn't want to be tarred with the same murderous brush.

He sat across from Lincoln looking diminished, as if the fight had gone out of him. 'When my son told me Hugh was doing an inventory of the paintings,' he said, 'I knew it wouldn't be long before he found out how many were missing. Frankie said he'd take care of it, he'd got an idea, accidents happen... Hugh wanted to meet, to work something out, so we arranged to meet at Rufus's apartment. Only Frankie would be there, not me.'

'Hugh wouldn't have been suspicious?'

'No, why? They'd known each other since they were children. I nearly called it off,' Rayner went on, 'but then Barbara Trent rang me. Hugh had been to see her, and she could tell he wasn't going to give up.' He hung his head with its peculiar halo of white hair. 'Hugh phoned me that evening to make sure our meeting was still on. That was the phone call you kept badgering me about.' He looked up, his eyes pleading. 'You realise I did this for Rufus, don't you? Because it's Frankie's money that's paying for the Old Shoddy Mill as well as his.'

Lincoln sat back, amazed. 'You really believe Rufus would've put a building project ahead of Hugh Buckthorn's life? He loved Hugh. Or is that why you let Frankie kill him after all?'

But Cornelius had nothing more to say.

'Essex Police have picked up Stewart Hubbard,' said Woody as Lincoln waited for the kettle to boil. 'They reckon he's stolen books and maps from libraries and bookshops all over the country.'

'Thank God Trish wasn't badly hurt. She could've broken her neck falling down the stairs.'

'Suki's gone over to pick her up from the hospital and take her back to the flat.'

'And then she's bringing her back here?'

Woody shrugged. 'Trish wants to clear up the mess that chap left behind. Suki's staying to help her.'

The door inched open and DCI Jacobs shoved his way in, walking stick first. He flopped down at Shauna's desk.

'The Cartland girl's come home with her tail between her legs,' he said. 'She's been hiding out at some old boyfriend's flat in Warminster. Know what she was doing when that guy caught her in the Abbey Suite? Fucking stealing! Made a habit of it, apparently, but he was the first to catch her at it. She'd go through coat pockets, suitcases, whatever. She was making a dash for it when she ran into Buckthorn, cooked up the story that some guy was trying to rape her, and Buckthorn fell for it.'

Lincoln felt stupid for so misjudging her. Not a vulnerable young victim but a quick-witted habitual thief who was probably under suspicion. No wonder the manager had been reluctant to call the police when Buckthorn took her to his office. 'She certainly took me in.'

'You weren't the only one. Don't beat yourself up about it.' Jacobs shoved himself onto his feet. 'And just to set the record straight... I put in for a transfer to Wiltshire because I needed a change of scenery after I split up with Donna. I'd heard Ross and Don were setting up home near Alicante, so I never expected them to be here. Whatever you've been thinking, I didn't come here to chase after my girlfriend. *Ex*-girlfriend.'

'And your tip-off about Press Vale? The sex workers coming in from Eastern Europe?'

'Maybe my informant got it wrong this time.' Jacobs tapped the side of his beaky nose. 'But I never betray my sources.'

Lincoln, still sceptical, let it go.

'Oh, and Youngman wants to see you Monday,' Jacobs added as he limped past Lincoln's desk. 'You might want to have your Fed rep on board.'

'I was nearly shot by the bloke *you* were supposed to have in custody, and *I'm* the one who's in trouble?'

'Yeah, well... You can explain it all to the DCS on Monday.'

When Jacobs had gone, Pam brought a mug of coffee and put it on Lincoln's desk. 'I put two sugars in,' she said.

'Thanks.' He stared into his mug. He'd been so sure Trish would come back after what had happened. How could she work with one arm in plaster?

'Why don't you go home, boss? You must be exhausted. When did you last sleep?'

'I had a doze at the hospital, but yes, I could do with going to bed. For about a week.'

His phone beeped. A text from Trish.

Coming home tomorrow. Can I stay with u?

He grinned as he texted back: *You already know the answer to that. xx*

CHAPTER 67

The corrugated iron sheets that had landed on Barbara Trent's lawn had not, luckily, done much damage after all. A man had come and taken them away, and now, she felt, life could return to normal.

This morning she'd picked a few of the first primroses and, with Corky in tow, had taken them up to Ploughboy's Pit, laying them gently on the shiny metal lid that now covered it. People would still dump their rubbish round it, of course. It was all you could expect these days. She said a little prayer for Yazmin, and went home.

Once indoors again, she did her usual dusting and tidying, straightening the pictures and ornaments she'd acquired over the years, many given to reward her for...well, for her discretion, turning a blind eye, being loyal.

In her parents' bedroom, which overlooked the back garden and the horses' field beyond, she dusted the frame of the marvellous painting Mr Howard had given her. She wasn't fond of religious paintings as a rule, but this one – *The Salvation of Saint Paul*, by Giacomo Scrabini – had the most exquisite little landscapes in the spaces in between the principal figures. She guessed it must be Italy rather than Damascus, but still...

She smiled to herself. This little house might not be Greywood Hall, but it was so uplifting, having beautiful things to look at.